G. P. Taylor liv   : was one of the first serving police officers to be ordained as a priest and continue in full-time police work. Following being seriously assaulted on duty, he became a full-time priest. In 2002, he published his first novel, Shadowmancer, which became a global success. He can be contacted at @gptaylorbooks on Twitter and Instagram.

Pig in the Pulpit TM & © 2024 GP Taylor. All Rights Reserved. Reproduction of any part of this work by any means without the written permission of the publisher is expressly forbidden. All names, characters and events in this publication are entirely fictional. Any resemblance to actual persons, living or dead is purely coincidental. Published by Markosia Enterprises, PO BOX 3477, Barnet, Hertfordshire, EN5 9HN. Harry Markos, Director.

First published in 2024
by Markosia Enterprises, Ltd
PO BOX 3477, Barnet,
Hertfordshire, EN5 9HN

Paperback: ISBN 978-1-916968-44-8
eBook: ISBN 978-1-916968-45-5

Editor: Alexia Markos

Book design by: Ian Sharman
Cover art by: sarahphotogirl.com

www.markosia.com

Pig In The Pulpit

G. P. Taylor

[1]
The Vicar of St Walstan's

The door to the Norman church stood open as the organ music that seeped from inside faded like the evening light. A covering of soft rain had given way to the final embers of the summer sun that now set over the Yorkshire moors. Long shadows of gnarled yew trees were cast over the broken gravestones and deep grass as a blackbird sang its evensong.

From within, the crowd of people spilled through the ancient doorway and down the stone steps. Their brook-babble conversations disappeared with them as they walked to the row of parked cars that filled the lane and the car park of the King Charles pub that had stood next to the church for three hundred years.

"A good service, Elsie," one old woman said to another as they moved slowly through the graveyard that would soon be their home. "I can't say I am thrilled with the fact that a priest has a day job. Whatever happened to a full-time vicar?"

"It is just what the bishop said," Elsie answered as she steadied herself with a bone-handled walking stick, and with the other hand, she thoughtfully smoothed the fine, white hairs on her chin. "We are too small a parish to have a paid priest. I think it is admirable that he does a job as well as looking after us. House for duty, a non-stipendiary minister."

"Well," interrupted the bespectacled man behind them as he struggled to pull on his coat and hold tight to the bundle of sheet music gripped in his fat fingers. "It means he doesn't have the freehold, and we can easily get rid of him if we don't like what he preaches. On a more positive note," the man stuttered, "at least God didn't send us a woman. He has a family, and that means children for the village school."

"God?" Elsie asked, unsure of whom Mr Gerald Griffin, organist and parish busybody spoke about.

"No, the vicar," he answered with a roll of the eyes.

"I pray he doesn't want a family service. The prospect of morning prayer and screaming children is quite unpalatable," Elsie chirped as they got to the lychgate. "Hands in the air and all that clapping is not a way to worship."

"I am sure he will do nothing of the sort, Mr Griffin. Morris told me the vicar has insisted on keeping the Book of Common Prayer for our eight o'clock service. As long as he does that, nothing else matters."

Her friend nodded in agreement as Griffin shrugged his sloped shoulders and gave up trying to put on his coat.

"My only doubt, Miss Hindle, is that he will not have the time for all the duties of the church. He works twenty miles away," Griffin said as he held the gate open and gave a half-smile.

"Is there not a conflict of interest between a policeman and a priest?" Elsie asked, taking hold of the gate to stop it closing on the spring hinge.

"Morris told me that the bishop said that the vicar would work for three days in the parish. If he celebrates Communion, he can do whatever job he wishes," Miss Hindle answered.

"As long as he does not spend his days in the King Charles. When Jack Green was found drunk in the hedge by the undertaker, it sealed his fate." Griffin's smile widened as he remembered the day when Reverend Jack Green was discovered by John Crowley, the undertaker, stuck headfirst in the blackthorn hedge that ran along the lane from the church. "On his way to take the funeral of

Lily Cowen. Still had the bottle in his hand. The man had relieved himself in his trousers and was so drunk that he couldn't speak."

"I heard it was the stress of the job and the breakdown of his marriage," Miss Hindle answered sympathetically. "It does that to the bladder."

"Dear Anne, I heard it was his love of gin. Many a Sunday morning, the man stank of it. It started long before his wife picked apples from the other side of the fence," Elsie chipped in caustically as her wrinkled, thin lips tightened into a wry smile.

"Apples, Elsie? What apples?" Miss Hindle asked as the final congregants from the installation of the new priest walked slowly by, each offering their goodnight.

"I believe Miss Groom means that his wife was seeing another man," Griffin said softly, as not to be overheard.

"Tragic. If only he had shared his troubles," Miss Hindle answered.

"He shared his troubles often. Usually whenever he came out of the pub. Shouted them at the top of his voice at the flower shop."

"Why ever should he do that?" Miss Hindle asked.

"I told you many times before, Anne," Elsie said as she held her friend by the arm. "It was the florist whom Mrs Green had been seeing."

"So you did, so you did," she answered softly to disguise her lack of memory. "It seems so long ago. How times change. St Walstan's has not had much luck with its incumbents. Some would say we are cursed with bad apples."

"Three in nine years," Griffin replied as he counted the former priests on his fingers. "I have played my organ for them all. Farrow died, Callow could not grasp that he could not spend church funds on himself, and poor Mr Green succumbed to drink."

"So, what of the Reverend Peter Barnes?" Miss Hindle asked. "What will be his misfortune? He is a redhead. That means he has a hidden temper."

"He's built like an ox, and I hear he isn't one for much drink," Griffin replied. "A little too evangelical for my liking, and he prays earnestly."

"He might be here for some time," Elsie continued. "I was told he has asked for a clock to be placed on the back wall of the church. Morris said that the vicar only preaches a sermon for ten minutes and likes to know the time. Vicar told Morris that if you haven't struck oil in ten minutes, stop boring."

"Thank God for that," Miss Hindle laughed for the first time in many days. "At least we shall not be browbeaten with mutterings of Mr Green."

"Goodnight, ladies. Thank you for coming tonight. Are you in need of a lift home?" A tall, strawberry-blond, well-built man asked as he walked towards them, his black cassock neatly folded over his arm.

"Thank you, but we only live a few yards away. Heather Cottage. Please call any time," Miss Hindle said politely.

"We make our own wine," Elsie added.

"So did Jesus," Barnes answered lightly.

"Vicar," Griffin butted in. "The hymns for Sunday? Do you have any preferences?"

"May I leave them to you, Griffin? You have been here far longer than me, and everyone speaks so highly of you."

Griffin tried to stifle the sudden blush that stirred in his cheeks. "Thank you, Vicar. I will do my best."

"Ladies, I bid you goodnight," Barnes answered as he nodded to Griffin, smiled, and walked down the short path that led towards the vicarage.

"It will be his good looks," Miss Hindle said when he was out of sight.

"Pardon?" Griffin asked.

"His misfortune," she added. "The church will be full of wide-eyed and hopeful middle-aged woman. They will be inviting him for tea and telling him their troubles."

"He has a wife—a very pretty, if not slightly plain, wife," Griffin said in several short breaths.

"That never matters. A handsome man in a clerical collar is like catnip to many a woman. Just mark my words, Mr Griffin.

Reverend Barnes is in danger. I once read a book called *The Thorn Birds*. The tragedy of a handsome priest littered the pages…"

"A police uniform by day and a cassock by night?" Griffin said in a thoughtful whisper as the blush returned to his face.

[2]
A Burger at the Vicarage

St Walstan's vicarage stood away from the village at the end of a long, tree-lined driveway. Its stone walls had endured since 1825 and held in place the flaking windows and leaded glass panes that reflected the last of the sun. The tall, purple beech were heavy, bent with leaves that hung like Christmas baubles. Their thick branches were filled with rook nests and calling birds settling to roost.

Peter Barnes counted his steps on the gravel drive that led to the house and the church field beyond. He could see the woman standing in the doorway, holding a glass. Her long, brown hair was draped over her shoulder and framed her thin face.

"Just what I need!" he shouted as he got near. "The bishop sends his regards and was sorry you couldn't come."

"What excuse did you give him? Did you tell him I was looking after the children?" she said as she stepped out of the doorway and offered him the glass.

"I didn't need to, Mary. He knows where you stand with God," Peter answered as he kissed her on the cheek. "They employed me as the priest. I made it clear you were a woman with your own career and wouldn't be the vicar's wife."

Mary laughed. "I am glad you did. The thought of sitting with a bunch of women praying to nothing is not my idea of fun."

"A bunch would be a blessing," he said as he wrapped his arm around her. "I looked at the parish attendance register. They have an average of six people at the eight o'clock and sometimes they are lucky to have twelve at the Eucharist."

"We have mice in the kitchen. Abigail took great pleasure in chasing them around before she went to bed."

"How is Harry?" Peter asked.

"He stopped throwing up about two hours ago," Mary replied as she took the cassock from his arm and put it over the back of the chair in the hallway. "I don't think it's a virus. Well, I hope not. The last thing I need is to be sick." She turned and kissed him on the lips. "God knows how I got involved with you, but I will always ditto you."

"That sounded like you are saying a goodbye."

"I am in a way. Saying goodbye to my husband the copper, and hello to the vicar," Mary sighed. "When you first said you wanted to pursue this, I never thought it would really happen. I didn't think the police would agree."

"I was always honest about what I believed. You should have told me before. I would never have done anything that you didn't want."

"What? Stand up against God? I knew how much you wanted this, how much you felt called to do both jobs. It'll take time, but I will get used to it." Mary kissed him again and then pulled away. "I often wonder if you love God more than me."

He thought for a moment as they walked through the hallway, past the empty packing boxes and into the kitchen. "I love you—always have and always will," he answered, his voice edged with frustration.

"You can't say that. You don't know what the future will bring," Mary answered, the thin smile hiding her heart. "I just hope we have time for each other and don't drift apart. You are working three days a week as a copper and three days in the parish. That leaves one day for me and the kids."

"Why didn't you tell me all this?" he asked, tapping the side of his glass with a finger and trying to hold back his impatience. "I have done it now."

"I could see how much you wanted it, and I didn't want to break your dream. It was only tonight when you were out and I was all alone in this rambling, gothic pile that it suddenly hit me."

Peter looked around the kitchen with its dated units and nicotine-stained ceiling and knew what she meant. "The diocese has promised to decorate for us and change the kitchen. They will start in a couple of weeks."

"Putting lipstick on a pig," Mary cut in. "We had a lovely home that we had worked hard for. Now we've rented it out."

"I'm sorry," he said as he tried to take her hand. "This will be our home."

"This is a vicarage, an open house for all the parishioners. It has a parish office and a meeting room. This isn't just our home." Mary slumped on the chair next to the table and flopped her face into her hands. "The churchwarden has a key, as does Martha, your lay reader. I met them this afternoon when you were at the rehearsal. They walked right in wanting to use the photocopier. The lay reader asked me to put the kettle on and then she called me 'my dear,'" Mary said, flicking her fingers as airborne quotation marks.

"I'll move the copier to the vestry," he answered, his mind scrambling to say the things that would make it right.

"You are now public property. Everybody will want a piece of you, and not just the people who go to church." Mary sat back in the chair and looked up at him as she sighed in relief for allowing all her concerns to punch him hard.

Peter pulled up a chair and sat next to her, offering his glass. "Want some?"

"I've had nearly a bottle already. When the kids went to bed, I sat in the garden with a pint glass."

"Did you watch the sun go down?" he asked, trying to take Mary away from her concerns.

"It rained. I could hear you all singing. So I sat under the oak tree and listened to the water splashing through the leaves."

"I wish I could have been with you."

"We would have argued. I am so angry that you have brought us here."

"Do you want to go back?" he asked as he got to his feet, took the opened bottle, and filled his glass.

Mary looked at him, tilted her head to one side, and smiled. It was a look she always used when she wanted to make up. "Are you hungry?"

"I would rather talk than eat."

"We are fine, Peter. I know we will make this work and it will be good for us. You know me, I can't keep things inside. I have to tell you how I feel. Ever since…" she stopped speaking suddenly as her words entered a forbidden land. "Hungry? We could take the wine and some food and eat under the tree."

"What you got?"

"Linda McCartney."

"I thought you were a vegetarian?"

"Very funny. It's burgers and salad."

"I think I would prefer to eat Linda McCartney…"

[3]
The Singing Ringing Tree

The phone in the hallway rang and rang. Its discordant chant broke through the first light of the summer morning. It echoed up the mahogany staircase and along the landing. Peter had not slept. The muted argument of the night had gone through his mind over and over. He thought he was to blame for all that Mary felt, and now the intrusion she had warned him of had arrived. Whoever was calling refused to stop.

"Shall I get it?" Mary asked sleepily. "I can tell them that you are not officially on duty until Sunday."

Peter kissed her, slipped on his robe, and got out of bed. "Better go before it wakes the children," he said as he crossed the bedroom floor.

"Thank you," she whispered as she closed her eyes and drifted into dreams.

It was twenty-five yards from the bedroom to the front door. Peter knew this because he had paced it out when they first saw the house. It was the one thing he liked about the vicarage. Six bedrooms, three bathrooms, living room, study, parish office, dining room, snug, orangery, and kitchen. The house was spacious, far bigger than the police house they had bought when the force was selling them off. Growing up in a council house, he had always dreamed of a big house—a very big house in the country. It was something he never thought possible. But, when they had driven along the lane on that cold, wet day in March and looked up at the ancient façade with its wisteria and old fig tree, he knew this would be their home.

The telephone was still ringing as he jumped the last three stairs and lifted the receiver. "Hello," he said, out of breath. "St Walstan's Vicarage." The voice was distant and far away as the telephone line crackled. "Yes… right… thank you… Truro?" Peter put the phone back on its cradle and walked slowly to the kitchen. Looking out of the window as he waited for the kettle to boil, he watched the fox sniffing along the hedge. Making the two cups of tea, he made his way back to the bedroom. Mary had opened the curtains and was standing by the window, looking into the garden.

"I saw a fox by the hedge. I think it was looking for mice," Mary said as she turned to him.

"It's not good news," he said, his voice hesitating with each word. "Truro Hospital. Your mother… a stroke."

"Is she?"

"Alive. The doctor said it was quite mild, but it has affected her right side and her speech. Your father is with her."

"What do I do?" Mary answered as she stood by the window.

"The doctor asked if you could go to be with your father. Your mother will be kept in for the next few days. She was worried how your father would cope."

"What about you? The parish?"

"I will be fine. I have some time before I am back at work. I can unpack, get things sorted for when you return. The children would love to see Grandpa and Cornwall is beautiful this time of year."

"You would be on your own."

"I will manage."

"About last night…" Mary said just above a whisper.

"There is nothing more to say," Peter answered as he walked to the window and wrapped his arms around her.

"I want to say sorry. It was the wrong time. I don't mind being here," Mary replied as they both looked out of the window to the distant hill and the edge of the woods.

"We can make this work, as a family," Peter said as he held her closer. "Your mum will be fine. She is as strong as an ox. A determined woman."

"Do you mind me going? Dad doesn't cope well on his own," Mary said softly.

David Knox, her father, was a small man in his eighties and had joyfully endured ill health for many years. He would often say that he would never see another Christmas, but he did. As his friends failed around him, he attended funerals as a social pastime. The man was a creaking gate that was well oiled, and any infirmity was always caught early due to his obsession with visiting the doctor's surgery at least weekly.

"It's important. You must be with your father," Peter answered, his words hiding how he really felt.

There was no love lost between the two men. Her father had told Mary on her wedding day that she would be better off marrying the best man. "After all," he said, "James has a farm and land. All Peter Barnes has is the possibility of a future police pension."

David himself had a pension and boasted about it regularly. He had retired from the Foreign Office at the age of sixty, just in time for his liver to recover from the endless nights spent drinking at the Consulate Club in Azerbaijan. His relationship with his son-in-law had ended long before Peter and Mary were married. Things had been fine until the day they met Peter's mother in the council house on Maple Street. She had served them tea in a mug and had not provided a saucer, a social failing of such consequences that it was mentioned several times on the car journey home.

Elizabeth, her mother, spoke little to Peter. Weekends with them in Cornwall were endured and not enjoyed. They insisted on a formal evening dinner with portions so small that they wouldn't feed a mouse. Food was often undercooked and was always preceded by sherry in the garden room of their large house. When Peter asked for a can of beer, his request was rejected with a shrug of the shoulders and the insinuation that he was an alcoholic.

They never asked Peter anything of his work and showed little interest in any aspect of his life. When he told them he was going to be ordained, Elizabeth said that they were the kind of family that spoke not of money, nor religion.

Mr and Mrs Knox had plenty of money, but not one ounce of faith. They attended the local Methodist church at Easter and Christmas and refused to kneel to pray. Elizabeth had been brought up as a Presbyterian and even though she didn't believe in a god, the dogma ran so deep in her Scotia blood that she oozed pious religiosity from every pore of her tight-lipped smile.

"I will go today and let you know how things are," Mary said as she held his hand tightly. "I don't know how long I will be away."

"Take as long as you need. The car is full of fuel, and I will help you pack."

Mary didn't answer. She stared out of the window; her attention was caught by a tree in the distance, the branches were hung with coloured ribbons that blew in the morning breeze.

"What's that tree on the top of the mound? I have never noticed it before."

"Oh, that? It's an old yew tree. Possibly a thousand years old. It was planted on a burial mound. The bishop warned me about it. The villagers call it the singing, ringing tree."

"What? That's the name of a television show when I was a child. It frightened me to death. Far worse than the Daleks."

"It caused my predecessor a lot of trouble."

"A tree?"

"Ancient Pagan site. Visited by people from around the country. Jack Green said it was evil and tried to get the tree chopped down. It became quite a local battle."

"What will you do about it? Aren't you supposed to fight against the works of the Devil?" Mary said with a sarcastic smile and a squeeze of his hand.

"I am going to leave it well alone. It is a tree, and if people believe it has magical powers, then that's fine by me."

"I suppose it's like you telling people that bread and wine suddenly become the body and blood of Jesus."

"Not quite," Peter said as he pulled the curtains across the window. "We still have time to sleep before the kids wake up."

"Just sleep? Perhaps something else?"

"What would you like?" he asked hopefully, knowing they had not lay in that way for the last two months.

"Toast," Mary laughed. "By the way, I found some letters addressed to a Frank Green, but you called him Jack."

"He was in the Navy. The bishop said Jack was his nick-name. Frank was his Sunday name. He went by both."

[4]
Tumulus

Peter watched the red Vauxhall Astra go through the vicarage gates as he waved Mary goodbye. The morning had been hectic. Bags packed, breakfast cooked, children loaded into the car as they begged to stay. Mary had second thoughts and said that she dreaded the journey. Peter had told her not to worry and promised to ring her every evening.

Now he waited until he could no longer hear the car, then turned and locked the front door. The bright morning sun was filtered through the leaves of the beech trees as he set off to walk. Peter had planned to hike along the boundaries of the parish. It was something priests of the past would do whenever they were called to a new church. He thought it would be a good way to get to know the land he was now called to serve. After all, an iron-age stone path ran through the garden of the vicarage towards the burial mound on the far hill. Peter decided he would follow the path until it met the river. From there, he could walk the boundary.

Crossing the stile, he was soon in the cornfield. All around him, staves of corn stood proud against the breeze. The path rose to meet him as his heart beat faster. In half a mile, he had crossed the fields. He sat on the fence and looked back to the village. The church tower cut through the trees. The vicarage was bathed in morning sunlight. All was well. This was Yorkshire, beautiful and bold.

Peter listened to the sound of a motorbike as it wound its way along the country lanes. Its deep growling engine broke the peace of the morning as it disappeared into the distance. High above him, a buzzard sparred with two crows. They spiralled, dipped, and dived in a mock dogfight until the raptor was shooed from the parish. The bird flew off to the north, climbing higher and higher on the summer thermals.

Far above, a jet crossed the sky leaving a thick, white contrail. Ahead was the yew tree. It was bigger than Peter had expected. The mound on which it stood was surrounded by a low, stone wall that had once stood much higher. Over the years, it had been robbed out and the gaps in the wall replaced with new stones.

At one side was a narrow gate that Peter went quickly through. He stood before the tree and looked up into the knotted branches. Hanging from each were brightly coloured ribbons. Some had faded with age and the remnants of those from far distant years were scattered on the stony ground. He noticed that many had writing upon them. Reaching up, he took hold of a red ribbon and read the words: *For Mother—make her well.* He wondered who had left the ribbon and what ailed their mother.

"They're prayers," the woman's voice came from behind him.

He turned quickly, taken by surprise. Before him was a woman with long, red hair. Her bare arms were heavily tattooed with images of snakes and fish. She was pretty, tall and thin faced with a shy smile. Peter thought she looked familiar and that he had seen her before but could not remember where.

"Morning," he said, his voice cracking with surprise. "I thought I was alone."

"Sorry, I saw you coming up the hill. I am working on the wall. The kids have been up from the village and some of the stones have fallen away."

"Do you do it for a living?"

"Is it strange that a woman works on a dry stone wall?" she asked as she rubbed her hands on her denim overalls and wiped the sweat from her forehead. "I have mended most of the walls around the village over the years."

"Tell me," he asked as he moved under the shade of the branches, "why do they have a wall around the mound?"

"It's a yew tree. Highly poisonous to sheep and cattle. The leaves and berries can kill in small doses and it's a sacred site. It's good to have it separated from the world in some way."

"The ribbons are prayers, I take it?" Peter asked.

"Folk come here every day from across the county and some from even further. People in need, people giving thanks, and some just wanting to step away from the world," the woman smiled at him. "I'm Estelle Smith, friends call me Stella. I live in Baytown."

Pete nodded. "I am…"

"I know who you are," she said before he could answer. "You're the copper. Peter Barnes. I saw your picture in the paper. The new vicar of St Walstan's. Don't you remember me? We have met before."

"You look familiar, but I can't think when we met."

"You arrested my husband three years ago for drunk driving and gave me a lift home on the way to the nick."

Peter realised who she was as he took a subconscious step backwards. "Sorry, just doing my job. A collision just outside Cloughton?"

"Don't apologise. He was a complete arse. Thankfully, he is now my ex-husband. He moved away. The man was always full of drink and anger. The two don't mix well."

"Sorry," he said again without thinking.

"You apologise a lot for a copper. Do you want a coffee? Fresh with cream, and I have a spare cup."

They sat on two large stones that stuck out from the mound and slowly drank the coffee. An hour passed quickly as they talked. Stella told him that the tree was once used to hang a witch and that on each solstice and equinox, Pagans would gather under its branches.

"Do you come here on the solstice?" he asked.

Stella laughed. "Are you asking me if I am Pagan?"

"Sort of," he replied.

"Do I look like one?"

"Do I look like a vicar?" he answered.

"Not like Jack Green. He was so miserable. He never took his dog collar off. I once saw him in shorts, sandals with socks, t-shirt and collar. I was here one day working on the wall, and he ordered me to leave in the name of Jesus. I told him that if Jesus was alive, he would be up here with the rest of us."

Peter laughed as she spoke. "What did he do?"

"Called me a witch and then stormed off all red-faced shouting that I would burn in Hell," she laughed to herself. "I don't believe in Hell."

"Was he right when he called you a witch?" Peter asked as he looked up at the branches of the tree.

"It was the priest of St Walstan's who had the woman hanged." As if she knew what he was thinking. "Her name was Esther Corbridge, she lived in your village and was a healer. She grew herbs and made medicines. The local priest couldn't understand why so many of his congregation went to her for help. He was jealous and accused her of sorcery. Esther used the water from the old spring in your churchyard and the priest wanted her to stop. He even pressed her family to help with the hanging. They did, for fear that they would also be accused. They hung her from this tree and buried her in the village."

"Where is she buried?"

"Under the double tree at the crossroads."

"The old oak and beech?" he asked.

"Planted on her body. Two saplings twisted together to form one tree. Consecrated ground was too good for her, they said. Buried her so that everyone who passed by would know their fate if they took up the old religion."

"A chapter of history that I wish had not happened. If she had lived today, she would have probably been a doctor," he answered as he sipped the last of his coffee and put the cup on the stone beside him. "I would not have objected to her taking the water."

"I had a sample analysed, it has a high magnesium and potassium content, as well as calcium. Many of these things were lacking in a diet. No wonder her patients were getting better," Stella spoke excitedly as if she had discovered a secret.

"Can the water be drunk now?" Peter asked.

"Of course, it is very pure. It has been filtered by the rock's miles below. You should try some."

"I was going to use it for baptisms and house blessings."

"They won't let you. Jack Green had a motion passed by your church council that the well should not be used for human consumption. He wanted the yew tree chopping down and the well bricking up. He thought they were both a conduit of evil—that's what he said in a sermon."

"You know a lot about my church," he answered.

"Your church wanted to ban me from coming here. I tend the wall for free and they wanted me to stop. I make no secret that I am a witch. We gather here and celebrate, and your church wanted us to stop," Stella spoke quickly as if she thought he would stop listening. "Green even rang the police and told them I was sacrificing animals."

"This isn't my beat. I work miles away. I never knew that."

"Sorry, I have spoken out of turn."

"I am glad you did. You have told me things that I never knew," Peter said thoughtfully as he got to his feet. "You are welcome to worship wherever you want. It is just as much your land as it is mine. If this is common land, then anyone can come here."

"Will you tell your church that?" she asked, her voice tinged with disbelief.

Peter thought quickly. "No, but you can."

"I have told them time and time again," she snapped.

"Then come to church and tell them from the pulpit."

Stella stopped speaking, the words she wanted to say taken from her mouth. "What?"

"Come and speak to the church. Tell them about how you worship God. We have a harvest festival in a few weeks. It would be a good time for you to speak."

Stella gave a roar of laughter. "Great joke, Vicar."

"I am serious. Lammas was a Pagan festival long before it was Christian," Peter said as he held out his hand towards her. "It's the least I can do to make amends for all that has happened to you."

She waited for a while before answering. The sun had risen higher and the yew tree no longer gave shade. Taking his hand, she looked him in the eyes.

"Do you really know what you are doing? There is a darkness in this village, and it will take more than me speaking in your church to rid us from it."

He gripped her hand tightly. "I am the vicar. It is my job to reach out and build bridges to those who believe differently to us."

"In my faith and in yours, there are people who thrive on our differences. I don't think it would be right for me to come anywhere near your church." Stella paused and pulled her hand from his. "You have a good heart and I trust you, but you lack judgement. For your sake, I do not want to speak in your church."

"Then I will pray that you change your mind," Peter said as he turned, said goodbye and walked away.

[5]
Miss Hindle's Attic

The boundary had been walked in four hours. The sun gave way to rain and then rain gave way to sun. After all, it was Yorkshire and having all the seasons of a year in one day was no surprise. Peter wearily walked the cobbled stones of the main street. Far ahead, he could see the church and the welcome sign of the King Charles. He had been told many times that the best way to get to know a parish was in the bar of the local pub.

Quickening his steps, he walked along the road. The cottages on either side were decorated with pots and baskets of summer flowers. Each door was neatly painted, every window cleaned. The pavement was swept and without litter. It was something he had not noticed before. There was a desire for perfection that he found unusual. Even the double yellow lines were crisp and pristine. All done by the people of the village whose pride verged on hubris.

"Afternoon, Vicar," the voice came from the doorway of Heather Cottage. "You look as if you have been on a safari."

"Miss Groom," he answered as he blocked the sun from his eyes with his hand. "I have been walking the boundary to get to know the parish."

"You look like a man who could do with a drink. I have made some lemonade for Anne. We are in the back garden. Come and join us," she said as if she had been lying in wait for him to pass.

Peter realised that this was an invitation he couldn't refuse. The misses Groom and Hindle had an influence within the church that he could clearly see. They had been part of St Walstan's for fifty years and had seen many priests come and go.

"I would love to join you," he said, giving a desperate glance to the pub and hoping his reluctance was not noticeable.

"Come on through. I am just going to the kitchen. Anne is in the garden."

Peter crossed the threshold of the cottage. The hallway was brightly painted with a solid, stone floor. On the walls were pictures of family and friends. A green telephone stood on an old coaching table. Four doors came off the hallway leading to different rooms. The back door was wide open, held back from slamming by a metal doorstop.

"Anne, we have a visitor," Miss Groom shouted from the kitchen. "The vicar is having a drink with us."

"I'm here, in the garden," Miss Hindle answered as Peter stepped through the back door and into the shade of the cottage.

"Good afternoon, Miss Hindle," Peter said as he admired the abundance of flowers that adorned the long, walled garden.

"Please, call me Anne. Keep Miss Hindle for the church porch," the old woman said with a youthful laugh. "How was your walk? Mrs Todd told us you were on your way."

"Mrs Todd?"

"From the butchers. She had been told by Gary Jones from the garage. He had seen you walking the footpath on the ten-acre field."

"The jungle drums of the parish," he answered, trying not to show concern that his every move was being watched and his journey telegraphed from house to house.

"We don't need drums or smoke signals," she giggled mischievously. "We have the telephone."

"What a beautiful garden and much bigger than I thought," Peter answered, hoping to steer the conversation away from his surveillance.

"Four hundred years old. During the war, my father had it all dug over and full of vegetables. We ate potatoes and carrots for every meal."

"Do you do all the work?" he asked.

"Elsie and I have worked hard for over forty years. Ever since my father died and left me the cottage," Anne replied as she moved along the painted garden seat to make room for him to sit down.

"You have done a very good job of it," Peter answered with genuine admiration. "It must take you many hours of work.

"We have Bruce. He is our gardener. Elsie and I like to potter in the potting shed," Anne said as Elsie brought out two tall glasses of fizzing lemonade poured over ice and garnished with herb leaves.

"We make a lemon cordial and then add some sparkling water."

"Interesting garnish," Peter said as he looked suspiciously at the leaf that floated in his glass.

"We love to have one of these in the afternoon. Always so relaxing," Anne replied.

Peter dipped his finger into the glass and examined the leaf and, without them noticing, dropped it to the ground.

"Where do you get the garnish?" Peter asked.

"Bruce takes care of the herb garden. We have some most unusual varieties."

"I would really love to see them," he answered.

"Elsie," Anne said. "Take the vicar to the herb garden."

Elsie guided him along the lawn, pointing out all the plants that filled the borders. Stands of foxgloves melted into swathes of delphiniums and hollyhocks, all confined in a neat putting green lawn.

"You must be very proud of all you have done over the years," he said as they walked towards a small hedge that divided the garden.

"Anne and I are very blessed. We want for nothing. We have been together since school."

"That is a wonderful thing, to find a trusted friend," he said as they walked into the herb garden.

"We fight like cat and dog, but we know each other so well, it is like living with yourself."

Peter stopped and looked at the herb garden in disbelief. Standing proud and mixed in with sage, borage, dill, and parsley was a tall plant with finger-like leaves covered in tight buds. They gave off a deep and pungent aroma that he was very familiar with.

"Is this what you put into the lemonade?" he asked Elsie.

"Bruce said that it has a soothing quality, but we had to have no more than one leaf a day," Elsie answered proudly. "They are magnificent and so beautiful."

"Did Bruce say what they were?" he asked.

"Salvia, a sort of sage plant from America."

"Really?" he said as he examined a plant that had been surgically pruned. "Does Bruce take care of them?"

"He comes every week and trims them so they grow and gives us enough leaves for the lemonade and salads."

"Salads?"

"Yes. They have a very distinct taste with rocket and borage. I have no trouble sleeping. Very calming. Bruce keeps a nursery of plants in the attic. He says it is the best place to bring on the plants. We have lighting and everything."

Peter laughed. Elsie echoed his Scythian joy, her face wrinkling into a broad smile. "When Bruce told you what they were, are you sure he didn't say sativa?"

"That's it," she answered with a deep laugh. "It was sativa and not salvia sage."

"And Miss Hindle's attic is full of them?"

"A couple of big ones," she said proudly.

"I need a gardener. Where do I find Bruce?"

"Did you enjoy the garden?" Anne Hindle asked as they returned to the bench in the shade of the cottage.

"You have a marvellous place. I can see why you have stayed so long."

"More lemonade?" Elsie asked as she walked towards the door.

Peter declined with a shake of his head as he sat next to Anne on the bench.

"Bruce does a fine job," she said as she sipped her drink with an ever-broadening smile on her face. "Tell me, Vicar, what are your plans for the church?"

Peter knew this was dangerous ground. He was priest in charge on a fixed term contract.

Miss Hindle was a stalwart of the early morning service.

"Plans for the church?" he said following a long pause. "My plans are to take my time and see what the parishioners want. I believe that you shouldn't fix anything that isn't broke."

"Broken, not broke," she answered, correcting his use of language. "The last vicar broke many things. The man was obviously mad. He had a guitar and insisted on playing it in church. The one before him filled the place with incense and candles. All he succeeded in doing was getting rid of the bats."

"You will be glad to know that I don't have a guitar," he answered as Miss Hindle laughed to herself.

"You will do something that gets all our backs up, vicars always do."

"I am here to take services and pray. St Walstan's belongs to the people and not the vicar," he answered.

"Do you say that because they are not paying you?" Elsie asked as she came out of the house, having obviously been listening to the conversation.

"No. I say that because it is how it should be. As a priest, I am a servant. Many priests have come and gone over the years and you both have seen them all. I may only be here for a few years. What right do I have to change your church?"

Elsie sat next to her companion. Peter noticed that she quietly held her hand. "I told you he was different," she said just above a whisper.

"So, you will be keeping the early morning service?" Miss Hindle asked.

"Eight o'clock every Sunday," he answered.

[6]
Bruce Jakes Loves Grass

The telephone rang three times and then stopped. It was the signal Mary always used to get him to call her back as her parents didn't like her using the phone to call home. Peter picked up the receiver and dialled his father-in-law's number. Mary answered.

"I arrived a couple of hours ago. Dad looked after the children, and I went to the hospital."

"How is she?"

"Not as bad as I thought. Her speech is slightly slurred, and she is weak, but the doctor said she could make a full recovery," Mary hesitated before going on. "I have a favour to ask."

"Anything."

"Dad has asked me to stay for a couple of weeks. He isn't coping very well. The place is a bit of a mess and I need to get things organised."

"That's fine. It is good that you can be there."

"Are you sure?" Mary asked.

"Yes," he answered, wrapping the phone cord around his fingers. "Kiss the kids for me."

"Love you," Mary said softly as if she was trying not to be overheard.

"Love you," he answered as the phone clicked and cut the call. Peter put the phone down and stood in the empty hallway decorated with someone else's taste in gigantic, green flowers and Rottweiler bees that seemed to stare at him.

There was a sudden, sharp knock at the door. Peter slipped the latch and opened the door. Standing there was a tall, muscular man in trainers, a t-shirt, and shorts, wearing a Halloween mask.

"Gary, what are you doing here?" Peter said as the man took off the mask and stepped inside the hall.

"I have come to take you out for a drink," Gary said as he put the mask on the table. "Mary rang Sarah and told her about her mother and that I was to make sure you were okay."

"I don't need a childminder."

"But you do need a friend. What's the pub like across the road?"

"I have no idea, I have never been," he answered.

"Well, now is your chance. I'm paying."

Peter knew it would be futile to argue. He and Gary Ross had been friends since police training school. They had lodged together in Scarborough when they were first sent out on the beat and were best men at each other's weddings. They were closer than brothers.

Gary owed his life to Peter. Four years ago, they had stopped a car late one night for a routine check. With no warning, the driver pulled a pistol from his coat and aimed at Gary. Without hesitating, Peter had grabbed the gun. Three shots were fired, one grazing his thigh. He knocked the man to the floor and handcuffed him. Gary had stood there frozen with fear. The arrest report made sure that everyone knew it had been a joint arrest and both men had acted bravely.

"Sarah says I can stay over, so we can have a drink. I don't want to get nicked for being over the limit. They serve food, and I bet you haven't had anything to eat."

"Well, you certainly looked dressed for the evening," Peter said as he took his jacket from the hook. "I could do with some food."

Stepping outside, Gary looked at the garden filled with shrubs and trees and surrounded by a high stone wall.

"Is this why you got ordained? I can now understand the attraction of becoming a part-time vicar."

"It wasn't about the house. I was fortunate that they needed someone. A matter of timing," Peter answered as they walked slowly along the drive as the warm summer breeze rustled the leaves above them.

"Does God have any more vacancies? I have a sudden sense of calling. If I can have a house like this." Gary slapped him on the back playfully.

"Three years part time at theological college. Using all my weekends and holidays to do the course. It wasn't easy."

"I have to be honest and say none of us thought you would do it," Gary said as they got to the gate. "A few of the lads think you are quite mad."

"So, what does the shift think?"

"A couple are worried that you might go soft. Can't have a vicar fighting someone during an arrest. You handed in your firearms ticket, and they are worried you might have lost your bottle."

"Anything else?"

"Inspector Hammond was laughing in the parade room saying that instead of Crime Squad you should be sent to the *God Squad*."

"Very funny," he answered. "Just seems like suddenly everyone has it in for me."

"You are a part-time vicar and part-time copper. What the hell is all that about? You are the only one in the country. How do you expect people to react? Your face was all over the newspapers. They even talked about you on the Jimmy Young Show. I am surprised the chief let you do it."

"They all knew what it would entail. The chief told me himself that it was good for the force," Peter snapped back.

"Don't shoot me, I am just the messenger. Just keep your head down when you get back and please don't get all godly," Gary answered as they got to the door of the pub.

"All godly? What do you mean?"

"Just be you. Don't put on a vicar voice or say stuff about God to prisoners. We have enough with Sergeant Isaiah. The other night, I took in a drunk for fighting. It took me forty-five minutes to get him from the custody desk and into the cell. Isaiah insisted on telling him all about his bloody Road to Damascus conversion and his salvation from booze. It was so boring. I nearly fell asleep. It must have been the tenth time I've heard it."

"He's Pentecostal. It means a lot to him."

"It meant a lot to the bloke I had arrested. The man pleaded with me not to leave him alone in case Isaiah came back."

"What did you do?"

"I told Isaiah that the man had expressed an interest in his beliefs. He ran into the cells like a rat up a drainpipe."

Peter never answered. As they were about to go into the pub, he noticed a yellow Ford Transit van parked across the road. On the side, painted in large, red letters were the words *'Bruce Jakes Loves Grass—Gardens Tended with Love and Care'*.

"Well, well," he said, turning to his companion. "Run me a vehicle check on that van next time you are in. I would love to know where he lives."

"Church or police business? I'm not getting the sack if you just want to convert him."

"It's a bit of both."

The bar of the King Charles was almost empty. Several locals stood under the beam and plaster ceiling in a tight group by the bar. At the back of the pub, two men in their mid-thirties were playing pool. The barman was standing by the sink, washing a pint mug. He was a thickset man with a broad face and short, cropped hair and looked up as they came in.

"Evening, Vicar," he said with a red-faced smile. "Would you like your first drink on the house?"

"Very kind, but my friend has promised to buy me a drink and as he still owes me one from when he was my best man, I would like to see the colour of his money," Peter answered, not wanting to take a favour from the barman.

"So, what will it be?" he asked.

They ordered two pints and sat in the corner of the room. The gathering at the bar occasionally looked over. It was obvious they were the subject of their conversation.

Three drinks, fish and chips, and two hours later, Peter looked at his watch in a way that was the universal signal that it was time to leave.

Gary stood up and stretched out his arms with a yawn.

"Past your bedtime?" shouted one of the men. "It's only nine o'clock. Still plenty of time yet."

"Early start tomorrow. Shift work," Gary answered as Peter began to follow him from the pub.

"You not going to introduce us to your wife then?" the man asked.

"Leave it, Bruce," the other man who had been playing pool said as he turned away.

"Bruce Jakes loves grass?" Peter asked. "The local gardener?"

"That's him," one of the men answered.

"See, Bruce, you are already a legend," another said with a pat on the back.

"What's your interest?" Bruce asked as he folded his arms and leant back on the bar.

"Sativa that is grown as a herb in the garden of old ladies," Peter answered as he nodded to the barman and walked from the bar.

"What was all that about?" Gary asked as they got outside.

"Give it a minute and I think you will find out."

The door to the pub opened and Bruce Jakes stepped out into the night with van keys in his hand.

"What were you on about in there?" he asked as he pulled back his shoulders.

"You are growing cannabis in the garden of Heather Cottage. There are also two plants in the attic," Peter answered as the three men stood in the road.

"What business is it of yours?" Bruce demanded.

"I am very interested in what my friend has just said," Gary answered as he opened his wallet and showed the man his warrant card. "Growing cannabis is a serious offence under the Misuse of Drugs Act. It will get the person locked up for a very long time."

"Sod it," Bruce Jakes said, looking remorsefully down at the ground. "I would never sell it. I'm not a dealer. Honest."

Peter thought for a moment. He could see the man's hand was trembling slightly and took him to one side by the van so that he could not be overheard. In the years he had been in the job, Peter had developed the copper's nous to know when someone was a villain. Bruce Jakes wasn't.

"You are lucky I am the local vicar and not the local copper. You have taken liberties with two old ladies who just happen to come to my church."

"It's not what you think. I wanted to help."

"How many other parishioners have you been trying to help?"

"Just Heather Cottage, honest," Jakes answered as he wiped a single bead of sweat from his forehead. "I just didn't want to be getting the stuff from a dealer. I'm not a criminal."

"They could have been hollyhocks," Peter said.

"Hollyhocks?" Bruce Jakes asked.

"My plant identification skills are not what they used to be. I may go back in a couple of days and see if I was right the first time," Peter answered, staring eye to eye with Bruce Jakes. "By the time I get to see them, they might have died. An accidental spraying of weed killer. Understand?"

"Weed killer?" Bruce Jake answered. "It happens all the time."

"Perfect."

"Will that be the end of it?"

"This isn't my patch," he answered as Jakes fumbled with the keys to the van door. "I wouldn't drive that if I were you. There's always a traffic car on the A174 at this time of night."

"Bugger," Jakes shrugged, realising he would have to walk.

[7]
Deliver Us From Evil

The water from the hot tap was lukewarm. It was early morning and the ancient heater had not yet warmed the tank. Peter boiled two kettles to do the washing up as the morning sun cascaded through the trees. He had cooked Gary breakfast before he went on shift and now wiped the remnants of egg and beans from the plate.

Early morning was never the time to talk about important things, Peter thought as he mulled over the fraught conversation they had before Gary left. There appeared to be a discreet opposition to him being a priest and keeping his job as a copper. The problem was that there seemed to be no place in the force for a man who also had God as a boss.

Gary had been honest. It was felt that out of all the jobs, being a copper and a priest was never going to work. Vicars were seen as soft, effeminate and kiddy fiddlers, not hardened police officers having to deal with violent offenders. Peter found his words hard, relentless, and not what he wanted to hear. There was no room for muscular Christianity, no room for a man with a faith. In his heart, he had a deep concern that already, there was a growing animosity towards him. He thought of what he would do when he went back on shift. Thankfully, that was many days away and he would face that nemesis nearer the time.

Looking out of the kitchen window, he saw that the fox was back. It sat under the hedge staring at him as it chewed on a rat that it had just killed.

Peter turned as he heard the telephone start to ring. It was not yet five-thirty. For a moment, he thought it was Mary and that something had happened to her mother. He threw the drying cloth onto the table as he made his way to the hallway.

Picking up the phone, he answered breathlessly. "Vicarage."

The woman on the phone was sobbing, unable to get out her words. "*Please*," she said as she gulped her breath. "*We haven't slept.*"

"What's wrong?" Peter asked.

"*Haunted*," was the one-word reply.

"Where are you?"

"*The Grange, we have only been in a few weeks. Please could you come and see us? Can you come now?*"

His drive to The Grange took ten minutes along the narrow, winding roads that led from the village, through the forestry and onto the moor edge. The house stood on the remnants of a moraine left behind by a glacier at the end of the Ice Age. It was an old country house with many windows that faced the south. At the entrance, a long driveway with raptor-topped stone pillars that stood at either side and held in place new, iron gates. On the right-hand side was a metal keypad and intercom.

Peter stopped the car and wound down the window and pressing the button he waited for the gates to open.

"*Hello?*" came the voice that he recognised as being the woman from the telephone conversation.

"Mrs Parker, it's me, Reverend Barnes."

"*I'll open the gate, drive straight up to the front door.*"

The gates slowly opened. Driving through, he noticed an old oak tree that had been felled and chopped for logs. It had fallen onto the dry stone wall and had left a hole in the tree canopy that was out of place, as if a scar that didn't need to be there. It gave him a view of The Grange. He could see the stone pillars on either side of the front door and the grey slate roof that hung over the building like the wings of a large corvid.

"Hello," shouted Mrs Parker as he stopped outside the house.

Peter was surprised when he saw her. She was much younger than her voice portrayed. He thought she would have been in her sixties. Yet, she was half that age and dressed in jeans and a long jumper. Her blonde hair fell across her shoulders and was blown across her face by the breeze.

"I'm sorry I took so long. I had to go to the church to get some things," he said as he got out of the car.

The front of the house was covered in honeysuckle that grew in and out of an old wisteria.

"I didn't know who to call. My husband is away. My mother is staying until he comes back. She is helping me look after my baby," Helen answered as she gestured for him to follow her into the house. "I thought it best to tell you when you got here rather than on the phone."

"You said you were being haunted. What has been happening?"

"It sounds so stupid in the daytime," she said as he followed her into the large kitchen. "We moved in a few weeks ago and everything was fine. My husband had some alterations done in the cellar. After that, I began to hear footsteps on the upstairs landing late at night. It also felt very cold, even on the hottest days. That's why I asked my mother to come and stay when George went to America. He's an architect. Two nights ago, I was in bed and just couldn't sleep. Agnes was in her cot next to the bed. When I looked, I am sure I saw a woman leaning over the cot looking at her. I screamed and put on the light. There was nothing there, so I brought Agnes into bed with me and gave her a feed. Later, I was just dropping to sleep, and I again heard footsteps. The door to the room opened, but there was no one there." Helen Parker took a deep breath and gulped as she flicked the switch on the kettle without thinking.

"What did the woman look like?" he asked as she took the cups from the rack and began the ritual of making a pot of tea as if it was something a vicar expected.

"Do you believe me or think that I am mad?" she asked stoically as she dropped the teabags into the pot and listened to the hissing of the kettle.

"I have no reason to think you are mad. People see things all the time. You obviously saw and heard something. Whether it is a ghost or spirit is open to interpretation."

"Do you believe in ghosts?" she asked.

"I believe in God and that there are things in this world beyond our understanding. I am to be convinced that a ghost is the return of a departed soul. More that it is like a video, a recording of someone from the past that under certain circumstances is replayed, and if we are in the right mind, we can see it."

"And these recordings throw books off shelves and slam all the doors in the house?" she asked as she poured water into the Cornishware teapot. "That is what we had to endure last night. It started when we went to bed and went on until first light. Every door in the house slammed. Footsteps went down the passageway and when I looked out of the bedroom door, a book was thrown from the shelf and landed at my feet. We didn't dare come out until it was dawn. That's when I rang you. We had the parish magazine put through our door and I got the number from there." Helen sighed in relief that someone had listened to her. "I didn't know who else to call."

"You have done the right thing," he said as she poured the tea into the cup. "I can help you. There is a phenomenon called a poltergeist."

"Poltergeist? Have you done this kind of thing before? It said in the magazine that you were new to the job."

"New to the parish, not to being a priest," he answered. "I think it would be best to have a house blessing. I could do it now, or when your husband gets back."

"He's away for another week. Anyway, he is such a realist, he would rather believe I was mad than in the supernatural," she said anxiously. "I felt something wasn't right here, but he insisted on buying the house."

"We can have the blessing now," Peter said as he sipped his tea.

"How does it work?" she asked.

"I pray and will sprinkle some salt and holy water in the rooms upstairs."

"Is that it? Will it work? What about tonight? I don't think I could face another night."

He smiled at her and took a sip from his cup and then emptied the rest down the sink. Without speaking, he took the teapot and filled the cup to the brim with hot tea. "Can you put the milk in?" he asked her.

"How can I? It's full," she answered with a confused frown.

"Exactly. I am not forcing anything to go but just inviting something good to come in. If this house is full of goodness and light, then negativity and darkness cannot dwell here."

Peter didn't waste any more time. He opened his bag and took out a small bottle of water with a silver cap and a vial of salt.

"Not exactly *Ghostbusters*," she laughed.

"But far more powerful," he replied as he looked around the vast kitchen with its gleaming, new Aga cooker that rumbled on the far side of the room. "You can stay here if you want. I will go upstairs to the landing."

Before he could leave the room, an older woman who looked like Helen came in carrying a small baby. She smiled at Peter and then looked towards her daughter.

"This is Reverend Barnes," Helen said. "Amanda, my mother."

"I didn't know you had called him. I fell asleep on the bed and Agnes has just woken up."

Peter could sense a tension from the way she spoke. "Nice to meet you," he said as she passed the child to its mother.

"Are you doing the right thing?" she asked him. "Will it work?"

"Would you like to come with me?" he asked.

The woman hesitated and looked from him to her daughter.

"Should I?" she asked Helen.

"Please," Helen said as she held her baby closer. Reluctantly, the woman followed Peter from the room.

"Is it the rooms on the landing?" he asked as they walked up the grand, open staircase that followed the walls of the double-vaulted hallway, its walls already filled with large pieces of modern art.

Amanda saw him looking at the painting. "Hugo has an obsession for them," she said as they reached the first half landing and looked back at a modernist painting of what could possibly be a horse. "They cost a fortune, but my daughter married a bottomless money pit."

"Have they been together a long time?"

"Two years," she answered curtly. "He is much older, married before, whirlwind romance," Amanda tried to smile as they walked up the next staircase.

He could see from her face that she was not happy with her daughter's situation. Peter felt a sudden chill in the air and gave a visible shiver.

"Is this the place?" he asked as the hairs on the back of his neck started to stand on end.

"Can you feel it?" Amanda asked.

"There is a change in the atmosphere at the top of the stairs. A draught?"

"A draught that slams doors and stamps along the floorboards?" she replied with a single raised eyebrow.

Peter unwrapped the thin, gold priest's stole that he took from his jacket pocket and put it over his shoulders. He twisted the silver stopper from the bottle of holy water and put it in his pocket. Then he looked around the long hallway. "I am going to say the Lord's Prayer and then go into each room and cast some water and salt. You can either stay here or follow me, it's up to you."

Amanda nodded. She had not prayed for many years. "Okay," she answered.

"Our Father, who art in heaven, Hallowed be thy name." A bedroom door suddenly slammed shut as a sudden gust sped up the stairs and along the passageway. Undaunted, Peter carried on praying. Amanda joined in. The words she had last said as a child came back to her from some lost vault in her memory. "The Power and the Glory," he went on, his voice getting stronger.

"Forever and ever," she echoed as another door slammed in the breeze.

"*Amen*," they said together.

Amanda breathed heavily as the adrenaline pulsed through her.

Peter said nothing as he handed her a small salt cellar. He turned and opened the door of the first room. "In the Name of Jesus, may all spirits be at peace and go to the place appointed for you. May the Holy Spirit be in this place. Amen," Peter said as he splashed holy water to the four corners of the room.

"Amen," she repeated as she instinctively sprinkled the salt then followed him to the next room where Peter repeated the prayer and the blessing.

They had soon prayed in all the rooms and now stood at the top of the stairs, looking down to the grand hallway with its open fire and long dining table with twelve chairs.

"The peace of God, which passes all understanding," Peter began the final prayer, his voice louder and stronger than before. Amanda could not concentrate. She closed her eyes and gripped tightly to the banister as she held back her tears. "The blessing of God almighty, the Father, the Son, and the Holy Spirit, be among you and remain with you always."

"Amen!" she shouted, her voice echoing around the galleried hallway.

"Amen," Peter answered softly as he put his hand on her shoulder. "How are you?"

The woman smiled. The smile broadened into an infectious laugh.

"I am fine. Thank you, Vicar. I feel as if a line has been drawn under what has happened.

"Is everything okay?" Helen shouted from below them.

"I'm fine, Helen," her mother answered as she leant over the banister and waved. Turning to Peter, she spoke quietly. "Thank you for coming. I feel that whatever it was had fed from my daughter's discontent. Do you think that is possible?"

He thought for a moment. "Is she very unhappy?" he asked.

"Helen liked the town. They had a lovely house on St Hilda's Terrace in the middle of Whitby. Hugo wanted a bigger place with land and bought The Grange without telling her. He treats her more like his child than his wife."

"And she stays with him regardless?"

"Helen has given up everything for him. Her job, her life, and most of her friends…" she stopped speaking as Helen walked towards them.

"Are you talking about me?" she said, holding the baby close.

"Just about the house," he answered. "It is a beautiful old place. You should invite your friends to come and stay when your husband is not here."

"And have them scared to death?" Helen replied with a shrug of her shoulders.

"I think all that is over," her mother answered as she looked back up the grand staircase.

"These old houses are amazingly built. I would suggest that you close any downstairs windows at night. The passageway in the east wing acts as a chimney. It sucks up the air from outside. I noticed the smell of honeysuckle when I was upstairs. It was coming from the bush outside the open window on the right-hand side of the front door."

"A draught caused the doors to slam?" her mother asked.

"Possibly. If each bedroom had an open door and an open window then the doors could close one after the other. There was a squall last night."

"What about the footsteps and the book flying off the shelf?" Helen replied.

"That I cannot explain. We have prayed and asked for peace. You will know over the next few days."

"And tonight?" she asked.

"You have my number. Call me if there is another problem. I will come straight over," he said as he took her hand and held it tightly. "Fill the house with your favourite music and laughter. Ghosts don't like it."

"Music?" her mother asked.

"Music, friends, and laughter. Make the house your own and fill it with your life and energy. This house has been empty for too long. Make it your home."

"I haven't had the chance to make any friends around here. I don't know where to start."

"My wife and I know how that feels," he replied as he walked to the door. "Perhaps we have to get out and find the people who we want in our lives."

[8]
Agincourt Fingers

The drive back to the village took longer than Peter expected. A tractor rattled ahead of him for most of the way and didn't even consider pulling over. It went on for mile after mile, and the young driver with a fat face and gap-toothed smile looked back, laughing to himself.

Instead of going straight to the vicarage, Peter drove to the petrol station on the main road to Pickering. He had thoughts of buying a newspaper, some coffee, and a bacon sandwich. His idea was to drink and eat in the car as he read the paper. Away from the vicarage, he was away from the phone, and he needed the space to think through what had happened at The Grange.

Pulling up on the forecourt, he parked his car and walked into the shop. He was the only customer. The curly-haired man behind the counter nodded and smiled.

"Morning, Vicar," he said as he shuffled the cigarettes along the shelf. "What will you be having?"

"Bacon butty, coffee, and a *Yorkshire Post*."

"Right," the man answered as he went into the back of the shop and grunted the request to his wife in the kitchen. He soon returned with a white paper bag and a tall paper cup. Peter handed him the money. "There you go," he said cheerfully. "Pick up your paper on the way out."

Peter thanked the man and left the shop. On the forecourt was an old, red pickup. It had seen better days. The front wing was crumpled at the side and the driver's door was badly dented.

"I had a fight with a lorry and the lorry won," a familiar voice said from behind him.

"Stella," he answered as he turned to greet her. "What are you doing here at such a time in the morning?"

"Early start. I want to finish the wall by the tree and then I have a couple of jobs that have been waiting for ages," she answered as she peaked inside the paper bag. "Dead pig?" Stella asked.

"Dead pig and coffee. I really need it."

"I hear you have been speaking to Bruce," Stella replied.

"News travels fast. Did he tell you or was it just gossip?"

"He's my cousin. Rang me last night and told me you have been giving him botanical advice."

"Possibly, I couldn't say," Peter answered.

"He is a good lad. Would never sell any of that stuff," Stella answered as she tied up her hair into a tight bun and then fixed it with a pencil.

"Not a very wise one growing dope in someone's back garden."

"It's medicinal. Bruce has the *black dog* and chronic arthritis. Since he has been taking it, he has got back to work and is so much better," she said, hoping for some sympathy.

"It's illegal. A controlled drug. He could get over five years in prison."

"Who has the right to say that a plant is illegal? I know plants in the fields ten times more dangerous. Alcohol is a killer and homewrecker, but you can get that everywhere. Without his herbs, Bruce will go downhill. Anne Hindle knows exactly what is growing in her garden, they both do. She was an industrial chemist in her time and her companion was a headteacher."

Peter put the sandwich down on the front of his car and took a sip of coffee. Stella folded her arms and gave him a tight-lipped stare.

"Okay. All I can say is that I won't be revisiting Miss Hindle in the near future."

Stella smiled. "You're not such a prat after all," she said sarcastically, as if she spoke to an old friend.

"I want something in return," he said before she could walk away.

"And what might that be?"

"Do you know The Grange?" he asked. "Just out of the forestry on the moor road?"

"Some new people have just moved in. Helen Parker is out there on her own and I thought that you might be able to help her not feel so isolated. They have a wall that has fallen down. Might be some work in it for you," Peter said as he opened the paper bag, took out the almost cold sandwich, and had a deep bite.

"You want me to nanny an incomer?" Stella asked.

"Yes," Peter nodded, unable to answer as he chewed the tough sinews.

"Rapunzel in her tower?" she asked.

"Helen is a nice person," he replied as he chewed a wad of meat and bread. "She is stuck out there with a new baby and I thought someone like you might make a good friend."

"What if I take her to the dark side?" Stella asked impishly.

"You are not on the dark side, so how can you take her there?"

"Your congregation might not like you introducing people to a witch."

"Then they will burn me at the stake and not you. So, will you go and see her?"

"You are one to be watched, Reverend Barnes. A very sneaky vicar."

"Do you want a bite of my sandwich?"

"Meat? I would rather eat my own foot. At least then, it would be only my life that is taken."

"Witch and vegetarian? You are a box of surprises," Peter said, taking another bite as the juices burst from within and trickled across his chin.

"Wrong. Typical police stereotyping. I sometimes will eat fish. By the way, I also live in a house. I am not a New Age traveller,"

Stella laughed as she walked away. "I will go and see your friend and convert her to devil worship."

"Thought you would, that's why I told you about her," he shouted back as she gave him a two-fingered answer as she went inside the shop.

[9]
The Holy Well

Peter spent the rest of the morning combing through the filing cabinet and reading the minutes of the church council meetings over many years. It was a sad indictment on his faith that Christians could fall out with each other over so many things. They had argued over what brand of coffee they should serve after the Eucharist, how tall the Christmas tree should be, what version of the Bible people should be allowed to read from and who should run the tombola at the annual church fête. These arguments had led to resignations and letters to the archbishop. All these petty squabbles were recorded in black ink with the names of the antagonists written alongside their complaints. Then there were copies of the letters sent to the bishop asking him to remove every priest over the last twenty years. They spoke of a parish riven with bitterness, that had obviously driven most of the ordinary people away. The arguments had left behind a hard core of stalwarts committed to continuing their resentments until the Angel of Death took them from this world.

Peter wondered if this was why most of his congregation were so old. Obviously, God did not want their company and the Devil had no intention of giving them house room for fear of them taking over Hell.

It was two hours later when he found the file he was looking for. It had been sealed in a brown envelope with thick tape and inscribed in large letters were the words *Holy Well*. Opening the envelope, he let the papers spill out over his desk. There were letters to and from the bishop, minutes of several meetings, a map of the location of the well and messages from parishioners. Walstan's Well was the cause of much consternation and anger.

As he read, he realised that it was visited as part of the pilgrimage to the yew tree. On the last Sunday of August each year, people would come to the village and gather at six o'clock in the evening by the double tree at the crossroads. From there they would walk to the well, fill flasks and bottles with the spring water and then make their way across the fields to the old yew. There, the pilgrims would water the roots of the tree and tie their prayers to its branches. It had been Reverend Green who had wanted to stop this. From the letters, he was adamant that this was evil and based on witchcraft. All his prose were filled with hate towards anyone who attended. Peter read on, realising that the date was the anniversary of the hanging of Esther Corbridge. Green had made it his sole purpose to put an end to the connection between the death of a witch and his church.

In pursuit of this, the minutes of a meeting held a year ago clearly stated that the spring was to be bricked up and the water piped into the drains. No one at the meeting had dared to disagree. The word of Mr Green was to be obeyed; he was the evangelical man who had the ear of God.

This was yet another issue that had been kept from him at his interview. He had been given the impression that St Walstan's was a typical rural parish with a few loyal, diehard parishioners. There had been no mention that they were financially insolvent and couldn't afford to pay one penny of the parish share. Nor had he been told that the tower of the church was in disrepair and needed ten thousand pounds spending urgently from funds they did not have. It was enough to turn a vicar to drink and had done so with the Reverend Green.

When he had walked through the churchyard, he couldn't find the well, such were the lengths the parish had gone to in allowing the bushes to become overgrown. Under the guise of rewilding, it had been hidden from everyone.

As he rustled through the paperwork, a handwritten note fell out. It was written in green ink by an educated hand. The words were a petition to Green to reconsider what he was doing. Peter read it quickly, his eyes darting to the signature. *Estelle Corbridge*. Across the note in thick, black capitals, written in another hand was the word, *witch*.

Folding the note, Peter slipped it into his wallet, put on his jacket, and locked his office door.

Outside the vicarage, the sun cracked the leaves of the trees with its heat. A cloudless sky went from horizon to horizon as swallows circled high above. Peter walked quickly from the vicarage to the churchyard. Opposite was the double tree that stood on a small green of mown grass. Its entwined branches were heavy with oak and birch leaves. The two trunks were wrapped around each other like a passionate embrace of secret lovers.

Pushing open the gate, he made his way through the ancient gravestones to a small dip in the ground where elder and buddleja had been allowed to grow unhindered. Clearing a way through, Peter found a small, templelike structure made of cut stone. The opening had been roughly bricked up with a plastic pipe sticking through and disappearing into the ground.

The mortar was breaking away in several places and the bricks were loose. Peter prodded the bricks as until one by one, they fell away. He took the bricks and stacked them to one side until the stone arch was opened to reveal a deep well of clear water. The plastic pipe was pulled from the water and pushed aside. Peter dipped his hands and washed away the heat of the day. He drank the water. It was cool and fresh.

"Don't let them see you doing that, Vicar," the voice came from several feet away.

He looked up. Morris Marsden, an old crow of a man, looked down at him from the footpath. In his hands were a bunch of keys on an old, iron bull ring. He had been the churchwarden for the last thirty years and had stood unopposed time and time again. Even on a hot summer's day, he wore a Dickensian, winter overcoat, its shoulders covered in a fall of dead skin that had escaped from under his age-worn Homburg hat.

"Morris, what are you doing here?"

"I was just going to the church to dress the altar."

"I found this old well. It looks as though it has been vandalised. I have taken out the bricks in case anyone is injured. I would hate for you to be sued for negligence as churchwarden."

"Indeed, Vicar. Very considerate of you to think that way," Morris answered nervously in his corvid-like voice as he wondered what the other members of the church council would think.

"The water tastes amazing, so cool and fresh. We should bottle it," Peter said getting to his feet. "What idiot had it bricked up? It is a resource for the parish. It must have a great deal of history."

"Reverend Green would differ on that opinion," Morris answered as if his friend, Mr Green, was still the vicar. "We passed a unanimous resolution."

"If Reverend Green had drunk this water and not sniffed so much of the barmaid's apron, he might still be here today."

"Indeed, Vicar. Indeed," he answered politely. "What exactly do you intend to do with the well? Have it bricked up again? Reverend Green—"

"Is in rehab for alcoholism and will be there for some time," Peter answered as he made his way up the slope towards the man. "Whatever he thought about the well or what he did will be voted on by the council. I have checked, and Walstan's Well is a listed monument, and bricking it up was illegal. I cannot find a faculty from the diocese for the work. As the only churchwarden, that makes you responsible. I might have to inform the English Heritage, the County Council, and the bishop as to what has been done here and see if they wish to take legal action. It might have to go to a consistory court."

Morris visibly shuddered at the threat of a consistory court. He touched his hat nervously. The idea the diocese might put him on trial for bricking up an ancient well made his mouth go dry and fingers shake. Morris was the only churchwarden and had been so for the last eleven years since Mrs Hinchcliffe had resigned. She had taken her bat, ball, and chequebook home with her and even moved out of the village, all because of an argument over a Victoria sponge. Undeterred, Morris had stuck to his guns. He was a churchman through and through. Anglicanism ran in his blood since becoming a choirboy at the age of seven, and too many Victoria sponges at the church fête could never be allowed.

"Court?" he answered thoughtfully as the lump in his thin neck bounced up and down. "*Court?*" his voice squeaked as he said the word again. "Perhaps Reverend Green was wrong in his disdain for the well. I will get Bruce to cut back the bushes and we can restore it to what it was before. Will it need a faculty?"

"I suggest it is a minor repair. It is not even worth mentioning this to the archdeacon. It could be just between you and me. Vicar and churchwarden. How do you feel about that?"

Morris gave a deep and relieved sigh.

"It's good to have someone so up on the law to guide us through all of these problems," he said as he fiddled with the keys in his hand.

Peter took out his wallet and unfolded the note. "Can you remember ever seeing this?" he asked him.

Morris read the note, his eyes skimming back and forth. "Where did you get this?" he asked.

"From the file. Surely, you would have been made aware of everything to do with the well?"

"Not this. I know nothing of it."

"One thing, who owns the green with the double tree?"

"It's the church. The red line plans are in the office. The whole of the village green is ours. We allow the village access."

"So, the double tree belongs to the parish?" Peter asked.

"The tree, the land, and the village green. All of it," Morris boasted as he held his arms wide. "We even own the high field that surrounds the yew tree up there," he said pointing to the tumuli.

"The place where they hung a woman for witchcraft," Peter said.

"Witchcraft? No. She was hung for theft of a pig," Morris answered.

"But I thought she was a witch?"

"That was what they wanted to hang her for but in 1815, you couldn't hang a woman for witchcraft. The vicar at the time was John Seagrave. His brother was the magistrate, he lived in The Grange. Between them, they made sure that Esther Corbridge could not escape the rope. A stolen pig was found in her cottage. That could not be denied. They hanged her for theft," Morris sighed as if he was speaking of an event he had observed himself. "It was obvious the pig had been smuggled into the cottage. As you would say, the evidence was planted, and she was fitted up," the man giggled.

"Esther Corbridge was murdered. Murdered by the vicar and his brother?"

"I suppose it could be seen that way. Things were different back then. I have been studying the history of this village for the last fifty years and a lot of the things that happened in the past would never happen today."

"Do you not think the murder of a woman should be put right?" Peter asked.

"What is the point? It all happened a long time ago," Morris answered as they walked towards the front door of the church.

"The sins of the father visited on the sons," Peter answered. "She was killed for a crime she did not commit. All the priests of this parish should have put it right, but they failed to do so. What was their fate?"

"Well, none of them stayed for very long. I admit it is a litany of early death, larceny, and dipsomania, but in their way, they were all good men." Morris thought for a while before continuing. "And of course, there was Albert Shepherd. He just vanished in 1966, never to be seen again. Some say he ran off with a chicken fancier he had met on a retreat."

"What was the fate of the Reverend Seagrave?" Peter asked.

"He was made the Archdeacon of Whitby. His brother bestowed a significant gift to the diocese."

"He was bought a promotion?"

"Seagrave was the third son. His eldest brother inherited The Grange estate. The family built the extension to the aisle and financed the church for many years. The middle brother was an army officer and Seaward, the younger, became a priest. He employed a perpetual curate to preach the sermon every Sunday. You have to understand that the living of St Walstan's was very profitable. The tithes and rents paid to the church at that time would be worth at least sixty thousand pounds today. Seagrave kept the living until the day he died."

"And got away with murder," Peter answered.

[10]
The Snake And The Frog

It had rained hard all night. The downpour had been relentless, smashing against the roof tiles of the vicarage as if it were the end of the world. A fox had howled throughout the dark hours. Its childlike cry pierced the windows and cut through the curtains. Peter had not slept. His restless mind had kept him awake. In his half-wake, half-slumber, he had waited for the phone to ring and for him to be called to The Grange. He thought of ghosts and spirits and in his mind, he went over and over the prayer of exorcism, unable to remember all the words.

By the time daylight crept over the windowsill, it had stopped raining. Finally, he fell asleep. He yawned deeply as he pulled the blankets up around him and slipped deeper into the pillow. The bed held him as if it would never let go, such was its comfort. Dreams came quickly. So did the cawing of the cockerel and the moaning of the cows in the church field. Every creature on earth had crawled from its hiding place to welcome the dawn with a deafening noise.

"Dear God," he said to himself as he rolled from the bed and went to the bathroom. He showered in cold water that warmed slightly with the dregs of the overnight tank. As the water flooded over him, he thought of ways to rid the village of the cockerel that he could still hear cackling in the village. Even though the shower water thundered down, somewhere very near, the cockerel welcomed the day.

Peter mused with the idea of catching the bird, taking it to another village, and releasing it there. He didn't think that chickens had a homing instinct, and it would be a long way for them to walk.

His thoughts were inspired by an incident with a drunken man late one night on the Whitby Road in Pickering. He had been parked in his patrol car and watched the man stagger up the street as if he was walking out of the town. As he did so, the man bounced off the stone wall and held onto a lamppost with whom he had a long and loud conversation.

Peter thought it best to intervene before the man injured himself or the lamppost. "What's your name? Where are you going?" he asked the man as he got out of the police car and walked towards him.

The middle-aged man was well dressed in a jacket and tie with casual trousers and didn't look like the usual Friday night drunk. He stared at Peter, a confused look on his face. "Sleights. Home," he managed to say after several attempts.

"You live in Sleights?" Peter asked, knowing that the village was a twenty-minute drive over the moors.

The man nodded with a drunken smile as he held onto the lamppost and hugged it as if it were his new best friend. "Yes. No taxi. Won't take me. I'm drunk."

"I didn't realise you were drunk," Peter said as he took hold of his arm.

He knew that he had two options. One was to arrest the man for being drunk and incapable. The other was to put him in the police car and drive him across the moor to Sleights. After all, Peter thought, he did have to check the gatehouse at RAF Fylingdales to see if there were any protesters, and it was on the way back.

"Are you the police?" the man asked.

"No, I am your local spaceman," he answered sarcastically.

"Thank you, spaceman," the man repeated.

Five minutes later, the man was in the car, fastened in, with a sick bucket in his lap, and the window open. Peter drove as steadily as he could. The man soon fell asleep with the motion of the car. His head lolled back, mouth open and beer dribble streaming across his chin.

In twenty minutes, he was in the village of Sleights and stopped on the corner of Coach Road by the fish and chip shop. "Where do you live?" he asked the man.

"There," the man drunkenly pointed to the telephone box.

"That house?" he asked.

"Yes," the man nodded insistently as he attempted to open the car door.

Peter helped the man out and made sure he was steady enough to be left.

"Shall I walk you to the door?" he asked.

"No," the man said, taking a house key from his pocket. "Wife asleep."

Peter got back in the car and watched the man walk off into the darkness. Driving back across the moors, he had checked the gatehouse of the early warning station and then drove back towards Pickering. As he passed the turn off to Levisham, the force radio crackled.

"*Delta Whisky to all units. We have just had a call from a man from Pickering who insists he was abducted by an alien and dumped in Sleights at the phone box. He seems to be drunk. Anyone seen anything unusual? Foxtrot-Papa-Three-Five, are you in Pickering?*"

Hearing his call sign, Peter pulled the car to the side of the road. He was filled with a sudden dread as he realised what had happened.

"Three-Five to control. I am in Levisham and haven't seen a thing all night. No aliens here," Peter answered. "What was the man's name?"

"*Sleightholme, Derek Sleightholme,*" the control room answered. "*I told him to sleep it off in the phone box and get the bus back in the morning.*"

"Ten-four," he replied, hoping he would never see the man again. *Sleights... home...* he thought, was his name and not his destination.

Stealing the cockerel and taking it to another village would be no good, he thought as he remembered Mr Sleightholme. The bird still crowed as Peter got dressed. It was five-thirty. He checked the phone to see if it was working and rang the speaking clock. The time, sponsored by Accurist, confirmed the early hour.

Peter made a flask of coffee and packed some bread and cheese. There was nothing in the diary until three in the afternoon. He had written his sermon for Sunday, and, looking out of the window, he could see that the sky to the west was clear of clouds.

As he got to the front door, he heard a vehicle on the driveway.

Outside, Greg Clark, the milkman jumped from his van and ran to the porch. He looked more a rugby player than a milkman. Winter or summer, he always wore shorts and trainers. Peter had known him for the last three years.

A milkman was the early morning eyes of the police who could roam the countryside and see things no copper ever could. They had met early one morning in mid-January when Greg had found a chemist had been broken into. He had driven to a phone box and called the police. Peter had caught the burglar in the back of the shop, stoned on the drugs he was trying to steal. From then on, Greg would always stop if he saw Peter in his patrol car and let him know who was out and about.

"Morning Greg. Glad I caught you," Peter said, thankful the milk wouldn't endure the heat of the day.

"You're an early bird, Peter," Greg answered. "You are the only one up in these parts. Where are you going at this time in the morning?"

"Onto the moor and then back through the woods," he answered as he took the milk from the milkman. "Just can't sleep."

"It's shift work. That's what does it," Greg answered. "Trouble is, I never get a day off."

"My days of shifts are over. Since I came here, I have gone part time. Nine to five and five to one. Occasional night to fill in for sick leave."

"Good stuff. Don't want to be a doom-monger, but watch out for the hagworms," Greg said as he turned to go back to the van with its engine still running.

"What?" he asked.

"Adders, vipers, hagworms. The moor is full of them. It's been a good summer for snakes and last night's rain will see them out looking for food."

"I certainly will," he answered.

"Found one last week up by the lake at the back of Ellerburn. It had choked on a frog. Poor snake was dead with the back legs of the frog sticking out of its mouth. A choked snake? Imagine that. Aren't you lot good at getting rid of them?"

"My lot?" he asked. "The police?"

"No. Saint Hilda and Patrick? Didn't they get rid of them?" the milkman asked as he leant against the bonnet of his van.

"Just a legend. A metaphor. I'm not sure if they actually got rid of them."

"There are no hagworms in Ireland, so something must have happened," Greg protested. "Not sure what a metaphor is. They either got rid of them or they didn't, and if they didn't, then it's all a load of bull, isn't it?"

Peter didn't think it was the right time to discuss the subtleties of medieval theology as he held two pints of full cream milk and a carton of orange juice, with a rucksack hanging off one shoulder and a rumbling milk wagon waking up the village.

"You are right," he answered quickly. "It's bullshit. Probably all made up," Peter replied. "Don't think they meant real snakes at all."

"I read all about it in the *Fortean Times*, the snakes were turned into stone." The milkman was adamant. "If that isn't true, then what about the rest of it?"

"Rest of what?" Peter asked, knowing it was the wrong thing to do.

"God. Jesus. Death?"

"What are you doing tonight?" Peter asked.

"Why?"
"Come around. We can talk. Have a beer? Half-six?"
"I go to bed at nine. Make it half-five."

[11]
The Twisted Tree

Greg Clark had insisted on giving Peter a lift in his van to the top of the village where the road faded and joined a forest track. He thought it would make up for the time he had wasted talking about saints getting rid of snakes. The milk bottles had rattled in the crates as Greg tried to miss the potholes in the road.

As the van drove off, Peter listened to the sounds of the forest. A group of pheasants called to each other through the clear morning air. It was as if they knew that in summer, they were safe from the guns that would come for them on the first day of October. Only the fox was a threat and many of these had gone to the towns to be free of the red-jacketed men and fat ladies on horseback who insisted on chasing them across the fields with a pack of dogs.

Peter walked on. The forest trail narrowed as it went uphill. The thick planting of pine trees blocked out the morning sun, giving a home to swirling clouds of tiny, black midges. He was soon covered. The beasts burrowed into his hair and up the sleeves of his shirt. The bites came quick and fast. Peter increased his pace and soon broke into a fast jog to escape the onslaught.

A hundred yards ahead, the forest opened to the moor. Here, a stiff breeze blew across the heather taking away the swarms of *Culicoides*. Peter took off his shirt and shook out the midges, then used it to rub his hair. He felt as if they were still crawling on his skin.

Tying the shirt around his waist, he set off. The morning sun beat down on the remnants of the Roman road on which he walked. After four miles he was at the head of the valley that overlooked The Grange. He could see the house below with its Georgian windows and side extensions. To the front of the house was the lake and the ha-ha that encircled it. Peter knew it would take him an hour to walk to The Grange. He wanted to call in to see what the night had brought for them.

As he walked down the track, Peter noticed an adder sunning itself on the bank. It lay curled, basking in the heat of the morning, unaware that it was being watched. Some distance away, two horses and riders hacked up the track. Peter put on his shirt as they got closer.

"Morning," he shouted as the riders ignored him. They kept their gaze firmly to the front as the horses plodded by. They looked like a mother and daughter out for a ride. The older woman was in her fifties. She had thin, suntanned arms with a gold Rolex watch that hung loosely from her wrist. The younger woman had long, blonde hair tied at the back in a tight knot. They were both dressed identically. White jodhpurs, blue polo shirts and cream gilets. Peter stood back to let them pass. "A good morning to be out."

Neither woman answered. It was as if he wasn't there. He had never seen them before or knew who they were. His greeting was that of someone wanting to be friendly, a country priest welcome with no menace or threat.

The horses passed by, their riders stoic in their avoidance of his smile. Peter shrugged and carried on walking. He was used to being ignored in a town if he said "hello" to a passerby, especially if he was wearing a clerical collar. It was as if, if they responded to his smile, he would drag them into some kind of cult.

In the country, it was a different matter. People usually spoke to fellow travellers. They passed the time of day with each other and chatted about the weather, the fields or how good the harvest would be. Not so much with the two riders. They acted as if they had met a servant who had overstepped his station and dared to even speak to them.

He gave them a second glance as he walked on and could see they were talking to each other, probably about him. After his years in the police, Peter had developed a thick skin and a broad back, and it would take more than two silent, rich women to get under his skin. He had met the type before, the parvenu of the countryside in their super clean Range Rovers and houses with Laura Ashley curtains.

When he arrived at the house, the gates to The Grange were shut. Climbing the wall, he noticed the red pickup parked in the copse of trees by the broken-down stone wall. Peter smiled to himself, knowing that Stella had come to the house and had got the job of building the wall. Yet, she was nowhere to be seen.

It was a ten-minute walk to the house. The long driveway twisted across the parkland along the edge of the lake and to the gravel forecourt outside the house. Peter took the direct route across the park. As he climbed the ha-ha, he saw a solitary tree. Going closer, he realised its thick branches were a mixture of oak and willow. Just like the witch-tree in his village, it was two trees planted together that had grown into an inosculation. Peter thought it was strange. This couldn't just be a coincidence. The willow-oak was obviously a lot younger than the witch tree by at least a hundred years. Its height was not as great, and the tree had the look of youth about it.

Looking to the house, he saw two women at the door. He could see it was Helen Parker and Stella. They both waved as he got closer.

"Morning," Helen shouted cheerfully as he got near. "To what do we owe this visit?"

"I came to see how you are?" he said, not wanting to break the confidence of his previous visit.

"Don't worry, Helen has told me everything," Stella answered. "You did a good job. They had a peaceful night. I'll have to watch out, you might have me exorcised."

"Legion?" he laughed. "Too many demons for me to handle."

"The only legion around here are the midge bites on your arms," Stella answered as Peter quickly rolled down the sleeves of his shirt to cover the marks.

"It was amazing. We had a peaceful night with no banging or footsteps," Helen said as she handed Stella the baby. "Fancy a cuppa? You look as though you need one. I'll bring a pot out and we can sit in the garden."

Stella nodded and wrapped the baby in her arms as if she had done it a thousand times before.

"Do you have children?" he asked.

"I wish. It is the one thing in life that has escaped me. I don't make good choices when it comes to men."

"Sorry," he answered.

"Apologising again. Is that what you are going to say when the blue rinse mob comes for you?"

"In what way?"

"I hear you opened up the well and threatened *Mad Morris* with a consistory court," Stella said, smiling broadly.

"News travels fast."

"Morris popped up the bar last night. He told everyone he was frightened you would tell English Heritage. Bruce rang me to let me know. Thought it would make me laugh."

"Did it?"

"I laughed like a drain," she answered. "Whose side are you on?"

"What do you mean?" he asked.

"You've only been vicar a few days and already you have upset half your congregation. They have a habit of being able to get rid of their clergy."

"There was no faculty. It was illegal. I do everything by the book and Jack Green was in the wrong."

"Always a copper."

"I certainly am, Estelle Corbridge. That is who you are, isn't it? Corbridge was your maiden name? The woman murdered was a maternal great, great, grandmother?"

"No shit, Sherlock. How did you work that one out?" Stella asked, shocked at the revelation.

"I found a letter from you to Jack Green and signed in your maiden name."

"Ah, that letter," she answered as she remembered what she had written. "Not my best use of the English language. I think I was drunk at the time."

"Block up the Holy Well and I will shove each brick up your arsehole, you fat, bald, git?" he said, quoting the words.

"You missed out the F-word," she answered, laughing.

"More tea, vicar?" Helen said jokingly as she came out of the house carrying a tray. "I have always wanted to say that."

"Wish I had a quid for every time someone had," he answered as he and Stella followed Helen to a rose-covered pergola over an outside dining table and oak chairs. "It's a beautiful house."

"I wish I had a quid," she answered. "Before we came here, we had a home in Whitby. It was all I ever wanted. George wanted something bigger, better and he bought this place."

"It has quite a lot of history," Stella added. "The Seagraves lived here for three hundred years. It was empty from '67 to '84."

"It was renovated ten years ago by the people we bought it from. They moved to London with work," Helen said as she poured the tea.

"That tree. The willow and oak. Do you know anything about it?" Peter said, pointing across the park. "We have a similar one in the village. Two trees growing together."

"Funny you mention that. I have a painting of the house from 1965. The tree hadn't been planted then."

"Seagrave's wife left him in '66," Stella said as she bad-eyed Peter for talking about the witch tree. "Took all her things, the dog and some money and was never seen again. That's what my mother told me when I was a bairn. Took off on the day of the World Cup final."

Peter looked at her but said nothing.

"I found a box of old clothes in the attic. It was the only part of the house the Hirst's hadn't renovated. They were from the sixties. All folded neatly and wrapped in tissue paper as if they had been kept for a reason and then forgotten."

"Where did Seagrave go when he left here?" Peter asked.

"My mother never said. That wasn't the gossip. His wife had been carrying on with someone in the village but no one ever found out who it was," Stella answered as she took a gulp of tea and then got up from the table. "Better be off. Wall won't mend itself. Call by when you go back to the vicarage. I have something in the van that will take the sting out of those midge bites on your arms."

[12]
Bog-Myrtle

The red pickup was parked under the trees. On the bonnet was a battered drinks flask and open packet of biscuits in a Tupperware bowl. Stella was in the ditch, stacking and sorting the stones into piles according to size and shape. She had stripped back the wall even further than it had been broken down by the fallen tree.

"Looks like hard work," Peter said as he stepped into the shade. Stella looked up.

"Thanks for the tip-off for the job. Helen wants me to sort all the walls of the estate," she said as she got up off her knees and wiped her hands on her dungarees. "I've got something for your midge bites."

"I have never been bitten so badly before," he answered.

"Did you drink alcohol last night?" she asked.

"Does that matter?"

"Midges love the booze and meat eaters. The female has to fill her stomach with blood before she can lay her eggs."

"Typical woman," he said under his breath as Stella walked to the pickup.

"Heard that, you misogynist."

"Sorry."

"Not accepted," Stella said as she reached into her bag, pulled out a small, glass jar and threw it at him.

"There you go. Bog myrtle and Calendula, it will ward the little buggers off and give you some relief."

"Is it any good with parishioners?"

"You are going to need something," she answered as she leant against the van. "You have picked your first fight over the well."

"What they did was wrong. They had no right to brick it up in the first place," Peter shrugged. "Pilgrimage is at the centre of faith, regardless of how the tradition started."

"Christmas, Easter, all stolen from Paganism," Stella added as she brought out a pouch of tobacco and hand-rolled a cigarette.

"We didn't steal them. We just changed the emphasis."

Stella laughed loudly as she lit the cigarette and took a long draw. "You have a cheek," she said as she exhaled the smoke. "They even built the church on a Pagan site."

"I agree. The well is for everyone, and I would like to see it used by everyone."

"What?" she said in surprise. "Would you let my coven worship there?"

"As long as you allow me to make sure no chickens are harmed in the service."

"Pillock," she answered as they both laughed. "I never know when you are being serious."

"What do you know about the Seagraves?" Peter asked, taking her by surprise.

"Make me laugh and then ask the question you wanted to ask in the first place?"

"They killed one of your relatives," Peter answered. "Hanged her for theft, as an excuse for her witchcraft."

"Who told you that?"

"Morris. He said they hanged her because she stole a pig, but it was really because they feared she was a witch."

"Did you know that a pig on a spear is the coat of arms of the Seagrave family? There is a heraldic shield above your pulpit and altar. They made sure that the Seagrave name was above the word of your god and above the sacrament of your god," Stella sighed. "I think that is why they said she had a pig put in her cottage. It was a symbol of their wealth and power. Esther never stole a pig. It was a fit up."

"How come it all came to an end and they sold the estate?"

"All I can think is, when the wife of Magnus Seagrave left, he sold the whole lot and went away. My mother worked here for a while when she was a young girl. She said the Seagraves were a power couple with a party of friends and fast cars. Beautiful people in the swinging sixties. John Lennon even stayed here. Then it all went wrong for them. As I said before, his wife ran away with another man. Why do you ask?"

"I would just like to know what kind of family would set someone up and have them murdered. It doesn't fit right. There must be something more to it. I want to find out."

"How are you going to do that? Seagrave is long gone. There is no family left. That's why the house was left empty. Nobody made a claim against the estate."

"Is there a land agent?"

"Grenville's in Malton. They seem to be the people who look after most of the big houses. I have worked for them before." Stella answered, unsure as to his motives. "Why are you so interested?"

"I would just like to find out what happened to them."

"Am I supposed to believe that?" she asked. "Typical answer from a copper."

[13]
Mr Griffin's Organ

The door to the church was wide open. From inside, the segued chords of *The Dam Busters March* and *The Old Wooden Cross* echoed around the oak-vaulted ceiling and out into the churchyard. Peter walked into the cool shade of the porch. The scent of the roses that clung to the stonework followed him. He stood by the oak door with its iron straps and listened. Every note was precise, accurate and executed. He couldn't understand why Gerald Griffin was the organist of a church in the backwater of a Yorkshire village. His playing could easily grace York Minster.

Yet Griffin was a private man with no musical ambition. A confirmed bachelor who lived alone on the edges of the village, he taught piano and organ as a peripatetic music teacher in schools around the county, as well as having a long list of private organ students. He was round-faced and fat-fingered, his joviality, hail-fellow-well-met and love of life was infectious to all. However, there was sometimes a sadness to his playing that betrayed the real state of his heart.

Peter listened for several minutes as Griffin jumped from tune to tune like a nightclub disc jockey. The sunlit, stained glass windows cast coloured lights across the medieval wall paintings of saints and dragons.

Finally, Griffin stopped and looked to the door.

"I didn't want to interrupt. It was beautiful," Peter said as he walked down the aisle.

"You are too kind," Griffin answered, giving him a small bow of the head. "It is so enjoyable to sit here on a warm day and lose myself in the music. Jack Green didn't have time for the old hymns. He wanted to play guitar and sing *Shine, Jesus, Shine* every Sunday as he sang in tongues."

"Quite a feat whilst playing guitar," Peter answered. "I hope you don't mind me handing the selection of music over to you. I always find the church organist knows what the congregation can cope with."

"That would be a relief and a joy. My organ has difficulty with modern tunes and the meagre bunch on Sunday just babble their way through every hymn, and this week we have a baptism during the service."

"I wasn't aware," he answered.

"A local family. Martha Storr has them well prepared."

"She's on holiday and hasn't left me the details," Peter answered, hating to be unprepared.

"Martha was very excited about her holiday. She has gone to see Jack Green at the sanatorium in Wanstead," Griffin said with an air of gossip in his voice.

"That is kind of her."

"They were very close. Martha had a strong affection for him. They sang from the same hymnbook."

"What do you mean by close?" Peter asked. He knew Martha was single. She had been a lay reader at St Walstan's for six years. A devout, plain woman, who dressed much older than her years and toured the parish on a bicycle.

"I wouldn't like to say," Griffin answered, just above a whisper, as if the walls could hear him. "They spent a lot of time together… praying in tongues. Every evening at five-thirty. I heard them several times when I came to rehearse. They were very devout. A comfort to one another. She followed his every word."

"Did you know him well?"

"Jack was a very shy man in some ways. He was obsessed with the dark arts and believed that this parish was in the grip of Satan. Every sermon was the same. We were sinners and had to repent as the Devil stalked us all day and night."

"He seemed to be the most tormented of you all," Peter answered. "Was he right in what he thought?"

"I have lived in the village most of my adult life. Jack was very black-and-white in what he believed. He insisted that I should find a wife. I told him that a bachelor aged sixty-three was so set in his ways that a wife wouldn't cope with him. He told me that God would find a way."

"You don't fancy getting married? Plenty of spinsters in the parish."

Griffin laughed and dramatically played the opening bars to Bach's *Toccata and Fugue in D minor*, his hands and arms flexing in the air.

"Jack wanted me to be prayed for and set free from whatever spirit bound me. I told him that the only spirit in my life was a single malt. He wasn't too pleased. There was talk that he would suspend me as organist. Luckily, he was found drunk in a hedge. The spirits must have got to him," Griffin laughed impishly, his whole face lighting up with a broad smile. "This church has been my life for nearly forty years. I love the place, the wall paintings, the smell, the atmosphere."

"Why should he want to suspend you?" Peter asked, as he thought he might already know the answer.

"In confidence. He didn't like my lifestyle, said it was incongruous to the Christian way. I told him I was just the organist. To be honest with you, Vicar, I do not have the greatest faith. I have trouble believing in God, let alone the spirits and demons that Jack Green was obsessed by."

"An obsession?" Peter asked as he looked up to the carved, oak screen above the altar.

"In his mind, they were everywhere. A spiritual zoo of malevolent creatures waiting to capture and possess us all."

"Then I shall have to be on my guard," he answered as he saw the speared, pig cartouche that was cut into the wood above the altar.

Griffin fumbled with a piece of paper and slid his spectacles to the end of his nose. "Hymns for Sunday?" he said, offering Peter the note. "Good, old-school favourites. The visitors might know some of these. I hate it when I start to play and no one sings. *When a Knight Won His Spurs* should get them going."

Peter looked at the note. The hymns Griffin had chosen reminded him of a school assembly. "How many people are you expecting for the baptism?" he asked.

"We should have a good turnout. Our numbers may swell to fifteen or twenty," Griffin said optimistically. "They bring their children for baptism and then we never see them again. We should baptise the bats. A great way to get rid of them," he laughed.

"Perhaps we should," Peter echoed as the sun moved the shadows of the window ledge across the walls, lighting the specks of dust in a rainbow of colour. "You are right, about the children. I find it frustrating, but the church is here for those who don't come that often."

"And you don't mind?" Griffin asked.

"Not at all. It's what we are here for."

"Jack Green didn't like it. He called them heathens," Griffin grumbled. "So, what about you? Do you disagree with my lifestyle choice as someone who is earnest?"

"Earnest? I have never heard it called that before. That is between you and your maker and none of my business. If I am right, then what you choose to do is no longer illegal. Yet, as I say, none of my business."

"It has been the subject of rumour and gossip," Griffin said as he bit his lip. "I have been so far in the closet, my postcode is Narnia."

"I listen to neither," Peter laughed as he answered. "I love Narnia."

"Sadly, there are those who do not think like you."

"They can think what they like. You are a good musician and that is all that matters," Peter said as he put a hand on his shoulder.

"It is good to have your support. I was wondering about my future here. Jack Green was a man of intense belief. He made it difficult for many of us in different ways." Griffin paused momentarily. "If

I may be so bold, please be careful of Martha. She has seen vicars come and go, and has fallen for every one of them."

[14]
The Co-Op

The kitchen was now clean. He had spent the evening washing the shelves and countertops. The grout around the tiles had been bleached until it looked liveable. The room stank of lemon, like a public lavatory at a railway station.

Greg Clark had rung earlier to tell Peter that he couldn't come over; a flat tyre and having to repair the van for work.

It was now ten past eight. Peter opened the door of the fridge and looked inside. There was milk and orange juice, but nothing else apart from a crust of *Mother's Pride* and a stale, end-crumb of cheese. He wanted something for breakfast.

Mary had rung earlier. It was not good news. She wanted to stay for a couple more weeks to make sure her father was going to cope and help settle in her mother when she was released from hospital. Peter had agreed; he knew it was the best thing. He could get the house sorted and by then, he hoped the place would be decorated. That thought came a poor second place to his need of food.

Peter looked at his watch. He knew he could make it to the Co-op before it closed. It was eight miles, and the shop closed at nine. Peter took the keys to the car, checked his wallet, and left the vicarage.

It was a warm summer evening. Peter opened the windows of the car and listened to the radio as the miles went by. Steve

Lamacq was talking over *Supersonic*, when he got to the outskirts of the town. Big houses with large gardens gave way to rows of semi-detached with hatchbacks on the driveways. The late-night shop was on an estate at the edge of the town, next to a hairdresser and a chip shop. They were both shut. Outside, the parking spaces were all empty. The door to the telephone box was open and as he pulled up, Peter noticed the handset had been ripped from the box and thrown to the floor.

The light above the door to the Co-op flickered as he turned off the engine and opened the car door. Chip boxes and crisp packets spilled out of the overflowing dustbin and were blown across the pavement by the warm evening breeze.

Walking to the door, Peter felt that there was something wrong. It was an instinct that gnawed at the pit of his stomach. He had felt it before and trusted the feeling. An unlocked pushbike was leant against the shop window. There was no one in the street and he wondered who would leave an expensive bike outside a shop.

Stepping closer to the door, he looked inside. He could hear raised voices. A man was shouting as a woman begged him to stop. Peter pressed himself against the wall so he could see more of what was happening inside and not activate the automatic door.

There were two men in balaclavas and hoodies. One had hold of the shop assistant and was forcing her to open the till. The woman was crying, begging them to stop.

Peter watched as she opened the till. The taller man pulled out the notes and filled his pockets as the other took a bottle of brandy from the shelf as he pushed the woman to the floor. Both men walked cockily towards the automatic door. It slid slowly open.

Peter blocked the way.

"What the feck?" the taller man said as he looked him up and down. "Vicar without a tart. Where's the fancy dress?"

"Put the money back," he answered.

"Get out of the way, or I will do you," the other man said as he pulled a screwdriver from his jeans pocket.

The blow was quick and precise. The punch was followed by a swift kick to the groin. The big man fell to the ground as screwdriver man ran at Peter. He stepped to the side, grabbed his attacker's wrist, and threw him to the floor.

Kneeling on his chest, he took the weapon from him and threw it to the roadway. He could hear the distant sirens of the police response car. The man looked up, trying in his drug-addled mind to make out what this creature in a clerical collar was.

"What the feck are you?" he screamed in a stream of spittle as the police car got closer.

"A priest," he answered.

"Good God," the man said.

"Possibly," Peter answered as the response car pulled up and two officers got out. "You're a feckin' zombie. Get off me, get off me," the man screamed as the drugs seared through his veins and warped his vision.

"Barney?" the sergeant said, recognising Peter. "You're a bit off your patch."

"Yeah, Prezzo," he answered. "Wrong place, wrong time."

Sergeant Preston was a brute of a man, as broad as he was tall with hands the size of a coal shovel. He was in his twenty-ninth year as a copper, with only seven months of his career left to do. Prezzo had fought most of the villains in the division but tonight, he was nursemaid to a young probationer.

"Right," he said to the junior officer. "Cuff them and get them locked up. Start with the big fella before he wakes up."

"He came at me with a weapon and a bottle of brandy. I had to defend myself."

"Good job. Two-nil to us, and a robbery solved within minutes," Preston said as Peter stood up. "What are you doing here?"

"Shopping. Bread and bacon."

"We'll take these two in. When are you next on duty? I'll need a statement."

"Two weeks. I am on leave."

"Typical... I want it tomorrow."

Peter handed him a business card.

"Send a car tomorrow morning. I will have it done for then."

Preston read the card and smiled as he ran his fingers through his thick Victorian beard. He was not a man of religion. His faith was his Masonic Lodge and those who shared its secrets. "I'd heard you were the vicar. How the hell are you going to level knocking out a robber and scaring the shit out of another with being a priest?"

"That is what I have to work out for myself," Peter replied as he looked up at the swallows as they stole insects from the dark-blue twilight sky.

"Rather you than me. Just wear that dog collar when this twat pleads not guilty at Crown Court and says you beat him up. You'll need the sympathy vote."

"How is the shop assistant? That one threw her to the floor," Peter said as he pointed to the smaller man who was being dragged to the car.

"Must be fine. She was able to press the panic alarm."

"I will go and see her," Peter replied. "Make sure she is okay."

"Don't forget to pay for your bacon. Can't be having you getting a freebie."

"I'll wait until you can send someone to take her statement."

"That offer of joining the Lodge is still open, Barney," Preston answered as he walked to the car and pushed the other man into the back seat.

"As someone once said, Prezzo, I refuse to join any club that would have me as a member."

"Groucho Marx," Preston shouted back in his gruff voice as he slammed the back door of the car. "By the way, we're not a bloody club. We are an ancient society."

[15]
Pleasant Valley Sunday

There was a strict routine for every church service that Peter took. He would check the altar, count the wafers for the Eucharist, make sure he had the hymn list and his sermon notes. This morning, he made sure all was ready for the baptism. Parents' names, what they would call the child, and who were the godparents. He knew that if people who were not religious had chosen to bring their child to church, then it must mean more to them than an excuse for a booze up and a party.

Morris Marsden had followed him round the dusty vestry like a handfed crow, picking at the registers and checking all the details. Peter put on his cassock and a gold, silk stole to mark the importance of baptism. He checked himself in the mirror. The feeling that he was an imposter was still in his mind. Growing up on a council estate and being kicked out of school didn't sit well with wearing clerical dress. For him, he was a working-class lad in a middle-class institution where belief was secondary to tradition. He had trained part time for the priesthood, and it made him feel he was a backdoor vicar. That, and being part time, gave him the deep anxiety that he was nearly, but not quite, a proper priest.

Now, he knew it would be right to pray. It had been part of his life long before he had the stirrings of a vocation in the church.

It was a timeout moment where he could stop and reflect within himself. Most of the time, he didn't know if God was listening, but he didn't care. Prayer felt good, a spiritual therapy where he could offload the issues in his life and the concern for others. He didn't believe that God was interested in the *give me, give me* prayers. Peter believed in God, not Father Christmas. It was more sitting in the presence of the Divine with the people on his mind, than muttering pleas and supplications.

This morning was no different. Finding a quiet corner of the church, he knelt on the tiles and closed his eyes. In his mind, he pictured the day ahead. A half-empty church, a crying child, and the posse of parishioners, who would doubtless queue up to complain about him unbricking the well.

As he tried to still his thoughts, the earworm of The Monkees singing *Pleasant Valley Sunday* went around and around, as if a loop of frustration. Peter went with it, accepting it for what it was and allowing the song to ebb away. It didn't go.

The singing got louder, like West Coast tinnitus. He listened to the words as if a radio played in his head. The weekend squire mowing his lawn. Mrs Gray, being proud today, because her roses are in bloom. Charcoal burning everywhere. Creature comfort goals that only burn the soul.

"*My thoughts all seem to stray to places far away*," he repeated over and over, realising he was missing Mary and the children.

Perhaps the song wasn't an intrusive earworm after all, he thought. God had a habit of using music to pull him up about things in his life that needed sorting. Peter found himself asking to be forgiven for being angry with Mary for going away. He hadn't told her, and never would, but she was always ready to pack her bag and run to her parents whenever they said they needed her.

In his heart, he felt it was just an excuse for her to get away. After all, he had taken her away from a wealthy family to live in a small police house on the edge of a council estate. She had a degree and a career. He had a hated uniform and five O-Levels.

If they hadn't had children so early, Peter thought that the marriage may not have survived. There was the pressure of his job, the times when he went to work and came back days later. The constant sniping of her parents about everything he did or didn't do. Her mother had accused him of being an alcoholic for drinking a can of beer before dinner. She had said his brown Fiat estate car was a disgrace and wondered how her daughter would allow herself to be driven around in it. It was a *drip, drip, drip* of malevolence that was slowly undermining their marriage. He wondered if his mother-in-law would ever be promoted to Heaven. Maybe then, Mary could be free from the shadow her mother had cast over her life. He wondered if Mary had stuck with him just to frustrate her parents. It was a thought he had many times, and one he was ashamed of.

Now, as the song finally faded, he bundled up his thoughts and dumped them on God with a whispered "*Amen*". It didn't matter if God was just an imaginary friend that didn't exist. As Peter stood up, he felt as if something had been taken from him.

The church bells rang in the tower as he picked up his prayer book from the vestry desk; Peter didn't know if he should go to the door to welcome people or just appear at the front of the church.

In the minute, his choice was taken from him. Gerald Griffin started to play. Peter suddenly realised he had prayed far too long.

Stepping from the vestry, he walked to the chancel steps and took a deep breath. The church was full. People were standing at the back. The baptismal family were Travellers, dressed in sharp suits and glittering dresses. The women all wore large hats. The older men were in shirts and waistcoats, their sleeves rolled up, and every man had both arms covered in tattoos.

At the back, leaning against the wall, was a giant of a man. His shaved head reflected the light from the stained glass windows. He was dressed in cord trousers and chockers.

Peter recognised him. Brendan Codona was the head of a Traveller family. A man suspected of crime, but a man who never got caught. He was far enough away from the scene and always had an alibi. He was the general of an army of willing followers who would do his bidding.

The last time they had met was late one autumn night in the middle of Farndale Moor. Peter was on solo patrol when he had stopped a car with four men and three lurcher dogs inside. When he asked what they were doing at that time, they told him they were looking for a lost dog. It was the usual excuse to cover poaching, burglary, or both. Codona had been polite, if not a little patronising and called Peter, *'son'*. He had shown him a wad of notes in his pocket that was a bundle of at least two thousand pounds. Codona had explained that a man always had a wad of money. It proved you could support your family.

As he watched the car drive away into the night, Peter had wondered if he would ever have that amount of money in the bank, let alone in his pocket.

As Peter welcomed the congregation and announced the first hymn, he couldn't help but notice that Codona was staring at him as if there was something about the vicar that he recognised.

Throughout the service, Codona kept looking at Peter with a furrowed brow, as if he tried to remember the name of a long-lost friend.

Three hymns, several prayers, and the collect later, Peter announced the baptism and walked with the proud mother in her frilly hat that resembled a gaudy, red sombrero to the font.

The whole church gathered around as cameras flashed and men at the back jostled to get a better view. Peter blessed the water with a sign of the cross and dutifully, the godparents and parents said their vows to God and the child.

The mother handed the baby to Peter. The child looked at him with a lopsided smile.

Taking the baby, he held the baby in his arms and lowered it over the font. "What name do you give this child?" Peter asked as a matter of tradition.

"Declan Theodore Churchill Nike O'Connor," the husband said proudly.

"You missed one," Brendan Codona chipped in with a broad Irish accent. "Brendan."

"Oh, yes," the husband answered, as if he had been given an instruction he could not refuse. "Brendan."

Peter repeated the list of names and then, taking his hand, cupped three palms of water over the child. "In the name of the Father, the Son, and the Holy Spirit... Amen," Peter said in blessing.

The baptismal party erupted into loud cheers and spontaneous applause. As the congregation quietened, Peter passed the baby back to the mother. As it did so, it let out an explosive, guttural release of gas as it filled its nappy to overflowing.

Bright yellow liquid oozed out of the handmade baptismal gown, and as it did, the child laughed uncontrollably. The infectious giggling spread quickly through the church. Peter laughed along. Even Miss Groom and Hindle tittered into their hands, both ladies smiling broadly.

"Love it, Vicar," Brendan Codona said as he slapped him on the back with his shovel-sized hands. "The wain is the image of his grandy."

Looking at the child and then to Codona, Peter could see the resemblance. Both were bald and amazingly ugly. "Just like you," he answered before announcing the final hymn. "Four hundred and thirty-four. *One More Step Along the Road*."

Suddenly, it was as if he was amongst the Kop at Anfield. The baptismal family erupted in many voices, a song they knew without even looking at the words. The church was filled with singing that swelled and roared, bringing everyone together. As the final verse ended, there was a raucous applause followed by happy laughter.

Peter stood at the door and shook the hands of everyone as they left. Outside, a crowd of villagers had gathered, drawn by the noise and wondering what was happening inside. Bruce Clark stood at the gate with his arms folded, taking everything in as the families left.

As the church emptied, Miss Hindle sidled up to Peter and pulled on his surplus.

"It was lovely," she said sincerely. "Handled very well, and what we would expect from a police officer."

"Lovely," echoed Miss Groom.

Several minutes later, Peter stood alone in the church. He took off his vestments and stole, folding them neatly and placing them on a pew by the door.

"Well done," Griffin said as he appeared from the vestry. "Reverend Green would have caused a riot if he had been here."

"They are good people. Sadly, they won't be here next Sunday to fill the pews," Peter answered with the realisation that this had certainly been a one of a kind.

"You are in need of a dry cleaner," Griffin answered, pointing to the sleeve of Peter's cassock.

Peter looked down to see the cuff of his *Wippell's* cassock was now covered in what was a bright orange stain. He wondered what the parents had fed the child to obtain such a vivid, dayglow colour.

"I hear it's a sign of luck, Gerald," he said with a smile. "Shame it smells of fish."

[16]
The Titanic

It had rained hard for three days. Mary had rung to say her mother would be delayed in leaving hospital and she wouldn't be home until after he had gone back to work. Peter had been ever so dutiful and said that she should take as long as she wanted. In return, Mary had been her usual unapologetic self. Her parents had her right where they wanted. A live-in child who could do the washing up, nursemaid her mother when she returned home, and cook for her father until then.

To fill the days, Peter had painted most of the house, emptied the shed, and that morning, had begun to clear out the cellar. For some reason, it appeared as if Jack Green had used it as a glass recycling centre. Box after box were filled with empty bottles. They followed a pattern. It was as if each box contained the hidden remnants of his drinking habit. Three bottles of beer. Two bottles of red wine. Two bottles of gin, and the occasional bottle of whisky. His alcohol habit was obviously very intense. Peter wondered how he had managed to run the parish for the time he did.

It was only when he came to the last box that he realised that the Reverend Green had another habit. There, in a taped-up box, were a stack of magazines. Opening the well-thumbed pages, Peter knew straight away what they were. Jack Green obviously loved to look at naked, fat ladies, most of them on the back of horses.

Putting them back in the box, he tried to restick the tape the best he could and stack the box near the steps, with the plan to take them outside and burn them when it stopped raining.

It was then that he heard the doorbell ring.

Wiping the dust from his shirt, he went up the stairs, along the passageway, and to the door.

John Crowley stood on the porch, shaking the rain from his bespoke *Crowley and Crowley Undertaker's* umbrella. He was dressed head to foot in black, had the look of a vintage film star, and knew it. Crowley was known as the Johnny Cash of the funeral trade. He was suave in dress and tongue and would never take no for an answer. Peter knew Crowley very well. His firm had the contract with the police to remove any dead body that came their way. Sudden deaths, suicides, accidents, and murders, John Crowley and his crew of undertakers would be there in an instant.

They had first met when Peter was a rookie copper in Scarborough. He had been sent to a suicide who had taken an overdose in a car park on the forest drive. Peter had been dropped off at the scene to preserve evidence and had been told to guard the car until backup eventually arrived.

One hour had passed uneventfully and then it had started to rain. Within a minute, it was a torrential downpour. With nowhere to shelter, Peter had decided to get in the car and sit in the passenger seat. It was the only place he could get out of the rain. In the driver's seat was a young man in his twenties. He was dressed in a white shirt and dark navy suit, and looked as though he had no troubles at all. His head was slumped forward as if he was asleep. In the footwell was an empty bottle of whisky and cartons of sleeping tablets.

Peter had only ever seen one dead body before at the mandatory post-mortem all junior officers had to endure on their first day out of training school. Now, here he was, miles from town, on his own, with a dead body. His radio had no signal, and he knew his colleague would not be back for some time.

"Hello," he said to the man. "My name is Peter. I'm sorry it has come to this in your life." Peter didn't know what else to do or say. He didn't just want to get in and sit there. He had been told that some faiths believed that the human soul stayed near the body for three days. If that was true, he thought, it would only be right for him to introduce himself.

Thankfully, the body didn't reply.

The rain pounded on the roof of the car. Peter waited and watched the windows slowly start to steam up with every breath he exhaled. In the warmth, he rested his head on the back of the seat, closed his eyes and dozed sleepily, listening to the rain.

There was a sudden knock on the window. Peter lurched awake. All he could see was the face of a man he didn't recognise staring through the glass. He jumped back away from the window, giving out a half scream. His elbow knocked the shoulder of the dead man, who slumped further forward, his head pressing down on the car horn.

The horn sounded loudly as the man outside pulled the car door open and pushed the body back in the seat.

"Frightened the life out of me," he said as Peter got out of the car. "I am John Crowley, the undertaker, and you must be a new boy?"

That night was twelve years ago. From then on, whenever there was a body, John Crowley or one of his men would be there to pick up the pieces.

"You busy?" he asked as he slicked back a mane of jet-black hair with his hand.

"Morning John, what can I do for you?" Peter replied.

"Funeral at the crem. Half an hour. I can take you."

"Why? Don't you have a minister?"

"Long story. I can explain on the way. I can tell you about the deceased as well. Get your stuff."

Peter changed his shirt, put on his cassock, grabbed his prayer book, and followed Crowley to the hearse. In the back was a wicker coffin, and by its side was a large wreath that spelled out the word *'Dad'*.

"Didn't realise you were actually on the way to the crematorium," Peter said as he got into the front.

Crowley jumped in the driver's seat, turned the ignition, and sped off. He drove quickly through the country lanes until he reached the main road. Then, as if he was a racing driver, put his foot down and headed to the town. The trees and hedges flashed by. Crowley overtook whenever he could as he weaved in and out of the traffic. As he drove, he explained that the Methodist minister had rung an hour before the service to say he was unwell. Crowley had attempted to find a replacement but could not.

"Why is it you lot all go on holiday at the same time? One whiff of sunshine and you all bugger off to France. Not a single vicar is at home and all the methies are at a conference. Bloody spiritual wasteland if you ask me."

"Am I the only one?" Peter asked as Crowley shoved a folded piece of paper into his hand.

"Yes. Thank God you were in. I had rung you several times with no answer. It was my last chance coming to the door. God knows what I would have done," he sighed. "I need a holiday, but the buggers keep dying. Six last week. It's the heat. Dropping like flies."

Peter read the details on the paper. "Frank West. Eighty-six. Retired fisherman. Husband to Elsie. Eleven children. Fourteen grandchildren. Watched *Countdown* and went to the pub every night. That's it?"

"What else do you need?" Crowley asked, taking a corner so fast that the coffin slid to one side.

"You to slow down for a start before there are three dead bodies in this hearse. Do you expect me to give a good service with no information?"

"They were big Methodists," he answered.

"Well," Peter replied. "They are not going to be very happy when a big Anglican turns up."

"They won't notice. You lot look the same. Just don't be too churchy."

"Brilliant. Now you want me to impersonate a Methodist?"

"Yes, and do it in under twenty minutes. Quick bit in the chapel and then a burial in the municipal graveyard."

"Not a cremation?"

"No. Family plot. He's been buried on top of his first wife," Crowley answered with a smile.

"What does his second wife think to that?" Peter asked.

"It's a triple grave. She's going in on top of them both when she pops it, so she'll be happy. It was a sod to dig. Had to get the JCB in. Full of clay, and that part of the cemetery is littered with freshwater springs."

As the car sped through the leafy streets, the sign for the crematorium came into sight. Crowley slowed the hearse to a walking pace as he turned into the gates. Peter could see a large crowd gathered around the entrance.

"He must have been popular," Peter said as the hearse drew closer.

"Where there's a will, there's a family," Crowley answered, looking in the rearview mirror and plucking a hair from his nostril.

"Give me a minute to talk to his widow before you get him out."

"Make it quick, we are almost ten minutes into our time slot, and I will get fined if you run late," Crowley answered as his face suddenly became sombre. "Break a leg, Vicar."

Peter felt like breaking his prayer book over the man's head. He stepped from the hearse and was greeted by a fat man in a tight-fitting suit.

"You're not Reverend Allerdice," the man complained.

"Sorry, he has been taken seriously ill," Peter answered as he made his way to the open doors and a gathering that he knew was the immediate family. Outside, the coffin was quickly loaded onto a trolley and soon caught up with the vicar.

A small, birdlike woman was surrounded by three burly men and an even bigger woman. "Minister?" the old woman said with a smile. "How is Mr Allerdice?"

"He is unwell, but everything is taken care of," Peter answered, taking her hand and trying to give her a reassuring smile as the taped organ music started to play.

Seventeen minutes later, the service was over. Peter had spoken some words of comfort and asked if any of the family would like to speak. The fat, tight-suited man had stood up and told the gathering how his uncle had been good to him as a child. Crowley had stood at the back of the chapel, drawing his hand across his neck as if it were a knife cutting his throat. When this failed, he began to cough loudly and spin his hand in ever smaller circles. Finally, the man stopped speaking.

The bright summer sun came out from the clouds as they left the chapel. The family followed the coffin and Peter to the graveside. The JCB had covered it in a carpet of false grass that made it look like a large, green, shaggy knoll. By its side was an anxious looking gravedigger. He summoned Peter over with a wave of the hand. "Vicar, we have a problem."

"What?" Peter answered, knowing this was about to turn into the worst day of his life.

"What problem?"

"It's the grave. Full of water. Think we hit the spring. It'll take a day or so to go down. I've filled it full of straw to hide the water. Get him in quick and we'll sort it out when the family have gone."

"Get him in quick?" Peter complained. "In front of two hundred mourners?"

"It's the only way. The sides might crumble in so we can't do an on-top committal," the digger answered as if he had been through every possible type of burial in his time. "It'll be alright if you just get him in quick."

The family gathered around the grave as the undertaker and his men lowered the coffin onto the bed of floating straw.

"He's not in very deep," the fat, tight-suited man complained.

"Ashes to ashes, dust to dust, in the sure and certain hope of—" Peter spoke loudly.

"Looks like he's bloody floating," the man whispered loudly.

"Amen," Peter said hurriedly as he turned to the mourners and bid them farewell. All but the family departed.

"Lovely service, and thank you," the widow said, supported by a big man who must have been her son.

"Lovely, great," the man echoed and then suddenly began to gawp at the grave.

There, like a wicker Titanic, the coffin was slowly upending as the heavier head end sank beneath the straw until the coffin was upright.

The gravedigger began to push at it with his shovel hoping it would go down further. All the coffin did was bob up and down with loud thump as the body of Frank West slumped to one end.

Peter could feel the clerical collar tightening around his neck as he turned a bright pink. He had no idea what to do next and watched in anger as Crowley and his henchmen made off to their cars, leaving him alone with the family.

As Elsie West looked at the coffin of her husband, her tears stopped. A broad smile came to her face and she started to laugh from the depths of her belly. Those around her joined in. Her burly son was slapping his thigh and howling, with tears rolling down his face. The family held each other up as they laughed and laughed.

"Are you alright?" Peter asked, not knowing why they found it so funny. Elsie West struggled to get a breath to answer him.

"He was a fisherman all his life," she wheezed through her teeth, trying to hold back another bout of laughter. "But he couldn't swim. He hated water and didn't like having a bath. Now he's bloody got one."

The woman laughed so loud, she spat out the bottom row of her false teeth. This caused her children to fall about in laughter.

By now, the gravedigger was hiding behind the grassy knoll of the JCB. Crowley was driving off, leaving Peter behind. The family were sat on the wet grass laughing as their mother picked up her teeth and slipped them back in her mouth, spitting out blades of grass.

Peter sat next to Elsie and held her hand. One by one, the family stopped laughing and gathered closer to her as behind them, the coffin slowly sank to the bottom of the grave.

"Crowley sold us a silk-lined, premier coffin," the son said as he watched it sink. "Thing must be full of chuffing holes."

"He always wanted to be buried at sea," Elsie said, trying not to laugh again.

[17]
The Mad - The Bad - The Sad

John Crowley remorsefully returned half an hour later. Peter had, by then, decided to set off and walk into town and catch a bus back to the village.

"Sorry, had to dash off. Forgot about an urgent job," he said as he opened the door to his black Mercedes, having dropped off the hearse. "Had to get the coffin carrier back to the shop. You didn't think I'd left you?"

"It looked that way," Peter answered, getting into the car. "You did go at a difficult time."

"Really? It looked like everything was tickety-boo."

"It was, if you call tickety-boo a coffin dropped into a grave of water and having to watch it sink in front of the family."

"How did they take it?"

"Hysterically. His widow didn't stop laughing until I got her to her car," Peter answered as Crowley drove off.

"Well," Crowley smiled. "Nothing ventured, eh?"

"She asked me what church I was from. I told her it was St Walstan's. Elsie didn't seem to have a problem that I was an Anglican."

"How are you settling in?" Crowley asked. "You know the place is cursed for vicars.

Every one of them has come to a grisly end."

"Thanks for that, John. Words of comfort never go amiss."

"Sorry. It's just that they do go through a lot of priests. Mad, bad, and sad. That's what my dad always said. St Walstan's either gets mad vicars, sad vicars, or bad vicars. Which one are you?"

"At this moment in time, I am the bloody annoyed vicar," Peter said in obvious discontent. "Did your father know the parish?"

"There have been Crowley's burying the dead since the time of George the First. We go back a long way. My father and grandfather and his father for over two hundred years. My dad knows more about what goes on in the churches around here than the vicars did."

"Is he still alive?"

"Alive? The man is unstoppable. Eighty and behaves like a teenager. He lives with me since my mother died. It's like having a kid in the house," Crowley tutted.

"I'd like to meet him."

"You got an hour? I need to pick some papers from the house and I can give you your cheque. Cup of tea?"

Peter nodded, and within twenty minutes, the car was pulling up outside a large, Victorian, detached house on a tree-lined street. The garden was immaculate, as if every fallen leaf had been hoovered up the moment it fell. Each blade of grass of the neatly manicured lawn was exactly the same, and looked as though it was a putting green surrounded by an abundance of flowering, bedding plants.

"Very nice," Peter said in surprise. "Death must pay well."

"Like my dad always says, no one gets out of life alive," Crowley answered with a smirk as he got out of the car and gestured for Peter to follow him into the house.

If the garden was perfect, then the house was doubly so. The solid wood floors were brightly polished, a vase of lilies stood on the grand piano in the centre of the hall, and not a thing was out of place.

"You live well," Peter commented as they walked into the Italian style kitchen and through the conservatory into the secluded back garden.

"Father, I have a guest who would like to meet you. Peter, this is my father," he said with affection. "James Crowley."

"Mr Crowley, a pleasure to meet you," he said to the tall, sprightly man who jumped up from the garden chair, dropping his copy of the *Evening News* to the ground.

"Call me Jim. My son is a pretentious little snipe who needs his backside kicking," the man laughed. "You must be the copper who is the new vicar at Walstan's?"

"Cup of tea, Dad?" John asked.

The older man nodded. Peter could not believe how young and well he looked. It was as if he could be a man half his age. Like his son, he had a full head of thick, black hair that was slightly greying at the sides. He was tall, muscular, and dressed in the style of a much younger man.

"How are you finding them out in the sticks? I think I knew you when you were a lad. Grew up on Maple Street. Your mother was a cook at the school and your dad drank in *The Newlands*."

"That's me," he answered.

"You have made good of yourself," Jim said. "And, you didn't have it handed on a plate to you. I like a self-made man. This family has always made money for the next generation, and we have done very well."

"John says that you think St Walstan's only gets the mad, the bad, and the sad."

Jim laughed. "He's telling tales. Though I must say, that parish can never hold on long to the incumbents. They all seem to meet a sticky end in one way or another. I took over running the firm in '44. I can just about remember all the priests back then. Seagrave was the vicar when I took over. He was there for many a year. A half-decent cricket player, and the last of the family to have the living. Seggy, as we called him, retired in '62 or '63. Then it was Shepherd, Albert Shepherd. That was when things started to go wrong for the church."

"You have a good memory. I have trouble remembering this morning," Peter replied as John came out of the house with a tray of tea and put it on the small garden table before going back inside.

"When you get old, you can remember the events long ago, but not the last time you had a pee."

"What was Shepherd like?" he asked.

"He didn't last long. He was married to a dowdy woman, older than him. She had the money. Shepherd went away on the day of the World Cup Final in '66. Never said anything, just upped and left."

"Did anyone know where he went?"

"Why the interest?" Jim asked, knowing it wasn't just out of politeness.

"Mad, bad, or sad? Just trying to work out which he was."

"Always a copper. If you are interested, he didn't run off with a chicken fancier. I know he was seeing Seagrave's wife. She was a beauty. Evelyn Seagrave. Long, blonde hair, and ruby-red lips with a smile for every man who came her way."

Jim sat back in his chair and contentedly sipped his tea. "Are you sure?" Peter asked.

"I buried his father. He was the brother of the last Seagrave vicar. His son's name was…" Jim thought as if the name was hidden from him momentarily. "…Magnus. It was his wife that Shepherd was seeing. I remember catching them one day when I was over at the church measuring up a grave to be dug. Couldn't find him anywhere. I saw him and her coming from that old mound in the fields. All that stuff about him running off with a woman he had met on a retreat was just a smokescreen to save Seagrave the embarrassment."

"So, they left together?" Peter asked.

"That is just pub gossip, but it's a good tale. Whether it is true or not is another thing. You better be watching yourself. St Walstan's is a funny place. My John found the last vicar drunk in the hedge. Not the first time that had happened. One Christmas Eve around '75, the vicar came out to take the midnight service. He was so full of whisky, he walked into the road and was hit by a car. So drunk, he didn't realise it had happened. Walked into church covered in blood. Car drove off into the night."

"Did they catch the driver?" Peter asked, wondering if a parish could be cursed.

"No one outside the pub got the number. Vicar got moved," Jim laughed as if it were a fond memory. "Seriously, watch yourself. I wasn't far wrong when I said mad, bad, or sad. There is always something that gets the incumbents before their time. I will pray it won't get you."

Peter felt unnerved. He could see that Jim Crowley was an honest man and spoke truths from his heart. Yet, even there on a sunny, summer afternoon in the shade of a tall willow with birds singing, he felt the hand of darkness on his life.

"What happened to Magnus Seagrave. Is he dead?"

"Went away sometime after his wife had left. I did hear he was dead. Buried somewhere near Aberdeen."

[18]
The Night Of The Long Butter Knives

The afternoon sun had given way to an evening of summer rain. The overgrown pathway to the church hall glistened as the light faded. Water dripped from the corrugated iron roof and onto the narrow bed of old roses that clung to the wooden wall.

Peter stepped inside the large, sparse room that was lit with several long, fluorescent tubes. The smell reminded him of his junior school. It had the odour of damp paper and old books, mixed with day-old, stewed cabbage. At one end was a low stage with faded, green curtains. In front of the stage were several trestle tables. Nestled against each of them was a row of hard-backed chairs.

Morris Marsden was sat at the head table, leafing through a pile of papers. He looked up and smiled. "Evening, Vicar," he said as he stood up. "I have sorted out the agenda and put the papers in order. Not a lot to talk of tonight, more way of getting to know each other."

"Excellent," Peter answered as he pulled out a chair at one of the side tables.

"Vicar, you are here at the head of the meeting," Morris said, gesturing for him to come to the top table.

Peter looked around as if he was eyeing up the room.

"Here would be better. I hope you will be chairing the meeting. After all, you are the churchwarden."

Morris was taken aback and took three paces to the side and looked at the papers on the table. "Chair the meeting?" he asked as several people came through the door. "I have never…"

"I am sure you will be wonderful. Pass me a copy of the agenda."

Morris nervously looked through the papers and slid the agenda to him as more people walked in and sat down.

Miss Hindle looked around the room and then went and closed the door.

"I think that is it," she said, sitting down. "The chairman usually sits on the top table, Vicar."

"Morris is the chairman. I am the vicar. This is your church, not mine, and you are responsible for everything that happens here. I am just a guide to help you walk the way." Anne Hindle slumped back in her chair and folded her arms as she muttered under her breath.

"Well, good evening," Morris said as he tapped the table with the tip of his pen. "Welcome to our first meeting of the year."

Peter looked around the room and realised that every one of the seven people gathered was looking at him as if he had committed an unforgivable sin. He was confronted by a wall of faces. Joseph Merton, retired schoolteacher with his grey beard, thin face, and the look of an unemployed archaeologist. Griffin, Hindle, and Groom huddled together like Act One extras in Macbeth. Next to them sat Mary Coleman, a middle-aged potter who wore a floral Laura Ashley dress and hardly ever spoke. She was the youngest by far, with a pretty but serious face. Finally, at the end of the table, sat noticeably away from the others, was a distinguished-looking woman whom Peter had never seen before. She wore a bright yellow summer jacket, white blouse, and silk scarf. Everything about her was perfect and in place, and only the laughter lines around her eyes gave away that she had easily reached seven decades.

"It is unusual that Morris should be chairman," Elsie Groom said before Morris could say another word. "Shouldn't we have a vote?"

"If I may speak, Mr Chairman. I believe your past incumbents may have overstepped the mark regarding church meetings. Rule fifteen states that I may ask Morris to chair the meeting, and he has all the powers vested in the chairman."

"Most irregular," Gerald Griffin added, "but I think we should allow it."

"It's not irregular at all. As you well know, St Walstan's cannot keep hold of its priests for very long. It would be far better for the parish to be able to run itself without a priest chairing the meetings."

The woman in the silk scarf raised her hand as if she wanted to speak. Morris nodded to her. "Amber, do you have a question?" he asked.

"I don't think we need a vote. It will be quite refreshing for you to be the chairman, Morris."

It was then that everyone at the table nodded in agreement as if the women had cast a spell over them.

"Very well," Morris said as he smiled at the woman in a way that thanked her. "We only have two items on the agenda. A report from the treasurer and any other business." Morris looked at the grey archaeologist. "Joe?"

Joseph Merton took out a wad of papers from his briefcase and slowly laid them out before him. "As you all know, I have only been looking after the books since the AGM. It is still not a good situation since we last met. If the parish was a business, we would be in the hands of the official receiver. Income last month was five hundred and seventy-five pounds less than expenditure. The diocese has stopped asking for the quota, and has even offered to pay half of the costs on the tower. I am sorry, Vicar, but your time here may be very short-lived."

The others ruffled in discontent as if the closing of a church was something they would never tolerate.

"What would be the answer?" Morris asked.

"We need an extra thousand pounds a month to show a profit," Merton answered stoically.

"We can't give any more," Anne Hindle said, looking at the vicar. "Do you have any idea what we could do? After all, it would be your job on the line if the church closed."

"Gamaliel Principle," he answered, knowing from the look on Anne Hindle's face that she did not understand.

"Does he live in the parish?" Elsie Groom asked as if Gamaliel was someone they could get the money from.

"If it is of God, then it will succeed, and if it is not, it will fail. Gamaliel was the leader of the Sanhedrin. You can read of him in the *Book of Acts*, Act Five," Amber said softly.

"Oh," Elsie Groom answered, lost for words.

"The same goes for this parish," Peter said as he leant forward and looked at each one in turn as he spoke. "We all have gifts and talents. Each of us does not want this church to fail. It is the responsibility of us all, but it must be the will of God."

Gerald Griffin gave an audible sigh as the thought of his church closing became a realisation he did not welcome.

"You sound fatalistic," Merton muttered in response.

"I suppose I do," Peter replied. "The answer is that the church needs to grow. You are not here to keep the doors of an old building open."

"But the church is the building," Anne Hindle answered. "It has stood here for nearly a thousand years."

"The church is the people and the building is the place you meet," he said, noting the look of horror on her face. "What would you do if the church burnt down?"

"Stay at home?" Elsie Groom asked.

For the next hour, the conversation was the same. They discussed fundraising and talked of bingo, jumble sales, raffles, and tombola. Throughout, Amber stayed silent, listening to all that was said. Even Mary Coleman chipped in, to the surprise of everyone.

"I think we should move on," Morris Marsden said as he tapped his fingers on the table. "Any other business?"

There was a moment of uncomfortable silence.

"The well," Mary Coleman said. "I heard that the vicar unbricked it."

"Yes," Morris answered, casting an anxious look towards Peter.

"Reverend Green said it was a place of evil," Mary Coleman, the one convert of Jack Green continued. "He said if we didn't shut up the well, then the evil would still walk the parish."

"He did not have authority to do it," Peter answered.

"But we voted for it," Miss Hindle insisted.

"You can vote for Hell to freeze over, but without a faculty, it will never happen," the vicar answered. "Brick it up again if you like, but I will have to report you all to the diocese."

"There will be no need to do that," Morris said quickly, fearing it would lead to him being taken to court. "I think the well is best left the way it is."

"But Reverend Green?" Mary protested.

"The Holy Well is not a place of evil. Neither will demons come from it," Peter answered. "It is a monument to an ancient time when water was spiritually more important than it is today. We should respect that. I intend to hold a service of blessing at the well this harvest time. It was once a place of pilgrimage."

"Witches," Mary barked. "That's all who come."

"Then we should welcome them," he answered. "They might leave something in the collection."

Mary Coleman stood up and slammed her papers on the table before turning and walking out of the room without speaking a word.

"And then there were six," Merton said, enjoying every minute of the drama.

"The woman is always hysterical," Anne Hindle replied, trying to break the following silence.

"Miss Hindle is right," Elsie Groom added. "Reverend Green got her to come to the church soon after he arrived here. Her husband had died at a young age, and she struggled with it."

"If that is everything?" Morris interrupted before Peter could answer.

"We are not always like this," Gerald Green said as he stood up. "We haven't even thanked the vicar for the wonderful service last Sunday."

"Here, here," Elsie Groom echoed as she helped Anne from her chair, handing her the walking stick from by the door. "It was good to see so many people in church."

Peter went to the door and said goodnight to each of them as they left. He noticed Amber held back. It was something he was used to. The parishioner with the most to say would hang on at the back of the line like a snake about to strike. They would always wait until last so they would not be interrupted and could have the vicar all to themselves.

He steeled himself, wondering what it was that she would bring forth. After reassuring Gerald that he would go and see Mary Coleman first thing in the morning, Amber was standing next to him.

"Sorry we didn't meet before your induction. I was away in Italy. I am Amber Hudson. I live at the Old Manor on the moor road. It is technically not in your parish, but I like coming here."

"And you are most welcome," he answered, waiting for the attack.

"I am glad you opened the well. It was all that your predecessor went on about. He had a fear of spirits."

"Thank you," he answered as she took hold of his hand. "Have you lived here for very long?"

"Born and bred. I have a house in London and another in Italy. I spend my time between them. Like the Queen, the flag is always up the pole when I am here. You can see it from the road. Call in if you are ever passing. I have some ideas about the church."

[19]
Gall Of Goat & Slips Of Yew

On the southern road out of the village, a double row of council houses sat incongruously at the edge of a small plantation of fir trees. Dales Terrace was built in the 1930s to house cheap land labour, and they were now occupied by a mix of people with little connection to the countryside.

Land labour was no longer needed, and the narrow green in front of the houses was a playground for children, made up of old cars, the occasional skip, and a pile of used tyres. It was the part of the village that had been purposely forgotten, and was even excluded from the neighbourhood watch scheme.

The red-bricked, slate-clad houses had plastic window frames and doors. Each house was a replica of the next. Some had well-tended gardens, whilst others were overgrown. The one on the corner had an old sofa under the front window next to the green wheelie bin. There was a coffee table with several empty beer cans crawling with wasps.

Peter counted the numbers on the doors as he walked along the row. Number seven seemed tidier than the rest. The wooden garden gate was nicely painted in a bright red, and the garden was planted with roses that had been carefully deadheaded of fading blooms. As he walked to the door, he saw a twitch of the net curtains.

Before he could knock, the door opened. Mary Coleman stood in the doorway in the same dress she had worn the night before. This time, it was covered in a yellow pinny tied around the waist.

"I didn't expect you to come," she said quickly. "I am finished with the church. All the work of Reverend Green is being undone."

"That is the last thing I want to do," he answered as he stood on the bottom step.

"You opened the well. We had prayed so hard that the water would be stopped, and you changed all that," Mary Coleman said as she twisted the pinny in her fingers.

"Things have to be done properly. That is the law of the church."

"What about the law of God? Do we ignore that?" she asked.

"There is no evil in the well. It is just spring water. Why do you think that the early Christians built the church there in the first place?" Peter asked. "It was a place of pilgrimage long before St Walstan's was built. The church was built there on purpose."

"Then why would Reverend Green want it blocking up?" she replied as she stepped back into the hallway. "You better come in. Can't have my neighbours hearing me arguing on the doorstep."

Peter stepped inside the house. It had a narrow hall with a set of stairs leading up. A passageway led to the back room and kitchen. To his left was the door to the front room. The wallpaper had seen better days and was starting to peel at the edges. He could smell a dog and see small dandelion-like tufts of hair floating up the stairs taken by the draught. Mary had tried to mask the smell with a heavily scented plug-in freshener. It mixed the fragrance of dog with strawberries that combined and stuck to the back of his throat.

Peter scanned the photographs on the wall to see if she had children. They were all of her and a man at various ages. The obligatory wedding picture took pride of place on the mantelpiece. Beside it was a fading photograph of her and the man on a foreign holiday, holding drinks as the sun set into the sea. On the far wall was a picture of an older couple that he thought must be her parents.

There was no sign of a man in the house. The shoes in the hallway were all women's. There wasn't a man's coat on the hooks.

"Do you live here alone?" he asked.

"My husband, David, died. It was a combine harvester accident. Reverend Green was very kind. He took the details for the funeral. After that, he came back every week to see me and share the good news," Mary said proudly. "Martha always came with him. They prayed for me, and I found Jesus."

Peter wanted to answer that he didn't know that Jesus had been lost. He thought it every time someone said the same thing. Perhaps he was wrong, but he didn't like to put the start of faith to a time, place, or person. He felt it was something that grew year by year and that the moment of enlightenment was when you just finally realised what had been going for a long time.

"I came to ask your forgiveness and to give me another chance."

"Already forgiven. I prayed for you this morning."

"Will you come back to church?" he asked.

"What else have I got? Jack and Martha were very good to me. They are like family."

"Do you have any relatives in the village?"

"None that take any notice. When David died, my friends all fell away. My sister-in-law lives across the green, but doesn't speak."

"Why?" he asked.

"They didn't want to listen. I tried to tell them about the truth, but they didn't want to know."

"You tried to tell them about faith?" Peter said.

"It was what Jack and Martha said I should do. He thought I was the one to bring these people out of darkness."

"Have you been in the village for very long?"

"Long?" she replied as if it was a flippant question. "Since I was born. I am adopted, and never knew my birth parents. It was a private arrangement between them and my birth mother. My adopted mum and dad lived in this house. They couldn't have children, so I was brought up as their own. They did the best for me and gave me all the love they had. Dad was fifty and Mum forty when I was born, so they were like grandparents."

"Are they still alive?" he asked.

"They died within a month of each other, just after the accident. I think it was the shock. My dad found David in the thresher of the combine. I think it was just too much. I lost David, our home, and everything else. We lived in a tied house on Holme Farm. No job, no house."

"You lost the house?"

"Notice to quit served the day after the funeral. Twelve years of loyalty gone in a day. Estate manager even blamed David for the accident. They got out of paying compensation. I came home to live with Mum and Dad and they were dead within three months. I lost my pottery business as I had no studio." Mary sat at the kitchen table as a slow trickle of tears crossed her cheeks.

"I have asked too much," Peter said as he offered her his handkerchief.

"I am glad you have. Jack has gone, Martha is away. I have had no one to talk to. The rest of the congregation are not friendly. I live in the wrong end of the village. My husband's passing is all so very fresh. Three deaths in a year is painful. It just bubbles through the cracks, and I can't keep it in. He died without knowing Jesus."

Peter made her a cup of coffee with the last of the milk in the fridge. He noticed there was little food, and what there was looked as if it was past its sell-by date. He sat with her for the next two hours as she unloaded all that was on her heart. Mary sobbed, laughed, and was then silent. She told him about her time at the now-closed village school. Her friends that had gone to live and work in York and Scarborough, and how the village had changed with incomers buying the pretty houses.

Mary talked about Jack Green as if he was her saviour. It was deeper than infatuation. Peter could see by her glowing face that when she mentioned his name, it was as if she spoke of someone with whom she had a deep, loving relationship. It was a situation that made him feel deeply uncomfortable.

"Were you a churchgoer before your husband died?" he asked.

"No. I had no desire or time for such things. Jack and Martha showed me the truth. They told me I had to change the way I lived and follow the Lord. So, I did."

"And the well, what did they say about the well?"

"A font of evil, a Pagan shrine on consecrated ground. It had to be blocked up. Jack had a message from God. He told Jack what to do, that it had to be done, and the witches stopped from using the water to feed the old yew tree on the mound. If you drink it, you drink evil."

"I have been researching the well, and in times gone by, it was the only source of pure water for the village. Every house drank from it, and we all do today," Peter answered.

"What do you mean?"

"I spoke to Yorkshire Water, and they told me that all the water around here comes from deep underground. The water that comes out of your tap is the same that comes out of the well. The well isn't evil. Evil comes from people's hearts and minds, not out of the ground."

"Are you saying Jack was a liar? He is a good man," Mary snapped back.

"Jack wasn't a well man. That is why he had to go away."

"Martha told me he was being attacked by demons because of the good work he was doing here. His wife was an adulterer and she brought evil into the house. She was seeing Fred Prescott from *Fred's Flowers*. It turned Jack to drink and made him sad. He would sit in that chair and cry like a child. He would tell me all that was on his mind. He would try to come here without Martha so we could be alone. Jack is a good man."

"He needed you?" Peter asked, already expecting what was to come.

"We needed each other. He would hold my hand. Jack said it would give me strength and that the Holy Spirit would come through him and into me. Sometimes, he would put his arms around me and hold me tight so that the power was stronger."

"Have you told anyone else about what Jack would do?"

"No. He told me it was a secret between us both. He said Martha wouldn't understand."

"A secret?"

"Yes, and I hold you as a priest to keep it and tell no one," she insisted.

"I never would," he paused momentarily. "One thing that will help me understand. Were you in love with him?"

Mary did not reply. Peter could see her bristle with anger, screwing up her eyes as she stared at him.

"I grew to love him, and he loved me… I know it."

"Does Martha know about you both?" he asked softly.

"No. Jack told me he would tell her when the time is right. He is going to find a place and we will live together once his divorce is settled and he is free to marry again. I will rent this house out. It was all my parents had to leave me when they died. Please," she insisted. "Don't tell anyone."

"I promise," Peter answered. "It is best you don't say anything about your plans."

"I am glad you understand. I thought they had sent you here to pull down everything Jack had built. He worked so hard for the parishioners and they didn't respect him. The bishop was always on the phone to him saying that someone or other had complained about this and that. *Sufferings of the cross* was what Jack said. We will be persecuted for our faith but have the promise of Heaven."

[20]
'Til Death Do Us Part

Saturday came around quickly. It was two hours until the wedding. The final touches to the church had been done. The pews were garlanded with flowers, the altar surrounded with columns of roses.

Peter sat in his stall, eyes closed, trying to still his mind. He had thought and prayed about what Mary Coleman had said to him. He had been tied to confidentiality and knew that he couldn't share it with anyone. At least in *the job*, Peter could share his concerns with the others on his shift. Often, it was the only way he coped. Death, violence, and heartbreak were a daily occurrence. All human tragedy presented itself on every shift. The days of *Dixon of Dock Green* had long gone.

The Church of England was different. Deanery meetings were sombre, middle-class, and out of touch with the world he inhabited day by day. His church colleagues had followed the same path in life. A good school, university, and then the church. Few had ever had a job in the outside world. They were religious professionals who were suspicious of him and spoke a coded language that he did not understand.

There had been times over the last few days when he had felt he had made a mistake. Perhaps Mary was right that the two jobs would never go together. She had said that he was too worldly to be a priest and too priestly to be a copper. Even Bishop Riley had his doubts. St Walstan's was an experiment, and one the bishop would closely watch.

"Vicar?" came the voice from the church door. "I have just come to check the flowers."

Peter looked up. There before him was a man in his late forties. He was tall, tanned, and smartly dressed in a casual shirt and trousers. His brown hair was brushed back from his thin face that was edged in a designer stubble.

"Hello," Peter said as he got up from his stall and walked down the central aisle. "Peter Barnes, nice to meet you."

"Freddy Prescott, from *Fred's Flowers*. Sorry I haven't had a chance to come and say hello. I have another shop in Scarborough, and the manager has been off sick, so I haven't been here," Freddy said with a wide smile and a firm handshake as strong as his aftershave.

"Good to meet you. The flowers look beautiful," Peter answered, unsure if he had met the man before.

"We try our best. My assistant, Ailsa, did these. She is very good at her job."

"They must have cost a fortune. Are they leaving the flowers or taking them to the reception?"

"They are all yours. The couple have paid for more flowers at the hotel. Or, should I say, their parents have."

"Lucky couple," Peter answered.

"The society wedding of the year in Yorkshire."

"I gathered at the rehearsal that there was no issue with money."

"Father owns a steel company in Sheffield," Freddy said as he looked around the church. "All seems fine," he stopped and looked at Peter. "How are you settling in?"

Peter paused before he answered. It was the kind of question that he knew led to something else. "Fine. The villagers haven't lynched me yet."

"Maggie was a good woman. She—" Freddy Prescott stopped mid-sentence as a large group of people came through the church door, followed by Gerald Griffin. "Perhaps later?"

"Of course," Peter answered, knowing that Maggie was the wife of Jack Green, who most of the village suspected of having an affair with Prescott.

"Vicar. Have you seen the order of service?" Griffin asked, waving a folded piece of card in his hand.

"Yes. Is there a problem?"

"Do I have to play the theme tune from *Goldfinger*?"

"The family thought it fitted the signing of the register. Could you give it a few bars?"

"Fitted? I feel like a cinema organist," he laughed as he walked on.

Peter never liked to refuse musical requests. There was always some reason why families chose certain songs. Having taken over a hundred funerals, he was now fluent in the words of *My Way*. He felt it the most inappropriate song to play, but if they wanted it, they could have it. Peter knew some priests who would refuse certain pieces of music in services. He had changed his mind when as a curate, he took a funeral for a young man who had fallen off the cliffs whilst on holiday at Whitby.

The whole service had been made up of pop songs instead of hymns. He had worked with the family to carefully fit the songs with each part of the liturgy. The packed church had wept and laughed; the music they were familiar with allowed them to grieve.

Now, he would endure the themes from *Goldfinger*, *Star Wars*, and *Grease*, all played reluctantly by Gerald Griffin in a classical style. It would be an assault on the ears, but it was what the family wanted.

The groom and best man fulfilled the custom to arrive first with an army of ushers. They all looked the same. Thin, muscular, and well dressed with short hair, southern accents, and worked in the city. *Bankers*, Peter thought as they fussed with the orders of service and showed people to their seats as if stewards at the Glyndebourne opera.

The bride was late. Uncomfortably, rudely, and annoyingly late. Peter had told her that being ten minutes was fine, but she had ignored his request of the night before, and now thirty minutes had passed. The church was hot, and the congregation bored.

The groom sat at the front of the church, twisting his cufflinks in his fingers as the best man read and reread his speech.

Finally, the bells stopped, and the lace-covered Edwina Melrose-Hirst stood at the church door, arm linked with her father, a preened man with thick, white hair combed back over his head. She smiled, the organ played, and the wedding service began.

Gerald Griffin played *Goldfinger* perfectly as the couple signed the registers and photographs were taken. Peter tried not to laugh, knowing what mental torture that such a purist as Gerald must be enduring.

Following the wedding blessing and prayers at the chancel steps, the couple followed him to the bottom of the bell tower. There, a single rope dangled as if set by the hangman. It was a long tradition at St Walstan's for the newlyweds to take the rope with joined hands and pull together as an act of union.

Peter trusted the ringers had set the bell before they had left, so that with a gentle pull it would tip and ring. Taking the rope, he pulled it slightly. The telltale stiffness was still there as he explained the tradition to the congregation and invited the couple to tell the world of their union in the tolling of the bell.

Edwina took the rope, and before her husband could take hold, she pulled long and hard. The bell rolled as the rope came down and upon returning, the bride went up, taken off her feet with a scream and a flourish of lace, like a butterfly pulled from a flower.

The congregation gasped and then, when she hit the floor, laughed. The bell rope snapped from its fastening and plunged to the floor. Her father rushed forward to protect his child. He tripped and fell on top of her as cameras flashed. The whole church applauded as her father got to his feet and raised his hands in victory as if he were a bare-knuckle fighter.

Peter waited for the laughing to subside and then gave the blessing.

At the door of the church, Edwina's father came up and shook his hand, pressing a thick wad of notes into his palm.

"Buy yourself a new rope," he said with a broad smile. "I hope someone caught it on camera."

Freddy Prescott had hung back from the crowds. He checked the flower stands and rearranged some of the blooms. It seemed obvious to Peter that he was waiting to speak and finish the conversation.

"Never seen a flying bride before," he laughed. "That was amazing."

"Such a slight thing. Light as a feather," Peter answered, waiting for the real question.

"I don't know what you have heard about Maggie and I, but I want to set the record straight for her sake," Freddy said as his face became more serious and his brow etched in a line.

"It's not my business," Peter answered. "Frank Green has gone, and what you do in your private life is up to you."

"We didn't have an affair. It would be impossible. Maggie is a very close friend. She came to my flower arranging classes and we just hit it off," Freddy spoke quickly as if he wanted to tell Peter as much as possible in the shortest possible time.

"You don't have to explain," Peter answered, trying to reassure him.

"Frank used to hit her. He would get drunk and hit her. Maggie thought he was messing about with the woman who takes the services. When she challenged him, he hit her. I told him that if he touched her again, I would see to him."

"You should have called the police."

"I did. Maggie wouldn't press charges. They didn't even come and see her."

"So why does half the village think she was having an affair with you?" Peter asked.

"Because I told Frank that I was. I wanted to protect Maggie from him. The man was a brute and had to be stopped." Freddy stepped closer as if he did not want to be overheard. "The thing is, I'm not into women. I have a partner, a man. We have been together for ten years."

"I heard Frank came to your shop shouting at you."

"He did. Swearing, drunk, and throwing handfuls of mud."

"Why didn't you get him arrested?"

"Maggie asked me not to. I have a block of flats in Scarborough. She lives in one rent-free. The church didn't want to help her.

Bishop Riley wanted to cover the whole thing up. He came to see me at the shop. He wanted Maggie out of the way as quickly as possible. There was even talk of letting Frank stay. He got a lot of support, but she got nothing. It was the least I could do."

"What evidence do you have that Frank was with Martha?" Peter asked.

"Maggie saw them late one night in the office at the vicarage. They were supposed to be photocopying the parish magazine. They were kissing."

"Did she challenge him about it?"

"At breakfast the next day. He said all they were doing was praying. Funny way to pray with your tongue down her throat," Freddy said, his voice tinged with anger. "Sorry. I shouldn't have said it, but it makes me mad that he got away with it."

"Do you think Maggie would talk to me?" Peter asked.

"Why, what good would it do? The bishop didn't want to know."

"He assaulted his wife, and you say he was intimate with Martha. He must answer for his actions."

"Frank Green is a dangerous man. I know, I have seen it in his eyes."

[21]
Nunc Dimittis

Evensong was without singing. It was the only service that Gerald Griffin refused to play at. He had said that there was a pressing engagement that he couldn't get out of. When Peter asked him in conversation where he was going, Gerald was vague and evasive.

The church was empty. Peter had rung the bell, but no one had come. He had stood at the church door, hoping that he would not be alone. The rain beat down from the darkening sky, and far to the west, he could hear the rumination of thunder.

The morning service had been poorly attended. Unlike the baptism of the week before, there had only been nine people who had braved the summer rain. Mary Coleman had stayed away, an absence that Morris Marsden had proudly pointed out. Anne Hindle had overheard the comment as she counted the meagre collection and added that it was a blessing in disguise.

Now, Peter sat in his stall reading from the prayer book and wondering why he was there. Like an automaton, he read the New Testament lesson and then the Nunc dimittis. It was a canticle that he had always liked. When he said the words, he felt at peace. Peter closed his eyes and repeated the first line several times in a low murmur.

It was then that he heard the sharp, stiletto-like footsteps clatter across the stone door slab. He looked up but could see no one. The footsteps had stopped, but he was sure there was someone there.

Again, he closed his eyes and continued to pray.

The footsteps came again as the hail rattled against the stained glass windows. Peter looked up. The church was empty, and yet he could hear footsteps now clattering on the metal heating grill behind the back pew. Clear and distinct, they came closer and then stopped. He could see no one but could hear deep, laboured breaths being taken.

"Hello!" he shouted, his words echoing around the empty church. There was no reply.

The footsteps came again, this time going back towards the door. They clattered and clanged on the metal grill and then clicked on the stone steps.

Peter sat back down. A shiver shot down his spine. He read the words of the psalm set for the evening. *Show us the light and be merciful.* The words stuck in his throat as the sound of footsteps came again as a crash of summer thunder exploded over the village. He sat further back, pushing into the carved oak stall, and listened. Peter could hear a hoof scraping against the stone floor. At that moment, a sudden gust of wind pulled the door shut. The bang echoed around the church as he got to his feet and prepared to meet whatever presence had come inside. In a dark and confused corner of his mind, he started to believe that Frank Green might be right.

"In the name of..." Peter shouted, fearing that a supernatural presence would appear. Then, it happened.

At the far end of the pew, a bearded and horned head appeared. A nanny goat slowly edged around the pew and stared at him. Trailing from a collar around its neck was a broken rope.

Peter sighed.

"Well," he said to the animal. "You scared the hell out of me. What are you doing here?"

The goat moaned as it started to chew a pew end bunch of summer flowers and walk towards him.

He could see that the creature was heavily pregnant. Her belly was swollen, the goat clawed the floor and moaned loudly.

Peter had the sudden realisation that the animal was going to give birth.

"You can't do it here," he said, taking hold of the collar and leading the beast to the far end of the church and a small side aisle.

He had no idea what to do next. The goat twisted around and then fell to its front knees with a loud groan. Peter could see from the rear of the animal that the kid was due very soon. He wondered why the animal had come into church and could only think it was escaping the storm.

There was a sudden issue of blood and water. The goat lay down and Peter could see the tip of a nose and two small hoof tips poking from her. The animal moaned loudly as she pushed but the kid didn't move. He knew he would have to help and quickly took off his robes, throwing them onto the floor. Rolling up his sleeve, he pushed his hand into the goat and took hold of the hooves. The goat pushed as Peter pulled as hard as he could. The kid moved forwards and slipped onto the stone floor. He cleared the airway with his fingers and rubbed the kid's chest.

The mother turned and licked the kid as she gave a shallow moan.

It was then that the door to the church burst open. A man stood there dripping with rain. He wore an old coat tied around the waist with bailing twine. His felt hat was flattened to his head and his chin was covered in a week of stubble.

"Gloria, you little beggar. I have been looking for you everywhere," he said, rushing towards her and kneeling on the floor.

"You could have been here sooner," Peter said. "How did you find us?"

"It was the thunder. Frightened her from the barn. Bruce saw her running into the churchyard. She would be looking for shelter." The man looked down at the bleating kid and the blood on his arms. "Did you deliver her?"

"I had to. The kid was stuck," Peter answered. "I saw it done on *Country File*, John Craven did it."

The man laughed.

"Well, Vicar, I'm glad you spend your time watching the telly. At least you are some earthly use, and not a chocolate fire-guard."

Peter laughed. He didn't know who smelt the worse, the farmer or the goat. Both stank like a wet dog that had swam in a ditch. The old man dripped water onto the stone floor as he held the mother goat in his arms and cradled it like a baby.

"She did well," Peter said.

"Aye. Gloria is a grand lass. Funny she came back here."

"Back?" Peter asked.

"Last Christmas. The school had the nativity here. They couldn't get a donkey, so they borrowed Gloria. Joseph and Mary walked her in," the man laughed out loud as he stroked the goat's head. "She peed on the floor and the woman vicar slipped on it. Just like that elephant on *Blue Peter*."

It was a childhood memory that had been repeated on every outtake programme ever since. He pictured the black and white images of a baby elephant pulling John Noakes, the presenter, around the BBC studio and through a pile of droppings on the nation's most popular children's show.

"You are showing your age," Peter said to the man. "That was years ago."

"I remember it well. It was two days after we got our first television," the man answered. "And we still have it in our back room."

[22]
The Old Manor

The morning walk was overcast. The rain of the night before had cleared and the woodland path from the village was overpoweringly humid in the heat of the morning. Peter hadn't slept. After the goat gave birth in the church, he had gone back to the vicarage and Mary had called. The news wasn't good. Her mother was being kept in hospital another week. The doctors had found a small growth on her kidney and wanted to operate. Mary insisted on staying with her father. Peter knew it was pointless to say how he really felt.

Thunder, like his troubled thoughts, echoed until the early hours. Both had kept him half waking, half sleeping until the sun rose. It was then he decided to get up, shower, eat, and then go for a long hike.

He had walked for three hours, stopping only to have coffee from his flask as he sat on a wall overlooking the moor and the old Roman marching camp. It was no more than a square ditch, but he was fascinated by the fact that once, a thousand Roman soldiers had lived there on their way to Hadrian's Wall. Now, it was a field of heather surrounded on three sides by a wall of conifers that formed the front line of the lifeless forest waiting to be cut down.

A mile further, he was at the gates of the Old Manor. The house was settled in a small valley surrounded by trees on three sides. To the front were several acres of grassland stretching down the valley.

It was a traditional Elizabethan manor with oak-beamed walls, framed with heavy, vertical timbers and diagonal supporting beams. The wattle walls between these timbers were daubed with whitewashed mortar.

It looked fragile, like a pack of cards waiting to be blown down by the slightest breeze. Yet, it had stood for nearly four hundred years, endured a civil war, disease, and incursions by rebellious Scots. The Old Manor was way off his police beat and wasn't in his parish. It was a house he had never seen before, and it held a magical charm as though it were the setting of a childhood story.

The long gravel drive was flanked along its length by fading rhododendrons. The ground beneath them was a carpet of discarded petals. He followed the track down the hill, through a stand of trees, and out into the open parkland.

On the far side of the valley, where the grassland met the trees, he could see a cluster of deer grazing as the sun broke through the clouds. Outside the house, on a trimmed circular lawn, was a tall, white-painted flagpole topped with a butcher's apron that hung limply as if a bloodstained tablecloth hung out to dry.

An old Mercedes station wagon was parked outside the house. Peter didn't know if he should call or carry on walking. His question was answered as a middle-aged man in a white shirt and black trousers stepped out of the tall front door.

"Can I help you?" he asked in a precise and refined accent. "I saw you coming down the drive."

"I was hoping to see Amber."

"Amber? Lady Hudson is not quite ready to receive guests. Who shall I say has called?"

He was about to answer when Amber Hudson came out of the house dressed in a flowing silk housecoat.

"Peter. You're an early bird," she said brightly. "Marcus has just made coffee. I am sure he can squeeze out another cup."

Peter thought that Marcus must obviously be the neatly preened man who now gave him a disappointed look.

"Yes, Lady Hudson, of course," Marcus said with a forced smile as he walked back into the house.

"He doesn't like people," she said when he was out of earshot. "Marcus has looked after me for thirty years. He is like a husband without the irritation," she laughed as she gestured for Peter to follow her into the house.

He gave an audible gasp as he walked into the entrance hall. The room was oak panelled from floor to ceiling. It had an intricate, vaulted, plaster ceiling with red-painted roses. The double-height leaded windows let in the morning sun that danced across the ten-seat Mouseman table. To one side was a stone fireplace. The opening was as tall as Peter and at least a fathom wide. Carved into the stones were the heads of forest animals.

"A beautiful room," Peter said as Amber gestured for him to sit down.

"It takes a hell of a lot of cleaning. It's what you think about when you get to my age. There have been Hudson's here since the Civil War," she said, pointing up to the portrait of a dower, bearded man in puritan dress that hung above the fireplace. "I am the last one. My father had two girls, and I did not have the womb for children."

"Your sister?" he asked.

"I knew you would ask. Evelyn was younger than me. She left her house one day and didn't go back. Haven't seen her for nearly thirty years and don't know if she is still alive. A long story, but I won't bore you with the details."

"Married to Magnus Seagrave of The Grange?" he asked.

"You have been a busy boy," Amber said as she sat down opposite him. "Do you know the whole story?"

"Just bits and pieces that have come up in conversation," he answered as Marcus came into the room and served coffee.

"Not the kind of subject I would have thought would crop up in conversation with the vicar," Amber answered, as if irritated.

"It was a retired undertaker who told me the history of the parish. Mad, bad, or sad."

Amber smiled as she sighed. "James Crowley?"

Peter nodded. "I was wondering what had gone wrong for my predecessors."

"James was a bit of a rogue in his day. A proper charmer. He had a thing for my sister, but my father said the only time he would have an undertaker in the house was when he was being carried out by one. Funny thing, it was James who did his funeral. If you spoke to James, then I am reassured you haven't been listening to parish gossip."

"Didn't Albert Shepherd go missing at the same time?" Peter asked.

Amber waited before answering. Her hand trembled slightly as she picked up the coffee cup. "From what I remember, gossip had it he was running away from his wife with a woman he had met. That was the word going around. I was living in London at the time. My husband had a gallery. We would come back for the occasional weekend."

"Do you think they went away together?" he asked.

"Why is it I suddenly get the feeling I am talking to you as a copper and not my parish priest?"

"Sorry. I am a believer that the history of a place can affect the future. Shepherd going missing seems to be the time things began to go wrong in the parish."

"I only come to St Walstan's because of Evelyn. It was a place that made her so happy. The church is a constant reminder of her. I feel she is there." Amber sipped her coffee. "Can I make a confession?"

"Go ahead."

"I don't believe in God."

"That's not a problem," Peter answered, specks of dust being illuminated by the shafts of sunlight to form a flickering rainbow. "Sometimes... neither do I."

"That would be a showstopper of a sermon," Amber replied.

"It's true. Sometimes I wake in the middle of the night and wonder if any of it is true. I have to be careful never to think about eternity or how big the universe is. I have a panic attack."

"And then what?" she asked.

"I cling onto what little faith I have, and I pray."

Amber looked him in the eyes. "I haven't prayed since the day Evelyn left."

"Did anyone report her missing?" he asked.

"Magnus said he had spoken to the police. He told them they had argued, and she had left him. Evelyn had taken her clothes and some money. Enough to keep her for a long time."

"Did she leave with Shepherd?" Peter asked.

"The rumour was he had gone off with a woman he had met on a church retreat. I don't think that is true." Amber looked away as if something distracted her outside. "Can I talk in confidence? I have never shared this with anyone, not even my husband. Evelyn was very much in love with Bertie, and Magnus knew about it."

"Where is Magnus now?" Peter asked.

"I went to see him the week after Evelyn had gone missing. He acted as if nothing had happened. The man could not have cared any less. Within the year, he was gone. I have no idea where he went. Everything was put into the hands of Meredith and Co., the solicitors in Malton."

"Not Grenville's, the land agents?"

"No. Magnus fell out with them soon after he married Evelyn." Amber stopped and looked at him. "You know a lot about this. What is your interest?"

"Honestly, it is just that… an interest. Maybe it's the copper in me wanting to know what happened. Two people cannot just vanish off the face of the earth."

Peter finished his coffee and put the cup down.

"Funny you say that. It is exactly what my husband used to go on about until the day he died." Amber looked at Peter and raised a knowing brow. "You are a stirrer of wasp nests, young man. What, with the Holy Well and Bertie Shepherd and my sister disappearing. Maybe God brought you here for a reason."

[23]
The Corniche

Marcus had insisted on giving Peter a lift back to the village. He had talked with Amber for a further two hours. In that time, they had spoken of her life in London, the death of her husband, and her overbearing father. The one thing that Peter realised was that she missed her sister, Evelyn. The only person she had in her life was the man who now drove him along the road in a ten-year-old Rolls Royce Corniche.

It was the first time Peter had ever been in a car like that. It glided silently down the road; it was not the kind of car he would have chosen, living at the end of a forest track.

"Have to take it for a service this morning," Marcus said as they drove up the long hill from the valley to the Roman fort. "It stays in the garage most of the year. It belonged to Sir John. I think Lady Amber keeps it for the memory."

"You have been with Lady Amber a long time," Peter answered.

"Every day has been a pleasure, but I think my time is coming to an end."

"Why?"

"I am seventy next year. I would like to travel and see the places I hear Lady Amber talking about."

"So, she doesn't take you with her?" he asked as they got to the main road. Marcus pulled the car over into a small lay-by, obviously ignoring what he said.

"I hope you don't mind. I have a ritual when I get the chance to drive this car," he said as he pressed the button on the console to lower the convertible roof. He then took a cassette tape from the glove box and slipped it into the machine. "I always thank the Romans for building a straight road two miles long."

Suddenly, and without warning, Marcus hit the accelerator with his right foot. The Corniche bolted forward along the empty road, gaining speed with every second. Freddie Mercury blasted from the speakers, filling the long lane with a song about a good time.

"She flies," Peter said, gripping the seat belt in his right hand.

"Just clearing the carburettor. It needs a quick blast."

The trees sped by as the wind blew through his hair, the sun shone, and music filled his ears. He looked at Marcus. The man had a broad smile. His fingers gripped the steering wheel as he sat back in the plush leather seat and intently watched the road ahead.

When the song finished, the car slowed down. Marcus pressed eject and the tape popped out from the player.

"I would never catch you in my police car," Peter said as he relaxed in his seat.

"I don't think you would anyway. Sir James liked rallying. I was his driver and he the navigator. Back in the day we won the RAC rally and a couple of Europeans."

"What made you stop?" he asked.

"Sir James died of throat cancer. I lost a good friend. He asked me to look after Lady Amber and I promised him I would."

"Then you can't retire. I believe she needs you more than you think."

"Perhaps," he answered. "She is a wonderful woman. I don't know what I would do without her in my life."

"Does she know you are in love with her?"

"With respect, Vicar, you are a cheeky bastard. I have punched a man in the face for less," Marcus answered jokingly. "Is it obvious?"

"You should tell her. Nothing to lose."

"My job? My home? Amber?"

"You love her, and she needs you."

"Sounds like you run a dating agency. How much do you charge?" Marcus asked.

"It's free. Payment for the lift home."

The rest of the journey took a matter of minutes. Marcus drove him to the gates of the church and dropped him off. He waved to Peter as he set off, the sounds of Freddie booming from the car again.

The village street was empty, as was the pub car park. *Bruce Loves Grass* was hitched on the verge outside Heather Cottage, the rear doors of the van open. Peter hoped that when he called again, the *pot plants* would be gone. He knew they wouldn't be destroyed, but just relocated, and he didn't really mind. There was some truth in the feeling that a destructive drug like alcohol was legal and a herb wasn't. Peter had seen how drink could wreck a family. His father had spent most of his life with a glass in his hand.

Walking back to the vicarage, his feelings of imposter syndrome were waning like the moon. Perhaps, he thought, he was in the right place at the right time.

As he turned into the vicarage driveway, he saw a woman sat on the bench by the front porch. She was hunched over, her head in her hands. When he walked towards her, she got up and walked towards him, wiping her face as she got closer.

"Reverend Barnes?" she asked as she got closer. "I'm Kelly Grant. I need a priest."

"How can I help?" he asked, seeing her distress.

"My mother is dying. She has asked for a priest. We live in Dales Terrace. Can you come straight away?"

In several minutes, he had changed, picked up a small bag containing his anointing oil and prayer book, and was walking out of the house.

Kelly had gone ahead, reassured the priest would follow.

Peter walked quickly and was soon outside the house. The door was open. A small Jack Russell barked in the weed-filled front garden as it stood on an old car tyre.

Kelly came to the door and ushered him inside.

The room was crowded with people. A woman lay on the sofa that had been pushed against the back wall. Two children sat on the fireside rug, surrounded by several adults. A man knelt at the head of the sofa, wiping the head of the woman with a face cloth. There was a palpable tension in the room, a fear of what was to come.

"That's my dad," Kelly said as the man looked up and smiled.

"Vince Grant," he said. "This is my wife, Dawn. Doctor says she's not got long. They let us bring her home from the hospice."

"What would you like me to do?" Peter asked.

"Before she fell asleep, she asked for a priest. She wanted a blessing."

The woman opened her eyes as she tried to turn her head towards him. Peter took out a small silver pyx filled with Holy oil from his bag. He rubbed his thumb on the cap as he looked around the room.

"I am going to pray for Dawn. If anyone wants to join in with me, you are welcome."

"Come on kids," one of the men said, leaning forward to take hold of the child.

"They can stay. You all can," Peter said as he knelt next to Vince. It was then that he drew a cross on her forehead with his thumb, "In the name of the Father, the Son, and the Holy Spirit. Now Lord, let your servant go in peace. May you bless her, keep her, and prepare a place in paradise. Amen."

Dawn sighed as if she repeated the word. The rise and fall of her chest slowed as the tension in her face appeared to ease. Peter knew that she was close to letting go. He had seen so many people on the edge of death. Some would fight to the bitter end, whilst others would gracefully give in and drift away.

Peter wasn't frightened of dying. He had seen so much death in the police that it was a daily occurrence. What scared him was the process and the pain. The long, laboured breaths and clinging on in fear of eternity. It was that fear that had pushed Peter towards Christianity. When he was fourteen, on a school trip to Whitby, he had seen the body of a man being pulled from the river. As the sodden corpse of the man was pulled from the water, there had been a sudden realisation of his own mortality.

From that moment, he had sojourned into spirituality. He had dabbled in spiritualism but never had a message from beyond the grave. Peter had found Jesus by accident at the death of a friend. Now he was here again.

Vince began to weep as he held her hand.

"I love you, darling. I always will," he sobbed as Kelly knelt with him.

"You can go home now, Mum," Kelly said as she squeezed her mum's hand.

"Perhaps Vince and Kelly might like some time alone with Dawn," Peter said to those gathered around the room, sensing the need for peace.

Kelly nodded in agreement. "It could be quite some time."

"Will you stay, Vicar?" Vince asked.

Peter nodded as the room cleared and people said quiet goodbyes. "Cup of tea?" Peter asked. "I can make it for you."

Kelly pointed to the kitchen and smiled. "Through there. It's a bit of a mess. Milk in the fridge."

The kitchen was more than a mess. A full sink was the least of the problems. It looked as though they had not had the time to clean it for weeks. Peter washed the cups, cleaned out the teapot, and made the drinks.

They sat together for two hours, hardly speaking. Vince held the hand of his wife as Kelly tore a paper tissue in her hands.

It was an hour later that Dawn's breathing changed. It became more laboured, exaggerated, and deeper. It was as if she struggled for breath.

"Doctor said I should ring him if her breathing changed," Vince said as he got to his feet.

"Good idea," Peter answered as Kelly took her father's place kneeling next to Dawn.

"How long will it be?" she asked.

"Anytime, I think," Peter answered as Vince came back into the room. "Would you pray, Vicar?" he asked.

Peter nodded as Vince knelt beside him. The three bowed their heads. Peter spoke the words of The Lord's Prayer.

"Amen," they said together as the prayer ended.

Kelly and Vince opened their eyes. Dawn had stopped breathing.

"Dawn... Dawn?" Vince said urgently.

"I think she has gone," Peter answered.

"Oh, God," Kelly groaned as Vince sobbed deeply.

Peter put his arms around them both and held them close.

"No more suffering. No more pain," Peter said as the father and daughter shed tears of fathomless grief.

[24]
The Cod Father

The lights on the fish and chip shop burnt brightly against the brick wall. Peter had driven around the town for half an hour. Every takeaway was shut. Getting food on a Monday night in a Yorkshire coastal town was impossible.

The Cod Father was his last chance. He had been in a fight there when he was new to the job. It was a traditional chippy with tiled walls, steel counter, and a bright fluorescent light. Next door was a beauty salon, post office, flower shop, and an out-of-place Italian restaurant that didn't do takeouts.

Peter pulled up outside, thankful that the chippy looked open. He had spent most of the day and early evening with Kelly Grant and her father. The doctor had signed the death certificate, and John Crowley had taken the body away. Now, Peter wanted to eat some food, and watch the sea and the passers-by on the promenade. He didn't want to go home. The vicarage was starting to feel empty. Its rooms echoed loneliness.

As he got out of his car, Peter saw a man smoking a cigarette outside the Italian restaurant. In the half-light, he thought the man look familiar, but was too far away to be sure. A thick cloud of blue smoke billowed up into the red lights above the door. The man looked towards him and then waved in recognition.

"Vicar!" the man shouted, throwing the cigarette to the floor and stamping upon it. "Can I have a moment?"

Peter stopped. He realised it was Freddy Prescott.

"Freddy," he answered as the man walked towards him, hand outstretched.

"What a coincidence. I was just talking about you before I came out for a smoke. We just finished the starters. Maggie is with us. She said she wants to talk to you."

"Anytime. Just tell her to give me a ring," Peter answered as he watched the owner of *The Cod Father* cleaning down the counter as he prepared to close the shop.

"Come and see her now. We have a seat at the table," Freddy replied.

"I came for some supper," Peter said, pointing to the chippy.

"Then have some with us."

His decision was made for him as the lights to the chip shop were turned off and the door was locked.

"Are you sure she won't mind? I don't want to spoil your night," he answered uncomfortably.

"It'll be fine," Freddy said, leading the way to the restaurant.

The *Bella Italia* was cosily dark. The room was crowded with glass-topped tables, lit with flickering electric candles. As he walked in, Peter could see Maggie Green sat at a corner table with a handsome looking man dressed in an expensive suit. She looked younger than the last time he had seen her when the bishop had taken him for a look around the vicarage. Maggie had straightened her hair and now wore makeup. She didn't look as stressed and worn out as she had at their first meeting.

"Maggie, look what the cat dragged in!" Freddy shouted across the empty restaurant. "I found him outside the chippy. He looked hungry."

Maggie smiled as she got to her feet to welcome Peter.

"We were just talking about you."

"How strange. What a coincidence," Maggie answered and then paused momentarily. "Perhaps... it wasn't a coincidence after all."

"This is Dan, my long-term companion," Freddy said, introducing his partner. "He hates flowers, so heaven knows what we have in common."

Dan stood up. He was a tall man with a shock of thick, blonde hair, a thin face and three-day stubble. Dan smiled a broad, perfect, white-toothed smile.

"Nice to meet you," he said in a deep, gravelly voice. "Come and sit with us."

"Amedeo," Freddy said to the waiter who hovered in a dark corner. "Could you make sure we have enough to share with our friend?"

The waiter nodded and vanished into the kitchen.

"I feel as if I have interrupted a good evening," Peter said as he sat down.

"How are you settling in?" Dan asked as Amedeo brought food to the table.

"Things have been interesting," he answered.

They ate and talked for the next hour, avoiding any mention of Frank Green. Peter felt as if he was being slowly prepared for what was to come.

It was only when coffee was being served that Maggie turned the conversation.

"I hope you believe that Freddy and I weren't having an affair," she said as she sipped a glass of red wine.

"Freddy told me in church, and I believed him. You have no need to explain," Peter answered.

"I feel I have to say something. There have been so many rumours. Bishop Riley just wanted me out of the way as soon as possible."

"What was Frank's relationship with Martha Storr?" Peter asked.

"They were very close. Too close. Martha had a thing for him, and I was in the way," Maggie answered. "We argued about her a lot. I said it wasn't right, the things they did, and people would talk."

"No one in the parish has mentioned any impropriety about them at all. The only thing that has been said was about Frank attacking the flower shop."

Dan and Freddy laughed.

"Not so much an attack as a tantrum with plant pots," Dan said as he squeezed Freddy on the arm. "He stood in the street shouting. Frank was drunk."

"What about Mary Coleman?"

"How did you find out about her?" she asked.

"It came up in conversation," he answered.

"Mary was besotted. She would sit at his feet in the Bible studies at the vicarage and eat up his every word. Frank believed she had to be set free from a spirit of grief. Everything was the result of spirits. You could never just be sick or have a cold. It always had to be some demon or other attacking you."

"He believed all that?" Peter asked.

"About five years ago, when we were in Middlesbrough, he went to a men's meeting to listen to a missionary. Frank came back speaking in tongues, saying he had been filled with the spirit. He didn't sleep for days and tried to pray for the whole congregation to get the gift. That is why we eventually got moved here. The church put up with it for quite a while, and then asked Bishop Riley to move us on. I think Riley believed he could do no harm in a backwater like St Walstan's."

"Did Frank carry on with the gift?" Peter asked.

"When it started, we were having problems in our marriage. Frank said that if I was like him then we would never be apart. He insisted on praying for me every day to be anointed, and when it didn't happen, he said that God had chosen not to bless me."

"Do you believe in all that stuff, Peter?" Dan asked.

"Yes. Nothing is impossible for God. Sadly, sometimes people get carried away with it all and God gets pushed out, and they carry on in their own strength."

"But speaking in a foreign language?" Dan asked.

"Some would say it is the language of angels. I just believe it's a way of praying through the emotions rather than the intellect. Others would argue that the gifts of the Holy Spirit died out with the early church."

"Anyway, he soon got Martha Storr babbling away," Mary said with a tinge of despair in her voice. "They would pray together," she paused and looked at Freddy. "Then I saw them. Wrapped around each other. Kissing."

"And you challenged him?" Peter asked.

"Of course, he was my husband. I wanted to know what was going on. Frank denied it. He said he was helping her. That's when he got angry and hit me. I should have left him there and then but... *vicar's wife syndrome...*"

"Did you tell Bishop Riley?"

"No. I didn't want to cause Frank any trouble. The church is his life, but the drink got in the way. He got drunk. Hit me and then asked to be forgiven the next morning."

"Did you ever say anything to Martha Storr?" Peter asked.

"There was no point. They were very close. She made it obvious to me that they had a special relationship."

[25]
Apples From The Tree

Morris Marsden picked his way through the shadows that danced on the gravel drive. He had been summoned to the vicarage but had been given no reason as to why. The call from the vicar had been brief. Now, as instructed, he was making his way to the vicarage as the church bells chimed the hour.

Peter stood by the front door. He was wearing a black clerical shirt and white collar underneath a black cassock.

"Vicar!" Morris shouted as he got near. "Ten o'clock, and not a minute late, and I am here."

"I am glad. I need to talk to you face-to-face."

"Something serious?" he asked.

"Extremely. I have been speaking to the bishop."

Morris followed him inside the house and to the office. Three chairs had been placed in a triangle on the floor.

"What's going on, Vicar? Not having a faculty for bricking up the well?" Morris asked as he sat on the chair opposite the door.

"No. I need you here as a witness. You are in a position of responsibility."

"Who else is coming?"

There was a knock on the door. Morris heard a voice he recognised.

"Hello? Peter?" Martha Storr shouted from the door.

"In here. In the office," Peter answered as Morris gave him a confused look.

Martha Storr walked into the room. She wore a safari jacket and matching trousers, with a leather handbag strapped across her chest. Her hair had been cropped short. Peter had only ever met Martha briefly, but he could see the difference in her. Gone were the dowdy clothes and plain face. Now, Martha was dressed much younger than her years and was wearing lipstick.

"Martha," Morris said getting to his feet and holding out his hand in welcome. "The holiday has done you good."

"Yes," she answered. "I needed to get away for a while."

Martha looked around the room wondering which seat she should take. It had changed since she had last been there. The photocopier was missing, as were the William Blake prints that once filled the walls. All had been replaced with large, framed Sutcliffe photographs of Whitby.

"How was Frank?" Peter asked as she sat down.

"Fine. Recovering," she said briskly, wondering how he knew where she had been. "Why is Morris here? I thought it was a meeting to plan services. Frank and I met every week."

"Morris is here because he is a churchwarden. I need to discuss something with you that had arisen whilst you were on holiday," Peter answered.

"What is that? What has happened?"

Morris shuffled uncomfortably in his chair.

"Are you having a relationship with Frank Green?" Peter asked. Martha sat back in her chair and defiantly folded her arms.

"That is none of your business. If I was, there would be no problem. Frank is getting divorced," Martha answered through steely lips. "The apple has fallen from the tree."

"I have reason to believe that the relationship started before he had left his wife."

"Did she tell you that?" Martha asked.

"I was approached by someone and given that information. I believe it to be true."

"It's none of your business. You're not a copper here. I am sure Bishop Riley will have something to say."

"Bishop Riley does have something to say. He called late last night and asked me to convene this meeting. I am not blaming you. Frank is a powerful man."

"Actually, he is a man that I love and have done for some time, but nothing happened until he had left Maggie. She was the one having an affair. That is what caused Frank to snap."

"Is Frank having a relationship with Mary Coleman?" Peter asked. Martha shuffled in her chair.

"In her dreams," Martha snapped. "Mary would love to get her hands on him. I warned Frank she was dangerous. Is that what this is all about? What has she said?"

"I would like to ask you to consider stepping back from parish duties."

"No," she snapped back. "I have been in this parish a long time and will be here long after you have gone. My ministry is from God."

"Is there any other way of sorting this out?" Morris asked.

"The request comes from the bishop. All I can say is that until this matter has been investigated, Martha will not be taking part in any services."

"My God!" Martha yelled. "How dare you?"

"I dare, because Bishop Riley has told me to tell you that he will ask a pastoral visitor to talk to you about this matter and find a resolution. Until that time, he believes it would be best for you to step back from your ministry," Peter answered calmly.

"What about the parishioners? For the sake of Martha, what do we tell them?" Morris asked.

Peter looked at her.

"What do you want me to say?" he asked. "I don't think anyone needs to know the details."

Martha took a deep, stoic breath. "I suppose I have no choice."

"What about a sabbatical?" Morris suggested. "The parish need not know anything else."

"You are totally wrong, you know. Frank is a man of God, more than you will ever be," Martha said angrily as she stood up to leave the room. "How long do I have to wait until the investigations are over?"

"Bishop Riley said he would contact you in a couple of days."

"Really?" she sneered. "Why is it that you look as if you are enjoying this? You have opened the well and let out the demon. Don't be surprised if it turns on you."

[26]
The Trimphone

Morris Marsden held the coffee cup in his hands as if it were a crystal ball. He stared into its depths as Peter looked out of the window.

"I really don't know what to say," Morris eventually replied. "I would never have thought that Frank Green would ever hit his wife and be inappropriate with a parishioner and a lay reader."

"Sadly, all true. But it has to stay between us. Mary Coleman was naïve in what she did, but I suspect Frank could be quite manipulative."

"He was so fervent in his beliefs. A devout evangelical, a man of the Bible," Morris answered.

"Often the case," Peter replied. "Frank had his weaknesses."

"Martha sounded like a stranger. I have known her for many years, but I have never heard her speak like she did. It was as if she was a different person."

"I think Frank might have made the same promises to her as he has to Mary Coleman."

"Then there will be two broken hearts," Morris answered as he finished his coffee. "I never married, and do not know the ways of women, but I can see that she loves him."

"The power of love is a curious thing," Peter answered. "Tell me, did you ever meet Evelyn Seagrave?"

"That is a name from the past. I remember her well. What a beauty. Tragic that she disappeared so suddenly. No trace. Just took her things and was gone. Her husband was broken-hearted. I remember him sitting in the pew, sobbing at evensong."

"Was he a religious man?" Peter asked.

"Deeply so," Morris answered. "He was the lay rector and had the power to appoint the vicar."

"So, he selected Albert Shepherd?"

"They went to the same university. Played cricket and rugby on the same team. Not that they were friends; far from it, actually. I often heard them arguing. Albert Shepherd was a bit of a bully. A big man who always got what he wanted. Seagrave always did what Shepherd said, and I could never understand why. They were both officers in the same regiment when they did national service. Shepherd was always boasting that he was one of the first officers in '47. He often tried to argue with Seagrave about the army, but Seagrave always backed down. It was as if Shepherd had something on him."

"How long have you been coming to St Walstan's?" Peter asked.

"Since I was a choirboy. I was at university during the war, so missed three years. I came back during the holidays and worked on The Grange Estate."

"So, why can't the church keep its priests?" Peter asked.

"The rot started with Albert Shepherd. He was a charismatic man, some would say a showman, with many followers. The church was always full on a Sunday morning, and at a festival, you couldn't get in the door. When he left, it was as if the heart went with him. People stopped coming," Morris said as he looked out of the window like a bird about to fly. "Frank Green thought it was a curse that he would break. He took down the engraved list of former priests from the church, said it was a reminder to all."

"It is unusual that you have had so many incumbents over the years. Tell me, Morris. Have you ever thought of leaving the village?"

"That is a question that I have often asked myself. The village can get a grip of you. I feel safe here, and I must admit, I have always been too afraid to leave. When I left university, I eventually got a job as a teacher at Ryedale School when it opened in '53 and stayed there all my career. I don't think I have the personality for adventure. The village is all I need."

"I never realised you were a teacher. I thought you must have been a lawyer," Peter said, offering him the cafetière of coffee.

"I am a history man. It is something that I love. You should come to the cottage, and I will show you all my research. I have an inventory of every dwelling and who has lived there over the last four hundred years."

"Tell me, Morris. Were there ever any rumours of Albert Shepherd and Evelyn Seagrave?"

Morris fell silent and ruffled his coat as if a roosting bird. He looked around the room as he filled his cup.

"Magnus Seagrave was a very jealous man. He hated anyone talking to his wife. I think that Albert Shepherd did it on purpose to irritate him. There was one occasion when I thought that Seagrave would hit him. It was after the Christmas Eve service in '65. His wife was in the vestry, counting the collection. I had gone in with the chalice and silver to lock it in the safe. Shepherd was wishing Mrs Seagrave a merry Christmas and kissed her on the cheek just as Magnus Seagrave walked in. There was a silence in the room that you could cut with a knife. I pretended to sort out the silverware in the safe until Shepherd and I were alone in the vestry. When I looked up, Shepherd joked about the whole thing. He said that Evelyn was a lovely woman and needed cheering up."

"What did Shepherd do before he was a clergyman?" Peter asked.

"I don't think he did anything in particular. His wife had a private income. National service, university, and then the church. They married quite young. Shepherd was a broad churchman, very liberal in his views. His sermons were very seldom about God, more your *Thought for the Day* sort of thing. Never anything to challenge or inspire, always full of jokes. I think that is why he was so popular. Can I ask, what is your interest in him?"

"I am just trying to get an understanding of the history of the church. I have discovered that Shepherd and Evelyn disappeared on the same day," Peter answered.

"Not exactly true. Evelyn left on the Saturday and Shepherd was seen driving his car, a brand new Hillman Hunter. They found it at Scarborough railway station."

"Do you think they ran off together?"

"I came into church on the Sunday morning. The place was packed. More people than usual, all talking about the World Cup. Everyone waited. There was no sign of the vicar. After about half an hour, his wife came in and said that the vicar had not gone home the night before and apologised for his absence. When we found out that Mrs Seagrave had vanished at the same time, people made assumptions. That is when Mrs Shepherd told the bishop about her husband and a woman he had met on a conference or some such thing." Morris took a long gulp of coffee and then wiped his lips. "She was adamant that her husband had gone off with another woman and not Evelyn Seagrave."

"What was Mrs Shepherd like with Magnus?" Peter asked.

"They were good friends. I think they found a bond with each other. When she left the parish, we never heard from her again. A sad woman. I believe she moved to Scotland to live with her sister."

There was a sudden shrill ring. The old, red trimphone bleated loudly.

"Sorry," Peter said. "Better get this."

"See you Sunday," Morris whispered as he put down his cup, nodded, and left the room.

[27]
The Realm Of Manners

The phone calls with Mary were becoming shorter and less frequent. When Peter rang her, there was never a reply. The call he took when Morris Marsden left the vicarage was just the same. Mary was distant and perfunctory. There was no familiarity. She gave an update on the symptoms of her mother and how the children had been. Then came the excuse to end the call long before Peter wanted.

He accepted the excuse without question and told Mary he loved her. Then the phone went dead. Peter put the receiver down and let it slowly click into the cradle. He got up from his desk and walked to the open door that led into the garden.

"Vicar!" Bruce Jakes shouted from the other side of the dry stone wall. "I need your help."

"What is it?" Peter asked as Bruce climbed over the wall.

"Can you come with me? I need help to get into Orchard House," Bruce said, out of breath. "I can see a body through the window. It looks like George Bateson."

Peter grabbed his jacket and set off at a pace, with Bruce Jakes following on as fast as he could.

Orchard House was on the other side of the churchyard. It was a Victorian villa, surrounded by apple and pear trees that grew out of a manicured lawn. A tall privet hedge ran up one side of the lane. The front fence was lined with rhododendron bushes and summer flowers.

"Where is he?" Peter shouted back to Bruce Jakes as they got to the white-painted gate.

"Around the back. In the orangery," Bruce answered as he struggled to keep pace.

Peter sprinted along the path and through the trees. He skirted the walls of the house until he reached the orangery. Looking inside, he could see the legs of a man stretching out from behind a leather sofa.

"When did you find him?"

"I came and cut the grass, and he always pays cash. I went to the kitchen door, and it was locked. Then I saw him on the floor."

It was then that Peter saw the splattering of blood and hair on the wall.

"Does he have a gun?" Peter asked as he pushed Bruce away from the window.

"He is a member of the local shoot. I think he had a few guns in the house," Bruce answered.

"Go to the pub. Call for the police and ambulance. I think he has been shot."

Bruce could see the serious look on his face.

"Right," he said as Peter turned to the patio doors of the orangery, stepped back, and then leapt forward, kicking them in.

Peter stepped inside and walked slowly to the other side of the room. The heat was unbearable. The radiators were piping hot. There was the usual sweet smell of a body that was starting to ferment. He slowly looked over the back of the sofa. There, between the wall and the sofa, was the body of a middle-aged man. He was wearing a pink golf sweater and blue slacks. Between his legs was a shotgun. On the wall behind him, were the remains of his cranium and brain. What was left of his face was covered with black flies that crawled in and out of his nostrils and mouth.

Peter had seen this numerous times before. He knew that the man had been dead for a while. The shotgun had been placed in his mouth and the blast would have instantly killed him. There was always a doubt about suicide, and murder could never be ruled out. There was nothing Peter could do apart from protect the scene until the police arrived.

"George?" the voice of a woman shouted from the door. Peter turned quickly.

Standing just outside the door was a blonde woman in an expensive summer dress. By her side was a small, blonde-haired boy.

"Please," Peter shouted. "Don't come in."

"Who the hell are you? Who broke the doors?" the woman demanded as she clutched her handbag.

"There has been an incident."

"Where is he? George is supposed to be having contact time with Harvey and he won't answer his bloody phone."

"Are you his wife?" Peter asked.

"About to be ex-wife, thankfully. What's the problem?" the woman said with little concern.

Peter ushered her into the garden under the shade of a tall apple tree. As he was about to speak, Bruce Jakes ran through the gate.

"Police and ambulance on its way," he said as he slumped against a tree, trying to get his breath.

"What the hell has happened?" the woman insisted. "What's wrong?"

"Please could we talk in private?" Peter asked.

The woman looked down at her child.

"Go and play, Harvey," she said to the boy.

Peter watched as the child ran to the far side of the garden and played with a tree swing. "There is the body of a man with shotgun wounds behind the sofa. I believe it may be your husband."

The woman showed no emotion. She looked to Bruce Jakes. "Did you find him, Bruce?" she asked.

"Yes, Mrs Bateson," Bruce answered softly. "I was doing the lawns and went to get paid, and I saw him on the floor."

"Right," she answered without a change in her face. "Bloody typical. What a coward."

"He's dead," Peter said, amazed at what he had just heard.

"Obviously," she replied. "He said he would do it if I divorced him, and he has. At least he was a man of his word," the woman laughed to herself. "Harvey!" she shouted. "We are going back home."

The boy turned and looked at her.

"The police will want a statement from you, and the body needs to be identified," Peter said as the boy ran back across the lawn.

"Well, they can find someone else," she said, taking a flip mirror from her pocket and checking her makeup. "I have my child to look after and I will have to see my lawyer." Before Peter could reply, the woman turned to leave. "Sorry you didn't get paid, Bruce. I don't think he will be needing you anymore, and I will be putting the house on the market tomorrow. Come on, Harvey."

The woman walked towards the gate as the two men looked at each other in disbelief. "I don't know what to say," Peter whispered.

"That's Bridget at her best. She's only been out of the house for three weeks. Traded George in for a new model."

"How long were they married?" Peter asked.

"Quite a long time," Bruce replied. "They had the boy a few years ago. She was having an affair for most of the time. George put up with a lot. He loved her. We would share a beer and have a fag, and he would always say how much he loved her."

Peter shook his head in obvious despair.

"Love that drove him to death," he answered as the sound of sirens echoed through the trees.

"Last time I saw him was in the pub a few nights ago. He was well loaded, bought everyone a drink. It was as if he was saying goodbye."

"Perhaps he was. Perhaps he had made up his mind," he answered as the police and ambulance arrived.

"Barney!" the deep voice shouted, as the tall, angular-jawed copper in a meticulously ironed shirt walked into the garden. "What the hell are you doing here?"

"Steve. I live next door," he answered as Steve Becket, an ex-Royal Marine commando as broad as he was tall, strode towards them.

"What's happened?" Steve asked.

"Body in the orangery. Shotgun wound to the head. He's been there a couple of days. Not a pretty sight."

"Next of kin?"

"She just left. Refused to do the identification or give a statement," Peter answered. "Recently separated and not in the mood."

"I know where she lives," Bruce cut in.

"And you are?" Steve asked.

"The gardener. *Bruce Loves Grass*. I found him."

The copper turned to Peter.

"Can you get a statement from Bruce, and do one yourself, Barney?" Steve asked as a paramedic ran towards them.

Peter nodded as the copper followed the paramedic towards the house.

"Do you think he killed himself?" Bruce asked as he rubbed his face, as if to wipe away the stress.

"Possibly," he answered. "There were no signs of a struggle, and it fits with what his wife said. That's when you take a deeper look and never take it for granted."

"Can I take my stuff away? I need my mower for later," Bruce asked, obviously in shock. "Leave it here for now and come to the vicarage. I have some statement forms and I can get it back to Steve before they wrap up here. Scenes of crime will have to come along, and doubtless an inspector."

"I knew he was dead when I saw his legs sticking out from behind the sofa."

"First time?" Peter asked.

"Yes. It's all a bit final. Brings it home."

[28]
Still Waters Run Deep

The statement took no time at all. After two cups of coffee and half a packet of biscuits, Bruce had told him everything he needed to know. *Bruce Loves Grass* had been cutting the lawn at Orchard House for the last ten years. George Bateson always paid on time and liked to share a beer with Bruce whenever he could.

In a short hour, they had talked of many things. Peter thought that Bruce was obviously a very intelligent man. He had dropped out of Durham University in his final year of reading English literature. Bruce admitted that, at the time, he had an LSD problem and spent most days tripping.

"I thought it would help my creativity," he said as he ate his final Bourbon biscuit. "If you take it every day for three weeks, it screws your brain. I had a mental breakdown and decided to dump literature and take up gardening."

"Did it help?" Peter asked.

"It is amazing what an hour in the garden can do for you. Once you have taken some acid, you never see the world the same way again. Yet, being outside straightens the brain."

"Why did you take so much?" Peter asked as he poured himself another cup of coffee.

"I wanted the answer about life and death. I was studying Shakespeare and *The Tempest*. There was a single line that permafried my brain. '*And thence retire me to my Milan, where every third thought shall be my grave.*' It was the words of Prospero. They scared me. I didn't know what would happen when I died. I had a fear of death."

"Are you still frightened of dying?" Peter asked.

"I have seen things on LSD. Things that give me hope that this isn't the whole world."

"It was a hallucinogen. It cannot be trusted," Peter answered.

"Whatever it was, I found an answer. I now know that I don't have to worry about the grave. I didn't worry about my life before I was born, so why do I have to worry about what happens after I die?"

Peter sat back against his desk and looked out of the window towards the yew tree on the burial mound. He wanted to tell Bruce how he felt about death. Even though he was a priest, he had doubts that sometimes led to disbelief. In the dark hours of the night, he would wake up with that same thought that everything he believed was a lie, a fairy story of jam today and glory tomorrow. Now, Bruce was telling him that he had found a kind of faith taking LSD.

"Perhaps I should prescribe it to my congregation," Peter answered jokingly.

"Well, it would liven things up in church," Bruce replied, feeling uncomfortable talking about his drug use to a copper.

"I don't think it would go down too well."

"Your lot are a funny bunch. I used to cut the grass in the churchyard. Then one day, Frank Green caught me drinking out of the well, and a week later I got the sack and the well was bricked up."

"Did you know Green well?" Peter asked, wondering what those in the village thought of his predecessor.

"I got the impression he thought I was weird. I wanted to create a nature zone at the back of the churchyard. Somewhere for the birds and butterflies. Frank Green demanded I cut the grass shorter. He wanted it like a bowling green, didn't like anything out of place."

"Do you want the job back?" Peter asked. "I could put it before the church council. A wild area would be good."

"If you are serious. Now that I am sacked from Orchard House, I'll need the work."

"Very serious," he paused. "One thing. Who did Bridget trade in George for?"

"A teacher in Scarborough. He wormed his way in as a tutor for their son and took her away."

"I thought she would be the kind of woman who liked money."

"She is, and he has lots of it. Big car, posh house, everything money can buy," Bruce gave a wide-eyed answer. "One minute he had nothing, and the next he was loaded."

"Does he have a name?"

"Simon, not sure of the surname," Bruce laughed. "Now that George is dead, Bridget will get everything… and George had a lot of cash."

"What did he do for work?"

"He traded commodities. Oil, sugar, anything he could buy and sell over the phone. He worked a lot from home and had an office in London. He was one stressed out bloke."

"Did you give him any of your medication?" Peter asked with a cheeky smile.

"Don't know what you mean. Medication?"

"Just thought you might have helped him relax a little."

"Are you speaking as a copper or a priest?" Bruce asked.

"Priest," he answered.

"George used stuff that was well out of my league. He was a fan of the Columbian marching powder. Took it all the time. He didn't need any weed."

"How did her boyfriend get all the money?" Peter asked.

"Now, that is the big question. He would come and drink in the pub. Kept everything close to his chest. Not a man for small talk," Bruce answered as he got up to leave. "However, it happened… it all came at once."

Looking out of the window, Peter saw Steve Becket walking up the driveway, his muscular arms filling the rolled sleeves of his shirt.

"Looks like someone wants to talk to us," Peter said as the copper approached. "I wouldn't mention the cocaine. That would be better coming from me."

[29]
Nostalgia Is A Seductive Liar

Friday night had been spent hurriedly researching for the Sunday sermon. Peter didn't like to write anything down. He wanted his words to be spontaneous and relevant to those around him. There was so much he felt he should talk about, and yet something inside him made him feel reluctant, even fearful, of a handful of old people.

There had already been an anonymous letter written to the bishop. It had complained about the opening of the well and baptising the children of *"unbelievers"*. A quick phone call from Bishop Riley had broken the news. The bishop did not seem concerned and told him not to worry. Peter knew from his job in the police that when the boss said don't worry, it usually meant you had to. Yet, Riley insisted that it was more of a tip-off rather than a correction.

Peter would have to watch out that someone in the congregation had a long knife at the ready.

In the Church of England, where there was one silent assassin, there were usually more.

The bishop thought the timing, a couple of days after Martha Storr was suspended, was a factor. He wondered if she had been the one who had sent it. Nevertheless, the bishop said he had sent Peter to St Walstan's because he had a thick skin and broad shoulders.

He knew that the right man was in the pulpit, regardless of what the letter-writer thought.

Despite broad shoulders and a thick skin, the conversation had left Peter feeling guarded. It had been the final straw that had broken his beliefs that church people were the living example of the gospel. In reality, he had so far found them petty, judgmental, rigid, and bitter. The people of St Walstan's didn't like each other, despite the commandment to love your neighbour as yourself. It seemed as if they had changed the words of the Bible to do unto others before they did it to you.

Now, Peter sat at his desk as the clock struck six in the morning. Outside, the early morning sun was breaking through the trees. He checked his diary. There, in bold letters, were the words *Jumble Sale*. He knew that the sale of rags and bric-à-brac were a great attraction. He would preach to a handful of people on a Sunday morning, and yet, a Saturday jumble would have a queue stretching across the church hall car park.

Today would be no different. The organisation of the jumble sale was in the hands of a secret society of several women, most of whom didn't even attend the church. As if by magic, they would gather mountains of old clothes and items people no longer wanted. They would be stacked on trestle tables and sold for whatever they could get for them. The clothes would have the odour of sweat and mould. It would cling to the nostrils and take days to go away.

The only difference at St Walstan's is that *jumble* had been renamed *rummage sale*. It gave it an air of being rural middle-class and not stocked with items no one really wanted.

Peter sat back and yawned, wondering if something urgent would come up so he could miss the sale. He had been booked to declare the rummage sale open. In reality, he knew that he would be dealing with a marauding mob of middle-aged mudlarks intent of getting as much stuff as they could carry for as little as they could part with. It was always the tradition that the vicar had to buy something before leaving and was allowed to scour the stalls before the doors opened to get the pick of anything he wanted at a premium price. This was a rite of passage and would be the subject of conversation amongst his parishioners. He knew he had to pick the right thing, nothing too ostentatious, nothing too cheap. He would be expected to set the standard and pay more than it was actually worth.

During his curacy, he had paid twenty-eight pounds for a cauliflower in the charity auction, only to be told later that the auctioneer had made Peter bid against himself without knowing.

The hours to the rummage opening passed slowly. Peter finished wallpapering the kitchen, put out the takeaway boxes from several lonely meals, and mowed the grass. The phone didn't ring, and no callers came to the door. It was a peaceful, four cups of tea type of day.

Everything in the garden had the colour of late summer. The leaves of the trees were tinged with yellow, like a subtle herald of autumn. It was a time of year that Peter liked. The smell of freshly cut grass was something that he loved. It reminded him of his childhood and the smell that would drift into the classroom when the school playing field was cut. His mind would wander away from what was being taught to thoughts of going home and playing on his bike on the old railway line to Whitby.

Peter would always go back to his childhood home, even though his parents had died. He would make his monthly pilgrimage and stop briefly outside the red brick, terraced house with its privet hedge and arch above the gate. Over the four years since they had both died, Peter had noticed how the street had changed. There were increasing numbers of cars and satellite dishes. The gardens were more unkempt, as if the occupants lacked any pride. The paintwork on the doors was old and tired. Here and there were discarded fridges and car tyres.

It was not how he remembered it as a child, when women in headscarves would talk to each other over the hedges and flirt with the milkman. Mrs Wilson at number ninety-eight would be in her garden, deadheading the flowers and picking any privet that dared to grow higher than she had trimmed the day before. She would always have a sweet in the pocket of her pinny to throw to him as he passed. He saw it as an ongoing apology for the fact that her son, who was six years older than Peter, enjoyed chasing him down the street with a nettle whip.

As Peter grew older, he found himself looking back to his childhood. It was only as an adult that he realised how poor his parents had been. The pantry was often empty. Bread and dripping were a staple part of the diet. Yorkshire puddings were served for dinner on Sunday to fill him up before a meagre slice of meat and a few vegetables. He now realised that it was cheap food, bought with the leftovers of the money his father earned from two jobs.

They had never gone without, but they had never had a lot. In all of this, there was the bitterness he felt towards his father. The man never told him that he was loved. He worked at two jobs, a cobbler by day, and barman at the local pub by night.

On Saturday and Sunday, he would never see his father. He would work at the pub on the lunchtime shift, come home, eat alone, sleep for an hour in front of the telly, and then get washed and shaved and go back to work. If he had a night off, it would be spent in the Corporation Club, always getting the last bus home. Sunday was the only day when Peter felt any kind of attention from his father, who would come in smelling of beer and give Peter a *Walnut Whip* chocolate bar. Peter hated the walnuts and would gouge out the fondant with his finger before eating the chocolate.

It wasn't unusual for Peter to be left home alone. He often thought of the night he had been left in the house and his parents had not come back. He had stayed downstairs with every light in the house switched on to conquer his fear of the dark. Just before midnight, there had been a knock at the door. Looking into the window were two coppers.

Peter had opened the door to be told that his mother and father had been locked up for fighting in a chip shop with two Dutch fishermen. A couple of hours later, his parents came back, still drunk and laughing. His father had scuffed knuckles from where he had punched the men, whilst his mother had broken the straps of her handbag from hitting them as they lay on the floor covered in chips.

The Christmas when Peter was fifteen, his father got drunk and told him that he was a mistake and should never have been born, the result of ten pints of Guinness in the *Newlands Hotel*. His father told him how disappointed he was that Peter wasn't a proper man. He said that men didn't read books or talk about God. Men went to work and then to the pub. It was then that he handed Peter a large, brown paper bag. Opening the gift, Peter unwrapped three porn magazines.

"That's what you should be reading, boy," his father had slurred. "Not all that queer stuff." It was a remark that still haunted Peter, and one that no matter how often he prayed, God didn't seem to want to take it away.

Yet, it was a different man who had travelled seventy miles in old age to watch Peter graduate from police training school. It was the only time that his father ever said the '*L*' word. Probably because he now thought his son was doing manly stuff. Peter had choked back the tears, knowing his father hated men who cried.

Then, two years later, Peter was driving his patrol car from headquarters back to his beat, when he got the radio message that his father had died from a sudden stroke. Funnily, he felt no grief and had no tears. They had all gone from him. As he drove, he remembered the day his father asked him if he was queer and then, before Peter could reply, took a swing at him. There wasn't anything he hated more than the thought of his son being a homosexual, and all because Peter had dyed his hair to be like David Bowie.

It was the first time Peter had ever punched a man. He knocked his father to the floor and walked out of the house. His father never told anyone what had happened, but the fight opened a Pandora's box.

Over the coming weeks, Peter found out that his father had been married before and had even slept with the sister of his wife. Both women had his children. All of this had been kept secret from Peter. He was not an only child. His father obviously had a bike and used it to get around and sow his seed wherever he found an open door and a warm bed.

[30]
The Grumble Jumble

The knock at the door broke his thoughts. Looking back into the past had stirred a malaise within. He knew there was nothing he could do to change it, but he wished he could. It was something he hated about memories. They were like bookmarks to the times in his life where he felt the most vulnerable. Many happy days lay locked in his mind. He was unable to recall them with the clarity of those that caused him pain.

The knock came again.

Peter could see the outline of a man through the door glass. From the shape and the shadow of a Trilby hat, he knew it was Gerald Griffin.

"One minute!" Peter shouted down the hallway.

"No worries," came the answer as Peter saw the doorknob turn and the door open. "Just the hymns for tomorrow. On my way to the *grumble jumble* and thought I would drop them off," he said as he slid an envelope onto the table by the door.

"Wait, and I will walk with you," Peter said, grabbing a jacket. "You can be my bodyguard."

Gerald Griffin appeared to blush.

"A pleasure," he answered with a cough in his throat. "I am sure you don't need one."

"Twenty women and a pile of jumble is a dangerous place," he laughed.

"And the dealers."

"Dealers?" Peter asked, wondering what he meant.

"Junk dealers. They come from all over the county looking for stray antiques that may have been given away by mistake. They virtually break down the door and push you out of the way to get to the stuff. It's like a scene from *Lovejoy*. Although none of them look like Ian McShane," Griffin said, as if giving away a secret fondness.

"More of a *Bergerac* man myself," he answered. "I like the car."

"Yes," Griffin answered, as if the word was a full stop. "I have been asked to play the piano throughout the sale. I thought I would do some songs from the sea and a little Moody and Sankey."

"Interesting," Peter answered as he shuddered at the thought. "I didn't realise you were a revivalist."

"I love a good singsong, and Ira Sankey clears the room quicker than a plague of rats," Griffin answered with a wink. "Should have the whole thing over within forty minutes. There's another jumble sale in the next village at three, and they will all clear off for that one."

"As long as I survive unscarred," he answered. "I have heard these sales are a dangerous place."

"Didn't they give you training in jumble sales at theological college? Knowing how to handle a jumble is more important than knowing the Bible. I suggest you say *hello* to all the helpers, pick something shiny from the bric-à-brac, and hide in the kitchen until the all-clear. Never leave until the very end and offer to help load the collecting van with all the leftover clothes. The ladies will have arranged the ragman to come, and he always needs a hand." Griffin took a wheezing breath as they walked slowly towards the church hall. "You will be more on show today than when you are in church. This is the chance for the village to get a look at you."

"Well, Gerald. Thank you for the heads-up. I feel more anxious than ever," Peter said, slapping Griffin on the back.

"Anxious? You take on villains in the dead of night. The ladies of the jumble sale are small beer in comparison."

"I can use my truncheon and handcuffs on a villain, but not on the ladies of the church," Griffin laughed.

"I don't think Bishop Riley would mind," Griffin answered as he mused the thought of the police leading the helpers at the village hall away in handcuffs. "Just check under the counters and see the stuff they hide away for themselves. A veritable black market of flowered tops and oversized knickers."

The queue at the church hall stretched across the car park and into the lane. Over one hundred grumbling people checked their watches, waiting in the afternoon sun for the doors to open. Peter smiled and nodded to everyone as he walked by. An old woman looked at him as if she tried to see inside his mind. Peter had never felt such scrutiny from a single look. As he passed by, the woman grunted something to her younger companion. They both laughed.

Griffin raised a doubtful eyebrow.

"I feel like I am being inspected by a gang of hungry meat butchers," Peter quipped to Griffin as they got to the door.

"You are, Vicar. You are."

A perm-haired, red-faced woman inside the hall opened the door as they approached, holding up a hand to the people at the front of the queue.

"Not ready yet," she growled like a small guard dog in the face of a lemon-lipped woman. "Afternoon, Vicar," she said in a softer tone as he and Griffin stepped inside.

"Afternoon," he answered, wondering what to do next.

Griffin must have read his mind and nodded towards the kitchen.

"Centre of operations," he gestured. "Capture the kitchen and win the battle."

Peter smiled as he looked around the hall. There was a loud hubbub of chattering as the room was made ready. Trestle tables stacked high with piles of old clothes formed a military square in the middle of the room. The jumble ladies stood steadfast, as if an embattled battalion of blue rinse soldiers awaiting the enemy.

As he walked to the kitchen, he greeted each volunteer with warm words and a handshake. Surprisingly, they all smiled at the greeting.

"You better watch out with all these women around you, Vicar," a younger woman in jeans and a t-shirt said as she held on to his hand longer than was comfortable. "Not used to having eye candy in the pulpit."

"Thank you," he replied with an embarrassed look. "Where is the bric-à-brac?"

The woman pointed to a table that stood alone next to the door to the toilets. "I can help you find something that takes your fancy, if you like," she said as she finally let go of his hand. "Or you could try the cake stall. I've got some nice buns."

"Will try it later," he answered as he stepped away.

"There'll be nothing left. Once those doors open, it's like a scene from *Jaws* in here. Total feeding frenzy and then it's all over." Griffin guided Peter towards the kitchen.

"That was Liz Morris. Known as the widow of Lastingham. Three husbands who have all died. All in the space of fifteen years. A veritable man-eater."

"She seemed very friendly," Peter answered.

"Beware," Griffin whispered. "The parishioners are not used to having a pleasant-faced vicar."

Before he could answer, the door to the kitchen opened and the hall fell silent. All the volunteers looked towards the tall, elderly woman dressed in a blue cardigan and white slacks. "Ladies," she said in a soft but commanding Yorkshire accent. "Mr Griffin will lead us in *Jerusalem* and the vicar will say a prayer. Then..." she paused, "the doors will be opened."

Griffin dashed to the piano as the woman turned to Peter and whispered, "Keep it short."

Griffin played the piano as the women sang. It was not a hymn that Peter liked. All that talk of satanic mills and a backpacking Jesus on a gap year, written by a man who said he saw angels in trees.

He muttered the words under the watchful eye of the woman before him. He felt like he was back in junior school being scrutinised by his headteacher, Miss Hornby, a tyrant who strongly resembled a malevolent witch. The woman had once given Peter the slipper for throwing a school cap belonging to Jack Jenkins on the roof, a matter made worse by the school caretaker falling off his ladder when he went up to get it.

As the hymn came to an end, Peter made his way towards the bric-à-brac table, hoping there would be something interesting to buy. Immediately, a bronze-coloured statue of Napoleon caught his eye. The emperor was on top of a ram's horn column. His hand was embedded in the jacket of his uniform. The figure stood at a foot tall and was finely carved.

As he picked it up for a closer look, he realised the hall had fallen silent. As he turned, he saw that the woman was staring at him.

"The prayer," Griffin whispered loudly.

"Let us pray," Peter answered, going on to ask God to bless the jumble sale and gave thanks for the time of the volunteers. All that went through his head was that God was probably not listening as there were far more important things on the agenda. World poverty, starvation, the war in Kuwait, and the melting ice cap.

Prayer was something Peter struggled with. He would prefer to sit in silence with the people on his mind than beseech God with a shopping list. "Amen," he said as he looked up. The woman in charge stared at him with a permanently raised eyebrow.

"Thank you, Vicar," she said, obviously disappointed as Gerald Griffin began to slowly play the cleverly disguised theme from *Jaws*.

The woman took a step towards Peter. "Better introduce myself," she said as the front door opened. "I am Margaret Barrie. Leader of the *Women's Institute*. You haven't been to one of our meetings yet."

"You haven't been to one of my services," he answered, already sensing that this was a woman he had to stand up to from the very beginning.

"And I never will," she replied as she turned to walk away. "If you want that piece of tat, it'll cost you ten pounds."

Peter looked at the statue and realised it would be the most expensive jumble he had ever been to. As he fumbled for his wallet, a hoard of bargain-hungry people rushed towards him.

Stepping back away from the advancing throng, Peter was suddenly dragged through the kitchen door.

"You'll be safe in here. I will make you a cup of tea," Liz Morris said as she looked at the statue he clutched in his hands. "Winston Churchill?" she asked.

[31]
Napoleon

The bronze statue stood proudly on the mantelpiece as if viewing its empire. Peter rolled the Antique Gold paint onto the wall that seemed to be taking several coats to cover. Speckles of paint covered his arm as the roller swished back and forth; the promise of drip-free was obviously a lie. He was thankful he had covered the furniture with old bed sheets. Mary would doubtless find something wrong with his handiwork, and as usual would insist that they get 'a man' in.

It was one of the things about her that was the least endearing, that and her sense of middle-class, Scottish privilege. *Marry in haste, repent in leisure,* was what his mother had said to him when she first met Mary.

Peter had ignored her. He was twenty-two, a failed student wanting to get his life back together after four years of misery trying to make a career living in London. It was there where he had become a Christian. It was a conscious decision to address the gnawing urge to discover what life and death was about.

The first book of faith he had read was the Quran; it had been given to him by a Muslim friend. The only thing that stopped him following Islam was that he didn't like the idea of giving up a beer with his friends. Yet, the book left a lasting impression on his life. It led to him searching out the prophet Jesus, and for the first time, he walked into a church as an enquirer rather than an attendant at a family wedding.

There was no Road to Damascus conversion, no flashing lights, no visions of angels. There was just a gradual acceptance that he was a Christian. A man had once asked him when he was born again. Peter couldn't really answer.

"Have you found Jesus?" the man insisted.

"I didn't know he was lost," Peter answered.

In some ways, not feeling born again and not finding Jesus made him feel as if he was a second-class believer. He had listened to people who had lived fallen lives and had a miraculous conversion. They had been saved from drink, drugs, and adultery by giving their lives to God. The more people he listened to, the more Peter realised they were in some kind of competition to see who could be saved from the deepest depths of sin. They wore their past wickedness like a trophy. The further they had fallen and been redeemed, the higher they were in Christian importance. It was as if they were a hierarchy of saved sinners.

A Scottish man he had gone to listen to in a small church room in Thornton-le-Dale had even said that he had fallen so far from God that the man had allowed his body to be tattooed, and he would carry the marks of sin until the day he died.

All Peter could boast of was smoking hash at college and kissing his male best friend in a drunken clinch as a teenager to see what it was like. When he had mentioned this to his vicar, Peter was told that if he ever wanted to get ordained, he should quickly find a wife, and this would stop his urges to kiss male friends.

Mary had been his quick fix. A quick fix to many things in his life. Within six months of meeting, they were married, and within a year, he was already having regrets. New marriage, new home, and a holiday with his in-laws on the shores of the Bosporus was all it had taken to make him want to pack his bags and leave. It had been the holiday that had turned his heart. Staying with the in-laws in their guarded apartment was a living hell.

It started the night he had a bath after the long train journey across Europe to Istanbul. As he got out of the water, he heard a crunch under his foot. There, squashed against the sole, was a small, brown scorpion. His mother-in-law had just laughed.

This unsettling incident was followed by a disastrous trip to the Dardanelles in a consulate car that was occasionally pulled over so that his father-in-law could throw up the booze he had drunk the night before.

From then on, he knew he would never be part of the family. His birth and upbringing had sealed his fate to be ever on the outside of the circle of trust. Peter was from a council house, and they would never let him forget it.

The news that Mary was pregnant with their first child stopped any of his thoughts about leaving. It was a total surprise, as Peter had been away from Mary on a course at the police college. They had only made love once during the whole time he was away.

As he finished painting the wall, he decided that decorating was not good for relationships. It allowed his mind to dwell on the things that he could never get answers for. Mulling was a habit that concerned him. Perhaps he would feel different when Mary had returned. Being alone made him think about the things of the past. His life was filled with *'if only'*.

He checked himself, knowing he could change nothing that had gone before. The past was the past. Peter had to believe that God had brought him to St Walstan's, and in a few days' time, he hoped that God would go before him as he returned to work.

[32]
Five-One

The serge uniform jacket felt uncomfortable. Peter hadn't worn it for a couple of weeks, and it felt tighter than he remembered. As he fastened up the silver tunic buttons, he stared in the mirror on the end wall of the locker room. Peter thought he looked different than before. He was not sure about returning to the beat. Four years ago, when he was accepted for the priesthood, it seemed such a good thing to do. The bishop had said that he would be one of the first ordained ministers in secular employment as a police officer. It was only the principal of his theological college who had pointed out the potential conflict.

As Peter opened the door of the locker room into the corridor that led to the parade room, he took a deep breath. He knew that in five paces, he would be back on the beat. There would be a pile of papers in the tray. The duty inspector didn't seem to care about an officer on leave. He would just allow the mail to pile up and for them to get on with it when they came back.

It was a common feeling to dread full-tray syndrome. Shotgun renewals, CPS advice files, internal memos, traffic files, and crime cases. Peter had one boomerang file. It had gone back and forth between Crown Prosecution Service, the superintendent, and his in-tray for several months. The theft by deception of a pigeon had caused Peter many hours of grief. A suspect in denial and a complainant who could not be trusted. Thirteen pounds fifty was the value of the theft. Peter had argued that it couldn't be theft if the pigeon had flown back to the loft it was sold from. There was no dishonest appropriation or intention to permanently deprive. All there was was a pigeon that had flown away. The CPS believed the man was running a scam where he would sell a pigeon that, when released, would fly back home so he could then sell it again and again.

Peter had explained that it is the fault of the buyer for letting the bird out too soon, and not a man running a scam. In return, the CPS asked for an expert witness. The only expert witness he could find was the man who sold the pigeon. Sometimes, he wanted to burn the file and hoped that it would be lost in the internal post or that the pigeon would die, just to put an end to it all.

As he walked into the parade room, he wondered how full his tray would be. Opening the door from the dark passageway, he stepped into the room. The bright strip lights over the desks flickered.

Sergeant Burley, a thin-bearded man in his fifties with an obvious missing tooth in the front of his mouth looked up.

"Now then, part-time Peter," he laughed. "Five-one, nine-five, five-one, three days a week and never on a Sunday. How the hell did you manage that?"

"New directive. They are even offering career breaks," Peter answered as he checked his tray that was surprisingly empty of all but two thin files. "Modern policing."

"What am I going to do when everyone in the nick wants to work part time? How can I roster a station? Superintendent thinks it's a stupid idea. You do realise the boss is using you as a poster boy, don't you?"

"I hadn't thought," he answered as he flicked through one of the files and read the CPS notes.

"He was looking like a Cheshire cat when he saw all the press reports of you being made a vicar with your own church. A right celebrity you have turned out to be. Not sure it's good for the job."

"Well, I just want to keep my head down and get on with the job. Nothing has changed. I am still the same copper," Peter answered quickly, quite prepared to fight his own corner.

He had known Joe Burley for three years. He had recently been promoted within the station, something that didn't go down well. A colleague that becomes a boss had its problems. Burley had fought hard for the promotion, so the extra money would enhance his pension. Now, he wanted to ride out his time without any problems. Peter going part time had him riled. "Why did you give in your ticket? Do you realise we will have to pull someone in who is firearms trained?"

"It had nothing to do with taking on a parish."

"The lads on the team think you have lost your bottle with all this God stuff," Burley snapped back as he got up from his chair. "They wonder what you will be like in a fight now that you are Vicar of St *Whatever*."

"So I gather."

"You called for backup when you went to that domestic last month. Couldn't you handle it?" he asked. "You have never done that before. Always sorted jobs out on your own."

"The man had a twelve-inch knife and was threatening to kill me. I had him arrested and cuffed before the backup arrived."

"Did you threaten to convert him? I heard he was crying like a baby when the van arrived."

"Look, Joe, if you have a problem with me, we can always take it higher. I am the same copper I have always been. We have worked together and there have never been any problems."

"Things change, people change. I think all this God stuff has sent you soft."

"Only time will tell," Peter answered.

"Have you ever thought of getting a desk job? They want an intelligence officer at Malton. I could have a word on your behalf. I'll be writing your performance report this year. It's due in three months."

There was an air of threat in what he said. Burley was serious. Peter knew that from now on, he would have to watch himself.

When he was a constable, Burley was a man who worked by the book. He would never warn or let someone off for a minor infringement of the law. Everyone had to be prosecuted, no matter how petty the offence. Rumour had it, that at his previous station, he was known as *gravel knees*. He had earned this title through years of climbing under parked cars to check the depths of the tread on the tyres. If he found any that were slightly worn, he would slap a ticket on the windscreen.

Burley had been moved from Richmond after he had been run over by a farmer who, on market day, had got into his Land Rover and, not seeing the copper underneath the back of his vehicle, had reversed over Burley as he measured the tread.

Burley had fatally wounded his pride and was a laughing stock of the town. Within weeks, he had been moved, and within three years, promoted.

"I have never seen myself as a desk man. Doubtless it might be out of my hands," Peter answered as he picked up the keys to his car. "Is there anything happening out there?"

"Quiet. Just as I like it. Try to keep it that way. I am off at ten. Quick changeover. Back at six tomorrow. Proper shifts. Please don't fill the cells with bodies for the early turn to sort out," Burley quipped as he raised an Elvis-like top lip into a smirk. "New inspector on tonight. A woman. Transfer from the Met. She is covering Scarborough to Sutton Bank. Her call sign is *Delta... Sierra... Zero... One*," Burley said, emphasising each word. "She might call you up."

"What's her name?" Peter asked.

"No idea. I just called her *Inspector*. Another woman in a man's job," Burley answered as he folded the duty file and walked out of the room.

[33]
Trout

The vehicle lights moved slowly along the tree-lined road that cut across Wheeldale Moor from Stape to Goathland. It was only just more than a forest track that followed the line of a Roman road. Peter would always park up there on summer nights. From his hiding place behind a dry stone wall, he could see from horizon to horizon.

The van's lights had taken ten minutes to get to him. They had stopped for most of that time and then slowly set off again. Peter sat in the patrol car and waited. The road was often used as a crime route out of Ryedale back towards Middlesborough.

It was a favourite road for travelling criminals. If stopped, they would often run off onto the moor, never to be seen again. He knew he was taking a chance to stop the vehicle on his own. There was no backup. It was just before midnight and an hour to the end of his shift. Peter toyed with the idea of just taking the registration number and checking it in back at the nick.

When the old Ford Transit van drove by, he could see that there was only the driver in the front. A rear taillight was out, and the van was tilted to one side as if the suspension was broken. Peter slowly drove onto the road, switched on his headlights, and began to follow.

Before he could radio in the registration, the Transit came to a sudden halt as the driver got out and stood by the open door.

Peter picked up the searchlight from the passenger seat and got out of the car.

"*Foxtrot-Papa*-Three-Five to *Delta-Sierra*. Blue Transit stopped. Wheeldale Moor. One up," Peter said as he opened the car door and got out of the car. "Why have you stopped?" he shouted, switching on the light and bathing the van in a blinding beam.

"No point running. You would have only got a car at the other end once you had checked the van," the man said as he pulled up the hood of his camouflage jacket and covered his eyes with his hand to stop the glare of the lamp.

"What's in the van?" Peter asked as he walked towards him.

"Four drunk mates. We have been out on the town in Pickering. I am the designated driver. Wouldn't risk my licence," the man answered as he nervously fiddled with the sleeves of his coat. "I'm teetotal, never touch the stuff."

"Why are you coming this way?"

The man laughed before he answered. "I am looking for flying saucers. A lot have been sighted up here. Something to do with Fylingdales Early Warning Station."

There was a groan from the back of the van.

"Is that one of your mates?" Peter asked as he took hold of the back door and pulled the handle.

A thin, dark-haired teenager rolled out of the van and onto the road. He looked about eighteen and, like the driver, was wearing camouflage clothing. The lad looked up at Peter and started to laugh. The sweet smell of cannabis coming out of the van was overpowering. It filled the night air and clung to the van as if it would never let go. Peter shone the searchlight into the van. Three men were sprawled across the floor, unconscious. One was propped up against two large plastic boxes. Next to him was a lorry battery and a broom handle with a metal plate nailed on the end and wires taped along the shaft.

"Told you," the driver said. "Billy isn't the worst one. They couldn't run if they wanted."

Peter shook them from their sleep and asked each one for their names and dates of birth. He went back to the police car and checked the identities.

Danny Cowen came back as recorded, but not currently wanted. He had an address in Brambles Farm and the Transit was his. Billy Graves had one offence as a minor with no details recorded. Both checked out.

"What else is in the van apart from your mates?" Peter asked.

"It's a fair cop, Guv," the lad on the floor squealed, unable to stop himself laughing. "We've been fishing."

"Fish," Cowen answered.

"Long way from the sea?" Peter replied.

"We have been trout fishing," Billy answered for his friend. "We electrocute them."

A flash of light cracked over the eastern horizon.

"Are you going to nick us then? The fish are from the trout farm, and before you ask, the miserable sod deserves to get robbed for the prices he charges to fish there," Cowen said, pointing up to the darkening sky. "We are going to get soaked if you hang around."

"Well, if you are so desperate to get locked up, I am happy to oblige," Peter replied before cautioning Cowen for theft of the fish.

"What about the lads?" Cowen asked.

"I will arrest them when they are less stoned," Peter said as he picked up laughing boy from the ground, walked him back to the police car, and radioed control. "Bringing in five for theft of fish from the trout farm. Can you send the van?"

It was not the answer he wanted. The only van in the division was off the road for a repair. *"We don't have a car free. All units are committed. Custody Sergeant at Malton. Can you take them there?"* the controller answered.

Peter sat back in the car seat and laughed. Here he was, fifteen miles from the nearest police station. The skies were about to open, and he had five suspects and two crates of stolen fish.

"Do you have enough fuel to get you to Malton Police Station?" he shouted to Cowen as heavy drops of rain began to fall and clatter on the roof of the patrol car.

"Half a tank... should be enough, why?"

"I'll take laughing boy with me and follow you to the station. Have you been there before?"

Cowen laughed.

"I admit to a crime without being questioned and now you want me to drive to the nick? Do you want me to take my own fingerprints?"

"Either that or wait here a couple of hours for a car to turn up," Peter replied as the thunder burst in the clouds a few miles away.

"I'll race you," Cowen joked as he closed the back door of the van and set off slowly up the road with the patrol car following behind.

"Will I go to prison?" Billy asked as he slowly sobered up from the cannabis.

"Doubt it. How many times you been locked up?" Peter asked.

"Got a caution for taking a bike, that's all."

"I wouldn't worry. Because you've been stoned, we will speak to you in the morning. Get the duty solicitor to sit in on the interview."

"My mother will kill me."

"Should have thought about that before you went out nicking fish," Peter answered as he wound down the side window to let out the odour of fish scales and old cannabis fumes.

Forty minutes later, the van and patrol car turned into Malton Police Station. Cowen got out of the van and opened the back doors as Peter and laughing boy parked next to him.

"Will this take long?" Cowen asked. "I'll take the lot and say these had nothing to do with it."

"Let's talk about that when we get you all inside," Peter said as three heavyset and hungover men got out of the van.

"Any chance of a coffee?" the tallest man said as he staggered towards the door of the station. "That, a bacon sandwich, and a comfy bed."

"In your dreams," Peter answered.

Before he could stop him, the man opened the door of the station and shouted into the darkness. "I want me mam."

"I'm your mother now, sonny," came the reply as a tall, athletic woman in a police uniform with short-cropped, blonde hair stepped outside.

Peter saw the pips on the shoulders of her uniform jacket and realised this must be the new inspector.

"Five arrested for theft from the trout farm, boss."

"I heard on the radio. How did they get here? The divisional carrier is off the road," she asked as the suspects formed an orderly queue to go into the station.

"I'll explain later," he said as she folded her arms and gave him a bemused smile. "They told me when I transferred that it was bloody weird in Yorkshire, but not that it would be this weird. You must be Peter Barnes. I am Carol Manning. Control joked you would have someone locked up before the end of your shift, but this takes the biscuit."

[34]
Many A True Word

One of the things Peter hated about a quick changeover was it was exactly that. By the time he had booked in the prisoners and driven back to the outlying police office, it was nearly two in the morning. From there, was a thirty-minute drive back to the vicarage. It was after three when he finally pulled back the quilt and got into bed.

Inspector Manning had signed the custody sheet to allow the men to be questioned the next morning when Peter came back on duty. He knew Burley would be livid that he had the cells filled up, and he would have to make sure they were fed before any interviews took place.

Manning was a breath of fresh air. She got on with the job without commenting on the fact that he had taken a risk getting them to drive back to Malton. She seemed to realise that in the sticks, policing was not the same as London. Over a late-night cup of tea, Manning had explained that if she shouted for help, ten coppers would be there within a minute, and no one went out single-crewed.

In London, she said, officers had a baton and stab vest. Peter had told her that he had a short truncheon and would get a copy of the Yellow Pages to stuff up the front of his jacket if there was any chance of a knife being involved.

Waking after three hours sleep was quite usual for him. Peter dressed quickly, slipped a civilian jacket over his uniform, and made a flask of coffee. He knew the day would be spent in the police station processing the prisoners. There was at least two thousand pounds worth of dead trout filling the fridges at the station. Peter would have to take them to the trout farm and have them dispose of the fish, keeping several on ice as evidence.

Peter radioed Force Control to say he had arrived at Malton. It was a habit he couldn't break. As he walked in the police station door, he could hear Burley in the office. The man had no control over the volume of his voice. Everything was said in a loud Yorkshire accent that always had a hint of aggression.

"Morning, Joe," Peter said as he stepped inside the office.

"What are you doing here?" Burley asked.

"I have some prisoners to interview," he answered.

"Not anymore. I gave them bail this morning. I checked for a suitable day. They are coming back at eighteen hundred next Wednesday. You are on a late."

"Inspector Manning signed them off to be interviewed this morning. I have come on duty early to do the job," Peter answered, pointing to the clock on the wall.

"Manning?" he asked, knowing fully well who she was.

"Female inspector."

"I decided that it would be better to let them go. Not worth keeping them over a few fish. You can interview them next week," Burley smiled. "After all, you are part time, and you'll need to get a statement of complaint."

Peter nodded. It was no use arguing with him. Burley did what Burley wanted. He knew no one would say anything to him so near to retirement. The man was a dinosaur, old school, with all the bad habits of his time. The thought of Burley being run over by the Land Rover flashed through his mind. He just wished the farmer had done a better job.

"I'll get up to the trout farm and take the fish back. I put some in the evidence freezer last night."

"Right," Burley answered as he read the front page of his newspaper. Peter left the room and stepped into the corridor.

"Barney. There is a call for you in the custody area," the front receptionist said through the glass screen. "Inspector Manning."

The red telephone in the custody suite rattled on the desk as if it was about to break.

Peter lifted it from the cradle. "Peter Barnes," he said. "Malton Custody."

"*Peter. Carol Manning. I heard you call up on the radio when you got to Malton. Early bird?*" she said with a yawn.

"Thought I would get a head start on the interviews."

"*I haven't managed to finish shift. I got called to Northallerton to review some prisoners. How are the trout thieves?*" she asked.

"Bailed."

There was a long silence.

"*Bailed? Have they been interviewed?*" her voice was edged in obvious concern.

"They were gone when I got here."

"*Who let them go? Was it Sergeant Burley?*"

"With respect, Inspector, this is something I don't want to get into."

"*I said they were to be kept until you could interview them,*" she answered, her voice exasperated.

"That's why I am in early. I am just as annoyed as you are."

"*It's enough to make a vicar swear. When have they been bailed to?*"

"Next week. At least I will have time to get the complaint sorted and the value of the fish," he answered.

"*How many did they take?*"

"I counted two hundred and seventy-three before I went off last night. I put a few in the freezer and will take the rest back to the farm."

"*Great job, by the way. Let's catch up tomorrow night. I am on lates,*" Manning paused. "*Leave Sergeant Burley to me.*"

Peter put down the phone and turned to leave the room. The door opened.

"What did she want?" Burley asked.

"She asked how the interviews were going."

"Typical. I suppose I will be getting a call from her. This isn't the bloody Met. You can't just keep people locked up. Just in the mood to give her a piece of my mind and tell her how it is."

[35]
Parable Of The Fishes

The two boxes of fish that were in the boot of his patrol car had already started to smell. Thirty trout had vanished overnight from the police station fridge. When he had mentioned this to Burley, he had just laughed and walked away.

Peter thought it typical. The first week he had arrived in the division, he had gone to a job where a red deer stag had been found in a residential garden. The beast appeared to be tame until you got near. Then it would drop its head and antlers, scraping the floor in anger.

The old lady who owned the bungalow wanted the deer gone. Peter had called supervision. The old duty sergeant had sent a marksman. Within an hour, the creature had been shot and picked up by a local butcher, and by the time the owner of a local estate had rung in to report his prized pet stag missing, it was hanging in a secret meat larder.

Peter had been in the office when the man had called. He handed the phone to the sergeant and went for a very long drive to a part of the moors where there was no radio reception.

It was not just things that were edible that went missing. Shortly after the stag murder, Peter had arrested two men in wetsuits for stealing golf balls from the pond of the local golf club. In one night, they had managed to get seven hundred balls from three golf courses. The balls were put into the property cupboard. By the time the case came to court to test if it was a theft, only ninety-six balls were left. The rest were being shot around the courses of North Yorkshire by various police officers who thought it was their right to help themselves to what was in the property cupboard.

Peter arrived at the trout farm a little after seven-thirty. He knew that Derek Robinson would be there by then. The man lived on-site, though that didn't do much good, as he had been burgled several times before. This was the first time anyone was caught for taking fish.

As he pulled into the yard, he could see Robinson by the feed sheds. He was a tall man in his late fifties, with a thick head of brown hair in tight curls. When he saw the police car pull in, he waved frantically.

"You must be psychic. I was just going to ring you," he shouted as he ran over. "I've been burgled. They have had everything from the shed. Strimmers, hedge cutters, and batteries. There is other stuff missing, but I won't know what until Jerry Ledham gets in at eight. I have cameras all around the place. They must have picked up something."

"You were robbed of some rainbows as well last night. I have some in the car."

"Did they dump them?" Robinson asked.

"No, I arrested five men from Middlesborough. Caught them on Stape Road," Peter said as they walked towards the shed. "Didn't even bother running."

"Bugger," Robinson shrugged in discontent. "I never heard a thing. Funny. We couldn't set the movement alarm last night. There was a fault on the system."

At the shed, Peter could see the door had been forced. The padlock and its clasp lay on the floor.

"If we leave everything. I will get scenes of crime to take some pictures and dust for prints."

Peter stopped and looked at the door. It was then he realised it hadn't been forced. The bolts that held the clasp had been undone from the inside.

"You thinking what I am?" Robinson asked.

"Is there another way in here?"

"A door at the back, but that is secure."

"Then that makes this even more worrying. Have you got any new staff?" Peter asked.

"No. Just had to lay a couple off. Takings are down. Nobody wants to pay for fishing."

"How much would two hundred trout cost to buy?"

Robinson thought for a moment.

"Heavy end of seven hundred quid at trade. Add on another two hundred retail. Do you think they had my equipment as well?" Robinson asked. "You'll be able to ask them when you talk to them."

"Yes," Peter replied, not wanting to tell him that Burley had let them go.

"Did they have any tools on them when they got caught?"

"No. They would likely hide the stuff and then come back for it later, usually during the day." Peter felt a twist of anger in his stomach. If Burley hadn't bailed them, there would have been a chance of finding the stash. Now, it was most probably long gone.

Together, they checked the perimeter fence. Then, they went back to the house to look over the CCTV. Peter had radioed in the burglary and asked for scenes of crime and C.I.D to attend. He hoped that news of the job would get back to Burley.

In the house, Robinson rewound the tape from the night before and then played it back on fast forward. A blip of shapes jumped across the screen.

"There they are," he said as he froze the screen. Camo gear and balaclavas. Bloody typical. Do they think they are in the Royal Marines?"

"That's them," Peter answered. "Sadly, it doesn't put them at the shed."

"Isn't that enough?" Robinson asked.

"They could just deny the burglary and say they were poaching your trout."

It was an hour before C.I.D arrived. Mick Botham was a broad man with a thick Yorkshire accent and sharp wit. Everyone called him *Columbo*, due to his knack of solving crimes without a shred of evidence. He always dressed like a farmer in a checked shirt, cord trousers, and dealer boots. Botham said it helped him fit in with the people he dealt with.

As Botham got out of the unmarked car, he could see that the detective was furious.

His face was blushing red, and blonde hair unbrushed.

Peter went out of the house to meet him.

"He let them go," Botham fumed as his dealer boots scattered the gravel. "Doesn't Burley realise we keep people in the next day to see if they have done any other jobs?"

Peter shrugged. "I guess not. None of them had any real form. I was supposed to interview them this morning, but when I got to Malton, they were long gone."

Peter took Botham to the shed and showed him the lock and clasp.

"Someone unbolted the clasp and left it in place. All they had to do was pull it off. Inside job," Botham said, rubbing his hands together.

"Best keep that to ourselves. Robinson has laid a couple of people off. They could have kept the keys and undid the bolts to make it look like a burglary."

"Good idea. D.I. has asked me to take on the job. Burley has been harping on that you're part time. Hope you don't mind."

"Loaves and fishes," Peter answered as he looked up to the moors.

"What?"

"Plenty to go around."

[36]
It Takes A Thief

The rain beat down on the roof of the patrol car. Peter had parked under the trees at the top of Rawcliffe Bank. He poured a coffee from his flask and sat back as he stared across the moors towards the coast. To the east, the sun still shone, but he knew it would soon be chased away by the squall that beat down above him.

People often joked that in Yorkshire, you could experience every season of the year in a single summer's day. So far, he had seen spring and autumn. Looking at the fast-moving clouds, he hoped summer was on the way. He liked being on a rural beat as it meant he could work on his own without a boss staring over his shoulder. As long as he kept the workbook full, then he knew he would be left alone. Peter had one of the highest arrest rates of the division, but this didn't make him many friends. The old guard begrudged this, and would gossip and moan every time he took someone in.

Only Malcolm Salt, a long-serving constable wasn't bothered. He was coming to the end of his time and would tip Peter off with anything he had heard with the words, "*Go get 'em, lad.*" Mal may have been well over fifty but was so fit, he could outrun Peter any day of the week. He knew everyone in the area and had a list of informants longer than the charge room desk.

Peter thought that if anyone knew where the machinery from the burglary was hidden, it would be Mal Salt. He had told Peter that to catch a thief, you had to think like one. It was advice that he had taken to heart. Mal had broken his ankle playing football and wouldn't be back for a few weeks. As Peter sat in the car, looking out at the changing landscape, he wondered where it could be.

Picking up the OS map from the passenger seat, he followed the route from the trout farm to the Roman road. Peter knew they would hide the stash somewhere near the road and yet far enough away so it wasn't accidentally found. As he moved his finger across the page, it stopped on a junction in the road before an elbow bend.

Thinking back to the night before, he knew that was the place where he had first seen the lights. It was only a couple of minutes' drive from where he had stopped them, yet he had watched the lights for at least ten minutes. A sudden realisation came over him that the place where they had hidden the machinery was just two miles away.

Peter quickly finished his coffee, reversed out of the clearing, and set off down the hill. He was soon through Stape, a moorland village of scattered houses, and in five minutes was at the junction before the elbow bend.

In the rough grass verge were deep tyre marks, as if a heavy vehicle had pulled off the road. Peter got out of the car and could clearly see where two tracks went into the pine wood.

Following one of the paths, Peter made his way to an old forester's hut. The moss-covered door had been propped up against the opening. All around, the pine needles that covered the ground had been scattered, as if several people had been there some time before.

Without moving the door, Peter looked inside. There, under a hessian sack in the gloom, he could see what looked like the handle of a hedge trimmer. Propped all around were other bits of machinery that has been hastily hidden under old sacks.

Peter couldn't believe his luck. He knew they would come back for it sooner rather than later. Thieves always did, they could not resist. It was their way of getting one-up over the law and sticking two fingers to the coppers.

Hiding the car fifty yards away, Peter radioed Mick Botham. "*Foxtrot-Papa*-Three-Five to *Foxtrot*-Mike-Two-Zero."

"*Go ahead*," Botham replied, the radio crackling.

"Got the stuff you are looking for."

"*What's your twenty?*" Botham said, asking for his location.

"Dog leg. Roman road," he answered quickly, knowing that even the people at the roundabout café in Pickering listened in to police broadcasts.

"*Ten-four. Twenty minutes.*"

As Mick Botham finished speaking, to his horror, Peter saw an old, white Renault Estate coming down the hill and slowing to stop at the side of the road. Through the trees, he could see that the driver was a woman in her thirties. In the passenger seat was Billy Graves.

"Two-Zero. We have visitors," Peter whispered and then pressed the talk key on the handset five times as a silent warning.

Slowly, he made his way behind the dead ground so that he could be closer to the hut. The woman got out of the car. She was smartly dressed in a green summer coat. Her short brown hair was cut in a bob. The woman looked around her.

Billy Graves got out of the car and followed her along the path to the hut. Peter watched, hidden in the bracken as they went to the door and pulled it open.

"Bloody hell," she said in a strong Teesside accent. "Danny said it was a grand worth of good stuff. This is just a pile of junk."

"He's got a buyer. Stolen to order. Fella in Stokesley is gonna take the lot," Graves replied cockily. "Inside man. Easy as hell."

"Well, I'm not going to get mucked up for that lot," the woman replied as she walked back to the car. "I'll have a fag and pretend to be enjoying the view. You can shift the stuff."

Bit by bit, Graves walked back and forth to the car carrying the tools and machinery. Peter watched as he filled the back of the estate with a couple of chainsaws, strimmers, hedge cutters, and batteries. The lad had no idea he was being watched and whistled *Relax* as he shifted the stuff.

When the last power drill was in the estate, Graves pulled down the back door and leant against it.

"We can take it direct to Stokesley or drop it off at yours," he said to the woman as he lit a cigarette.

She didn't reply. The woman was staring at the figure coming through the trees about ten feet away.

"We're going nowhere," she said finally.

"Danny wants us back by three. He told the fella."

"Shut up, Billy," she answered. "We're nicked."

"What?" Billy said as he turned and saw Peter Barnes a few feet away. "Sod it."

"Morning, Billy. I didn't think I would see you until next week," Peter said.

"Smart-arse," the woman answered. "Don't you have a home to go to? You must be some sort of weirdo lurking around in the woods. Anyway, we just found the stuff and were going to take it to the police station and hand it in."

"Stokesley by chance?" Peter asked as he stepped forward and took the car keys from her hand.

"You're taking a chance out here on your own, aren't you?" the woman said. Billy slipped his hand under the back of his camouflage jacket.

"Not really," Peter answered. "Cavalry on the way."

"Give her back the keys," Graves said as he held out a long-bladed knife towards Peter.

"Put it away and I won't mention that you are so stupid."

"Give her the keys," he shouted.

The blow was quick. The fist hit Graves full in the face. The lad dropped to the floor, his nose broken.

Peter picked up the knife and threw it across the road. Then, he unclipped the handcuffs from his belt and looked at the woman.

"Bracelets?" she said, with no concern for Billy Graves. "Do you think I need them?"

Peter said nothing. He clipped a cuff on her wrist, led her to the open door of the Renault, and fastened her to the steering wheel.

Billy Graves was lying on the road, crying. Peter picked him up, opened the passenger side door, and pushed him in.

"You don't have to say anything, unless you wish to do so. Anything you do say may be given in evidence. You are both under arrest on suspicion of handling stolen goods."

"You must love yourself," the woman snarled. "I bet you get off on this, don't you?"

Graves sat in the car, head in hands, sobbing.

[37]
The Grim Reaper

The day had passed slowly. Morning prayer had been said alone. The Eucharist was celebrated with just two others. If God was blessing his ministry at St Walstan's, it was difficult to see.

By early afternoon, Peter was looking forward to going to work. Mick Botham had interviewed Billy Graves. The woman turned out to be the girlfriend of Danny Cowen. Both had been charged with handling stolen goods. Cowen and the others had been rearrested on suspicion of burglary and there was enough forensic evidence to charge them all.

As Peter walked into the police station, he looked forward to the evening ahead. In the car park was a Toyota people carrier. He noticed the two blue lights hidden discreetly in the front grill and wondered which top brass was visiting.

"Peter," came the voice from the main office. "I hear you have been busy on your first night back."

Peter recognised the voice. David Turner was the divisional superintendent. A Bramshill man selected to go far, and a member of the accelerated training programme. Everyone knew he was being groomed for further promotion. To see him out after five o'clock was a very rare thing. His safe place was in his bland office at headquarters, with a copy of *The Guardian* on his desk. He was known to many as *the Grim Reaper* for his ability to kill off the career of anyone he saw as a threat. Sadly, he treated everyone with suspicion and disdain.

Peter stepped inside the room with its white gloss walls and bright strip lights. It was more like a public toilet than a police office. Against the wall was a long, tea-stained desk with three computer monitors and a dial phone. Next to the phone was the police repeater radio and handset. To one side was a makeshift custody desk ready in case any of his colleagues should make an arrest when a sergeant was on duty. That was a rarity.

"Evening, Superintendent," Peter answered as he stepped inside the office and saw Turner sat next to Carol Manning.

"I hear you have met Inspector Manning," Turner said as he pointed to the empty chair in an obvious invitation for Peter to sit down. "Thought I would come to the *outpost* and see how you are getting on."

"Thanks," Peter answered. "Busy couple of days."

"I was just wondering if you have thought anything about applying for promotion?" Turner asked. "I am sure that now you have got time on your hands since you finished your ordination training."

"It is something I have thought about for a couple of years."

"I just thought you might like to broaden your experiences and see some different departments."

Peter wondered if this was Burley's doing. He knew he wanted him out, but not this quickly.

"There is a vacancy in Force Intelligence. You could be the right fit for it," Carol Manning added, as if it had already been decided.

"Nine to five. Part time. Plain clothes and in the heart of the division. A chance to be seen," Turner added.

"It's something to consider. Could I have a couple of weeks to think things through?" Peter asked.

"Glad we are singing from the same hymnbook," Turner laughed as he got to his feet and wiped the biscuit crumbs from his trousers. "Better get off. Dinner at Castle Howard. I believe your bishop is a guest." Turner gave his goodbyes and left.

Carol Manning waited until she heard the door click shut.

"Well, that was interesting," she said as she poured Peter a cup of tea. "He was here when I arrived. Got the shock of my life."

"I feel as if I am being set up. Joe Burley told me about the job. I don't think he wants me here."

"From what I gather, he doesn't like the idea of part-time coppers," Manning answered as she sipped her tea. "I hear that he is peeved that you are a vicar, and doesn't believe the two jobs are compatible."

"I keep a divide between them and have done for a year as a curate."

"But what about when the two collide? It is only a matter of time."

"Then I will have to face it then. I hope being a priest helps me in the job."

"Just watch your back. Joe Burley isn't a happy man. He believes he is king of this outpost and doesn't want a troublesome priest hanging around," she paused and smiled. "Why did you get ordained? What is God all about? This job killed off any faith I had. Death, violence, and hatred. It's all we see."

"My faith gives me hope that the world is somehow better than all that," Peter answered. "I am genuinely interested. You are one of the first officers to do this. It is a landmark in policing."

Manning leant forward. "How can God be real if he... she... it... allows so much suffering?"

"I'm still trying to work that one out," he answered honestly. "Suffering is part of the world we live in. As a priest, I try to offer a different way to live our lives. If anything, seeing the evil people can do makes me believe there must be a force for good in the world."

"I get that," she answered. "But what about the parents of the child who was killed in the fatal on the A64 last week? What would you say to them? How can you explain it away?"

"It's heartbreaking. My belief in God is stretched every day. Some would say that suffering is because humanity abandoned God. It's the human condition. We inflict it on each other, cause wars, commit murder, poison the atmosphere..."

"I don't buy that," Manning answered as she stood up. "That doesn't give me an answer."

"Sometimes, there just isn't an answer. I pray and give it all to God."

"I used to pray," she answered as she walked to the door. "I used to pray every day for my husband to get better. Then one day, he died. He was twenty-seven. God and I are not on speaking terms," Manning nodded to him as she tried to smile. A single tear trickled across her cheek. She turned back and drew a breath. "You did a good job yesterday. I have recommended a commendation."

"Thank you," he answered softly.

"You are the only person that knows about my husband, and I want to keep it that way."

"Is that why you transferred from the Met?"

"Yes... too many memories."

[38]
Come Quick Kee-Tat, Big Fight

The rain beat down on the roof of the patrol car. Peter had been parked for the last hour on the edge of the town, waiting for the pubs to close and the drunks to go home. It was divisional policy that all rural beat officers would park near to town for the last hour of the pubs being open and be on hand to back up the double-crewed town car.

As he sat watching raindrops trickle across the windscreen, racing each other across the glass, Peter would occasionally flick the wiper switch to clear them away and imagine he was playing *Space Invaders*.

Time dragged. The rain would quickly clear any revellers who wanted a fight. Checking his watch, he knew he was in for a long night.

Suddenly, the force radio crackled. The *click, click, click* was a signal that a message was coming.

"*Come quick... Kee-Tat... big fight,*" the female controller said repeating the words of the three-nine's call that came in nearly every night from the only Chinese takeaway in town. "*All units respond. Several males fighting inside.*"

It was a call that Peter was used to. Flicking on the headlights, he started the car and set off into town. There was no use in speeding there. Fights at the Kee-Tat were always over the moment they started.

The radio crackled again.

"Delta-Sierra-Two-Nine. Ten-Five at the scene."

The town car had beat him to the fight. Turning the corner, Peter could see the flashing blue lights reflecting off the building and wet pavement.

"*Foxtrot-Papa*-Three-Five. Ten-five," Peter said as he pulled up behind the new Range Rover patrol car that had arrived at Malton a week before.

"That was quick, Barney," Steve Becket said as he stood on the rain-soaked pavement outside the takeaway in shirt sleeves rolled up tightly over his muscular arms. "Nothing happening here. The owner panicked when some lads started throwing chips at the windows and ran off."

"Typical," Peter answered as he looked at the two women in fake fur coats, leaning against the glass window of the takeaway. "You've given him advice?"

"Told him to wait until the fight started before calling it in," Steve laughed.

"How did you manage to get the keys to the Range Rover?" he asked. "I thought mere mortals were not allowed to drive it."

"The town car is over mileage. The lease company will charge a penny a mile. This was the only thing left; had to prize the keys from the inspector's fingers."

"Over mileage, what's that about?"

"All the cars in D Division were leased with a penalty if they went over one hundred thousand miles. Superintendent Evans did the deal and never asked what the average mileage was. There is a year left to go on the contract and a couple of the cars are over mileage. One has had its wheels taken off so it can't be used, the other is on a twenty mile a shift limit," Steve said as he shook his head in bewilderment.

"Typical," Peter answered.

"By the way, and off the record, that neighbour of yours had enough cocaine and alcohol in his blood to drop an elephant. I am surprised he managed to shoot himself."

"Poor man," he answered. "I have the funeral next week. His wife refuses to speak to me and insists she wants nothing to do with him. Thankfully, his sister is making all the arrangements."

"Funny thing," Becket paused for a moment. "I had a call from the fraud squad. George Bateson was a person of interest. Apparently, he was being investigated for insider trading. They believed he was getting someone to buy stocks of companies Bateson was working for. He was making a lot of money. His wife won't speak to me either. She lives in a flash house with her toy boy."

Before he could answer, one of the women outside the takeaway shouted over. "Thought I recognised you," the blonde in tight jeans said as her friend laughed.

Steve turned and smiled. "It's because I am famous," he answered.

"Not you," she said, "Peter, Peter Barnes. I know your missus."

"Really? How?" he replied.

"We worked together. A right party animal, that one. Proper cougar."

Suddenly, a Rover Vanden Plas lurched through the stone archway of the backyard of the Masonic Lodge. The car glided slowly along the road, the driver slumped over the steering wheel.

"Good grief," Peter said as the car rubbed along the kerb stone, grating its wheels on the concrete. "He was asleep."

The car slowed to a halt as the engine shuddered and then stalled with a sudden lurch.

Peter ran to the car.

The woman at the takeaway shouted, "We had a hell of a time when you were away on your course. When the cat's away. Tell her Hazel Connor sends her love."

Peter ignored her. The woman was drunk.

Looking inside the car, he could see that the driver was a man in his fifties, wearing a dinner jacket and black tie. His head was slumped against the side window. For a fleeting moment, Peter thought the man was dead.

Carefully, he opened the door of the car. The man slumped out before Peter could stop him. He groaned, opening his eyes and looking at Peter.

"What the bloody hell are you doing?" the man questioned him with slurred words.

"I was going to ask you the same," he answered as the whisky fumes oozed out of the car.

"Looks like he is trolleyed," Steve Becket said as he and Peter helped the man to his feet.

"I need you to provide me with a sample of breath for a roadside breath test," Peter said to the man.

"No bloody way. Take me home," the man managed to say in semi-coherence.

"Are you refusing?" Becket asked him.

"Bugger off. Do you know who I am?" the man replied.

"You are drunk, that's all I know."

"And you are nicked for not provided a sample of breath," Peter added as he took the man by the arm and began to lead him towards his car.

"Do you know who I am? I am the worshipful Master of the Lodge," the man slurred. "The chief constable is a friend of mine."

"Well, he is probably fast asleep, and I don't think he will be of any help," Peter said as he placed the man in the back of his car. "This isn't the Lodge, and anyway, he has just retired."

"I'll have you out of the job by Friday, you bloody upstart."

"Coming in with one for failing to provide," Peter radioed the controller as he pulled on his seat belt and started the car.

"*Ten-Four. Take him to Malton. Custody suite is open,*" the woman answered.

"I will make it difficult for you," the man said, the shock of being arrested sobering him up.

"That's fine. People make it difficult all the time. One more won't make a difference," Peter answered as the man lolled his head drunkenly with the motion of the car.

The man muttered all the way to Malton. Turning into the police station yard, he looked up. "You are making a big mistake," he said.

"So you keep saying," Peter answered, pulling up into the only free space in the car park.

"I suggest you let me out here and I will get a taxi, and we will forget all about it," the man said sternly as he tapped the seat in front of him with an outstretched hand.

"Let's talk about it inside. You were in a road, driving a motor vehicle, and you are drunk. No one will want to forget about that."

"A fool," the man muttered as he was helped from the car and led to the station.

Once inside, Peter soon realised that something was wrong. As he walked the man into the brightly lit custody area, Geoff Haslem, Duty Sergeant, stood up.

"Now then, Barney," Haslem said with an obvious look of embarrassment on his face. "Is this man under arrest?"

"Yes," Peter answered. "Failing to provide a sample of breath."

"Let him take a seat in the interview room and we can see where we are going," Haslem said, putting down his pen and nodding to the man.

"He needs to go on the CAMIC. He should provide a sample of breath," Peter argued, never having known a prisoner to be put in the interview room without having details taken.

"Let's not be hasty. I just need to make a call," Haslem answered as he turned and left the room. "Make him a coffee and put him in room one."

"I told you the crap was about to fall on your head," the man said with a drunken smile. "A career-ending decision."

The door opened and Haslem walked back into the room followed by Derek Grant, a tall sticklike man who was the night inspector.

"Evening, Peter," Grant said, trying not to look at the man. "You can leave the prisoner with us and we will process him."

"Thanks, Inspector. I would rather stay and see it through for the continuity of evidence," Peter answered as the feeling that something was drastically wrong grew even more intense. "Procedure states that he should be booked in and put on the CAMIC as soon as possible."

Haslem looked at Grant. "He is right," he said in a voice just above a whisper.

"The CAMIC machine hasn't been calibrated. We will have to get a doctor. Get a blood sample," Grant answered.

"So, we wait?" Peter asked.

"What time do you finish?" Grant asked.

"When my prisoner is bailed to court," Peter replied. "Can we book him in? I sense you don't need to ask him for his details as you know who he is already."

Grant nodded to Haslem. "I'll ring Doc Craven and get him to come down. You better book him in," Grant said as he pushed the door open. "Don't put him in a cell."

Peter walked the man to interview room one. He sat on a chair, head in hands, as if to rid himself of the drink.

"What's going on?" Peter asked Haslem outside the room.

"I don't know what you mean," Haslem answered.

"You are not following procedure. You haven't even asked for his details. Do you know him? Is he a friend of yours?"

"Ridiculous," Haslem answered curtly.

"You are a Freemason and so is this man. I locked him up coming out the back of the Lodge. He said he was the Worshipful Master." Peter drew breath. "Why are you protecting him?"

"You'll be walking the streets of Selby if you rock this boat," Haslem snarled back. "Just because you are a bloody vicar, it won't protect you."

"Divided loyalties? What about without fear of favour?"

"I know where my loyalties lie," Haslem answered.

It was an hour before Doctor Craven came to take the blood. Peter noticed that he smelt of drink, and without introduction, was on first name terms with the prisoner. As the prisoner was bailed, the doctor offered to give the *Worshipful Master* a lift home.

Haslem and Grant looked at Peter as he closed the door behind Craven as they left the custody suite.

"If you give me the paperwork, I'll make sure it gets to CPS once we have the blood alcohol back," Grant said as he finished the dregs of his tea.

"Will do," Peter said as he picked up the paperwork from the custody desk, smiled at the two men, and walked out of the room.

[39]
Day Follows Night

It had finally stopped raining just before dawn. The night had been hot, close, and airless. There was no breeze. The curtains at the open windows hung loosely. Peter lay, wide-eyed, staring at the freshly painted ceiling. He traced a faint mark in the lining paper that crossed the room from wall to wall.

On the bedside table, the digital clock flashed four thirty-seven. He had been awake most of the night. Peter knew that Haslem would do his best to make things tough for him. The thought troubled him. He wondered if the right thing to do was to take the job in Force Intelligence and stay off the streets. Never had he come across the problems of the night before. The Masons were a tight-knit group in the division. Half the station was on the square, hoodwinked and cable towed. They would all drink in the same pub and wear the little square and compass badge on their uniform ties. Peter never thought they would ever try to use their influence to pervert the course of justice. Now, he knew he just might be wrong. Before he had left the station, he had gone into the CAMIC room. Peter checked the machine and the calibration log. The CAMIC machine had been calibrated at the beginning of the night shift. Grant had lied.

It wasn't long before the church clock chimed the hour.

The bedside clock flashed six. He must have slept since he last looked. Outside, he heard the milk van pull up and the clatter of bottles on the doorstep. Birds sang, a cockerel crowed, cows moaned, and the whole of nature conspired to keep him awake.

Rolling from the bed, Peter slipped his dressing gown over his t-shirt and pyjama trousers and went downstairs. In the kitchen, he flicked the switch on the kettle, put two teaspoons of coffee in the cup, and poured in the milk. It was a move that made him feel dishonest. There was no one to confess to that he had tipped out all the Fairtrade coffee in the church hall and replaced it with Nescafé Gold.

The bishop had sent an edict that all parishes should only use Fairtrade coffee for any church gatherings. Peter hated the taste and hated being told what to do even more. Switching the coffee was an act of rebellion. It was his secret, and every time someone said how Fairtrade coffee had improved and didn't taste the same at home, he would smile to himself, proud of the deception.

By the garden hedge, the fox searched for mice. Peter had left it the remnants of his latest takeaway. The fox hadn't touched the leftover kebab, a worrying sign that neither should have Peter. Since Mary had been away, he had glutted on meat. Marriage had made him a reluctant vegetarian. It was something he did to keep the peace.

Whenever she was away, Peter made up for his meat fast. He would make sure there was no trace of any chicken bones, pizza boxes, or burger wrappers before she came back.

Her return had not been mentioned. The infrequent phone calls dwindled even further. His mother-in-law was home from hospital. Mary would be looking after her, as well as her father and the children.

The last time Peter had spoken to her, the conversation was brief. Mary seemed to be distracted, and yet she was adamant that she would stay on as long as she could to help her mother recover.

As he looked out of the window, he wondered what Hazel Connor had meant by 'party animal' and 'proper cougar'. The last thing he thought Mary could ever be was a cougar, and as for party animal, that was out of the question.

He could count on one hand the times Mary had been drunk. Even then, she always stopped herself.

Mary was controlled in every aspect of her life. Everything was done in moderation. Procreation was rationed and fitted into the diary, usually in the afternoon, and since the children had been born, had become increasingly more perfunctory and infrequent to the point of abstinence. More and more, to get relief whilst showering, he would find himself in the company of Onan, patron saint of lonely men. It was a part of his life that troubled him. Peter had promised God that he would never imagine being with another woman. Yet, with Mary away, it was a hard road to follow.

As he looked out of the window, what nagged in his mind was that his first child was not his own. It was an irrational thought. Peter had no real reason to doubt that Mary had always been faithful, but it was the timing of the conception that worried him. Now, Hazel Connor had managed to make his mind whir with anxious thoughts that sometime in the past, her fidelity might be questioned.

The fox sat by the gate that opened into the field. It looked back to the vicarage as it scratched the fleas from its belly with its clawed foot. Fox gazed at the clouds, ears flicking from side to side, as if it could sense a sound that no one else could perceive. For a brief moment, Peter and the fox stared eye to eye, beast to man. There was an honesty in the eye of the fox that Peter had never seen in the eye of any man. It was the honesty of a creature that killed to live. A creature that would kill every hen in a run and only take one. That is how God had made it. The fox had nothing to apologise and lie for. Its life was simple and uncomplicated.

The kettle boiled. It clicked obediently, like it had done a thousand times before. Peter filled the cup, opened the back door, and looked into the garden. The fox had gone, vanished as if a will-o'-the-wisp. He walked to the end of the hedge at the back of the garden and leant against the dry stone wall that stood as a boundary to the field.

In the distance, the old yew tree swayed in the breeze.

"You're up early," the voice said from his right.

He turned, startled. In the field by the side of the wall stood Stella Smith. Her hair was tied back and held in place by a red bandana.

"Rather early? What are you doing here?" Peter asked.

"Morris has asked me to come and fix your wall. He noticed some of the stones had fallen away. I have a job up at The Grange later. I thought I could get this done before I went there."

"How is Mrs Parker?"

"Very formal. Helen is fine. No more noises in the house. What you been up to since I last saw you?" Stella asked as she pulled up the shoulder strap of her overalls.

"Back to work. Copper stuff."

"Shame about George from Orchard House," Stella said as she leant against the wall, taking a pouch from her pocket and beginning to roll a cigarette.

"Did you know him?" Peter asked.

"Everyone knew George. Life and soul of the pub. A nice man," Stella answered. "Strange that he should choose to end his life the way he did."

"All over in a second," she said with a grimace. "Not a way to go."

"I am taking the funeral next week. His widow is not very helpful and doesn't want anything to do with it. House going up for sale."

"Their marriage was over a long time ago. She has been playing around since they got here. Anyway, I heard she was moving back in. Her boyfriend has dumped her."

"How do you find all this out?" he asked.

"People tell me stuff and I listen," Stella said as she rolled up her shirt sleeves, revealing the green serpent tattoo that wound its way up her arm. "I was over in Scarborough in The Merchant, and this bloke comes up and starts talking. He says he has seen me in the village pub where his ex-girlfriend lived. I played dumb and he told me that they had broken up. She was too controlling, but he didn't care. He even said that her husband had died. I got the impression he was more interested in George than Bridget. He kept talking about George knowing what was going on with stocks and trades. The man was well stoned. He was drinking quad vodka and coke."

"Does this drunken Casanova have a name?"

"Simon Tindall. He said he was a teacher but was now playing the stock market. Offered to take me on a holiday," Stella smiled.

"Are you going?"

"Ha, ha. What he didn't say was that he already had another girlfriend. She turned up ten minutes later and whisked him away."

"Disappointed?" Peter asked.

"No thanks," she said with a smile. "I have had my fill of men. More trouble than they are worth."

"We are not all like that," he answered, looking at her intently.

"Men are just children that never grow up," she replied, lighting the cigarette as she put it to her lips. "And just think, your God put them in charge over the whole world."

"Glad you regard us so highly. I was going to ask if you would like to come to the blessing of the well. I asked Morris to have it restored."

"He gave me the job; wondered if you had anything to do with it."

"So, will you come?" Peter said as their eyes met in an awkward glance.

"Let me restore the well and then I will let you know," Stella answered as she looked away and took a long drag from the cigarette, then blew the smoke into the morning air. "Why are you so keen on the well anyway?"

"Every time I pray, it just comes to mind. Whenever I close my eyes, I see three things: the well, the yew, and the grave tree. It is as if God wants me to do something. That is why I want to have a well blessing. It is a place to start putting things right."

"You are playing with fire. Doesn't your book say you wrestle not against flesh and blood, but against principalities, against powers, and against the rulers of the darkness of this world? There is more here than I could handle."

"I thought Pagans believed in making things right in the world?"

"If you look back at what is wrong in this place, it always comes from the hearts of men. There is a power here that feeds on weakness. It finds the chink in the armour and exploits it. That's what it did to Seagrave, Shepherd, and Frank Green. It will do the same to you."

[40]
Daniel

The rest of the morning was spent reading the minutes of the church meetings as far back as 1964. It was a depressing account of lack of funds, dwindling congregations, and bitter infighting. The only hope was for a brief period in the sixties. Albert Shepherd had brought in more people. Finances were abundant and there were many social events. The church was the centre of village life, with the good Shepherd steering the ship through a calm and prosperous sea.

From what Peter read, the man was much loved and admired. Everything he did was blessed, even though he was a man of little prayer. The daily office was never said in church. Services were kept to a minimum. There was no Bible study or faith gatherings. Shepherd ran the church as if it were a club. Film nights, bingo, beetle drives, and talent shows filled the winter evenings. All were well attended and each made money for the church.

Peter got the impression that Shepherd was like an event director at a holiday camp.

In one of the files at the back of the cabinet were notes of his sermons, written in hand by a now-dead churchwarden. Shepherd talked about life with very little mention of God. The talks were brief and stayed clear of any mention of salvation or Heaven.

The only indication of faith that Peter could find was at Christmas in 1965. Shepherd read from the Book of Genesis and spoke about the guilt of Eve, a strange subject for Midnight Mass. There were thick underlinings in the notes. The word 'sin' was picked out in several places, 'nakedness' in another. He talked of going the way of man, and not of God, and eating fruit that did not belong to him. It was as if Shepherd was making a confession to the people he served.

Peter thought of what Stella had said. The late morning light grew dim as a passing shower beat against the window glass. It was as if she was saying that each priest came to the parish as a good man, and something here changed them.

Maggie Green had said just that when they first arrived, her husband was an open-minded man who hardly drank, and within a few months of being vicar, all that had changed. Frank Green had become a radical Pentecostalist. He saw everything as a battle between the forces of light and darkness. Yet within him was a darkness that took him away drunkenly from his wife and into the arms of one or even two lovers.

It was as Morris had told him about all the other incumbents. Each had fallen to their very own vice. Theft, drunkenness, greed, pride, and adultery.

Peter did not believe in spiritual warfare; that, he left for God. However, the evidence was there before him, every priest sent to the parish had fallen within a few months of their arrival. All except Seagrave.

A sudden, sharp knock at the office door dragged him from his thoughts. He could see the shape of a woman through the glass. He knew it was Stella. For an instance, he thought not to answer it. The knock came again.

"Come in!" he shouted.

The door opened. Stella smiled, rain dripping across her face as she looked around the office walls that were now covered with old photographs and a large print of *The Lady of Shalott* above the gas fire.

"Nice poster. Handy having an office with an outside door, keeps the riffraff out of the house."

"They still try to get in," he answered.

"Last time I was in here, Frank Green was telling me I was going to burn in Hell."

"And have you?" he asked. "It must be a very crowded place. Priests must go somewhere when they are dead."

Stella smiled. It was broad and welcoming. Her eyes tightened, forming laughter lines on her sunbathed skin.

"Just about to start on the well. I wondered what you wanted it to look like?" she asked as she leant against the doorframe. "I was thinking a small cairn, just how it was before Frank had it bricked up."

"That would be good. Are you starting today? I thought you were going up to The Grange?"

"Just on my way. Wanted to check in first. Hope to start the well tomorrow."

"Tell me..." he started as he sat back in his chair. "You said I was playing with fire. Do you really believe it?"

"Maybe I used the wrong words. I just want you to be careful. This church has a bad history and I don't want you to fall into it. My beliefs tell me that there are positive and negative forces. St Walstan's is a place of darkness. I would never practice a ritual here. The energy is too strong."

"Harmful?" he asked.

"Cursed. Malevolent. Call it what you wish."

"Demons?"

"Negative attitudes and energy. Jealousy. Bitterness. Anger. The three horsemen of St Walston's," she laughed, trying to take the sting out of her words.

"And you really believe that?"

"Yes. There has been a lot of hate in this parish."

Peter sat for a moment and thought. "You believe it can make good men bad?"

"They become sympathetic to the nature of the power. Frank Green slowly became an angry man. I saw it happen over the months. When we first met, he was like you. He talked to me about my beliefs, and the welcome was slowly eroded until he hated the ground I walked on."

"And you think this will happen to me?"

"I don't think it is a coincidence. That's all I can say," Stella smiled and said her goodbye, leaving him alone.

He was confused. Peter was a man of evidence. He needed facts, even for his belief in God. That is what made faith so hard. There were few facts. It was all down to belief, but that could change quickly and easily. As a child, Peter had believed in the Tooth Fairy and Father Christmas, yet these had disappeared as the age of disbelieving came upon him. He often worried that the same thing would happen to his faith in God, that this too would be taken from him with the complexities and cruelties of life.

As he stared at the Waterhouse print that hung in a gold frame on the wall above the fire, he found himself repeating the same words over and over as if a childhood mantra. *"Jesus loves me, this I know because the Bible tells me so."*

They were the words he always went back to when his faith was weak. With all the talk of curses, powers and principalities, Peter no longer knew what to believe. He looked at the phone on the desk and had the sudden urge to ring Mary. Peter wanted to hear her voice, the voice of a benign atheist who believed in nothing other than humanity.

Dialling the number, he listened as the call connected.

"*Hello, David Knox,*" her father answered.

"David, it's Peter. I was wondering if Mary was around?" he asked bluntly, knowing there was no need for pleasantries or small talk.

"*Just missed her. I gave her the morning off. She's gone to the beach with the children. Daniel has taken them.*"

"Daniel?"

"*Yes. Just moved in next door. Nice chap. Been helping me with the hedge.*"

[41]
Ashes To Ashes

Morris Marsden could not contain his discontent as he strutted along the driveway towards the vicarage. In his hands, he carried a small wooden box with brass handles.

Peter waved as he sat drinking the last of his coffee, leaning against the doorway in the late morning sun.

"Hello, Morris," he shouted as his churchwarden got closer. "A lovely day after the rain."

"I wish it was," Morris crowed. "We have a problem, and I am unable to rectify it. I have nowhere to put Elsie Berryman."

"Why? The internment of ashes isn't for another hour."

"The undertaker left her in church, but she hasn't got a hole," Morris muttered loudly as he slumped onto the bench by the front door. "Elsie can't be scattered; she was a very tidy woman."

"Hole?" Peter asked as Morris sighed deeply.

"I went to make sure everything was in order, and the undertaker hasn't sent a gravedigger. Nothing is ready. I even laid out a roll of false grass. She wanted to go in the grave on top of her husband. That was her last request. On top of him in life and on top of him in death. The poor man suffered."

"Out of interest, when did she die?"

"Just after Frank Green came to the parish. She left instructions that she wasn't to be buried until he was gone. They did not get on, and she insisted that it wasn't to be a woman."

"She died before the first ordinations of women?"

"Elsie had a deep sense of foreboding. She was the parish representative of *Forward in Faith*. A founder member, November '92, just after the vote in Synod to allow the ordination of women."

"Forward in faith, backward in belief. That's what Trevor, my old college principal, used to say," Peter answered.

"Serious business having a woman priest. We had to have several emergency meetings to stop Bishop Riley sending one when Frank left us."

Morris sighed again. His face was edged with the strain. "But you managed to fend them off?"

"St Walstan's is no place for a female priest. We are traditionalists. Elsie would be spinning in her grave if a woman got their hands on her box."

"Don't worry, Morris, I will handle Elsie's box with care, and I'll dig the hole to give her enough room to spin. That's not a problem. You take my cassock and surplus to the church and I will see you there."

Morris gave a relieved smile as if a weight had been taken from him.

"If you are sure? It isn't a thing a priest should normally do. I don't want to impose."

Peter took the ashes and walked to the churchyard. Taking the keys from the pocket of his jeans, he opened the small wooden tool store at the back of the church.

The gravestone was etched with lichen. The words were plain, clear, and cold. *Jack Berryman. Born 1910. Died 1984.* There was no loving words or kind farewell. To one side of the stone was a piece of false grass, and next to that a square of plywood board.

Peter presumed this was for the soil to be placed on. From what he remembered from the lesson on burials at theological college, a casket had to be buried at least six inches below the ground. This meant that the hole had to be two feet deep. He wondered how far down Jack had been buried.

The spade cut through the turf quickly. Peter had watched numerous episodes of *Time Team* and had always wanted to cut an archaeological trench. He dug quickly, keeping the sides of the trench as neat as he could. In half an hour, the grave was two feet deep and square. Peter knelt on the grass and took out the last of the soil with his hands. There had been no ancient discoveries or any sign of Jack Berryman.

Wiping the sweat from his forehead with the back of his hand, he stood up.

"That's not deep enough," said the sharp voice from behind him. "Foxes. It needs to be at a depth where they can't get to the coffin."

Peter turned. There, using an old gravestone as a perch to rest against, was a birdlike woman dressed in a long, funeral-black coat with a dead mink wrapped around her neck. She peered at him over the rims of her Pince-Nez spectacles. Her eyes were creased with age and jowls hung at either side of her lipstick-soaked mouth.

"Sorry?" he asked.

"The grave. You will have to dig it deeper. The sides are too narrow. Is the vicar around?" the woman asked, flashing her lipstick-stained teeth as she bobbed her head back and forth like an enquiring owl.

"He's around somewhere."

"Idling in the vicarage no doubt. I shall tell him I am not satisfied with the grave."

"Are you a relative of the deceased?" he asked.

"She was married to my brother. Not that it is any of your business," the woman paused momentarily. "Where is the man? I have heard he is not right for this parish. Vicar and policeman. He arrested my neighbour for no reason. All the man did was drive his car back from the Lodge."

Peter knew he could not admit who he was. This old woman had presumed from the way he was dressed and the mud on his hands that he was the gravedigger. The deceit had now gone too far. Yet his inner impertinence urged him to go on.

"If you knew the things about him that I do, it would turn your hair green. He is a very sinful man."

"I can imagine. Jack of all trades, master of none. How long have you known him?" she asked as she tapped her walking stick on the ground.

"Over thirty years."

Peter smiled and walked away as a gathering of funeral guests began drifting from gate to grave.

"Tell the vicar he is late," the woman shouted as Peter walked towards the church and smiled at Morris, who was standing at the porch gate.

"Was Mrs. Barrie having her say?" Morris asked. "I heard her voice."

"Mrs Barrie? Any relation to Margaret Barrie from the W.I?"

"Like mother, like daughter. They don't speak to each other. Margaret won't be seen within a mile of her mother," Morris answered with a shrug of the shoulders, his look of discontent not needing a reply.

"Mrs Barrie must be quite old," Peter said.

"At least ninety, but as sharp as a pin."

"I will get washed, changed, and see you by the grave," Peter said as he looked at the darkening sky. "We better get going."

The crowd gathered at the grave stood in silence as Peter walked towards them. Mrs Barrie looked at him and squinted her eyes in disbelief. It was obvious that she wondered if the gravedigger was the thick twin of the vicar.

Peter stood by the grave and looked at those gathered eye to eye. As his stare met with Mrs Barrie, she looked away. Morris placed the box of ashes into the chamber as Peter spoke the words of internment.

"Not deep enough," Mrs Barrie grumbled as Peter said the final prayer. "Fox will be eating well off old Elsie."

"Amen," Peter answered as if in reply.

"Thank you, Vicar. I am the nephew. John Barton," a fat, bald man said in a high-pitched voice.

"A nice gathering. She must have been a popular woman," Peter answered.

"Where there's a will, there's a family," he answered. "See that fat man in the long coat? That is the family solicitor. Today, we all find out what Aunt Elsie has left us. She said the money wasn't to be released until she was in the ground."

"Well, I wish you luck," Peter answered as he noticed Mrs Barrie waiting by the gate.

"That grave is not deep enough," she said as he walked towards her. "Foxes are notorious for digging up the dead."

"With respect, Mrs Barrie, I don't think the foxes will want to eat cremated remains."

"Matters not. What if a child digs her up? What then?" she asked curmudgeonly.

"I will make sure I keep a look out for Burke and Hare," he answered.

"What will you do? Arrest them like you did me neighbour, poor Mr Jepson, on his way home from the Masonic?"

"Probably," he answered with a smile.

"And another thing," she went on. "Your footwear is highly inappropriate for a priest. Hiking boots do not look well under a cassock. They send mixed messages. They should be black shoes, patent if possible. I shall write to Bishop Riley for an opinion."

"Suitable footwear for a gravedigger? Do you go to church, Mrs Barrie?" he asked.

"When you get to my age, you go to church far more often than you would ever like. Dropping like flies. I wonder when it will be my turn. There will be no one at my funeral, as I have outlived them all. Don't get any ideas that you'll be doing the service. I want to be buried deep enough so nothing can dig me up. I doubt you have the strength to dig a grave that deep."

[42]
Dan Rosslyn

As Peter walked through the vicarage doorway, he could hear the telephone ringing. He hoped it was Mary. The thought of her calling filled him with a mix of pleasure and anxiety. All day, he had wondered who Daniel was and why a man should be taking his wife and children to the beach. Jealousy was his nemesis. It was kryptonite of the soul. There had always been a morsel of distrust in their relationship.

Peter walked to the telephone. He rehearsed his lines. First, he would ask how she was; enquire about the children, and then quietly ask what she had been doing, hoping she would give an explanation as to who Daniel was. Peter even thought he would ask her about Hazel Connor. Reluctantly, he reached for the phone.

"Hello. Peter Barnes."

"*Barney?*" Carol Manning said cheerfully. "*I need a favour. We are down on staff. Could you come in and work a four-midnight?*"

He thought for a moment. "You desperate?" he asked.

"*And some,*" she said. "*Any chance?*"

"Give me an hour," he answered. "Just back from a funeral."

"*You are a total star. I have to cover C and D Divisions with three officers. You will make four,*" she spoke, then paused. "*Word of warning. Derek Grant mentioned you in dispatches. You locked up a bloke called Jepson. Derek has suggested a transfer for you to a desk job. Nest of vipers.*"

Had enough of them in the Met. Let me know when you get in and we can meet up for a coffee."

Peter put the handset back in its cradle, got changed, and set off to work. As he passed the village pub, he saw Mrs Barrie waving her finger at the family solicitor. From the troubled look on her face, he could see all was not well with her. Peter smiled.

"Schadenfreude," he said to himself as he acknowledged the warm, smug feeling that came over him.

The outpost was empty when he unlocked the door and went inside. As usual, there was the crackle of the radio, but no usual chatter. Four officers to cover half of the North Riding was stretching the thin blue line to snapping point.

The white-painted walls looked less drab. The toilet-like paint had been decorated with information posters on the danger of New Age Travellers. It was a photo of a man with long hair and a waistcoat sat in an old Luton van. The writing underneath suggested that the government wanted names and information on anyone with long hair sleeping in a van. Every division had to supply statistics. The last line made him laugh. 'NATs are a fifth column of anarchists and need to be stopped.'

How could people living a different lifestyle be such a threat? Peter thought as he sat at the desk, logged on to the CAFS monitor, and scrolled through all the reported crimes and incidents for that day.

Thankfully, it had been a quiet morning. The only outstanding job was an overnight burglary from the records office at a Meredith and Co., a local solicitor. Scenes of crime had examined the break-in, but the senior partner had been in court all morning and wouldn't be back until three, so no one knew what, if anything, had been taken. The incident had been given to Peter to follow up that afternoon.

It was a job he didn't mind doing. A two-page crime report, some local inquiries, and doubtless C.I.D. would demand it wasn't their job.

Peter checked his in-tray. In a brown envelope was a returned blood form for Charles Jepson. It said that the man was four times over the legal limit to drive a car, the highest ever recorded in Yorkshire. Surely Derek Grant could not argue with that.

As he read the report, the radio crackled to life. *"Foxtrot-Papa from Delta-Sierra-Zero-Two."*

"Go ahead," Peter answered.

"Are you in the office?"

"Affirmative."

"See you in ten."

Peter knew the voice well. Dan Rosslyn was the detective inspector who covered D Division. Everyone called him *the silver fox*. His black, Walter Raleigh-style beard, salt and pepper hair, snappy dressing, and good looks gave him the appearance of a TV soap actor. Rosslyn was an articulate man with an interest in medieval history who kept his personal life to himself. Apart from that, all Peter knew of him was that he lived alone in a cottage next to a pub.

It was only a few minutes later that Peter heard a car pull up in the car park by the back door. Peter went outside. Dan Rosslyn sat in his brown Fiesta with the window down, taking the final drags from a cigarette that he then casually tossed from the window. He could see a large, black plastic dustbin in the back of the car.

"What you got in the back?" Peter asked as Rosslyn got out of the driver's seat and smoothed back his hair with his fingers.

"Republican arms cache. Found it up in Dalby," Rosslyn answered proudly. "Pistols, ammunition, and a pack of Semtex," Rosslyn said as he opened the hatchback and pulled out the dustbin. "Brought it here as it is more out of the way than Scarborough and I didn't fancy taking it that far. I just want to ring Catterick and get their opinion."

Peter stepped back. "Are you sure you should take it inside?" he asked.

"Well, I'm not going to leave it out here, am I?" Rosslyn laughed as he carried the bin towards the back door.

"Leave it in the car. You're not taking it into the nick," Peter insisted.

"Tail wagging the dog?" Rosslyn asked.

"Operation Satan Force," Peter answered. "Force procedure when dealing with explosives," Peter continued. "I went to the urban combat training last month. Leave it in the car and I will ring Catterick."

Rosslyn didn't argue. He looked as though he could suddenly see the mountain of paperwork that was about to fall on him. "Shit rolls downhill," was all he could say as he put the bin on the ground and stepped back.

"You are lucky to be alive," Peter said. "Provisionals usually place a hand grenade with the pin out. They jam it underneath so when the bin is pulled out, it explodes." Peter watched the colour drain from the face of the inspector.

"Are you serious?" he asked as he leant against the wall and lit a cigarette.

"All part of the training. I saw the demonstration. A couple of ounces of Semtex would take the roof off your car," Peter added, not knowing if it were true or not. "I'll ring Catterick."

"Thanks," Rosslyn muttered. "Put the kettle on?"

The call was made quickly. As Peter explained to the duty major what Rosslyn had done, he could hear the loud laughter in the background.

The advice was given with military firmness: *Evacuate the station. Set up a hundred-yard cordon. Await Bomb Disposal.*

Peter picked up the radio handset and took a deep breath.

"*Foxtrot-Papa* to all units and stations. *Foxtrot-Papa* is now code *Tango*. Bomb disposal on route. Hundred-yard cordon to be set up. No one to approach."

"*Foxtrot-Papa from Delta-Sierra-Zero-One. Landline now,*" Carol Manning's voice cut in as the phone immediately rang.

"PC Barnes," he answered.

"*What's happening?*" Manning asked as the force radio clattered in the background with panicked voices and sirens.

"Rosslyn has brought an IRA arms cache in a dustbin. Semtex and guns."

"*Dear God. Where is it?*"

"I told him to leave it in the car. He wanted to bring it into the station."

"*Where is he?*" she asked, her voice shrill and angry.

"Having a cigarette outside."

It was then Peter heard the call on the force radio.

"*XN to Foxtrot-Papa. Alpha-Romeo units coming towards you. Sending Tango units,*" the calm voice of the controller said.

"Did you hear that?" he asked Manning.

"*I am on my way.*"

[43]
Semtex

The explosion echoed through the forest. It shook the trees, and even from two hundred yards, the blast hit him in the chest like a fist. The low rumble moved slowly down the valley as a mushroom cloud rose majestically in the late evening sun.

"Grenade?" Peter asked the young army lieutenant who was now calmly winding in a long wire.

"From the sound, it was a grenade and Semtex. It's an industrial explosive. Military munitions sound harsher," the man answered in perfect received pronunciation.

"Booby trap?" he asked.

The officer leant against the back of the army Transit.

"The idiot who pulled that bin out of the ground is lucky to be alive. It was only because the hole had filled with water. The mud held the safety lever in place, so it didn't detonate. They had left a bar of Semtex next to it for good measure."

"Safe to approach the site?" Peter asked.

"I better go first," the man answered as he walked towards the site of the explosion winding the red wire onto its metal spool. "Typical place for an arms cache," he said, looking around the forest. "I wonder who they were planning to take out? In Ireland, they would always hide the guns near to where they were going to use them. Got any targets around here?"

Before Peter could answer, a car came up the forest track and pulled up behind the Transit. Carol Manning waved as she got out of the car.

"It's the boss," Peter said as she got nearer.

"How did it go?" she asked.

"All sorted, ma'am," the officer said politely. "Were you the inspector that pulled out the bin?"

"Do I look stupid?" she asked as the three of them began to laugh. "You can have the nick back now. All the explosives have been taken care of. Rosslyn has gone home."

"Job to do," the soldier said as he walked up the forest path, leaving Peter and Manning alone.

"Is Rosslyn okay?" Peter asked. "He is a very lucky man."

"I think he realised how lucky he was when they found the Semtex in the bin had been attached to a rocker switch. God knows why it didn't go off. How are you?" she asked. "Hell of an afternoon."

"I got the blood results back for Jepson. The man was four times over. If found guilty, he will lose his licence for a couple of years or more. He was convicted for the same two years ago in Cornwall when he was on holiday. He had only got his licence back a week before he got nicked."

"Have you got the paperwork?" she asked.

"It's in the car. I didn't want to leave it in my tray," Peter answered.

"Let me take it to prosecutions. I will deliver it by hand," Manning answered. "Better safe than sorry."

"I was warned that I would be walking the streets of Selby for nicking Jepson."

"Have you ever considered a complaint?" she asked.

"Pointless," he replied. "Hoping they move on."

"When I was a young officer, before I was married, my shift sergeant made a pass at me. I said nothing. Every night shift, he would always want to double-crew with me. Every night, he would touch my leg and suggest we drove somewhere dark."

"Did you complain about him?" he asked.

"No. I thought he would lose interest."

"Did it stop?"

"Yes. After six weeks of it, I got a friend to ring his wife. She told her he was having an affair with me. His wife made him move stations. I was promoted to sergeant and then inspector. A year later, I was chief inspector. I was his boss and made his life hell. He transferred out to Norfolk," Manning smiled. "When my husband died, I took a cut in rank to come here. It was worth it."

"I am considering taking the desk job," he said reluctantly. "It just might make things easier."

"Why not get promoted? I had a look on the system. You passed your exam and yet you didn't put in for promotion."

"I saw what it did to some people, and anyway, I like being out here."

Manning looked around her. The evening wind sped through the trees, blowing away the smoke from the detonation.

"One of the reasons I came back to Yorkshire. In London, you forget what it is like to stand in a forest," Manning said as she watched a hawk making lazy circles in the sky. "You could almost get me to believe in God looking at all this."

"Evolution or intelligent design?" Peter asked.

"Myth or legend?" she answered. "By the way," she went on quickly before he could reply. "Mr Meredith rang in to ask when someone was going to call about his burglary. I noticed that you were allocated the job. I told him you would call in tomorrow."

"Tomorrow? I am on a rest day."

She laughed. "That was the other thing I was going to ask you. Any chance of you working your rest day?"

[44]
Meredith & Co

The door to the solicitor's office was open. An old iron key was twisted in the lock. Hanging from it was a leather fob. The brass door plate was stained with finger marks and had not been cleaned for some time.

James Meredith sat behind a kneehole desk that was stacked with files and tomes on law. Casually, he plucked a long, white hair from his nostril and placed it on the desk. Hearing the footsteps on the stairs, he sat back in his leather chair and waited.

"Come in, Constable," he said as, through the gap in the door, he saw the shadow cross the hall. "I hear that you have had your hands full."

Peter stepped inside the untidy office. The wood-panelled walls gave it a Dickensian glow, as if Ebenezer himself could be sat at the desk. A stack of papers littered the floor, an overcoat was thrown in the corner, and three bags of shopping were stacked behind the door. Meredith was a spindly, spider-like man with a bush of thick, black hair that topped a wrinkled, thin face. The black tie and waistcoat he had on were splattered here and there with the remains of his breakfast.

"Sorry for the delay," Peter answered. "Quite an unusual time yesterday."

"I feel I have got you here under false pretences. The villains didn't take a thing," Meredith said as he stood up and shook the officer's hand in welcome. "I am sure you have better things to be doing."

"I am glad they took nothing, but I would like to know why they broke in," he answered.

"That will be forever a mystery," Meredith answered. "We never keep money here overnight and the documents are worthless. The store they broke into contains paperwork from many years ago."

"I have made some local inquiries, and no one was seen. Perhaps we will get some forensic evidence."

"I don't hold out any hope," Meredith stopped for a moment. "I hear that apart from your police duties, you are the priest at St Walstan's. An interesting combination."

"News travels fast," he answered.

"I am a friend of Amber Hudson. She speaks very highly of you. I had dinner there last night."

"When I visited her, I was given a thrilling lift home in her Rolls Royce," Peter laughed.

"You have inherited probably one of the most troubled parishes in the diocese. I am not a churchman but have watched the comings and goings of St Walstan's with much interest. My family used to look after the legal matters for the Seagrave family, who held the gift of the title. You must be made of strong stuff."

"I hope so," Peter answered. "Have the Seagraves died out?"

"That I cannot say. My father dealt with the transfer of the estate into a trust. Again, another tragedy of your parish. There are rumours he is dead. The last I heard of Magnus Seagrave, he was living in a village on the Moray Firth. At one time he was a good friend of my father. They shared the same lodge. Then they fell out. A petty squabble that was never resolved."

"How old would Seagrave be now?"

"If he is alive, Magnus will not be a day over eighty. My father said that he became a shadow of a man when his wife went off. He was constantly worried. Strangely, we were given instructions by the trust not to sell off the estate until a few years ago. It was a time I remember well. We oversaw the inspections and repairs. Grenville's did the work. My father was glad to be shot of the account."

"Do you have an address for the trust?" Peter asked.

"Are you asking as a police officer or a priest?" Meredith smiled liked a contented otter. "A strange question and not one that I should answer. It's all a matter of client confidentiality."

"I was just interested. The Seagraves were important in the history of the parish, and I was going to invite the trust to the blessing of the restored well," Peter answered, thinking quickly.

"My goodness," Meredith said in surprise. "You have restored St Walstan's well? I remember that from when I was a boy. My grandmother would get a flask of well water and make some tea with it every Christmas. She swore by it and said it protected her from bronchitis."

"My predecessor had it bricked up. He believed it to be a conduit of evil forces," Peter answered.

"Yes, I know all about him. A hard act to follow. In confidence, he asked me to handle his divorce. I made an excuse that I was too busy. The truth of it was that with what Amber had told me, I would have been on the side of his poor wife."

"I fully understand," Peter answered.

"That is the thing about the parish. It has ended the marriage of every priest who has been there. Are you married?"

[45]
Funeral

The handful of people that had been in the church now stood by the porch in the late afternoon sun. A large green and silver dragonfly buzzed back and forth, as if it had flown out of a carboniferous swamp. Peter watched as it danced over the heads of the mourners and then darted upwards, disappearing over the trees.

There was something about the funeral that saddened his heart. There had been no real grief, no remorse, and no sadness. It was as if those who had come were there out of duty, rather than love or friendship. They were mainly fellow drinkers from the pub. The only person to show any sign of mourning was Hannah Bateson, a small, shrew-like woman who, like her dead brother, appeared to be alone in life.

The funeral of someone who committed suicide was never easy. People always wanted answers, and often there were never any to give. Peter had dealt with twenty suicides since joining the police force. Each one had been a tragedy for those left behind. He had once dragged a man from an exhaust-filled car and tried to give him mouth-to-mouth. The fumes coming from within the man made him feel sick. A doctor had arrived at the scene and told him to stop. Peter looked up. He stared at the woman on the doorstep and nodded to the doctor. It was then that the doctor realised that what Peter was doing was for the sake of the wife.

The doctor and copper worked on the man until the ambulance arrived. Both knew what they did was futile. The paramedics picked the body from the driveway, placing an oxygen mask on a man who was already dead, just for the sake of the living.

As the doctor walked away, Peter was left to tell the woman the news she did not want to hear. She crumpled into his arms, thanking him for trying to save her husband.

Peter had given the eulogy with the memories that Hannah had given to him and embellished it with the bits and pieces he had picked out from conversations with Stella and Bruce. His widow wouldn't speak to him. All she would say is that he got what he deserved.

Now, Bridget Bateson stood alone, pretending to read the names on the gravestones. Cutting through the people, Peter walked towards her and put a hand on her shoulder. "I am glad that you came," he said softly. "It means a lot."

"Really?" she asked. "I am only here to make sure he is dead."

"I can assure you he is," Peter replied. "I am sorry that you feel that way."

"Life is full of surprises," she said as tears began to roll down her face. "We were happy at first, and then I found out he had a cocaine habit. He said it was so that he could work the long hours and pay for everything. I was his country wife. Alone through the week, and housekeeper and cook at the weekends. In all honesty, I was not a good wife, or a loyal one, but I suspect that you probably know all about that, considering the people here today."

"I don't listen to gossip," he answered.

"It's not gossip. All perfectly true. I can't deny it. Yet I don't think I should be blamed for it. George had his dalliances in London and paid for them. I got mine for free."

"What will you do now?" Peter asked, hoping to change the conversation.

"Move back into Orchard House for a while. Give my son a settled life. I was going to ask if you would come and pray in the room where it happened. I am superstitious like that."

"Of course. Will you be moving in alone?"

"Simon? My now ex-partner? He is long gone. I have my son and that is all I want."

"I am sorry that has happened," he said.

"He was a leech. I should have realised that when we met. George did try to warn me, but I didn't listen. Simon fancied himself as a stockbroker. I was just a means of information. When I left George, Simon was horrified. He wanted me in the house so he could get insider information. Then it was too late. I moved in with him and realised I had made a big mistake."

"Why didn't you go back to George?"

"I am too stubborn. I will never admit to making a mistake."

"He would have taken you back."

"I know that now, but it's too late. Life is like that. He's dead, and no matter how angry I feel towards him, I wish it had never happened."

"Do you fancy a drink in the pub, Bridget?" Stella interrupted, sensing the situation. "We are all going," she said as she turned to Peter before continuing. "Are you going to join us?"

Peter didn't hesitate. He nodded in agreement. "I'll go if you will," he said to Bridget.

"I don't know," she hesitated.

"Come on, Bridget," Stella said as she took hold of her hand. "We would love you to be there."

Peter left his robes in the church and followed the last of the mourners to the pub. The double tree hung its branches, draped heavily with summer leaves that showed the first signs of change. Stella stood underneath the tree with a drink in hand. Her long, black dress etched the shape of her legs as she leant back against the trunk.

"You should be a priest," he said as he walked into the shade. "It was a good idea to invite Bridget. Where is she?"

"Bruce took her to the bar. She needs a beer to lighten up," Stella answered. "Are you getting one?"

"Not yet. If I drink at this time of day, I will soon be asleep."

"Lightweight," she replied with a smile.

"I take it you are not driving home?" he asked as he took the glass of wine from her hand and took a sip.

"Bruce is the designated driver. I wouldn't want you coming after me."

"I don't think I could catch you," Peter answered. "Bridget has some difficult times ahead."

"She will get through. Bridget was married to George, and that would take nerves of steel," Stella answered. "He could be a difficult man."

"Did you know him well?"

"Just from the pub," she answered. "Life and soul of the party."

"Why do you think he did it?" Peter asked as he watched the strap of her dress slip from her shoulders.

Stella smiled. She had seen that look before and realised he was no different from every other man who had looked at her in that way.

"You can never tell what goes through a man's mind," she answered. "Sometimes life is too difficult for some people to cope with. We are fragile souls that shouldn't live the lives we do. We marry the wrong people, do the wrong jobs, and live in the wrong houses. Then we are surprised when it all goes wrong." Stella watched as he swallowed deeply.

"But that is the world we live in," he answered, stepping from one foot to the other.

"It doesn't have to be. We can change our lives. Leave when a relationship goes bad. Change our jobs. Move to the place we feel at home in. I woke up one morning and realised the man I was with was bad for me. I left that day. No hard feelings. I told him straight that it would destroy us both if I stayed. He sighed the biggest sigh of relief, as he felt the same but didn't want to say so. Our lives changed for the better that day."

"You can't just walk out of a marriage. I vowed to stay married until I died. That is the meaning of Christian marriage. Lifelong togetherness."

"Are you happy in your marriage?" she asked.

Peter hesitated. It was a question he had never asked himself. "I am very content," he said.

"Content is not happy," she answered quickly.

"Happiness is transitory. It can be changed by the weather. Contentment is something different."

"That is a sentence from a sermon. It may fool your Sunday morning followers, but it doesn't fool me. You can be honest, Peter. This isn't holy ground. Your God isn't listening."

"I am in the right marriage, the right job, and the right place. God brought me here." He paused momentarily. "The church owns this land and I have asked Bishop Riley to consecrate it. Esther Corbridge is buried beneath our feet. I checked the parish registers, and she was baptised in St Walston's. I must make things right."

Stella gripped the stem of her glass and fought the urge to throw the wine in his face. Her ancestor lay beneath their feet, murdered by the priest. Now, another priest offered solace, wanting to make the ground holy by the scattering of water and salt, as if it would recompense the death. "And it will make things right? Atone for the murder?"

"Something must be done. I pass this tree every day and it is a constant reminder of what Seagrave did," Peter answered trying to remain calm. "As you say, there is a blight on this parish. It has to change."

"So, blessing the ground will make things right?" she asked. "Typical Christian attitude. Steal all the Pagan festivals and build your churches on our sites. Is your magic better than mine?"

[46]
Summer Fox

The late afternoon alfresco sleep was broken by the jagged sound of the telephone. Peter got up from the deckchair and shook the lingering images from his mind. It had been a disjointed dream. The type that jumps from scene to scene, and intertwined within it was that he had lost his trousers and still had to do traffic control at the crossroads in Malton on bank holiday Monday. Peter was thankful to wake. His last remembrance was that of Mary, stood by the side of the road with the children in the pram. An obvious look of discontent was etched on her face as she raised a disapproving brow.

"St Waltan's Vicarage," he said as he picked up the handset.

"*Hi, Peter. It's me,*" Mary answered. "*It's been a while… sorry.*"

"How are the children? When are you back?" Peter said as he noted the sombre tone of her voice that was a harbinger of what she would say next.

"*Listen. Things are a bit difficult here. I need to stay longer. Are you okay with that?*"

"How is your mum?"

"*Fine. Doing well,*" Mary said with a sigh, as if she searched for the right words.

"I rang and your father said you had gone to the beach. How was it?"

"*Good. A couple of hours out at Porthtowan with the children,*" she answered without mention of who had taken her.

Peter fought to keep jealousy out of his voice. It was a battle he quickly lost.

"Who is Daniel?"

"*Daniel?*" she asked, buying time. "*He's...*" she paused, "*the next-door neighbour; he gave us a lift to the beach. He was going that way.*"

"Your father said it was an outing."

"*My God,*" she snapped. "*What are you trying to say?*"

"Nothing," he drew breath. "Daniel was thrown into the conversation by your father. Just wondered why he was taking my wife and children to the beach."

"*He took me because I didn't want to go on my own. I had been looking after my parents and needed a break.*"

"Are you coming home?" he asked.

"*That is not my home. We have rented our home out, remember?*" she snapped.

"A home is where we are," Peter said, hoping to calm her down.

"*I lost my home when you got that job. The children were uprooted and lost their friends. You are so selfish. You and that bloody God of yours. I don't know if I want to come back.*"

"What do you mean?" he gasped in shock. "Abigail starts school in September."

"*There is a school here. A Steiner school. My dad says he will pay.*"

"You have had that conversation?" he asked in surprise. "What are you trying to say?"

"*I think we need some time apart. I need to think things through,*" Mary said, her voice on the edge of tears. "*I need space.*" The words were simple. Three short syllables. The struggling thoughts behind them were complex, multifaceted, undefined, and unspoken.

"We need to talk. Face to face. It's important. Our marriage."

"*I don't want to talk. I have had a lot of time to think,*" Mary demanded.

Peter thought for a while as he stared through the window and watched the fox as it hunted in the summer hedgerow. All the while, Mary spoke, repeating her need for space and what was right for the children. It was obvious that the time apart that she wanted would go on and on as she slowly drifted further away from him.

Perhaps, he thought, it was his fault. The years of working all hours and studying at theological college had pulled them apart. He knew they had lost the closeness they once had. Laughter had been replaced by stilted conversations as they both became expert walkers on broken glass.

Mary would never back down and always pushed for an argument. Peter would meet her anger with silence, in the belief that least said, soonest mended. There had been times of respite, usually after several glasses of wine, when life didn't seem so bad. These were short-lived, and Mary would soon retreat into her own world.

"Are you trying to say you want a divorce?" he asked.

There was a long silence.

"*It's not a word I like,*" she answered. "*I just need to sort out my parents without the stress of worrying that I am not the good wife.*"

"I told you to take as long as you wanted. I am not pressuring you to come back."

"*It's there. The elephant in the room. Every time I look at my ring finger. A constant reminder that my husband is miles away.*"

"Can I speak to the children? I haven't heard from them in ages," he asked.

"*They are next door. With Daniel.*"

[47]
Wisteria

The shower finally began to run cold. Peter watched the water cascade over his face and down the tiled walls of the bathroom. He could hear the ancient plumbing rattle and moan as it tried to refill the copper water tank in the attic. Throughout, he could think of nothing else but Mary and the children. The conversation had come as a complete surprise, and now it twisted in his stomach.

Peter knew he could do nothing. Mary was a woman who would never change her mind.

She wanted space, and nothing he could say or do would alter that.

Stepping from the shower, he dried himself and then dressed quickly. Within half an hour, he was sat in his car. In his hand, he looked at the gilded invitation to Bishop's garden party. It was an event he had been to many times.

Gordon Riley invited all the clergy in his diocese, he even had his own marquee in case of rain. The bishop would make sure that he spoke to everyone. Each priest was given two minutes of his time. In his head, they were divided into friends, terrorists, and enemies. Riley called it *the management of change.*

Friends could be trusted, as they were absolutely and sycophantically loyal. He knew they expected that loyalty be repaid with favours, but he didn't mind. They each had a yellow file that contained particulars of their lives. Riley would always help them. After all, it was his duty.

Enemies were to be kept close and spied upon by his friends. Riley kept a red file for each priest. It had every scrap of information about what they did and did not do. He would use the information against them if they ever stepped out of line.

Terrorists on the other hand had to be routed out one by one and evicted from the diocese, with a good reference to make sure they went. These priests could never be trusted. They ran with the fox and the hounds. Each was given a blue file. Riley found that terrorists were always ready to inform on any priest with a peculiar vice or opinion. They were his useful idiots.

Set amongst the neat lawns and roses, his garden party was an ideal opportunity to press flesh and gauge the level of discontent within his diocese. Riley tried to be all things to all people, but he knew in so many ways that he failed. There was upset within the ranks. Some priests felt overlooked for the plum jobs. Others were bitter at the state of their houses and blamed Riley for inaction, even though they knew his hands were tied by lack of finances.

It took an hour for Peter to drive to the party. The three-storey, Georgian house was at the end of the square in the old part of town. It formed part of the façade of ancient houses made of Tudor brick. A high wall and a grass verge separated it from the road.

As he got out of the car, he could hear raised voices in the garden beyond. At this, Peter was overwhelmed with the feeling that he was an imposter. If there were those within the police that didn't want a priest in their midst, then there were priests who didn't want a copper in theirs.

Peter was one of the first priests that had trained part time. He knew there would be several clergymen at the party who would make it very clear that they believed he was a second-class priest.

Peter opened the carved wooden gate and stepped into the garden. It was a gathering of men. Apart from a handful, all were approaching retirement age, overweight, and dressed in clerical garb. In the corner of the garden, standing in the fading evening sun, was a tight gathering of grumbling black shirts. Peter knew they were the traditionalists who didn't want women priests. Nor did they want part-time priests. As they saw him walk towards them, they all turned away.

"Peter," Bishop Riley said as he broke away from a small huddle of balding men that he was entertaining with his stories of a recent fishing trip. He was wearing a red clerical shirt with a tight collar that dug into his double chin. "I am so glad you could come. No crime busting tonight?"

"Not until later," he answered with a smile.

"All well in the force?"

"So far, so good. The parish is going well, and thank you for coming to hallow the ground."

"I knew that you would be the man to sort it out. I did mention it to Frank Green, but he just wanted to chop the tree down. You have a thick skin and broad shoulders. Just the man needed for that parish."

"It's not a bad place. Different to what I expected," he answered.

"I had a letter from Martha Storr. She has resigned from being a reader and is moving away. I believe she is going to train as a pastor for a charismatic church. She will be happy there," Riley smiled at Peter and put a hand on his shoulder.

"I am relieved. Frank is a powerful man; a heavy shepherd."

"I think they call it gaslighting," Riley replied as he led Peter by the arm away from the party. "Let me show you the wisteria. I have had a surprise second bloom that came overnight before I was going to summer prune."

"Beautiful," he answered. "It is the same colour as one in my parish."

"The Seagrave's old house?" he answered. "This is grown from a cutting from there. I bought it at a summer sale many years ago."

"Did you ever come across a priest called Albert Shepherd?" Peter asked.

"My goodness, Peter," Riley laughed. "You sound like a copper."

"Sorry."

"Funnily enough, I knew him when I was in the first year of my curacy," Riley went on, knowing what the next question would be. "He was similar to Frank Green. A very charismatic man and one for the ladies. The bishop at the time made it quite clear it was a relief he went off. So, what is your interest in Bertie?"

"There is no trace of the man. Missing people usually turn up somewhere."

"I remember it well. One of the great mysteries of the diocese. The bishop was livid. It was even covered in the newspapers. Bertie's wife was adamant he had run off with one of his women."

"One?" Peter asked.

Riley took out a metal comb and slowly ran it through his grey hair, pushing it away from his face. "Why do I feel I am being interviewed by the police?"

"Sorry. Just tying up loose ends," Peter answered.

"Perhaps loose ends should be left that way." Riley paused for a moment. "I am passing your way in a couple of weeks. Let's go for a walk together."

[48]
Dogging

The journey to the police station was quicker than expected. The road across Fylingdales Moor was empty. Peter watched as the sun began to set over Bransdale. He left the thoughts of the party far behind, taking the chance to leave early. He was glad that the bishop had not asked about Mary. Before he could, Peter made excuses that he was due at work earlier than he really was. The less time he had to take off his card, the better. It would be a quick shift, nine until one, and then home. Friday could sometimes be busy, especially on a warm summer's night when there was no rain to rush the drunks away.

The one thing Peter liked about being part time was the lack of paperwork. The fewer people he locked up, the less forms he had to fill out. He knew that some of the sergeants used him as a filler. They had already asked him to cover for sick leave and tried to make him squeeze in an extra shift each week. So far, he had managed to resist, but he knew that doing the two roles could not be sustained forever.

The pull on both sides was getting stronger. None of his superiors in the police could understand his role as a priest. Peter knew from the brief conversations he had with them that they felt slightly intimidated. It was as if they knew he answered to a higher power other than the chief constable.

As he dropped down from the Hole of Horcum, he knew that something in his life would have to give. His marriage was hanging by a thread, and forces within the police were wanting him gone. Peter wondered if this was the price he would have to pay.

Jehovah Jireh, the Lord who provides, usually opened a window before he closed a door. So far, since taking on the parish, all the doors in his life appeared to be being slammed in his face, and the windows painted shut.

As usual, when he got to the police station, it was empty. There was a note pinned to the monitor of the computer telling him that everyone was in Malton and he had the town to himself.

Peter rang control and checked in as he looked through all the reported crimes and incidents of the day. Everything had been written off. It had been a quiet day with only three jobs on the system. It was an omen of what was to come—quiet days were always followed by busy nights.

Getting in the patrol car, Peter toured the town. It was one long street with a couple of pubs, four charity shops, a church at the top, and a railway station at the bottom. At both ends was a fish and chip shop. The street was empty and the pubs looked quiet. Perhaps he was wrong. The night might be quiet after all. There was nothing on the car radio, just the summer static and the overlap of a foreign trawler far out at sea using the same bandwidth.

As day turned to night, Peter checked some of the outlying villages and, like the town, found them sleepily empty. He laughed to himself, wondering if the world had been raptured and only he had been left behind. The thought that God could take the chosen to Heaven and leave him behind made him smile. It was not a concept he had thought often about. The Book of Revelation was not one of his favourites. Peter left all the end-time stuff to others. He knew he only had enough faith for the day he was in rather than the future.

There were no signs of the Four Horsemen of the Apocalypse on the road to Ellerburn. A local priest had told him that he had seen an angel at the trout lake there, but Peter admitted that he had never had a supernatural experience.

When he was younger, he had gone to every place that he was told was haunted. Peter would stay there overnight, waiting to catch the ghost and yet, he never saw or felt a single thing. It was as if he was spiritually blind to everything other than the world he lived in.

Fellow priests told him about being filled with the Holy Spirit and feeling overwhelmed by the joy of God. All he had experienced was a slight warming of the heart that he thought was indigestion. Even so, he had faith. It was simple and childlike, and he was content with that, knowing only God could change it. It was faith based on the hope that death was not the end to life and that God could, in some way, change him for the better.

There was no place in his theology for a God that answered every prayer. He knew that wasn't the way it worked. Peter had a list of requests that he had no answer for. Perhaps they were selfish or fickle. However, he would often pray for something that had already happened, believing that a God who stood outside time could somehow influence the event for the better. *After all*, he thought, *it was up to God.*

"Thy will be done," he found himself muttering as a blue Ford Escort sped up the hill. Instinctively, he followed. The car had four occupants and was travelling too fast for the road. "*Foxtrot-Papa-Three-Five to Control.*"

"*Go ahead,*" the operator answered.

"Vehicle check. Blue Ford Escort. Forest Drive."

Peter gave the registration number and waited for a reply.

"*No trace suspect or stolen. Keeper comes from Scarborough.*"

He knew that Forest Drive was a back road used by drunk drivers to avoid being stopped. The Escort was heading in that direction and getting faster. Accelerating, Peter tried to keep pace. The driver ahead had obviously realised he was being followed and was trying to put tarmac between them.

With a flick of a switch, Peter put on the blue top lights and flashed the main beam. It was as if he had given the car ahead an invitation to race.

"Vehicle failed to stop," Peter shouted into the handset as he geared down and pushed his foot on the accelerator. "Roads clear, no traffic, permission to pursue?"

There was a brief pause.

"*Permission granted,*" Carol Manning answered. "*All units to assist. Forest Drive.*"

The radio crackled to life as cars across the division responded. It was as if everyone wanted in on the chase.

"*K-Nine to Three-Five. I am fifteen minutes away, coming from Langdale End. Bruno wants a run, so don't lock them up before I get there.*"

"Ten-Four," he answered, knowing that Gary Webb and his dog Bruno would be all he needed if the car decamped in the forest. The last time he had met Bruno, the Alsatian had cornered him in the office and had not let him get away until Gary gave the nod. Peter had never seen such a big dog. It was more like a rhino with a scarred face where a knifeman had slashed it during a fight. Bruno was one of the most aggressive dogs in the county and would never back down. It could track for miles and never wanted to give up. "Vehicle on Forest Drive. Seven-zero miles per hour. No traffic. Road conditions good."

Peter could see the car gaining on him. He could never understand why he had to drive underpowered town cars when the bosses had the high-performance vehicles that sat outside Malton Police Station and were only used for driving back and forth to headquarters.

As he approached the toll booth to the Forest Drive, he saw the car ahead disappear into the night. Peter knew that once out of sight, they could pull off the road onto any of the tracks and he would lose them.

"*Location?*" Manning asked.

"Toll booth towards Dalby village. Vehicle out of sight," he answered.

"*Received. K-Nine, location?*" she asked.

Gary Webb didn't answer. Peter knew that he would only call up when he was minutes away, in case someone in the fleeing car was using a scanner and listening in.

"*No signal at Langdale,*" a voice chipped in as Peter took the brow of the hill, the tyres of the car leaving the road.

Ahead, he could see the brake lights and then headlights of the Escort. The vehicle spun in the road, coming to an abrupt stop as the front offside tyre punctured. The doors to the car burst open. Four teenagers jumped out, dressed in dinner suits and black bow ties, and ran into the dark woods.

"Decamp, half a mile from Dalby village. Four occupants. Male. White. Teens. Dinner suits. Into the woods," Peter said before he threw the handset onto the passenger seat, stopped the car, and set the brake.

"*Five minutes,*" Gary Webb shouted, the noise of Bruno barking in the back of his van almost drowning out his voice. "*Tell them I'm coming. Bruno's already up for this one.*"

Peter didn't answer. He switched off the engine and got out of the car. In the forest, he could hear the trampling of sticks and the occasional moan. The stars glistened above him. The forest was still. Far away, he could hear a lorry along Scarborough Road. He smiled. *Why wait for Gary Webb*, he thought to himself.

"Police dog handler. Come out of the woods or I will send the dog in. You have one minute," Peter shouted, then stuck his head back into the police car and began to bark like a mad dog with a sore throat. It was something he had never done before but thought it was worth a try. In the dark of night, lit only by blue flashing lights and a bright moon, he had no other way of getting them to come out of the trees.

Within the minute, a dark shadow emerged from the forest with hands above its head.

"Don't send your dog in. I give up," the muddy teen said as he walked towards the flashing lights, his bow tie hanging limply from his shirt.

"You the driver?" Peter asked.

"Yes," he answered. "Where are your mates?"

"I was alone. There is no one else."

"Yeah. I believe you."

After several stark questions, Peter had the truth. The driver had panicked and made off. The lad insisted they had tried to stop him.

Peter handcuffed the teen.

"Where's the dog?" the lad asked as Peter was about to put him into the back of the car.

"Woof," Peter answered, trying not to laugh.

"He doesn't have a dog. He's on his own," the lad shouted to warn his friends, the words echoing around the forest.

"Why did you do that?" Peter asked.

"Because you are a bloody cheat. I thought you had a dog."

Suddenly, the headlights of the dog van lit the other side of the valley. It wasn't long before Gary Webb arrived.

"Are they still in there?" he asked as he got out of the van.

"Got one, three outstanding," Peter answered as Webb looked at the lad in the back of the van and started to laugh.

"Very well-dressed villains you get out here," he answered.

"Where have you been?" Webb asked the lad.

"Cricket club summer dinner," he answered sheepishly.

"Well, son, your friends are going to meet Bruno," Webb said, walking back to his van as if a gunslinger waiting for a fight.

"Is he in a good mood?" Peter asked.

"Bruno has been fed up all week. He keeps looking at me as if I am his next meal."

"Right," Peter answered as he got back in his patrol car and shut the door.

"Why you got in?" the lad in the back asked.

"You will see in a minute."

Webb opened the back door of his van and in the dimmed headlamps, a shadow moved slowly into the road. Standing between the two vehicles was a large, long-haired dog. It had the appearance of a red-eyed wolf. Its tongue hung from the side of its mouth as the beast slowly licked its lips.

"My God. What the hell is that?" the lad asked.

"That is Bruno," Peter answered.

"Police dog handler. You have two minutes to come out before I put the dog in," Webb shouted into the silent darkness.

The minutes passed slowly. Bruno stood silently next to his handler. It was as if the dog knew that it would be best to be quiet.

"What's he doing?" the lad asked.

"Giving them time to come out. If they don't, he will send Bruno to find them."

Webb bent down and stroked the dog. "You know what to do, fella. Go get them."

It was as if the dog suddenly grew in size. Bruno shook with excitement and then leapt from the road, with Webb close behind. Dog and man vanished into the forest.

"I hope for their sake they don't try to run," Peter said as he got out of the car, taking the handheld searchlight from the boot and scanning the trees with the instant daylight.

It was then that he heard the first scream as Bruno found his victim.

"Walk to the light," Webb shouted as a dark-haired teenager in a ripped dinner suit got to his feet and tried to back away from Bruno. "Last chance for anyone else. Make yourself known or the dog will have you."

Instantly, two lads stood up in the undergrowth, hands covering their groins as Bruno growled. Their rented dinner suits were covered in mud and vegetation.

"We give up," the taller one shouted as his companion cowered at his side, fearful the dog would attack.

"Go to the car," Webb ordered as he slipped the snarling Bruno on a short leash.

The three men walked towards the searchlight. Each held his hands above his head.

Their muddied faces were smeared with tears of fear.

"Who is the driver?" Peter asked.

"Me," the taller lad said.
"Your car?"
"No…" the lad hesitated. "We borrowed it."

[49]
Hunt

The quick changeover from the night before had gone faster than Peter had expected. One moment he was resting his head on the pillow, and the next he was listening to the bedside alarm shouting for him to get up. His first thought was the deep regret of agreeing to work an extra day. For a moment, he thought about ringing in sick, but couldn't dream up a good excuse.

The joyriders of the night before had all been bailed. They had borrowed the car from a friend and the driver had been insured. He was borderline on breath alcohol and had opted for a blood test. Peter hoped he it would come back negative. They were decent lads who panicked. The driver had made off because he thought he was not insured. After a little digging, Peter found out the lad's own insurance covered him to drive.

It was only the making off from police that the inspector bailed them for. Peter knew that would go nowhere. The driver had learnt his lesson, and a criminal offence wouldn't do his chances any good.

Saturday usually was a quiet day. As he parked his car outside the station, he could see that Carol Manning was already there.

"Morning," he said as he walked in through the back doorway.

"Coffee and a doughnut," she answered as she turned from the computer monitor. "Is your sermon done for tomorrow? It looks like we could be in for a long day."

"What's happening?" Peter asked as he took off his jacket.

"The Upper Dale Hunt has decided to go cubbing before the season starts to get away from the sabs."

"It's a bit early for that. They usually wait until late August."

"What is cubbing?" she asked.

"The hunt goes out to train their hounds to catch foxes. They usually surround a patch of woodland where they know there are fox cubs and send the hounds in."

"Sounds barbaric," she replied with a grimace on her face.

"Not everyone's cup of tea, but this is the country. How did you find out?"

"We had an anonymous call. She asked to leave a message for you that it was happening. She said she was a hunt saboteur and that you would know why she rang in. Any ideas?"

"Yes. She is no threat. Always a peaceful protest. Her and her husband. He can run as fast as a horse. Never any bother."

"Why did she call it in?"

"Protection. She will be going on her own. Her husband will be working. Fox hunters can sometimes get a bit physical with protesters around here, especially the hunt followers."

"I have put the division on standby."

"Let me go and have a look and I will call in if I need any backup."

"Are you sure?" she asked. "I have never policed a fox hunt before. Not something you have to do in Islington."

Peter drank the coffee and left the doughnut. An hour later he was ten miles north of the town at the junction of two roads that headed out across the moor. A long copse of oak and sycamore trees followed the road, falling away down the slight incline until it met the stream. Several horseboxes and mud-covered, four-by-fours were parked on the verge.

A crowd of twenty people were gathered around three horsemen, each dressed in tweed jackets, riding hats, and jodhpurs. A gaggle of foxhounds blocked the grit road. They barked, howled, and bounded as if they knew what was to come. A solitary woman stood on the other side of the road carrying a placard. Her curled, blonde hair blew in the breeze.

Carry Johnson was his informant. A thirty-something ardent vegetarian and animal rights campaigner who was prepared to take on the hunt.

Peter got out of the patrol car. He could smell the scent of the faraway heather. As he walked down the road, a middle-aged man on a seventeen-hand Dutch warmblood horse turned towards him.

"My man!" he shouted as he spurred the horse towards him. "Get rid of that bloody woman."

Peter looked around to see if the man was talking to him. "Sorry, are you talking to me?" Peter asked.

"Of course I am. Who the bloody hell is there around here?" the man shouted.

"I thought there must be one of your dogs around here."

"Do you know who I am?" the man asked as he slapped his crop against his riding boot.

"No," Peter answered.

"I know the chief constable."

"He retired. Hasn't been replaced."

"Get rid of that sab," the man shouted, pointing to Carry Johnson as spittle spewed from his mouth.

"No. She has every right to protest."

"What is your name?"

"Reverend Peter Barnes. What's yours?"

"Bugger off," the man answered as he pulled the sweating horse around and rode off. "You'll regret that, you cocky sod. I thought coppers were supposed to help the law abiding?"

"We are. She has done nothing wrong."

The rider pulled up his horse and turned the beast around as its metal shoes slipped on the surface of the road.

"Nothing wrong?" the man shouted as the horse rose on its hind legs. "She is a bloody nuisance, and I can't be responsible if anything happens to her."

"But I can," Peter shouted back. "She has every right in the world to be here."

"Bugger you. Stupid little man."

"One more comment like that and I will lock you up for a breach of the peace."

The horseman looked at Peter, took a deep breath, and then spat on the ground.

Carry Johnson walked towards him. She was a small woman in her early thirties, wrapped in an oversized jacket and wellington boots.

"I didn't know if you were on duty," she said as she adjusted her red beret.

"I got your message. Why are they cubbing so early?" he asked.

"Don't want to get stabbed. Terrier men have been in there for hours. They will be blocking up the holes in the hope the cubs make a run for it," she answered anxiously.

"Have you been here long?"

"I came first thing. When I saw them, I went to the phone box and rang it in. They shouldn't be allowed."

"Have they said anything to you?" he asked.

"Just the usual. Water off a duck's back."

Peter could see that her hand was shaking. Her eyes flickered back and forth. "You should never come out alone. It's too dangerous."

"There will be more of us the next time. A group is coming up from London. They are going to disrupt the grouse shoot at the same time."

"How many?"

"A couple of hundred. Twelfth of August, a national day of action," Carry hesitated. "Don't drop me in it. I am only telling you because I don't like some of the things they do. I am not one for violence and these people are edging for a fight. The hunt won't stand a chance. Neither will the guns."

"Next Saturday? Guns and protesters are not a happy mix."

[50]
Old Rugged Cross

The space on the pew next to Anne Hindle was empty. It was unusual for Elsie Groom not to be with her companion. They lived every aspect of their life together, even down to the twin set, pearls, and tweed skirts that they wore as identical uniforms of age and class.

Peter hadn't seen her in the village. Every time he had passed the cottage, the door was unusually shut. The roses around the door had not been deadheaded. Their petals dropped in piles along the path like fading confetti.

As he looked down from the pulpit, he could see that Anne was in another world. She would always be an attentive parishioner, giving either approving or disapproving grunts, or a burst of flatulence throughout his sermon. Today, she sat in silence, looking into the distance as if she were not there.

It was always usual for Peter to stand at the door of the church to say goodbye to all who had bothered to get out of bed and not go to the car boot sale on a Sunday morning. The congregation was slowly growing. Helen Parker sat with Amber Hudson most Sundays since he had gone to her house. Even Fred Prescott had been twice, much to the concern of Morris Marsden, who had questioned whether it was safe to use the same communion cup as '*that kind of gentleman*'.

Gerald Griffin had been openly offended. His retort in the PPC meeting could easily have been taken for his coming out. Peter had agreed with him, arguing that it would be virtually impossible to catch AIDS from the cup, and that it was highly unlikely that just being gay meant you had HIV.

Morris had remained unconvinced. He had insisted that if that kind of person was in the congregation, then he would dip and not sip.

That was the last time he had seen Elsie Groom. She was not one to miss church. As he said goodbye to the last worshippers, Anne walked towards him. Peter knew from the look on her face that something was wrong.

"How is Elsie?" he asked.

"I was wondering if you would mind coming back with me and bring communion for her? Elsie has not been well," Anne said, her words laboured with worry.

"Have you called the doctor?" he asked.

"Elsie insists she is just tired and would never want to trouble the doctor."

"If you wait, we can walk down together, I will just get my bag," Peter put a reassuring hand on her shoulder as he spoke.

Anne put her hand on his as tears came to her eyes.

"Do you know something?" she asked, not waiting for an answer. "People my age seldom are comforted by a warm hand."

"Sorry," he answered without thinking.

The walk from the church was laboured. Anne Hindle was not her usual robust self and stopped often, changing her walking stick from one hand to another. She seemed relieved when she arrived at the cottage. Taking the key for the door that was never usually locked, she slid it in the lock and pushed it open.

The cottage sighed as the air was pulled from inside. It was a sad, exhausted sigh, as if a chased animal had finally surrendered.

"Elsie," she shouted in a broken voice. "The vicar has come to give you Holy Communion."

There was no answer, just the deep silence of the house.

"She was in the conservatory. I will go and see if she is still there."

"No, let me," Peter answered, sensing that all was not right.

As he walked into the conservatory that overlooked the garden, he could see the outline of a woman resting against the sloping back of the day bed.

"Elsie?" he asked, knowing she would not answer.

"Elsie," Anne repeated in frustration.

Peter walked towards the woman and took hold of her hand, feeling for the pulse in her wrist.

"I am sorry, Miss Hindle. Elsie has passed."

The woman crumbled and slumped on the nearby sofa. She sobbed deeply as Peter sat with her.

"I've dreaded this day all my life. Now she has gone on alone. First day I have not been with her in all these years," Anne sobbed as she spoke. It was the first time Peter had seen any real emotion come from her. She had always been so proper and controlled. "She is younger than me. How can God call her before me?"

"There is a time for all of us," he answered awkwardly.

"What do I do now?"

"We have to telephone her doctor and also inform the police."

"She's not been murdered, for God's sake," Anne snapped.

"It's a procedure, that's all."

"Will you pray for her?"

Peter nodded and, taking the stole from his bag, placed it around his neck. He knelt by the side of the chair and put his hand on her head.

As he prayed, Anne sobbed, twisting the silk handkerchief in her fingers.

"Amen," he said as he anointed Elsie with oil. "May you rest in peace and rise in glory."

"She was the love of my life; more than just a companion."

"I don't believe love can be broken by death."

"I have dreaded this day. I hoped that I would be taken first, but that is not meant to be," Anne said as she wiped her face. "Elsie has planned her funeral, hymns, and everything. She even wrote her own eulogy. *The Old Rugged Cross*. It was one of her favourite hymns."

"A popular choice."

"I hate it. Sentimental rubbish. Just like *My Way*. Narcissist's anthem. I was at a funeral in Scarborough Crematorium the other week and it was played as the final hymn. It was the first time I have ever really listened to the words. Not exactly Shakespeare."

"I should call the doctor. He will have to examine her."

"Too bloody late," Anne said stoically. "Did you know, Vicar, the only time we ever argued was nearly thirty years ago? Elsie gave one hundred pounds to the priest to get him out of trouble. I told her it was a mistake. I think she had a shine for him. He was a handsome man. She never got the money back."

"Albert Shepherd?"

"A name I don't like to hear."

[51]
Happy Monday

The August rain had been relentless. The gutters overflowed as the water flowed down the walls of the cottages that lined the road from the church to The Holt, an old, detached house set in its own grounds behind a row of copper beech.

As Peter got out of the patrol car, he could see the woman at the door. She was dressed in a padded gilet, riding boots, and jodhpurs. Her blonde hair was tied back in a tight bun.

"Suspicious package?" Peter asked as he walked along the driveway towards her. It was all control had said to him when he was given the first job of the morning.

"I put it under the oak tree in the paddock. It was the only thing I could think to do," she answered. "The postman left it in the porch. When I got back from the hack, I saw it and thought it didn't look right. It is a small parcel with something square in the middle and a thick tube on one side. My husband got a warning from the police that Masters of the Hunt could be targets of letter bombs. He is Hector Winstanley, the Master of the Upper Dale Hunt."

Peter smiled to himself, realising this must be the man on the horse. "I think I have met your husband. Is he around?" he asked.

"No. He works in London during the week. I can't contact him as he is on the train and doesn't get into town until eleven."

"Are you expecting any parcels?" Peter asked as he hid from the rain under the eaves of the porch.

"Nothing that I know of. Handwritten in felt tip in my husband's name. It was misspelt." The woman gave a shrug. "Bloody sabs. They think they can change the history of the countryside by threats of violence. They will never win. We will hunt foxes and they will never stop us."

"I'll go take a look at the parcel."

Peter walked across the grass paddock to the tall oak tree that knitted its ancient roots into the bank of the stream. Leaning against the trunk was a large, brown envelope. He could clearly see a tubular shape and something square edged in the soaked parcel. Something about it didn't look right.

"*Foxtrot-Papa*-Three-Five. At the scene of the package. Request you call Catterick to attend."

The answer came quickly. "*Ten-Four*."

Peter spent the next two hours in the Aga-warmed kitchen of The Holt as he waited for bomb squad to arrive. The shelves were stacked with Cornishware pots and bowls. Everything was neat and in order. It looked as though it could be a set from *Good Housekeeping*.

Mrs Winstanley had fed him fruit scones and cups of tea. She even bemoaned the fact that one of his colleagues was obviously anti-hunting and regaled the story of her husband having words with the officer at the cub hunting.

Peter had smiled to himself, not wanting to let her know who he really was.

When the doorbell rang, he had learnt that Mrs Winstanley was not as happily married as the world would believe. She had everything that she needed except love. The overwhelming reason she stayed with her husband was because of the horses. They gave her a purpose, the will to get up each morning and pretend to be happy. The horses helped her endure, knowing that Hector had a double life. Weekdays in London. Weekends in the country. He had a city mistress and a country wife. That was the way of the world in the social circle in which she lived.

It was a trade-off in a society where the men had the money, and the women who wanted it had to obey the rules and put up with their male peccadillos.

Peter answered the door.

"You again?" the officer said with a smile as he brushed back a flop of hair with his fingers. "This is becoming a habit. What have you got this time?"

"Suspicious package for the Master of the Hunt."

Peter explained the situation as they walked to the oak tree. The officer looked around the empty fields.

"Nearest neighbour?" he asked.

"Eight hundred yards."

"The further the neighbour, the bigger the bang," the man laughed. "It doesn't look suspicious, but I always love the chance to blow something up."

"It might be valuable," Peter joked. "They look like they can afford it."

It was not long before the bomb disposal officer had attached the detonator on the small pack of explosives set against the parcel. The man walked the one hundred yards back to Peter and offered him the small metal box and firing button.

"Really?" Peter asked, relishing the experience.

"Your turn," he answered.

"Fire," Peter said as he pressed the button.

Instantly, there was a loud explosion. The package was blown into the air. Torn, singed pages of magazines and broken video tape slowly fell like grounded kites and tails. The oak tree dropped three branches that clattered to the ground, breaking the fence by the stream as a mushroom cloud billowed upwards. A long, dull rumble rolled up the valley towards Ellerburn.

"Nice," the officer said as he took a cigarette out of his pocket and lit it.

"Magazines?" Peter asked.

"Porn. I took the liberty to cut open the wrapper before I set the explosive."

"So you knew it wasn't a bomb?" Peter asked as they walked towards the tree.

"I wasn't coming all this way without the chance to blow something up. A job in the countryside is a rarity. I am going to Ireland in a couple of weeks and need to get some practice in. Shouldn't have set it against the tree, but what the hell."

As they got to the site of the detonation, ripped and burnt pages of the magazines littered the ground. Peter bent down and picked up what was left of a plastic tube with a motor hanging out.

"Is this what I think it is?" he asked.

"Feminine relief massager," the man said with a broad smile.

"His wife doesn't look like the type," Peter answered as he scooped up the pages of the magazines and stacked them in a pile.

"Whatever are you doing?" the officer asked.

"I'm going to burn the evidence," he answered. "Mrs Winstanley doesn't have to know."

The officer shrugged his shoulders as he said goodbye. "You would do that for her?" he asked.

"Yes," Peter answered as he picked up the remains of a video cartridge and then set fire to the magazines.

He watched as the soldier walked across the field back to the house and collected the coil of wire and the detonator button. The fire burnt slowly, given shelter from the now light rain by the canopy of the tree. Mrs Winstanley appeared by the fence and looked as though she was in deep conversation.

Peter put the remains of the video and the massager onto the fire, helped by the sticks he had collected.

"What are you doing?" Mrs Winstanley shouted as she marched across the field.

"Making sure there is no trace of any explosives on the package. They could be dangerous," he said quickly.

"I want to see what was there!" she insisted, screaming at the top of her voice and punching the air with her fists. "The soldier said it was pornographic magazines and other stuff. What kind of pervert orders that kind of thing?"

"You don't need to know," Peter answered, trying to calm her down. "He might not have ordered it. It could be a joke sent by a friend."

"I'll give him a bloody vibrator. The officer was quite descriptive," she said as she kicked the fire with her riding boot, trying to scatter and douse the burning pages. "This is the last. Bloody. Straw!" the woman screamed with tears streaming down her face. "He has made me look like a fool for the last time. Half the village is at the end of the drive."

"No one needs to know," Peter said.

"They will know, because I am going to tell them," Mrs Winstanley screamed as she cried. "I know they all laugh at me behind my back. They think I am a fool for putting up with him. Last year, it was one of the stable girls, and this year, it is the cashier at the petrol station. Plenty of time for them and none for his wife."

"Don't say anything to them. Pray about it first."

"You sound like a bloody vicar."

"I am," he answered.

The woman didn't answer as the sudden realisation as to who he was crossed her face.

[52]
Least Said

The vicarage telephone rang several times and then abruptly stopped, just as Peter picked up the handset. He had been in the garden watching the sun set behind the hills. The yew tree on the old mound had cast a long shadow across the field towards the house. Its gnarled branches reached out, as if to scoop up the earth. When the phone had rung, he wondered if he should answer it. Since he had last spoken to Mary, he had thought long and hard about his future.

Divorce was something he felt he couldn't share with anyone at work, let alone another priest. Clergy were renowned for sharing gossip for '*prayer purposes*'. The last thing he wanted was the bishop finding out his marriage had hit a bump in the road and that his wife was having trips to the beach with some bloke called Daniel.

When the phone kept on ringing, he had second thoughts and had reluctantly walked to the office, knowing it would be Sod's law that it stopped as he got there. Peter was right.

He put the handset back on the cradle. It gave a reassuring click and then suddenly rang.

"Peter Barnes," he said, expecting to hear Mary reply.

"Barney. *Jeff Langley from Force Intelligence.*"

"Bit late for a social call, Jeff."

"*You put in a report of sabs coming up to disrupt the first shoot of the year.*"

"Yes. Information from a trusted source," he answered.

"*We had the Met check it out and they say that your informant is wrong. They have no intelligence and we should take no action*," Langley said with an air of self-importance.

"It's the Met. You can never trust them to get it right. Look how they messed the miners' strike."

"*They are adamant that there will be no sabs travelling to Yorkshire on Saturday.*"

"Why the late-night call?" he asked.

"*I was coming to that,*" Langley answered with a smirk in his voice. "*You have been re-rostered. Superintendent wants to play safe. He said you knew most of the sabs in Yorkshire and he wants you to police the shoot.*"

"It was my day off," he answered.

"*Not anymore. We are five men down and pulling in people off rest days. Federation said we must give people notice for a change of shift. Sorry.*"

"Bugger," he muttered under his breath.

Langley laughed. "*Finally made a vicar swear. I've been waiting all my life to do that.*"

"How many officers will be with me?" Peter answered, ignoring the man's laughter.

"*Just you. Peter Barnes is the thin blue line. I have done an intelligence analysis and there is no threat. You will be there to fly the flag. None of the guns are of any note. A couple of celebrities and a bloke who owns a hotel chain. Nobody on the Irish hit list.*"

"That's reassuring. Any backup if it hits the fan?"

"*You won't need any. They are not telling anyone which part of the moor they will be on until the morning. You will get a call at eight-thirty.*"

The call ended without any pleasantries. Jeff Langley was not the kind of man for small talk.

Peter put down the phone and thought about calling Mary. The children would be in bed and it had been a while since they last spoke. He lifted the handset and began to dial the number, then quickly put the phone down. *Now was not the time*, Peter thought as he walked from the room. He was far too angry and knew they would argue. "Least said..." he said the words out loud as he opened the front door and took in a deep breath.

[53]
Cider with Gravy

Last orders had been called five minutes before Peter got to the pub. There was no sign of the five men at the bar making a move, and as he walked in, each nodded in turn. One man even attempted a half-smile.

Having left the vicarage with no money, the landlord gave him a pint of cider and told him to pay for it the next time he was in. Peter thanked him, took the drink outside, and sat on the bench under the double tree.

The late evening had a warm breeze that came from the south. Peter could smell the scent of roses that it had collected as it swirled through the village. Bats flew in and out of the branches of the tree above him. As he drank the cider, he wondered where his life would take him.

All he could think of was Mary and the children. He felt selfish for changing their lives and blindly following what he thought was his vocation. God had called him, or so he thought. Yet now he wondered if it had been his own desire, a dream brought on by cheese before bedtime.

Peter knew that if he was divorced, the bishop was within his right to move him, even though he had just got there. He didn't have the freehold of the parish and was only a priest in charge. Technically, he wasn't employed. His family were just tenants without a contract and had no security.

"Lord, please sort this all out," Peter said in a half-whisper, hoping his words would be carried away by the breeze.

"First sign of madness. Talking to yourself," the voice came from behind him.

Peter didn't turn. He knew the voice well. "Stella, are you talking to me? I thought after the last time we spoke under this tree you would never speak to me again."

"That? All forgotten. You are a man, and men speak before thinking," she answered. "It's all to do with where their brains are located."

"And where exactly is that?" he asked.

"Three inches from what they usually talk out of," Stella laughed to herself. "Anyway, what are you asking your imaginary friend to sort out?"

"Was I that loud?"

"Got the gist of it."

"Does a witch pray?" Peter asked as he sipped his drink.

"Bring your pint and I will show you what I have been up to tonight," Stella said as she began to cross the road towards the churchyard.

Peter hesitated.

"Come on, Vicar. I want to show you the well."

"It's dark," he answered, annoyed that, as usual, she had avoided a question.

"Frightened I might turn you into a frog?" she answered as she opened the gate and began to walk through the graves.

"More that I may be seen going into a churchyard with a woman at night."

"I wouldn't worry about that; Frank Green was doing it all the time."

"If only the trees could talk," Peter answered as he followed her.

"They can, Vicar. They can."

Stella led him to the well. In the half-light of the late evening, Peter could see what she had done. The well was now restored to how it was when it was first built.

"How have you done this?" he asked. "It is beautiful."

"I went to County Hall and found some drawings that were done in the 1600s. I checked with Morris, who said it would be okay. I rebuilt the pool. It's lined with clay and the stones are inlaid into it. The water comes out from the spring and over the stones into the pool."

"Where does the water go?" he asked as a full moon broke over the trees and bathed the well in a deep blue light.

"Back into the ground. Possibly an underground stream. Mother Earth loans the water to us and then drinks it back up."

"When was it finished?"

"Tonight. I was going to wait until tomorrow to show you."

The limestone cairn looked as if it had been in place for hundreds of years. Each stone fitted close to the next. It needed no mortar as it was locked tightly together. The spring water oozed from between a stone slot as if it came from the mouth of an oracle. The small pool of water was crystal clear.

It was then that Peter noticed the outline of a fish made of coloured stones. Even in the moonlight, it was clearly visible.

"Did you make the fish?" he asked.

"I thought you might like it. I hear that fishes play a big part in your faith," Stella answered as she took hold of his glass and helped herself to the cider. "A toast. To new beginnings?"

"New beginnings," he echoed. "Why the change of heart? I thought our friendship was nearly over."

"I'm a redhead. Sometimes I lose my temper, then go away and think about it. Perhaps you are right about consecrating the ground where Esther is buried. It would be good if there was a headstone or something that tells her story."

"I was planning the blessing for harvest," he answered as he took back the glass. There was a sudden flash of torchlight.

"Vicar, I didn't realise it was you," Morris Marsden said as he walked, torch in hand, down the low bank towards the well. "I heard voices as I was just locking up the church."

"Stella was showing me what she has done to the well," Peter answered.

"Please don't say we needed a faculty," Morris stuttered.

"A minor repair, that's all. No faculty," Peter said reassuringly.

Morris gasped like a thirsty crow.

"Appreciated. I gave Stella the go-ahead. I thought you wouldn't mind."

"It's beautiful. I couldn't have wished for more."

"I have to say, it is a weight off my mind," Morris replied with a further sigh. "Things have changed for the better."

"In some ways," Peter answered. "In some ways."

[54]
The Lion Inn

St Walstan's well was the least of his worries. As he drove the marked police Transit van across the sunlit moor with its flowering heather towards Blakey Ridge, Peter could see a large gathering of people and cars in the Atchin Tan, a layby used for centuries by Travellers, overlooking Rosedale Abbey.

Immediately, he knew that these people were not the ones with guns waiting to wage war on the grouse. Their location had been released in a telephone call that morning, five miles from where he now was.

As he drove closer, he could see the balaclavas, face masks, and dark clothing that was the uniform of the sabs. Pulling into the gravelled layby and getting out of the van, he was greeted with a loud cheer. He looked around at the collection of vehicles; some didn't look like they were fit to be on the road.

"One copper and seventy of us," said the middle-aged, bearded man in a combat jacket and high-vis tabard. "The odds aren't looking good for you."

"Just passing through. Wondered what you were all doing," he answered, not wanting to give anything away.

"Glorious twelfth. Well, it will be for us," the man answered as a woman in jeans and a long coat handed him a cup of coffee that she had just poured from a flask. "We are here to save the grouse."

"Peacefully, I hope," Peter answered as he looked around at the gathering of men and women dressed for confrontation, some with handheld radios, others with binoculars and walking sticks.

"We like to keep it that way," the man answered.

"Are you the leader?" Peter asked as the man sipped the coffee.

"We have no leaders. I just saw you first. Thought you were the advanced troops when I saw the van. Didn't realise there would just be you."

Peter could feel a certain tension in his words. As the man spoke, others drew closure to form a human wall behind him.

"There are plenty more where I came from," Peter replied. "I am just on my way to a report of a dog worrying sheep. As long as you don't break the law and keep to the public paths, you have every right to be on the moors. Just watch out for the guns."

Peter knew his words wouldn't be enough to put them off. The last thing he wanted was for them to know he was the only one on duty for miles.

"Very kind sentiments. We will do as you say," the man said as those around him laughed.

Peter knew what their intention would be. Find the guns. Stop the shoot. They would already have spotters driving around the moors, looking for where the guns were. Even with over five hundred square miles of the National Park, the shoot could still easily be found.

"Well, have a safe day," Peter said as he turned and walked back to the van.

As he got in the vehicle, he could feel every sab staring at him. He was miles from anywhere, and the only copper between Pickering and Whitby. In his pocket was the location of the guns. Closing the door of the van and starting the engine, he waved to the man and smiled. He hoped no one would see his rising sense of panic.

It was obvious the saboteurs were well-equipped. He knew they would have scanners to listen in to the police radio. As he drove to the top of the ridge, he saw in his wing mirror that a small blue Fiat had pulled out of the layby. He was being followed.

Peter pressed his foot on the accelerator. The Transit wasn't the best vehicle for speed. Two miles up the road was a pub. He knew that they had a telephone. It was the safest way to inform control.

The futile words of Jeff Langley echoed through his mind: "*Peter Barnes is the thin blue line. I have done an intelligence analysis and there is no threat. You will be there to fly the flag.*"

"The only flag the guns will be flying is a white one," he said to himself, knowing in his heart that men drunk on money and early morning champagne would not go quietly.

The police van sped up the hill, every gear grinding as he left the Fiat far behind. If he could get around the next bend, into the dip, and up the small hill, he could hide the van around the back of the pub.

Checking his wing mirror, the Fiat was out of sight. Peter drove faster, hoping the Transit had the legs to make it. In the distance, he saw the pub. The car park was empty.

Pulling off the road, he sped through the narrow entrance at the side of the pub and, pulling the handbrake, skidded to a halt behind an old cowshed. A shroud of dust billowed up in the morning air, something that could tell his pursuers where he was hiding.

The back door of the pub opened and before Peter could get out of the van, the landlord, Derek Spivey, was in the yard, his shirt open to the waist and half a bacon butty in his hand.

"What the hell's going on?" the man shouted as he wondered why a police van had done a handbrake stop outside his kitchen window.

"I need to use your phone," Peter answered as he got out of the van and saw the Fiat speed by. "There's going to be trouble. Seventy sabs to disrupt the shoot."

"There better bloody not be trouble. I have the guns booked in here for lunch. Phone's in the kitchen," he said as Peter pushed by him and went in the back door of the pub.

Dialling the number, Peter tried to calm his breath. He could feel his heart racing as the adrenaline pumped. It was three minutes before he finally got through to control.

"Seventy sabs. All equipped for the day. Walking sticks, radios, and binoculars. There could be more in other places."

"*Ten-Four*," the woman answered. "*We'll get as many as we can from other divisions. We might be able to get ten or fifteen to you in an hour or so.*"

"Ring Cleveland and ask for assistance," Peter said. "Stay off the radio. I think they have scanners. Is there a traffic car and vehicle inspection unit? I have an idea on what we can do."

"*What's your location?*" the controller asked.

"Lion Inn. Blakey Ridge."

"*At least they have a bar*," the woman laughed. "*Stay there and I will ring you back in five minutes.*"

"Tell Inspector Manning I am going to the car park on Chimney Bank. It's a mile from the shoot. If all units could meet there." Peter put down the phone as he realised that the landlord was stood behind him.

"You are the only one on duty? No wonder you looked like you'd been chased by the devil. Shoot doesn't start for two hours," Derek said as he slid a plate and a freshly cooked bacon roll onto the table. "Better have that. It might be quite some time before you see food again."

[55]
The Battle Of Atchin Tan

The hour passed slowly. The sun climbed higher in the clear sky to heat the August day. Across the moor, honeybees sped back and forth from the row of hives in the garden of Keeper's Cottage, an isolated house by the side of a disused railway track. It had once been the manager's house for the long-gone mine. Now, it was the home of David Harness, the young gamekeeper for the estate that covered the moors.

As Peter pulled up in the Transit, Harness was already waiting. As he had left the pub, the landlord had phoned Harness to tell him the copper was on his way.

"Sabs?" Harness asked as he stroked his red beard.

"Seventy and probably more," Peter answered. "Can we call off the shoot?"

"No way. There's a bloody member of the cabinet and that bloke off *News at Ten*. More than my job is worth," Harness sighed. "Good thing they are running late. They are still having breakfast in the White Horse."

"How long have we got? Do you have anyone on the moors that could be spotted?" Peter asked.

"We set up yesterday. The tractor and carts are in the pub car park, ready to take the guns to the first drive. That's if we can get them out."

"Anyone else down there?"

"Just an old couple in a Fiat car. Looked like hikers. They were having a flask of tea."

"Sabs," Peter answered. "They were sent to find out where you are going. They will have a two-way radio."

"Sly buggers," Harness answered, as if he had been taken for a fool for not realising who they were. "They looked normal. Not the usual beardy-weirdy."

Before he could answer, a winding procession of five police vehicles slowly made their way up Chimney Bank towards the car park.

"It's the boss," Peter said as the police Range Rover pulled up, followed by a traffic car, a rural patrol, a Cleveland dog van, and a vehicle inspection truck.

"Morning, Peter. I got what you asked for, but why did you want the VIU?"

"Thanks, boss. I know it was a strange request. There are about thirty to forty cars down at Atchin Tan. Some of them look like they shouldn't be on the road. We could delay them from leaving and take some off the road."

"What's your reasonable suspicion? We can't go around harassing them," Manning answered.

Peter smiled. "I saw the state of them before I phoned into control. We could block them in."

The driver of the traffic car got out and walked slowly across. He looked as though he had just got out of bed. His shirt was crumpled, and tie covered in what looked like an egg breakfast.

Morris Stone had been in traffic longer than anyone could remember. He was a no nonsense, hit first, ask questions later type of copper.

"Why the hell do you want us?" he asked, pointing to the VIU truck.

"Vehicle checks at Atchin Tan. I thought it would be a good way to delay the sabs. There could be problems if they get near the shoot."

Stone laughed and raised his eyebrows, as if he could see great sport ahead.

"What do you think?" Carol Manning asked.

"Could be fun," Stone replied. "When do we strike?"

"As soon as we can. The shoot will be starting when they get out of the White Horse." Peter thought for a moment. "There are a couple of sabs in the car park down there. They will try to follow the guns to the first drive."

"I can stop them," Harness answered, stepping into the conversation.

"Who are you?" Manning asked suspiciously.

"David Harness. Gamekeeper. These are my moors."

Manning smiled.

"What would you do?"

"My wife has a very temperamental car. She could break down in the car park. It has a narrow entrance. Nothing would get out from behind her."

"Morris, take the beat car with you and the TIU. I will follow you down. There will doubtless be a lawyer with them to argue the case," Manning said as she checked her watch and turned to Peter. "How the hell did this happen? Why are we so unprepared?"

"I told Jeff Langley in Force Intelligence it was going to happen. He said they had checked it out and there would be no sabs," Peter answered. "There's also another problem. I was told there was no one of note on the shoot. Turns out there is a member of the cabinet with them."

Carol Manning rolled her eyes in disbelief. "I should radio it in," she answered.

"With respect, boss," Morris butted in. "Better to wait until we have them boxed in before we say anything on the radio."

"You can use the phone in the house," Harness said, pointing to the isolated building by the side of the disused railway track high on the edge of the moor.

"Nice view," she replied, looking out over the vast expanse of purple moorland with the small village nestled deep in the protective arms of the valley below.

"Hard to believe that a couple of hundred years ago this was nothing more than an industrial estate. The sky would be black with chimney smoke," Harness answered, pointing to the ruins of the old mine workings.

Fifteen minutes later, the convoy was heading back down the road towards Atchin Tan layby. The Cleveland patrol car followed Mrs Harness to the pub. The plan was to let out the tractor and bus cart carrying the guns and then block in the Fiat.

No plan was foolproof, and Peter knew they were outnumbered.

As he pulled up behind the TIU van, Morris Stone was already tapping the tyres of an old Bedford van.

Manning had blocked the exit with the Range Rover and Peter saw her take a deep breath before getting out. He was glad she was his shift inspector. She knew the job and wasn't afraid to get stuck in. Manning reminded him of his first shift sergeant who had taken him under her wing. She was always the first into a fight, a copper's copper.

As Manning walked across the layby to the parked vehicles, she was surrounded by a grumbling mob. A tall man with three-day stubble and a London accent prodded her in the chest with a long finger as he hurled abuse in her face.

The retaliation was instant, Manning grabbed him by the hand, and with a twist of her arm, spun the man to the floor. Instinctively, Peter drew his truncheon, ready for what was to come.

"Next one to do that gets locked up. Understand?" Manning screamed at the top of her voice.

The crowd parted as the bearded man in a combat jacket stepped through the mob.

"We are here to stop a shoot. Not pick fights with the police," he said loudly as he helped the man up from the floor. "Let them do what they want to do."

"Thought you weren't the leader?" Peter asked, slipping the truncheon back in its pocket.

"I am the spokesperson," the man answered. "It would seem you weren't after a dog after all."

There was a sudden blast of gunfire from the moor across the valley. It echoed across the heathered uplands, as if the start of a trench war.

All those gathered looked across to where the sound had come from. Far away on the other side of the valley, wisps of ghost-like smoke drifted from the grouse butts. Flag-waving beaters made their way like a line of ants across the moor. As if one, the sabs set off at a pace over the edge of the moor and into the trees. Only the bearded man was left behind.

"What now?" Manning asked Peter.

"They'll be there before you," the man said. "No stopping them now."

"He's right," Peter echoed. "We best be going. I know a shortcut."

"What about our vehicles?" the man asked casually as the two-way in his pocket clicked.

"I have all the time in the world, and by the look of some of these motors, they will be going nowhere," Stone said as he stepped into the conversation.

"We are here to protect the grouse, and you are in the pockets of a few rich men." It was the first time the man had raised his voice. For a moment, he raised a finger towards Carol Manning and then quickly pulled back his hand. "Just like the miners' strike. Maggie's Army."

[56]
The Outpost

Carol Manning put the receiver onto its cradle. Relieved, she gave a great sigh of relief as she sat back in the office chair.

"Acting Chief Constable. Very pleased with the outcome. Tea and medals all around," Manning said as she sighed again.

"It was a close thing. Good job they couldn't get across the river. It bought us some time," Peter answered.

"He did say that Jeff Langley is going to get carpeted. Turns out he hadn't even bothered following your up intel properly. He had just rung a mate of his in the Met for a chat. Langley has visions of transferring to SO15. Some chance of that," Manning smiled. "Turns out the cabinet member was the Deputy Prime Minister, and he had left his close protection officer back at the pub."

"Lucky that Cleveland turned up when they did. All's well that ends well," Peter said as he ate the last remnants of the newspaper-wrapped fish and chips that he had shared with Manning.

"So, what's the sermon for tomorrow?" she asked.

"I'm going to have to busk it. With working extra days, I haven't had the chance. Not even sure what the Bible readings are," Peter replied as he looked at the clock and realised that by the time he got home, there would be no time to write anything unless he stayed up half the night.

"Do you get stage fright? All those eyes staring up at you."

"If I had a big audience, I possibly would. The faithful of St Walstan's are few. We are up against the car boot sale and junior football."

"Why not have a service on a weeknight and don't have it clash with *Coronation Street*?"

"They are a traditional lot and might protest about coming any time other than a Sunday," Peter answered as he wiped up the last dribble of vinegar from the greased paper with the final fat chip.

"I used to go to a mid-week evening service in London," she answered.

"Church?" Peter smiled.

"What's so funny about that? I went to Holy Trinity. Next to the Brompton Oratory."

"Sorry."

"I took my husband. It was a healing service, but things…"

Her words faded.

[57]
Letterbox

The church clock struck the ninth hour as Peter got out of his car and took in a deep breath of warm evening air. Above his head, the leaves of the beech trees dryly rattled with the first hint of autumn. He knew it would not be long before they started to fall. August was a month that he did not like. Already, the evenings were drawing in. Slowly, the night crept upon the world, as if an unwelcome guest of a long summer.

Walking to the door, Peter noticed the tip of a brown envelope sticking from the letterbox. Opening the door and stepping inside, he slipped the letter from the box. It had no name or address and had obviously been hand-delivered.

Sliding his finger under the flap, he quickly opened the envelope. Inside was a single piece of paper. All that was on it was a few brief words written in an educated hand.

'*I bind you to priestly confidence, Magnus Seagrave is still with us.*'

Peter read the note twice over. He knew where the information had come from. The writing was the same as that he had seen in the office of James Meredith. "So much for client confidentiality," he muttered as he went to the kitchen and poured a glass of wine from last night's bottle.

Peter wondered why Meredith should take the time to let him know about Seagrave. More than that, he had been bound to a priestly confidence.

As he took a mouthful of wine, the telephone began to chime. He swallowed hard before picking up the handset from the wall phone.

Before he could answer, he heard Mary's voice. "*Peter... I was hoping to catch you before you went to bed.*"

"Just got in. It's been a long day. Hunt saboteurs," Peter answered, unsure that he wanted to talk to his wife.

"*Was everything okay?*" she asked, her voice unusually soft. "*I have just got the kids to bed and sorted some food for Dad.*"

"I am missing you all. How are they?" he asked.

"*They have been asking about you. I just wish I could get things sorted here and then could come back.*"

"I thought you wanted space? That's why I haven't called."

"*I have missed you. I was wrong. I was stressed,*" she said, as if the excuses had been rehearsed. "*I regret the conversation. It should never have happened.*"

"So do I," he answered. "I wish you were here. The house feels so empty."

"*I want to come back, but Mum and Dad have to get sorted. You can't believe what it is like. It is as if I am still a teenager,*" Mary answered.

"I thought you weren't going to come back. I was worried," Peter replied.

"*It was wrong of me. The pressure of being down here with Mum and Dad.*"

"I thought you would run off with Daniel."

"*Don't be ridiculous. Why would you think that?*"

"Days on the beach?" he asked, realising it was the wrong thing to say.

"*Daniel would be more interested in you than me. He isn't into women. Anyway, that would be the last thing I would ever do.*"

"Sorry," he said. "I should never have said anything."

"*How are things with the church?*" Mary said, knowing when to change the subject for the sake of peace.

"Difficult. The bishop did warn me that it wouldn't be an easy ride." Peter took a deep breath, hoping that this wasn't just small talk. He wanted to ask her what Helen Connor had meant when she had called Mary a party animal. Peter knew that now was not the right time.

"*We can get through this*," she answered. "*Change is always difficult.*"

"Thank you. I have been so worried about us," Peter answered, holding back the tears as his voice began to crack.

"*It's my fault. I am sorry. Forgive me.*"

"There is no need to ask. Everything will be good. I can't wait to see you all again."

"*I will be back as soon as I can. I promise.*"

"We are having a blessing of the well and t h e harvest festival on the bank holiday weekend. Could you be back for then?"

"*Blessing of a well?*"

Peter explained all that had gone on, describing each member of the parish and the events around them.

Mary had laughed as he told her of Morris Marsden and his fear of breaking church rules.

"*It's a different world,*" she said, breaking into what he was saying. "*Promise me you will give more time to me and the children. That is my only fear.*"

"I promise," Peter answered, knowing that it had already been broken.

[58]
Storm

Evensong had been said alone. It had rained all Sunday afternoon and the first chill of autumn had fallen on the village. Not even Morris Marsden had joined him for prayers. At the morning Eucharist, Gerald had told Peter that he was not feeling well and asked to be excused for duty that evening.

As he had preached that morning, he could see from the pulpit the slow change in the congregation. The church was gradually growing. Occasional visitors had become regular attendees.

Anne Hindle sat alone, dressed in widow's weeds of an old black hat and lace veil. She did not stand for any of the hymns. Instead, she knelt forward in prayer as those around her murdered yet another, once fine, song of praise.

The death of Elsie Groom had touched the heart of all the parishioners. There was no doubt that they all knew how much the two old ladies had loved each other.

When Morris Marsden had found out about her death, he had simply said to Peter that Elsie had been promoted to glory.

As Peter locked the church door and stepped out into the evening light, he thought it was an apt way to talk about death. There was no promise of a physical heaven—a replica of this world with endless days of sunshine and meadow walks. A land where the lion will lay down with the lamb. That was a picture of the afterlife that he didn't think possible, nor did he want. Death was the one thing that could bring about a sense of rising panic in his chest. It was the thought of endless time, an eternal eternity, that made him sometimes wish he had never been born at all.

At theological college, there were often arguments as to what the afterlife would be like. They seemed to be split along partisan lines as to where on the church candle you hung your faith.

The Anglo-Catholics that he knew pressed for a long sleep and then the resurrection of the dead, as if a final Easter morning, when all those who have gone before, wake from the grave.

Several evangelicals on his course insisted with certainty that God would divide the sheep from the goats, a divine judgement on those who were not born again. Hellfire and damnation to those who did not believe.

Peter felt it was far more complicated than that—more fudged, grey, and unclear. It was as if life after death had no real meaning. For him, his faith was about who we were in this world and not the next. Life was the sacrament of the present moment.

Peter hoped that there would be something after death, but felt he wouldn't be cheated if it was just *The Big Sleep*, or even reincarnation.

He had expressed this during a formal dinner as he sat next to the principal of his college and the archbishop of York. The archbishop had nearly choked on a roast potato, spluttering his surprise that anyone about to be ordained had to have some principled thought on one of the biggest questions that faced humanity.

The goose fat potato had wedged somewhere in his upper throat and pieces were blown out of his mouth as he coughed and grunted that Peter should consider what he had to offer the Church of England if he had no solid belief in life after death.

Peter could not assemble a single original, theological thought as he watched the archbishop go red in the face and gasp for breath. The man insisted on continuing the debate on the final Christian hope. All Peter could think was that his doubting faith would be responsible for killing the shocked archbishop.

Finally, the offending vegetable had been coughed back into his mouth to be rechewed and eaten. The situation had been rescued by the college principal, who had echoed what Peter had said by quoting Origen and the early Church Fathers.

As Peter walked back to the house, he could hear the start of a new rainfall as fat drops of water struck the leaves of the beech trees above his head. With each step, the rain beat down heavier and heavier. Looking to the north, he could see the high grey clouds, more fitting for winter than August. They were blown by a strong wind that was whipping up from across the North Sea.

There had been no mention on the lunchtime radio of bad weather. Yet now, the sky grew darker, as if a thick veil was cast over the evening sun. The tops of the trees began to blow and the thin upper branches rattled like the swords of an advancing army.

Thoughts of going for an evening walk were soon cut short as he ran the last few yards to the front door of the house. Peter had decided in that time to drink wine and watch television. *The Tales of Para Handy* soon merged into *Commonwealth Games Grandstand*.

Outside the house, the wind beat at the trees and rain crashed against the roof. Peter knew he would never sleep. Tomorrow was a day off, and he would stay in bed when the storm subsided. As he drank a final glass of wine, he lay back on the sofa as his eyes slowly closed.

The telephone woke him from his sleep. Peter realised it was morning, as the curtains were edged in sunlight. Next to the sofa was the empty wine glass. The longcase clock in the hall struck seven times. He wondered who could be ringing at this time in the morning.

Making his way to the phone in the hall, he lifted the receiver.

"Peter. It's Carol Manning," she said in a hopeful voice.

"Inspector," he answered, hoping she wasn't going to ask him to come in.

"*There is a house in your parish called The Grange. Do you know it?*"

It was a question that made him fully awake.

"Yes. Helen Parker was in church yesterday. Is everything okay?"

"*Got a bit of a garbled message from control. Apparently, a tree came down overnight in her garden. She has found some human bones in the roots. The informant said they looked old. More archaeological than criminal.*" Manning paused for a moment before continuing. "*I have no one to send. Could you get up there and hold the fort until I can get scenes of crime? The division is carnage. The storm has blocked three major roads and ripped the roof off several houses. I don't have enough officers.*"

"I will be there in twenty minutes."

"*Thank you. I've told her you will be on your way.*"

"You owe me one," he answered.

"*I was joking. I'll get control to ring her now and put sixteen hours on your time off card.*"

The one good thing about falling asleep on the sofa was that he was still fully dressed.

In ten minutes, he was in the car and heading out of the village. Carol Manning had been right. The storm of the night before had caused chaos. Several beech branches had snapped from the trees in the churchyard and hung like broken limbs. Old rook nests were scattered in piles on the driveway. At the lane to the moor, the football club caravan lay on its side, pressed up against the gate of the playing fields.

As he drove towards The Grange, he weaved in and out of fallen branches. The summer bloom had been beaten from the trees. The copse of oak at the top of the hill had been stripped of leaves. The gnarled branches looked as if they were reaching upwards on a December day.

Turning the corner to the house, he stopped suddenly, his way blocked by a small herd of fallow deer who stood in the middle of the road not wanting to move. It was as if the forest had become their enemy and that the winds of the night had beaten them from their home. The animals stood motionless as he got out of the car, and only moved to the verge when he shooed them away.

The deer stood and watched as he walked away, as if they were too frightened to move.

[59]
Dead Men Tell Tales

The gates to the house were open as he went up the drive; he could see that the tall double tree that had stood so proudly at the front of the house was now on its side, in a mass of broken branches and a twisted trunk.

Helen Parker was ready to greet him as he parked the car at the side of the house. She looked forlorn and anxious; her long, blue, silk robe trailed on the damp gravel.

"I am so glad they have sent you. It's such a horrible sight," Helen said as tears rolled down her face.

"When did you find the oak-willow had fallen?" Peter asked as he took her hand and walked with her.

"About an hour ago. My husband is away golfing with clients. I got up and looked out of the window and saw the tree had fallen. My mother was looking after my baby so I came outside. It was then that I found them."

"Them? I was told it was just some old bones," he answered.

"It's two bodies," she said, her face giving away her concern. "I rang the emergency number and told them. They must have got the message wrong. I wondered why they seemed so calm when they rang back. It's a man and a woman. The man is a priest. You can see his dog collar."

"Go in the house," Peter said as he set off towards the tree at a pace. "Ring the police station and ask for Inspector Manning. Tell her I need C.I.D."

As he approached the tree, Peter slowed his pace to a walk. The double tree had fallen and had lifted the root ball from the stony ground. There, like a macabre tableau wrapped in tree roots, were two bodies.

It was obvious that one was a man and the other a woman. Both were dressed formally. The man wore a dark suit and, as Helen had said, a clerical collar. The woman was in a summer dress. The hair of the corpse was tied back. Both skeletons were well preserved, the mummified facial features still recognisable.

Peter knew who the man was. His picture hung in the vestry of the church along with those of all the former priests as if a roll of honour.

Albert Shepherd dangled in the roots, his bone hand clutching that of the woman he was interned with. There was a small hole in his forehead. Peter could see that the back of the cranium was gone. The woman had been shot through the side of the head. The left side of her skull was missing, and both bodies had, at some time, been gnawed by rats.

Suddenly, all that he had been told began to make sense. Bertie Shepherd had not run away with a lover. He had been murdered.

Peter presumed the woman was Evelyn Seagrave. It was as if they had been executed where they were buried, and the two trees planted on them as if to keep them in the grave. If the storm had not come then they might never have been discovered. Peter took a step back.

In the hole left by the fallen tree were what looked like two old suitcases. The linen covers had rotted, and all that was left were the frames and a bundle of clothes. Next to that, Peter could see the carcass of a small dog on a long, red lead.

Far to the south, the last of the clouds cleared and a warm sun beat down. Peter looked out over the fields that led to the forest. Above the trees the birds spiralled in the still air. It was a picture of rural bliss. A fine summer day in Yorkshire. Yet, just feet away, was the scene of a double murder. It was incongruous to the landscape it inhabited, and yet to nature, it was of no more concern than two dead badgers at the roadside.

"Peter," Helen shouted from the French window of the dining room. "Inspector on the phone for you."

He turned and walked towards the house, the sun reflecting off the limestone walls. The door was surrounded by the same wisteria that Bishop Riley had taken a cutting from years before. It made him think how everything in life appeared to be linked, joined in an unseen way through time.

Peter felt that Albert Shepherd had reached out to him. There had been too much coincidence. It was as if time meant nothing and was just the passing of the earth around the sun. For thirty years, the earth had kept its secret, and now, Albert and Evelyn were back in the world. They had been born again. The sun would shine on them once more as they gave up their secrets and told their tales.

The oak and willow tree had been grown together. Their trunks were entwined, and perhaps that was their weakness. As Peter got to the French window, he looked back and wondered if that was what the murderer had done back in '66.

"Where is the phone?" he asked Helen as the cool of the house wrapped around him. Helen pointed to the oak sideboard in the alcove by the fireplace.

"If you pick it up, I will hang up in the kitchen."

Peter waited for the reassuring click before he began to speak. "Inspector," he said when he heard the sound.

"*What have you got, Peter? Mrs Parker said you needed to speak.*"

"There are two bodies, and I think I know who they are. They have both been shot through the head. The skeletons are well preserved."

"*My God. Seriously?*"

"Very."

"*How long would you say they have been buried?*" she asked.

"Since just after the '66 World Cup," he answered.

"*Are you joking?*"

"No. One of the bodies is a former priest. He went missing in '66. The other is a woman. I believe they are the remains of

Evelyn Seagrave, who once lived in this house. She disappeared at the same time."

There was a long silence. Peter could hear Manning breathing heavily.

"*Preserve the scene. I will be there as soon as I can,*" Manning answered.

Peter put down the telephone and turned around. Helen Parker was standing in the doorway holding a Cornishware cup of coffee in her hand.

"I'm sorry, Peter. I overheard what you said. Is it Evelyn Seagrave?"

[60]
Tongue Stone

It was an hour before Peter heard the sound of the diesel engine. The police Range Rover powered up the driveway towards the house as he waited by the fallen tree.

The scene had been preserved. Helen and her mother had stayed in the house, and neither had the desire for breakfast. Peter had drunk two cups of coffee and had checked the scene. He knew no one would come anywhere near, but he had to be sure.

Helen had rung Stella and asked her to come to the house. She had told Peter that she needed to have her friend. Peter had agreed but wondered why she hadn't wanted to call her husband. When he asked her, Helen answered that she would call him later as he wasn't that good in the mornings. There had been an edge of resentment in her voice, as if she knew something that she didn't want to talk about.

Peter had asked her who her husband was away with. Helen had answered with one word: *clients*.

As Carol Manning opened the door of the car, Peter saw the SOCO van come through the open entrance gates. The driver had a cigarette hanging from his lip. His right arm was resting on the open window. It was a sight Peter knew well.

Gerry Dunning was one of the first civilian SOCO officers in North Yorkshire. He had grown up on a farm in the Falklands. The first time he had met Peter, he had told him about how, during the war, two SAS soldiers had secretly stayed on his farm for a week before the British landed to take back the island. An Argentinian patrol had visited the farm. The SAS officers had taken them out quickly. Gerry and his dad had used the digger to carve out a large hole and had buried the Jeep and the men in the wilds of Lafonia.

It was an act that meant the SAS soldiers were not discovered, a vital part of the British attack on Goose Green.

Peter thought that it must have affected Gerry in some deep way and wondered if that was the reason why he had left the Falklands and come to England.

"That's a big tree," Manning said as she walked towards Peter. "What is it?"

"It is two trees: an oak and a willow. There is a similar, much older one in the village. There is a body under that one as well."

"Seriously? Is burying people under trees a local tradition?" she asked sarcastically.

"Yes," Peter answered as Manning laughed, obviously thinking he was joking.

"Good job it fell that way. It could have taken out the house," she answered.

"The slope helped it fall away. That and the fact there is a bed of rock only a few feet from the surface," Peter said as they walked towards the scene.

Carol Manning stopped and took a deep breath. "Well, I wasn't expecting this," she said with a sigh. "It's like a macabre art installation. Somehow it doesn't look real."

"The roots have lifted the skeletons from the ground."

"They are so well preserved. I would never have thought that after all this time they would look like this."

"Perhaps Gerry will have some answers," Peter replied as Gerry Dunning marched across the lawn carrying his large black case.

"Morning all," he said cheerily. "Nice day for it."

"What do you think?" Manning asked him as Gerry opened his case and took out a camera.

"Fantastic. Never seen anything like this before. I will get some snaps and have a closer look."

Before Manning could reply, there was a rumble of tyres on the drive as a red pickup sped up the hill.

"Visitors," Manning said warily.

"It's Stella. She is a friend of Helen. A bit of support," Peter answered.

"Can she be trusted to keep this quiet? I don't want anything getting out just yet."

"I know her well," Peter nodded his approval.

Gerry Dunning worked on the scene as Peter and Manning looked on. A hundred photographs later, Gerry stepped into the grave to take a closer look at the corpses.

Using a long metal probe, he pushed it inside the mouth of Albert Shepherd and prised out a round, black stone.

"Interesting," he said as he took the stone and put it on an exhibit board, ready to be photographed. "Never seen that before."

"It's a tongue stone," Stella said as she walked towards them with a tray of coffee and some sandwiches. "They are used to keep the undead in the grave, especially vampires."

Manning looked at Peter as if she didn't know what to do.

"Stella, this is Inspector Manning and Officer Dunning. Tell me, how do you know what it is?"

"It was a tradition when someone died to put a stone in the mouth to stop them rising from the grave. They would sometimes wrap the body in holly wands so they couldn't dig themselves out of the ground."

"A ritual burial?" Manning asked.

"Stella is an authority on the occult," Peter butted in.

"I think this was done more to ease the conscience of the killer rather than the afterlife of the victim," Stella said, as if a criminal expert. "From all accounts, my great-great-great-grandmother had the same thing done to her when she was murdered."

Manning looked at Peter again, as if she did not know what to say.

"Stella had an ancestor, Esther Corbridge, who was hanged for theft of a pig and buried under the double tree in my village. She had been set up with the crime because they thought she was a witch," Peter answered.

"Good God. Is this place safe?" Manning asked with a deep exhale of breath. "Just goes to show… I did years in the Met and never saw anything like this."

"This is Yorkshire. We do murder differently up here," Stella added as she put the tray on the ground, brushed a strand of deep red hair from her face, then turned to walk back to the house. "The family that killed Esther lived here. They have a history of getting rid of people they didn't like."

[61]
Rags And Bones

The late afternoon had clouded over as a fresh breeze blew in from the coast. The sky threatened rain as Gerry Dunning placed the last of the bones into the plastic body boxes that were always used for skeletons and decomposing cadavers. They were better than body bags and kept even the most rotting corpse in one piece.

It had taken five hours to take all the skeletons from within the roots of the tree. Each bone was photographed in place before it was moved. Clothing was removed as intact as possible.

Gerry worked alone, watched by the occasional visiting detective inspector, superintendent, or assistant chief constable. Claire Manning thought it highly funny that they were prepared to turn out on a bank holiday Monday.

By six o'clock, all that remained was the hole in the ground and the fallen tree.

"Good job, Gerry," Manning said as she patted him on the back as he took off his forensic suit and wiped the sweat from his face.

"Not really... no real evidence and I couldn't find the bullets. I have seen similar gunshot wounds in the past at close range with a military pistol. They were killed with a small handgun, probably a thirty-eight calibre. Looks like they were both shot at close range. Executed."

"No signs of a struggle?" Peter asked.

"They died too long ago to tell. Death would have been instant. Strange thing is, that from the way they were, it looks as if they were killed somewhere else and then placed in the grave. The hands had been put together and there are gouges and scrapings in the rock, similar to that of a mechanical digger."

"Premeditated?" Manning asked.

"Not necessarily," Peter answered. "They could have been killed elsewhere and then brought here after the grave had been dug."

Manning looked at him suspiciously.

"I ask you this as a copper and not as a priest. Do you have any suspicion as to who did this?"

"Magnus Seagrave. He was the husband of Evelyn. She was probably having a relationship with Albert Shepherd," Peter answered. "That's just from what I have picked up as vicar."

"Do you know where he is?" Manning asked.

Peter dreaded the question. "No," he answered. "He would be of an age by now. He could possibly be dead. All I know is that he left the house soon after his wife went missing and wasn't seen again. People put it down to him being heartbroken."

Before he could say any more, Helen came out of the door with a tray of coffee.

"I thought you might like this. I saw you were all packed up. I had a call from the undertaker. They said they will be here in forty-five minutes for the collection," Helen stopped and looked at the black plastic lids of the body boxes. "Strange word, *collection*. So sanitised."

"This is Inspector Manning and Gerry Dunning," Peter said by way of introduction. "Sorry I haven't been out before. It is all a bit of a shock."

"Are you Helen Robinson. Raincliffe School, Scarborough?" Manning asked.

"Yes," she answered.

"I am Carol Burley. Manning is my married name. You were a year below me. We were in the orchestra together. You played the flute."

"Very badly," Helen answered. "I remember you. Didn't you move away?"

"Long story... back now. Still in my dad's house on Stepney Drive. I was left it when he died. Mum and Dad divorced. That's why I moved away," Manning answered as they stood around the body boxes, drinking coffee and talking of the old school days.

"What can I do with the grave?" Helen asked, as if to end the conversation.

"I've got everything I need: samples from the soil and fragments of clothing. I was going to ask if it would be okay for me to put a tarp over it, just in case I need anything else?"

"Can I get someone to chop up the tree?" Stella asked as she walked out of the house. "It's not a reminder you want to be looking at every day."

"I'm fine with that," Gerry answered. "What about you, boss?"

Manning nodded. "The superintendent said it was my case and not for C.I.D... Detective Inspector Roberts didn't seem to be bothered when he came up here. Apparently, they are short-staffed. Can you get someone easily?"

"*Bruce Loves Grass*?" Peter asked Stella.

"I could get him here tomorrow," she answered.

"One thing," Helen asked softly as if she was breaking an unwritten rule. "What happens to the remains?"

"They will be reburied and given a proper funeral," Peter answered.

"Who will tell Amber Hudson?" Stella asked.

"Evelyn was the sister of Amber Hudson. She lives a few miles away. She comes to my church."

"Would you do that?" Manning asked Peter. "I am going to put out a press release that will say that we have found the body of a missing woman, but won't go into details. I would prefer if we could keep this to ourselves for the time being."

"I can come with you," Stella said. "Amber is a good friend."

[62]
Whisky

The road to the Old Manor was littered with the debris of the storm. Stella drove her pickup and Peter clung to the door handle, stomping on the imaginary brake with his foot before every bend. It was a subconscious act, in the hope that she would slow down. She had insisted on taking her pickup as it had four-wheel drive.

It wasn't long before they were at the gates of the house. Stella had not said a word the entire journey. Her eyes were fixed on the road, and the sleeves of her shirt were rolled back to reveal the tattoos on her arms.

"How do you think Amber will take it?" Peter asked as he realised he had said something stupid.

Stella caught the look on his face and resisted being sarcastic.

"I think she will find closure. Amber often talks about Evelyn and what has happened to her."

"How do you know her?" he asked.

"I did some walling for her when I first started out, and we became good friends. I see her most weeks for a coffee. I stayed here for a few weeks when I split from my ex-husband."

"Do you want to tell her?" Peter asked.

"You're the copper and the priest. Isn't that your job?" Stella didn't wait for an answer. "Let me tell her."

Peter nodded in agreement as the pickup drove slowly down the hill towards the house. As it pulled up outside, Peter saw Amber and Marcus clearing away some fallen branches of a tall monkey puzzle tree that towered over the front lawn.

Amber turned and waved with a warm smile. Then she saw Peter. Her face changed, as if she knew something bad was about to happen.

"Stella, what brings you? Have you kidnapped the vicar?" Amber asked as she walked towards the vehicle.

"It's Evelyn," Stella answered. "Her body has been found."

Amber stiffened her back as she took off her gardening gloves and turned to Marcus. "I need a drink," she shouted to him. "Something strong. In the main hall. Evelyn has been found."

"Two minutes," he answered as he put down the branch he was holding and made towards the back of the house.

Amber walked purposefully into the house. She showed no real signs of emotion. Everything was kept together, as if she had mourned for many years and there were no more tears left.

"Where was she found?" Amber asked as she sat at the long oak table and gestured for Peter and Stella to do the same.

"The Grange," Stella answered, her words dulled by the wooden panelling that encompassed the room. "The double tree fell down in the storm and Evelyn was underneath."

"How is Helen? It must be a great shock?"

"She has taken it well, so far. I don't think it has sunk in yet," Peter added.

Stella paused before she went on. "There was another body in the grave."

"Bertie Shepherd?" Amber asked. "Were they murdered?"

"Yes," Peter answered. "They were buried together. It's very important that their identities do not get out. The police are going to put out a press release to say that the body of a missing person has been found. They will not give any names."

"What about Magnus Seagrave? He killed them. My husband was right all along. He always said Evelyn was murdered."

"It isn't known where Seagrave is, or if he is still alive," Pete

"Is it worth pursuing him? He will have paid his price, knowing what he has done for so long and living with the fear that the bodies would be found," Amber said as Marcus brought in a tray of crystal glasses filled with whisky.

"If he is alive, he needs to face justice. No one should be allowed to kill and get away with it," Peter answered as he declined the glass that Marcus was offering him.

"How will you find him?" Amber asked.

"There are many ways. If he has a bank account, credit card, or is registered to vote. We all leave a trace as to where we are," Peter said as Amber sipped from her glass.

"And what about Evelyn? What happens to her?" she asked.

"She will be returned to you for burial. To be at peace."

"I need to see where she was all these years," Amber said as she turned to Marcus.

"I am sure it can be arranged," Stella answered.

"No. I want to go now, before it gets dark."

[63]
Old Stone

Four long shadows were cast as the gathering stood by the shallow grave. The evening sun was settling below the hills to the west as it let go of its grip on The Grange. The fallen tree still had life within it. Several birds had settled to roost in its broken branches. The leaves had not yet been starved of life.

Amber sobbed as she twisted the handkerchief in her hand as Marcus put a strong arm around her back and held her close. Peter and Stella looked on. Both felt like outsiders in the grief of another.

Peter knew there were no words that would help at this time. Silence was often best. He saw that Stella had a tear that rolled across her cheek and down the side of her face. Her stoniness was broken. Peter reached out and put a hand on her shoulder as they all shared the solemn moment.

"Would it be right to pray?" Amber asked. "I have been so angry with Evelyn for so long. I thought she had run away and was too pigheaded to get in touch. She has been here all along."

"Dear Lord. We pray for the repose of the souls of Evelyn and Bertie. May they rest in peace and rise in glory. Bless us in our lives, in our mistakes, in our sadness. Keep with us in life and in death. May your peace be upon this place and all spirits be at rest. In the name of Jesus. Amen."

"Amen," they all repeated, as if it was the only way to end the spell.

The door of the house suddenly slammed shut as if someone had run outside to be with them. A squall of wind rattled the wisteria, scattering a pungent scent of lilacs across the garden.

Amber jumped and gave a shivered laugh.

"That was unexpected," she said as she held Marcus by the hand.

"Do you believe in life after death?" Marcus asked as he turned to Peter.

"I do," Helen said as she came through the French windows and walked towards them. "Especially after living here. I think Evelyn was trying to tell us something. We had all sorts of things going on in the house. Peter came and blessed the place for us."

"Evelyn was always one for making herself known," Amber answered as she smiled at Marcus. "I am glad she has been found and I am glad that she is free. Thank you, Helen, for letting me come and see where she was resting. It brings an end to all my worries. I thought that Evelyn didn't like me and that's why she hadn't been in touch. Now I know why."

"You are welcome here anytime," Helen answered. "I was going to ask you what you would like us to do with the…" she stopped, not knowing how to describe the hole in the ground where Evelyn had been buried.

"A small quern-stone with their initials? She loved Bertie, even though he was a rogue," Amber answered, knowing exactly what Helen had meant. "I have one in the garden at home."

"That would be perfect," Helen answered.

"Will you preside over the burial of her remains, Peter? She loved your church. Would it be possible to have her buried in the churchyard?"

"Of course," Peter answered. "Hopefully this will bring about a resolution."

"It has already," Amber replied as she turned to Marcus and took his hand. "Now that this is all over, I wondered if you would finally like to ask me to marry? After all, we have been more than friends for so long, we might as well make it official."

Marcus pulled Amber towards him and kissed her.

"I think he just said yes," Stella said as Marcus held Amber in his arms.

"That was a perfect proposal," Amber said as Marcus ended the kiss.

[64]
Solid Air

The window of the red pickup was open. The dented vehicle looked out of place as it stood on the gravel drive of The Grange. Stella walked slowly towards the pickup. Her hands were buried deep into the pockets of the baggy denim dungarees that hung on long shoulder straps. Her red hair had fallen from the once-tight bun tied with a pencil and now hung in strands.

Each step she took was slow and deliberate, as if she was thinking deeply about what to say.

Peter walked on behind and, looking back, waved at Marcus and Amber, who were arm in arm by the fallen tree.

"You have brought something to this place, Reverend Barnes. Circles are being completed. Secrets uncovered," Stella said as she leant against the side of the pickup. "I wonder what will happen next?"

"Hopefully nothing," Peter answered as he looked towards the darkening forest and the hills beyond. "I am a great believer in coincidences, and they never come in threes."

"I don't think any of this is a coincidence. Since you came here, things have changed. The Holy Well. The Corbridge tree... and now this. Not every day a storm comes along and uncovers a thirty-year-old murder."

Peter smiled.

"Funny thing. I never believed they had just run off at the same time."

"A story that should have been forgotten?"

"It was something that had obviously touched a lot of people. For me, it started with Esther Corbridge. The injustice and cruelty of what a priest did."

"Aided by his brother, the magistrate," she answered. "There is a lot of hate in the Seagrave family."

"Hopefully that will now be over."

"Will the police look for Magnus?"

"There will be a post-mortem of the remains. As much evidence as possible will be examined. Inquiries will be made to find Magnus Seagrave, and eventually he will be put before the court."

"Just in time for the harvest festival and blessing of the well."

"I doubt it. Finding him might take a little longer. That's if he is still alive."

Stella laughed.

"What's so funny?" Peter asked.

"You know he is alive," Stella answered with a raised, chastising brow.

"Do I?"

"The note. Did you not read it? I put it through your door."

"You posted the note? Why?" Peter asked, wanting to know how she was involved.

"I was asked to drop it in when I came to finish off the wall at the back of the churchyard. I did knock, but you weren't in."

"Who by?"

"Not at liberty to say. A concerned parishioner," Stella answered, folding her arms across her chest defensively.

"You worry me. Is James Meredith in your coven? I recognised the handwriting," Peter stuttered the words. "I feel like I am being treated like a dinlo. Did he tell you what was in it?"

"He's my uncle on my mother's side, and he is definitely not part of a coven," Stella laughed. "Uncle James wanted to help you out but didn't want to be seen. Client details and all that. He just wanted me to drop the note off."

"Then why did he tell you the contents?" Peter asked, trying to keep his anger within.

"He didn't. The envelope was open, so I had a sneaky peak. Sorry," Stella smiled, sensing his annoyance. "When I read it, I realised it was confidential. I shouldn't have said anything to you, but sometimes you can be bloody annoying. One minute a priest, the next a copper. Who are you, Peter Barnes?"

Peter stepped back, as if he had been shot in the chest with a bullet of solid air.

It was a question he had often asked himself, and not one that he wanted to answer. Peter turned away from her to watch the sun finally fade as it sunk into the ground.

Stella stepped towards him and put her hand on his shoulder. He could feel the sudden warmth through his shirt. He wanted to take hold of her hand, intertwine his fingers, and hold her close. Peter stepped away and cast the thought from his mind.

"I don't know if I can do this anymore," he answered. "I don't know who I am sometimes. The bishop did say that it would be difficult, but I thought I could wing it. Perhaps I was wrong."

"Are you afraid they will find out you are human?"

Peter stumbled over his words. "This isn't easy."

[65]
Blackmore Farm

Carol Manning sat in the passenger seat of the patrol car with her arms folded.

"Bloody typical," she seethed. "Give you a cold case and then take it from you when there is the prospect of an arrest. Thanks for picking me up, I didn't want to hang around the *outpost*."

"No problem," Peter answered as he drove out of the town towards Whitby. "I wondered why *Dippy Dinlo* was at the station."

"He came to give me the good news; Detective Chief Inspector Browning obviously didn't want to tell me himself. So, he sent his laughing boy," Manning scoffed. "C.I.D want the collar, and don't think a thirty-year-old murder can be solved by uniformed officers. They let us investigate for two weeks and then snatched the case back. Lack of officers. Stupid excuse."

"Do they have any leads?"

"They don't know if he is alive. Magnus Seagrave vanished off the map. I went to his old solicitor and he said he couldn't tell me anything."

"You spoke to James Meredith?" Peter asked, unable to tell her what he knew.

"Yes, not the most helpful of people. He didn't reply to several of my questions. The only thing he said was that they hadn't heard from Seagrave for some considerable time."

Peter nodded. He knew that for some reason Meredith was lying, and he couldn't understand why.

"Meredith Senior and Seagrave were in the same masonic lodge."

"Isn't everybody around here? I wonder if Browning is on the square?" Manning answered as the radio juddered into life.

"Foxtrot-Papa-Three-Five from control."

"Go ahead," Manning said as she pressed the key on the handset.

"Report of a missing person. Blackmore Farm. He hasn't been seen for three weeks. Gerry Blair. A bit of a recluse. Informant waiting at the scene."

"Ten-Four," Manning answered.

"Fifteen minutes away," Peter said. "I met Gerry Blair last year. A strange man. I had to take his shotgun from him for trying to shoot seagulls. No family. Lives on his own."

"Probably gone on holiday and never told anyone. How do you want to handle it?"

"You're the boss."

"It's your beat," she answered.

Blackmore Farm was the last house in the village. From there, the road dropped away and meandered through the forestry until it reached Egton.

Old and stone-built, the house had seen better days. The land around it had been long sold off, and the pub next door had closed down. The paint on the windows was peeling away, dried by wind and sun. Each glass was covered on the inside by thick, dirty net curtains.

Peter pulled the car up to the gate. Standing by the telephone box outside the pub was the postman. He was a tall man with the look of a soldier. His postman shorts had sharp creases pressed into them, and his walking boots laced in army fashion. The man waved as Peter and Inspector Manning got out of the car.

"Morning, Barney," the man said as he began to walk towards them. "Hope it's not a wild goose chase. Gerry hasn't been seen for a while. He's a funny old bugger at the best of times. I have never known him to go away for this long before," the postman stopped and looked at Manning. "Nice pips on the shoulders, ma'am," he said, giving her a military salute. "Never expected you to bring your boss with you, Barney. I am Nick Selby. Postman." Selby gave a subtle bow.

"Nick was in the army. Paratrooper. Only became a postie a couple of years ago," Peter added.

"Enough pension to retire, but I got bored sitting at home, looking at my wife's ankles. So, I took this job. They leave me alone. I do five villages every day. From Goathland to Lastingham."

"How come you rang it in today?" Manning asked.

"Milkman. He stopped me and said that things didn't look right. Every time he knocked, there was no reply. He asked me if I had seen him. Today I had a letter that needed signing for," Selby paused and looked up at a first-floor window. "And there's the flies."

The postman pointed to the shabby square window above them. The net curtain was black—thick with a seething mass of bluebottles. The flies clung to the netting, crawling over each other in a vast swarm.

"That's a lot of flies," Peter answered as he went to the boot of the patrol car and took out two pairs of goggles and face masks.

"Am I out of the loop here?" Manning asked. "It's a missing person."

"Vomitoria," Selby said proudly. "I was a survival trainer in the army. I know my flies."

"And?" she asked.

"For that many flies to be on the curtains, it means they have a plentiful food supply for the maggots. It's a bedroom window, so I think I know what we might find," Peter said as he took a small container of *Vicks VapoRub* and smeared it under his nose.

"You are joking?" Manning asked as he handed her the container.

"It'll stop you throwing up with the smell," he answered.

"Do you want me to come in with you?" Selby asked.

"No. If you could hang on for five minutes. We'll go in and have a look," he said, handing Manning a pair of goggles and a face mask.

"Do I need these?" she asked, not wanting to shrink back from the task.

"It's August. He hasn't been seen for a few weeks and the weather has been warm. If he is dead, then it will stink in there."

"In the Met, we would just call the clean-up team."

"In North Yorkshire, we are the clean-up team," Peter answered with a smile.

[66]
Bones Picked Bare

The back door was unlocked. The brass handle had not been cleaned in years and the wood was deeply scratched by a long-dead dog.

Peter pushed against the door. It opened slowly. Even with masked faces, the stench of rotting flesh and maggot faeces was overwhelming.

The cluttered kitchen was filled with black flies that swarmed like a dark cloud. All around them was the detritus of a fractured life. Piles of newspapers were stacked against the walls as if to insulate against the outside world. The old, cold Aga was inch-thick in grease. The remnants of a forgotten meal were left in the frying pan. Now long-cold, the sausage and egg were cocooned in white mould.

Carol Manning gave a visible shudder as Peter walked through the kitchen and into the living room. The mess was even worse. The corpse of a dog lay on the fireside rug. Its stomach had burst open and was being slowly eaten by a hoard of maggots.

"Poor sod," she said, pointing at the animal. "Why did it die?"

"No water," Peter answered as he opened the door to the stairway. "Hasn't been dead for long."

"I know what you mean about the smell. My stomach is twitching."

"Don't worry. I have grown immune to it," Peter answered as he began to walk slowly up the enclosed staircase that was filled with a swirling mass of black flies.

He stopped at the dog-scratched bedroom door and brushed the flies from his face as Manning coughed.

"I don't think I can go in," she shouted from the landing below. "Feel like I am going to throw up."

"Take a deep breath. It will go away," he answered as he turned the handle of the door and slowly opened it.

There was a sudden rush as the swarm billowed from the room. The hallway was filled with a frantic, black, clinging mass of flies. Manning made her way slowly up the stairs towards him as he stepped inside.

On top of the bed was what remained of the man. Most of the flesh had been eaten away, leaving a pyjama-covered skeleton. The skull still had hair, and what was left of the beard covered one side of what was once his face.

Maggots slowly crawled in and out of the decaying nostrils. They were much smaller than Carol Manning thought they should be. The creatures were nothing like the ones her father had used for fishing and kept in the fridge, much to the annoyance of her mother. They seemed to move as one, turning this way and that way as they looked for more flesh.

On the bedside table was an empty bottle of vodka. Next to the bottle was a discarded box of Valium.

Carol Manning reached out and picked up the box. "Suicide?" she asked.

"I think we better get SOCO," Peter answered. "It's a bit too obvious."

[67]
Kalashnikov

The quarterly meeting of the parochial church council had come around quicker than Peter had liked. It had rained most of the day and the browning leaves of the August trees dripped onto the vicarage drive as he made his way to the church hall.

He hoped the rain would stop a big turnout. It often worked in the police that when PC Rain turned up, crime went down. Sadly, as he turned into the car park, he could see that it wasn't going to be the case. The discovery of the bodies at The Grange had probably prompted a desire for gossip. After all, their vicar was the man who was first on the scene; perhaps he would share some of the more gruesome elements of what was now being treated as a cold case murder.

As he stepped towards the door, it suddenly opened. Morris Marsden smiled. "Just coming out for a breath of fresh air. We have rather a full house."

"How? We don't have that many on the PCC," Peter answered.

"Frank Green insisted that the meeting should be open to everyone in the parish, though only those on the council can speak or vote," Marsden answered with a ruffle of his hair, as if he was shaking lice from his feathers. "Here's the agenda, sorry I didn't drop it off before now."

"Interesting," Peter answered as he scanned the sheet of paper and stepped into the room, only to be greeted by a sea of faces.

Joseph Merton held court at one end of the trestle table. His grey beard had grown even longer, and now he combed it methodically with his fingers. Before him was a pile of papers, obviously a testimony to the financial dire straits of the church.

As Peter sat down, Merton middle-fingered his spectacles up his nose and gave a wry smile. The rest of the council sat facing the audience. Morris walked towards the table and sat down as Peter tapped the table with his knuckle to calm the crowd. Then, he looked at the agenda. On it were only two pieces of discussion. *Harvest. Namibia.*

"Thank you, Vicar," Morris said as he looked about the room. "So good to see so many of you taking an interest in the matters of the church. There are apologies for absence from Anne Hindle and Lady Amber Hudson, and our prayers are with them both. Helen Parker will be joining the council at our next meeting. Tonight, we have only two items on the agenda. Vicar, the first is yours. Harvest festival events."

Peter stood up and cleared his throat, not knowing how his words would be received.

"On the Sunday of the bank holiday, the bishop has agreed to consecrate the ground where Esther Corbridge is buried. We will then proceed to church for the harvest celebration. Then the bishop will bless the well, and people will be invited to take water to the old yew tree. It is to be a day of thanks and putting things right from the past. There will be a memorial plaque, and the tree will be known as the Corbridge tree."

Peter took a long breath as he finished. He looked at those gathered. Many of the faces were familiar, many were not. Before him were most of the people that had entered his life in the parish.

Kelly Grant sat with her father. To one side, Fred Prescott, Bruce Jakes and Liz Morris were huddled on the back row. Most surprising of all was the sight of Stella Smith standing by the emergency exit under the portrait of Queen Elizabeth that hung on the wall in a broken frame.

Worryingly, Mary Coleman was in the front row. Her hands were clasped, handbag perched on her knees as she slowly rocked back and forth. "Paganism," she grumbled loudly as Peter spoke. "Witchcraft."

"There will be a market and rides for children. It is hoped that everyone in the village and beyond will feel welcome. It will be more than just a harvest festival. It will be a new start."

Mary Coleman got to her feet and stepped towards him.

"You will pay for this. God will not let you go unpunished. The door has been opened and the Devil welcomed. *Mene, Mene, Tekel, Upharsin*. You have been held in the balance and found wanting."

Peter reached out his hand over the table towards her in a gesture of friendship. "Mary, please."

The woman slapped his hand away and spat in his face. "You will burn in Hell," she said as she clutched her handbag, turned, and walked from the room.

The audience sat in stunned silence as the vicar casually wiped his face with a tissue and sat down.

"Moving on. Next item," Morris said calmly as if nothing had happened whilst the door to the hall slammed shut. "We have had a parcel from Namibia. Before Reverend Green left us, we raised money for a tribe that was sent in cash by a missionary friend."

Peter sat back in his chair and smiled, trying to hide his anxiety. "In cash?" he asked.

"That is what the missionary wanted, and Reverend Green insisted. The money was for bibles for the church," Morris answered as he turned to the long, thin cardboard box propped against the wall. "This has arrived today as a gift to us from Namibia," he said as he ripped open the top flap and looked nervously inside.

"What is it, Morris?" Joseph Merton asked.

"A letter and a photograph," he answered as he rummaged in the box and then handed the photograph and a piece of paper to the vicar. "There is also what looks like a bow and arrow."

"Interesting," Merton said with a smirk. "Would you care to read it to us, Vicar?"

Peter closed his eyes for a moment and took a deep breath and then read the words.

"*Many thanks for the money you sent with the missionary. We no longer need our bows to hunt or protect ourselves. We have bought Kalashnikovs.*" He paused momentarily after reading before continuing. "Does that satisfy your interest, Joseph?" he asked.

"I warned him that we should not send money, but he would not listen," Merton answered. "He insisted that it was what God wanted. We could all be locked up for inadvertently supplying guns."

The dull hum of restrained laughter grew louder. Stella Smith stood in the corner, holding her face in her hands as she tried not to laugh.

"It's not every day a church sponsors a desert war," Fred Prescott muttered loudly from the back of the room.

At that, everyone but Morris Marsden began to laugh. It was hearty and deep, as if it broke the absurdity of the moment.

Peter pushed the photograph across the table and then reached out and put his hand on Morris. The image clearly showed a group of men, each holding an automatic rifle, their faces glowing with large smiles.

"Don't worry, it is not your fault. Frank Green was a fool to do such a thing."

Morris turned, looked at the photo, smiled, and then started to laugh. "Any other business?" Morris asked as the laughter subsided.

Joseph Merton leant forward and rustled the papers before him.

"I only have one thing. It concerns us all. There has been a donation to church funds," Merton paused, drew a breath, and looked around the room. "There has been a bequest of two hundred thousand pounds. I was asked not to mention it to anyone until tonight, so I apologise, Vicar, that you have been kept in the dark. It is an anonymous bequest, but one that if invested wisely, our church will have no further financial worries."

Peter could see Morris begin to shake. His hand trembled as he held onto the table. Gerald Griffin moved quickly towards him and wrapped Morris in his arms as the man began to cry. It was as if the burden of years of financial worry had been lifted from him. Man and boy, he had been faithful to his God and worried and toiled to keep the doors of the church open, the roof free from leaks, the walls from falling in, and the vestry toilet streak-free.

Priests had come and gone with no concern for what was to come. Morris was there every day. He would clean and polish in his quiet service without any public reward.

The church had scrimped and picked, supported by jumble sales and begrudging donations. Now, Morris knew that time was over.

"I'm sorry," he said as Gerald released him from his grip. "I am just overcome with thanks. We have been truly blessed by God, and for that I give thanks."

Peter looked about the room. Fred Prescott wiped a tear from his eye as Liz Morris sat crying. It was as if the whole room had been filled with a spirit of love and gratitude that touched the hearts of everyone there.

"Lord, we give you thanks for the wonders you perform in all our lives and the blessings you pour upon us all. Help us be wise in all we do. In the name of the Saviour, Amen."

His final word was echoed by every voice in the hall. Peter smiled. For the first time, he didn't feel alone, and inside, his heart was no longer afraid that he wasn't the right priest for the parish.

As he looked around the room, it was as if it was slowly filling with the Holy Spirit as faint wisps of mist spiralled from under the door and into the room.

It was at that moment he could smell petrol.

There was a sudden explosion. A fireball rolled across the room. The doors to the hall were quickly lapped in flames as the petrol that had seeped underneath set alight.

The mist quickly turned into black, acrid smoke. The fluorescent lights flickered and then failed as the room was plunged into darkness, lit only by the burning doors.

"Open the fire escape!" Peter shouted.

Stella Smith pushed against the handle. It was held fast.

"It won't open," she answered as the flames from the door burnt against the polystyrene tiles stuck to the ceiling that began to drip burning bullets on the floor. The sudden heat was intense. It cracked the glass of the window by the door. Hot shards shot across the room.

"Get out of the way!" Peter shouted, running across the room. He dived at the door. It smashed open. The door fell off its rotten hinges. Peter rolled onto the grass outside. One by one, people ran from the hall. He got to his feet and went back inside.

"All clear," he shouted as he came outside. "Can someone ring for the police and fire brigade?"

Without an answer, Bruce and Stella ran off. In the burning light of the fire, Peter noticed the woman by the front door of the hall. The flames lit her face and cast a long shadow. The front wall was now engulfed in flames. The wooden boards peeled back and away from the roof. As they did, the flames grew more intense.

Mary Coleman stood in the light of the fire with an empty petrol can in her hands. She was motionless. As Mary stared at the growing inferno, Peter could hear her softly singing *Amazing Grace* to herself, as if in a trance.

He began to walk towards her and as he did, he noticed she was soaked from head to foot in fluid.

"Stay back!" she shouted. "This is how it ends."

"Don't do it, Mary. It is not worth it. God would not want it," Peter answered as he walked slowly towards her.

Mary stepped towards the flames. Peter knew that if she went any closer the petrol fumes coming from her on a warm summer night would suddenly ignite.

"God? What do you know of God? You are a servant of Satan!" Mary screamed, eyes filled with tears.

"It is not what God would want. God brings life, not death," Peter answered, edging closer.

"I am a martyr for the faith. Frank said it was worth giving my life for Jesus."

At that moment, Mary stepped towards the flames.

Peter dived towards her, striking Mary in the chest with one hand. She fell backwards onto the ground as petrol flames flashed across the grass. From the darkness, Fred Prescott dashed towards them, his hands gripping the fire extinguisher from his car.

As Mary and the vicar lay on the floor, about to be engulfed in fire, he doused them both in a cloud of white powder.

Behind them, the flames of the burning hall grew higher and higher, leaping towards the branches of the trees. Long, dark, flickering shadows were cast across the ground, as if they were surrounded by long-dead dancers. There was a sudden crash as the roof collapsed, sending thousands of bright sparks high into the air.

Peter lifted Mary from the grass and began to drag her away from the flames. The woman put up no fight. She hung limply from his arms and sobbed and sobbed. One by one, all who were there followed on.

[68]
Epilogue

The long wooden kitchen table had never been surrounded by so many people. It seemed only right that they should gather there. Bruce Jakes had brought six bottles of wine from his van that went well with the single malt that had miraculously appeared from the briefcase belonging to Joseph Merton.

It had been three hours since they had left the fire, yet it was all they could think and talk about. The wine bottles had been emptied, and the conversation ebbed and dulled as the adrenaline subsided.

"I can't understand why I couldn't open the door," Stella said as she sipped the malt. "It just wouldn't move."

"You were all very lucky," Carol Manning answered. "It was wedged with an iron bar. Good job your vicar is the size he is."

"Did she want to kill us?" Bruce asked as he held Stella by the hand.

"That is something we will have to find out," Manning answered.

Peter walked in, his hair was still wet from the shower he had taken to rid himself of the smell of petrol and extinguisher powder. "Did I miss something?" he asked. "Thanks to Freddy, I didn't go up in flames."

Fred Prescott gave an embarrassed laugh.

"I have had that in my car for ages and never thought it would be used," he answered.

"Good job you did," Manning said. "The woman had covered herself in petrol and could have gone up at any time."

"But why did she do it?" Merton asked as he hugged the bottle of single malt.

"I don't think she is mentally stable. Mary has been through so much. All I can say is that she needs our help and prayers," Peter answered. "She believed that the well was evil, and I opened it up again."

"She tried to burn us all alive," Bruce replied indignantly as the large, round station clock on the far wall of the kitchen struck midnight. "She needs to go to prison for attempted murder."

"Possibly," Manning answered. "I suggest you lot need to go to bed. I will want statements from you all in the morning."

Peter turned to Fred Prescott. "Thanks for tonight. Things could have ended differently."

"I am just glad the bloody thing worked," he answered as he gave Peter a long hug. "Never thought I would get involved with you lot, but I'm glad I did."

Peter didn't know what to say. Words seemed pointless.

"Likewise," he mumbled in reply as Carol Manning patted him on his shoulder.

"Better be going. I will send someone to pick up your statement tomorrow."

"Thanks, boss," Peter said with a nod of the head.

"Never a dull moment in your parish. I spend so much time here, I might start coming to church myself," she quipped as she guided a drunken Joseph Merton out of the house, followed by Fred Prescott.

"We better be going too," Stella echoed as she helped Bruce up from his chair. "Mary meant what she said about burning in Hell. Didn't realise she wanted us all to go with you."

"The Lord gives and takes away," Peter answered.

"The Women's Institute will not be pleased you have burnt the hall down," Bruce butted in with a smile. "They'll have to meet in the pub."

"Joking aside," Peter said seriously. "I really appreciated you both being there. It meant a lot to me."

"We wouldn't have missed it for the world. Not every night you see someone spit in the face of the vicar and then try to burn him alive. I thought they only did that to witches?" Stella said as she gave an unconvincing laugh.

Peter reached out to her and then pulled his hand back. "I am starting to believe there is a force at work in this place. Perhaps you have been right all along."

Stella leant towards him and kissed him on the cheek. Peter caught her worried look as she stepped away. "Look after yourself. I don't think everyone is pleased with what you are trying to do."

[69]
Bridestones

The evening sun slowly faded behind the trees as Peter walked up the hill from the car park by Staindale Lake. He followed the footpath across the stream and through the woods until it broke through the trees. Peter turned down the babble on his police radio and looked out across the rising moor to the large sandstone carbuncle that grew out of the ground. The rock had stood there since the Ice Age. Carved by a retreating glacier and then weathered by rain and frost until it looked as if it had been dropped from the sky.

There was no sign of the missing teenager he had been tasked to find. The path he had followed had been trodden on that day by a thousand people visiting the stones. There was no way he would be able to pick out the pattern of the Doc Marten boots that the lad was wearing.

Peter leant against the stone and looked back across the canopy of the forest. The trees stretched into the distance. From where he stood, he could make out the village of Dalby that now served as a forward station for the search. Several plumes of smoke came up through the trees from the chimneys of the forester houses. Even for late August, the nights were colder than he expected for late summer.

The babble on the radio grew more intense. Peter could hear voices of the civilian search teams cutting across each other on the open channel. He couldn't make out what they were saying as they excitedly screeched their locations and every small detail of their search.

"Barney!" the voice shouted from beyond the stones. "Barney!"

"Here," he answered as he stepped out from the cover of the rock and waved at Carol Manning as she came along the path from the moor.

"I got dropped off on the Whitby Road and was told to come across to the stones and meet you here," Manning answered as she slumped against the tall pepperpot stone and took a deep breath. "It's a bloody long way. The boss gave me a map."

"When did they make a detective gold commander?" Peter asked.

"When they gave Superintendent Siddons annual leave and didn't realise the only super left was in C.I.D."

Peter laughed, swung the bag from his shoulder, and brought out a large flask. "Coffee?" he asked.

"Legend," Manning answered with a sigh of relief.

Peter poured two cups and sat next to Manning. "Biscuit?" he asked as he took out a packet of Bourbons and offered one to her.

"What else do you have in that bag?" Manning asked.

"Night sight, coffee, chocolate, torch, and a survival bag. Just the usual stuff."

"Do you think he is still out here?" she asked.

"He's sixteen. As soon as it gets dark, that's when he will realise he is alone in a forest."

"Gold commander was talking about bringing in a helicopter, but he doesn't know if we can afford it. The parents think he is going to top himself."

"The tree cover is too thick for a helicopter. They would never see him. Why do his parents think he came all the way from Scarborough to kill himself in the woods?"

"They found something in his diary about him wanting to die at the Bridestones. He thinks he is Rambo," Manning said as she tapped the metal cup on the side of the rock and looked out into the growing gloom. "What are we going to do when it gets dark?"

"Sit and listen. The forest is very quiet. If he is coming to the Bridestones, we will hear him."

They sat in silence through the next hour. The day slowly dimmed as darkness began to consume them and as the light went from blue to black. The forest was not as quiet as Peter had said. A mile to the west, they could hear the traffic on the Whitby Road. Within the forest itself, the wind stirred the trees so the branches clashed as if clattering staves. The far-off call of an owl echoed through the trees as high on the moor, a vixen cried like a small child.

"She admitted it," Manning said in a whisper as if afraid to speak. "Mary Coleman coughed the lot. She had prepared the whole thing and had planned to leave the meeting before the end and set fire to the hall."

"Did she say why?" he asked, equally quiet.

"Satan. That's all she said. Repeated the name over and over. I had the detective send over the interview notes today."

"Why did they take her to Northallerton to be interviewed?" Peter asked. "Not the usual thing to do."

"Not every day someone tries to murder a copper. In that, we have a problem. The chairman of the police committee is gunning for you. She doesn't like the idea of having a copper and a priest getting bigger headlines than she does. The acting chief is her lapdog."

"What should I do?" he asked in a low whisper as he poured coffee into both cups.

"Low profile. You have four weeks of leave on your card, and your time in lieu is maxed out."

"Hide?"

"Karen Benton wants blood. The acting chief said it looked bad for the force, having one of its own attacked by a madwoman. You have become the story," Manning sighed. "I think it will blow over. Coleman will be remanded in custody to Low Newton. Things will go quiet until the trial. From what she said in her interview, she can only plead guilty with diminished responsibility. The defence want to have her examined by a psychiatrist."

"I feel sorry for Mary. She has been through so much."

"She wanted you dead. Is the Church of England full of nutters?" Manning asked with a whispered laugh.

"Yes," he replied as he sipped his coffee. "I even have an imaginary friend and talk to myself."

"The other hot news is that I have been given back the Seagrave cold case. C.I.D. say they are overwhelmed with work, as three of their officers have been seconded to the murder in Skipton."

"Does that mean they couldn't find Magnus Seagrave?" he asked.

"I don't think they even tried. From the file they gave me, it looks as though Seagrave disappeared."

"Getting away with murder."

His words were cut short by the sound of someone clumsily walking through the woods. Peter reached into his bag and took out his night sight binoculars. There, coming up the path to the stones, was a cloaked figure. Long hair was tied back in a ponytail. The thin face and slight build fitted the description of the missing lad.

"Is it him?" Manning whispered.

Peter put down the binoculars and nodded as the figure walked towards the stones.

The lad came closer and sat on a large rock, unaware that he was being watched from several feet away.

"Fancy a coffee, Michael?" Peter asked the figure in a loud voice. "I have biscuits."

[70]
Park-Drive

The ashes of the church hall were edged in burnt grass. The building had collapsed inward. Its wooden walls had disintegrated and the metal struts that had held up the roof were slumped on the ground like the rib cage of a large dead elephant. Even a week later, the smell of smoke hung in the air.

Bishop Riley stood on the gravel of the car park. His belly hung over the rim of his Marks & Spencer trousers as a sweat stain under the armpits of his clerical shirt grew in the heat of the afternoon.

"My God, Peter. She must have wanted you dead," Riley said as he sucked on the last of his Park Drive cigarette. "I went to visit her in prison. Apparently, Frank Green had sent her a letter saying that there could never be anything between them. It must have been that which pushed her over the edge."

"So much so that she would have burnt us all to death?" he asked.

"It would appear that Frank had gaslighted her all along. You will be aware of his intentions?"

"I have heard nothing."

"He is to marry Martha Storr and is coming back to live in the parish. Frank believes God is calling him here to fight evil. That is what he told Mary Coleman. Worryingly, she believed he wanted her to martyr herself in the name of Jesus."

"That is what she said on the night. Frank had said it would be fitting to die for Jesus," Peter answered.

"As a police officer, what do you make of it?" Riley asked.

"There seems to be a sense of encouragement."

"My thoughts exactly," Riley replied as he walked slowly around the ruins of the hall with Peter following two paces behind. "Frank Green is a dangerous man. I have had word that he is to set up services in the pub."

"That'll be handy for him."

"Glad to see you haven't lost your sense of humour. He has gone teetotal and given up the demon gin. Poor sod. Despite what has gone on here, I still think you are the man for the job, but there are dangers."

"Dangers?" Peter asked, wondering what the man meant.

"I had a telephone call from Karen Benton, the chair *whatever* of the police committee. She wanted me to move you; asked if you could be given a job in York Minster, away from people."

"And?" Peter asked, wondering if his time in the parish would soon be over.

"I told her to bugger off and asked what right she had over the ministry of the church. Before she hung up, I made it very clear you were here for five years, and that the parish wanted you."

"Thank you. Do they?" Peter asked, knowing that Riley was a spymaster that even the KGB would envy.

"Morris Marsden speaks highly of you. He said you were a breath of fresh air. I had coffee with him this morning. I also called in on Amber Hudson. She is a very old friend and one of your greatest supporters. You have made a great impression here. It's not your fault that a murdered priest turns up in the roots of a tree. You have rocked the boat for all the right reasons."

"That's a relief. I was beginning to wonder if I was the right man," Peter answered as Riley lit another cigarette.

"Do you feel like an imposter? That one day you are going to be found out?" Riley asked with a smirk.

"Yes."

"I'm glad. So do I," Riley laughed. "Doubt is a good sign of a true vocation. I never trust any of these buggers who come along with a rock-solid faith and Jesus on speed dial."

"How do you see me going forward with the parish?"

"Just keep doing what you are doing." Riley stopped and turned to Peter. "How is your other job going? I got the impression that Benton is a little upset."

"They want me to move to a desk job. When Mary gets back, I will talk with her about it. I am on leave for a couple of weeks until the press gets bored."

"Might not be a bad thing," Riley answered as he put his hand on Peter's shoulder. "How is Mary doing?"

"She rang last night. Hopefully, Mary is coming home for the harvest festival. Her mother is making a good recovery."

"Harvest," Riley said with a jowled smile. "I was told by Mary Coleman that if I consecrated the ground of a witch, then I too would burn in the fires of Hades."

"Soon there will not be enough room. Hell will be full of priests."

"Perhaps it already is," Riley laughed. "I told her that I was consecrating the grave of a woman who had been wrongfully hanged for theft. It will be a wonderful day, rain or shine."

"We were going to have refreshments in the church hall. That is not going to happen now," Peter replied as he kicked the ash by his foot. "Morris has suggested a marquee."

Riley did not answer, obviously distracted by his wristwatch.

"My God. Is that the time?" he said briskly. "I must get along the road. Why is it that a priest cannot find a mistress in Leeds instead of their parish? This will be the second time this month."

"Anyone I know?" Peter asked, not knowing what else to say.

"You won't have to wait too long to find out. The editor of *The Mail on Sunday* joyfully informed me that he will be running a double-page spread tomorrow. They even have photographs taken by a secret camera hidden in the wardrobe. I am going to tell the man now that his days are over. Then, it's tea with the local lord who has the right of the parish appointment. He is in for the shock of his life."

"Rather you than me," Peter replied.

"I could never do your job, Peter. All that death and misery," Riley smiled. "One minute dealing with a suicide, and the next, giving out tickets for not wearing a seat belt. I am surprised you haven't gone mad."

"Good days and bad days," Peter answered as Riley began to walk back to his car.

"See you next Sunday. Be with you by early afternoon."

Peter watched as the car drove slowly away. He turned to look at what was once the church hall and wondered if there really was a force for evil at work around him.

[71]
Bonaparte

It was late in the afternoon when the police Range Rover cracked the gravel on the driveway of the vicarage. The tyres scattered pebbles into the wheel arches and fired them into the hedges as it braked quickly.

Steve Becket jumped out of the car and slammed the door. He hugged a thick file under his arm as he strode towards the door.

"Becky? Unexpected visit?" Peter asked as he came around the side of the vicarage, his face stained with dirt and sweat.

"I have been ringing you for an hour and got no reply," Becket answered with a smile. "Gardening leave?"

"Yes. Keeping my head down, but I expect *the gossip factory* has you fully informed."

"Talk of the town, mate," Becket answered. "Dead bodies in tree roots. Crazed parishioners wanting to burn the vicar alive. What next?"

"What do you want, Becky?" Peter asked as he wiped his face with the back of his gardening glove.

"Carol Manning has got me as her bag carrier. I am tasked with picking up a few loose ends from the cold case," Becket replied as he offered Peter the thick file from under his arm. "She thought you might like to have a look at some of the stuff that has turned up."

"Have you found Seagrave?"

"That's the problem," Becket said as he opened the file and pulled out a long piece of official-looking paper. "Case closed. He's dead."

Peter took the certificate and looked at the typing.

"*14th of July, 1967. Elgin. Scotland.* I thought he had changed his name?"

"So did we. That was duff info," Becket answered. "The man has been dead all this time. Manning wants you to have some holiday reading. She wanted some fresh eyes to see if something has been missed."

Becket handed Peter the file.

"Thanks," he answered as he sat on the wooden bench by the front door. "Cuppa?"

"I've got to get back," Becket paused and folded his muscular arms across his neatly ironed shirt. "One more thing. The *crown procrastination service* has lost the file on the drunken Freemason you locked up."

"Lost? How?" he asked.

"No idea. I only found out as I was on the witness list and got a notification that I would no longer be needed. I asked the file preparation inspector what was happening and he said the paperwork had been lost between the two offices."

"Typical," Peter answered. "I never thought it would get to court."

"For God's sake, don't do anything," Becket insisted. "He will come again. They always do."

"He has friends on the inside," Peter argued.

"Now is not the time to make any more enemies," Becket replied. "The only reason I am here is because Manning wants to put some distance between you and her. She has a career to think about."

"What's that supposed to mean?"

"Your name is on everyone's lips. Manning doesn't want to get dragged into it."

"*It*?" Peter snapped back. "I haven't done anything wrong."

"You are famous. Copper becomes a priest that someone tries to kill. They don't think it's good for the job," Becket answered defensively.

"They?"

"Supervision."

"Carol Manning?" Peter asked, feeling betrayed.

"No. She is well on your side and about the only one who is defending you. Manning has a lot on her plate. You have been replaced at the *outpost* by Dave Raw."

"I thought he was set to get locked up for assaulting a prisoner?" Peter asked in disbelief.

"He got off at Crown Court. Raw said he punched the man in the face to defend himself," Becket replied with a smile. "He saw the man clench his fist and was about to break free of the officer holding him, so he decked the prisoner."

Peter slumped down on the wooden seat and shook his head in disbelief. "My God."

"You are better away from it all. The division is in chaos. Custody Office at Malton is closed due to lack of staff. All prisoners must go to Scarborough or Northallerton. Sergeant Burley has done a *Blackadder* and gone all wibble with stress and won't be back for six weeks, if at all. Three more traffic cars are over mileage, and the keys have been locked away," Becket laughed in exasperation. "Sod it. I will have that cup of tea."

"Follow me," Peter answered as he stood up and opened the front door, stepping inside the house with Becket following on. "Grab a seat in the office and I will get some tea."

Steve Becket stepped into the large office, his attention grabbed by the statue of Napoleon Bonaparte on the mantelpiece. Picking it up, he checked the base.

"Admiring my artefacts?" Peter asked as he put the tray of tea and biscuits on the desk.

"It's nicked."

"What? It can't be. I bought that from the parish jumble sale," Peter answered.

"It's still nicked. I attended the burglary at Mulgrave Castle a year ago. It has the letters MC on the base."

"Are you sure?"

"Positive. It was one of the things the Marquis said he would really miss. We got two lads from Middlesbrough for the job. The Carter brothers."

Peter laughed. "You are joking? I took Brian Carter to HMP Durham on prisoner escort."

"The Marquis will be well pleased. Can I tell him who found it?" Becket said as he held Napoleon up to the light coming through the window.

"You can tell him it cost me ten quid," Peter answered.

"Valued at twenty grand. One of a kind. Made in France for the man himself," Becket answered proudly. "You got a bargain. If only a temporary one."

[72]
Mary – Mary

Mickey Dolenz sang the last line of *Mary, Mary*, his voice coming from the tinny speaker of the kitchen radio. It was a song that always made him think of his wife. He had flippantly called it *their* song, something that Mary thought was a sour joke. Yet, like the song, Mary had left him six months into their courtship and Peter had gone after her.

Peter finished the washing up and stacked the final cup on the steel draining board.

It was at times like this that he thought he had made a mistake. Perhaps he should have let her go forever. Perhaps he might have forced the hand of God, and that his being with Mary was not what God wanted after all.

The line '*What did I do to make you leave me?*' was an earworm he couldn't get out of his head.

The argument had been about his faith. Mary always thought Peter loved God more than he did her. It rubbed at their marriage most days when they were together. Mary didn't need to say it— the irritation was always there. God was the third wheel, the triangle in their relationship that she resented.

Peter wiped his hands on the drying cloth then placed it over the plate rack as the phone in the office began to ring. It was stark, shrill, and echoed along the corridor.

Walking quickly through the hall, he knew it would be Mary. Since Peter had gone on gardening leave, she had rung every day.

"*How are things?*" Mary asked when he picked up the phone.

"Better now I can hear your voice," he answered.

"*We are all packed and setting off first thing. The children are so excited. I told Mum and Dad we would all try and get down in a week or so. Did you manage to get cover for the services?*"

"I asked Frank Green."

"*What?*"

"Joking. Bishop Riley said he will take them for me. He likes the idea of being back in the pulpit on a normal Sunday," Peter answered. "What time do you think you'll be back?"

"*What time is the harvest?*" Mary asked.

"It all starts at lunchtime with a street market, and the consecration of the grave is at two, and the service in church at three. Will you be back in time?"

"*We should be. The road out of Cornwall is usually clear first thing. I just hope the motorway doesn't have any hold ups.*" Mary paused momentarily. "*I am really looking forward to seeing you. I know I don't say it often enough, but I really love you.*"

Peter smiled to himself. *Love* was a word that she seldom said. Whenever Peter said it to Mary, she always replied with 'ditto'.

"Thank you," he answered. "That means a lot."

"*I mean it. We have all missed you so much. I should have been there for you. The idea that someone wanted to kill you…*" Mary trailed off, her voice strained.

"Don't worry. We will be together again tomorrow, and that's all that matters."

"*Peter?*" she lilted.

"Yes?" he answered, knowing her saying his name was a preface to something that was on her mind.

"*Can things be different when I get back? Promise me that you will give us more of your time?*"

"I promise. I have learnt a lot whilst you have been away," Peter replied, his voice deepening. "Life and work balance. I have prayed about it and realised I had got it all wrong."

"*I have been telling you that for years. Why is it that you listen to God more than you do to me?*"

[73]
Blessed Bones

The large crowd around the tree blocked the road and filled the pavement. A warm breeze gently blew through the branches under a cloudless Yorkshire sky. Unusually, for an August bank holiday Sunday, the weather was perfect; it hadn't snowed.

Peter and Bishop Riley stood under the crown of leaves. Both were dressed simply in black cassocks. Each had a white stole draped over their shoulders.

Gathered around them were an amalgamation of people. The curious, with no connection to the church, had come to gawp and wonder why an old grave should need prayers to be said and water splashed upon it, as they waited for the street market to open.

Rory Brown, a local copper, leant against the church gate, the sleeves of his blue shirt rolled up over his elbows. He was three weeks from retirement and had seen everything the world had to offer. Before he joined the force, he was a semi-professional footballer. A man well-considered by villain and copper alike.

Stella and a garner of companions stood next to Riley in critical solidarity. She wore a green velvet cloak over a matching long dress that was uncomfortably warm for the weather. Her hair was woven into a long plait, intertwined with red and gold thread. It was the first time that Peter had seen her wearing makeup. Both of her eyes were etched in deep black kajal liner.

The twelve women with her all looked the same, though none were as thin or tall as Stella. Each carried a short, carved staff—a sign of their faith. The only man in the group dragged neat fingers through the strands of his grey beard. The shorter woman next to him clutched his cloak, as if to claim him as her own.

Around them were members of most of the local churches under the order of the bishop to attend. Three priests in dark suits were intermingled amongst the flock. Their presence was out of reluctant duty. Bishop Riley was always to be obeyed, even if it meant forgoing the Sunday afternoon sleep taken by most of the clergy between morning prayer and evensong.

As the church clock struck the hour, Riley stamped his staff on the ground three times.

Peter looked around the crowd, hoping to see his wife.

"Prevent us, O Lord, in all our doings with thy most gracious favour," Riley said loudly as he began the rite of consecration.

Peter wasn't listening. His eyes searched the crowd for Mary and the children as a nagging concern twisted in his stomach. He took some comfort in the faces of those he knew: Morris Marsden, Amber Hudson, Helen Parker, and Fred Prescott.

"Amen," he answered automatically as Riley came to the end of the first prayer.

Peter noticed that Riley smiled at Stella as she repeated the 'Amen'. It was as if it transcended any tradition. A word of unity and agreement. A '*so mote it be*' that joined them all in common purpose.

Riley took his staff and etched a cross in the ground as he began to speak.

"By virtue of our sacred office in the church of God, we do now consecrate, and set apart from all profane and common uses, this ground to be a resting place for Esther Corbridge, who departed this life. May God forgive our sinfulness and corruption for what we did to her in life, and make satisfaction in death."

There was an eerie silence. The large crowd looked on as Peter took a flask of holy water from his pocket and sprinkled it on the ground. The wind blew through the branches as leaves began to fall.

"From this time, may this tree be a symbol of life and not death," Peter said as the water fell like tears. "Amen."

The word was again repeated by the crowd that had now come closer to the old tree, as if drawn by the ritual.

A man caught his eye. Peter had never seen him before. The man was striking in appearance, steel-blue eyes, old, tall, thin, and well dressed in a summer blazer, Panama hat, and cream trousers. He had the bearing of a man of means, aristocratic in demeanour and looked out of place amongst the crowd.

Their eyes met. The man smiled.

"May the Lord of his mercy grant to us, with all the faithful departed, rest and peace. Amen," Riley said the final prayer as Peter realised that he had not heard anything that had been said. The crowd clapped spontaneously. "I believe the street market is now open and the harvest festival will take place in the church at three."

The crowd clapped again as Riley turned to Stella. "Thank you for your presence."

"Pagans at a consecration?" she answered.

"We are all children of God," Riley answered with a warm smile. "We both dress up and say our magic spells. God is far bigger than all of us."

"Brave thing to say, Bishop. There are those who would disagree with you. Frank Green is one of them," she answered.

"We have our ways and you have yours. The church wronged your ancestor, and Peter was correct in wanting to make things right. I believe God stands outside of time and I hope that Esther is somehow aware of what we have done today," Riley said as he tapped his staff against the gnarled trunk of the tree. "This is a marker better than any gravestone. A living memory of a life wrongly taken." Riley turned to Peter. "More tea, Vicar?" he said with a laugh.

As the crowds parted and Peter set off to follow Bishop Riley, the tall man in the Panama hat stopped him.

"Vicar. Would it be possible for me to talk to you later?" he said in a soft and refined voice.

"Of course," Peter answered. "I will be free after the service."

"Vestry?"

"Yes," Peter answered cautiously. "Was there anything in particular you wanted to talk about?"

"I would just like your opinion on life after death. It is something drawing close and I want to know what might be in store."

[74]
Coda

Peter folded his white liturgical scarf and placed it in the drawer of his vestry desk. Morris Marsden fussed around him, putting the collection in the gun-grey, steel safe and hanging the cassock in the oak vestment locker.

"I cannot believe the number of people who came to the service," Morris said with the excitement of a schoolboy. "The church was full, and they were standing at the back."

"Are you coming to the blessing of the well?" Peter asked.

"Of course," Morris answered with an even bigger smile as he pulled at the frayed cuffs of his jacket. "All very wonderful and a candlelit walk to the old tree."

"Atmospheric," Peter answered. "I was hoping Mary would have been here by now. She must be delayed in traffic."

"Bank holiday weekend and it is a long way to Cornwall. I have never been myself, but I hear it is quite beautiful," Morris answered eagerly "I have never seen so much produce brought as a harvest offering. It was usually just a couple of cans of peas and a Fray Bentos steak pie."

"I nearly laughed when the goat yelled at Bishop Riley during the sermon. The look on his face."

"Don't they say never work with children or animals?" Morris answered. "I am glad you have come to minister to us, Vicar. Things have changed for the better."

Peter could see that Morris held back tears.

"It's your parish, Morris. All those years of your hard work," he answered.

"Amber Hudson has asked if she could join me as churchwarden and Fred Prescott would like to be co-opted onto the PCC."

"Good news. I agree to both. More hands make—"

His words were curtailed by a knock at the vestry door.

Morris took hold of the brass handle, opened the door, and then stepped back in surprise as if he had seen a ghost.

"I have an appointment to see the vicar," the man said as he stepped inside the room.

"I was just leaving," Morris answered, his voice strained.

"See you later, Morris," Peter said as he gestured for the man to sit down.

"Yes," Morris answered sullenly as he stepped out of the room without looking at the man.

"Sorry to catch you at the end of a busy day," the man said seriously. "But I have a pressing concern."

"Life after death?" Peter asked. "I don't know if I will be much help. Are you from the parish?"

"Many years ago. My family had a house here. I moved away. I wanted see the place for one last time," the man stopped and drew a long, deep breath as he looked around the room. "I have been told that I do not have long to live. A silent cancer that has taken over my body and it is only a matter of time. I suppose it is God's way of getting rid of the aged. After all, no one gets out of life alive."

Peter sat down next to the man. A sudden burst of afternoon sunlight came in through the vestry and lit up the shards of dust in the air. They danced, fairy-like, across the room, blown by an unseen draft.

"I don't think that human life ends with death. It would be a cruel of God to do that. I believe in something, but to be truthful, I don't know what form that will take."

"An honest answer. How then should I prepare myself for what is to come?" he asked as he fidgeted with the brim of his hat.

"Make sure you are at peace with everyone in this world before you go to the next."

"Does God forgive every wrongdoing?" he asked.

"Everything," Peter answered.

"Even murder?"

"If it is a true repentance," he replied warily as the man produced a pistol from his jacket.

"Fear not. It isn't loaded. I would like you to dispose of it for me. Take the gun, and hopefully take my wrongdoing as well."

Peter took the pistol from the man and placed it on the vestry table out of reach. "What have you done?"

"Forgive me, for I have sinned," the man answered. "All these years, I have carried what I have done, and the pain of it is finally killing me."

"Evelyn?" Peter asked.

"You know who I am?"

"Magnus Seagrave. From the moment I saw you by the tree. There is a photo of you in the church file. You have aged well."

"I had to come back, and when I heard of what you were doing, I thought today would be the right time. When I lived in the village, the tree was a constant reminder of what my family did to Esther Corbridge. It was a curse on my family, and now it has been lifted. Hopefully, you can lift the curse that is upon me. I speak to you as a priest. I know of your other work. James Meredith told me. He rang to say you were consecrating the tree and opening the well. He believes you are an honourable man."

"You killed your wife and her lover," Peter answered. "Is that what you wish to repent of?"

"I only killed her lover. Albert Shepherd. I loved Evelyn, and he tried to take her from me. He was a bully of a man. We were officers in the same regiment. He made my life hell."

"Why did you appoint him as priest?" Peter asked.

"He had a hold on me. When I was at Sandhurst, I had a forbidden relationship with a fellow officer and Shepherd discovered us and threatened to expose me. I would have been arrested and my dalliance exposed. Being a homosexual was a criminal offence. My marriage to Evelyn was one of convenience. I needed a wife and she needed to escape from her father. Yet, I grew to love her. She had her desires filled with male friends and I skulked the public toilets of York."

"Did she know?" he asked.

"We never spoke of our lovers. There was an unspoken agreement that we never brought them home."

"They were both shot dead. Executed," Peter answered.

"Shepherd had asked her to leave with him. Evelyn refused. She told him that despite my "condition", she wanted to stay with me. One night, he came to the house. Shepherd was drunk. I was upstairs and I heard them arguing on the lawn. I ran down and as I did, I heard a shot. Evelyn was dead. Shepherd stood over her with the gun in his hand. There was a struggle. I grabbed the gun, and it went off."

"You buried them hand in hand and put a suitcase of clothes and a dead dog in the grave. Was it your idea to plant two entwined trees in the grave?"

"For the afterlife. Evelyn loved her clothes and her dog. I thought it fitting. Planting two trees on the grave of someone murdered keeps the crime in the grave. It worked for Esther Corbridge. I thought it would work for me," Magnus Seagrave said as he started to cry. "Will your God forgive me of that?"

"And you took his car to Scarborough and left it at the station?" Peter asked.

"I panicked. Tried to make it look like he disappeared, that they had run away together."

"You could have claimed self-defence," Peter said. "Reasonable force. The man had a gun."

"It is engraved with his name and army number. I have kept it all these years."

"If you had told the police…"

"I was afraid they would bring back hanging. I thought of going to the police. By then, I had changed my name and started a new life."

"I saw your death certificate. 14th of July 1967. Elgin. Scotland."

"A deception. The coroner was an old friend. He produced a certificate for me, and for that, I am ashamed. I took the identity of a man who had died. The trust fund supplied me with all I needed."

"James Meredith helped you?"

"He was a keeper of my secret. Yet, it was James who told me that now would be the time to give myself up."

"Did he know what you did?" Peter asked.

"When the bodies were discovered, he realised why I had left. James contacted me and I admitted what I had done," Seagrave said as he stared into the light streaming through the vestry window. "'Ill blows the wind that profits nobody. This man, whom hand to hand I slew in fight.'"

"Henry the Fifth?"

"Will you give me absolution?" Seagrave said, his voiced edged in desperation.

"Do you truly repent?" Peter asked.

"I do," Seagrave answered as tears rolled across his lined cheeks.

"You will go to the police?"

"Yes."

For a moment, both men sat in silence.

"May God give you pardon and peace. I absolve you from your sins in the name of the Father, and of the Son, and of the Holy Spirit. Amen," Peter said as he reached forward and etched the sign of a cross on the man's forehead.

The vestry door opened. Amber Hudson stood in the archway with Morris at her side.

"Amber?" Seagrave said with a welcome surprise as he got to his feet.

"Sorry," Morris said quietly.

"I knew you must have recognised me, young Morris."

"I heard everything, Magnus. Why did you not tell us at the time?" Amber asked as she reached out and took his hand. "We would have stood by you."

"I was frightened. I did not know what to do," Seagrave answered.

"What happens now?" she asked Peter, who picked up the pistol and put it in the pocket of his jacket.

"Morris, is Rory Brown still here?" Peter asked.

"Yes."

"Shall we all go together?" Peter asked.

"It would be a great relief," Seagrave answered. "A weight has been taken from me."

[75]
Finem Mundi

The village street was still filled with people. Music played as Morris dancers clattered their staves in the late afternoon sun. The double tree looked taller and more magnificent. Its branches hung heavy with leaves that had begun to have an autumn crisp of yellow and brown. Peter Barnes stood at the church door and looked on the beauty of the village. From where he was, Peter could see Rory Brown help Magnus Seagrave into the back of the police car with Amber at his side.

In his heart, he knew that the confession would lead to more conflict within the police.

It was yet another clash between the two worlds he now inhabited.

In a strange way, he was glad that it had been overheard. At least there would be another witness.

It was a beautiful day and as he scanned the crowd looking for Mary. From far away, came the drone of a police siren that drew ever closer. It broke the magic of the day with the mundanity of modern life and a tragedy about to unfurl for someone.

The noise grew louder, and then stopped suddenly. Seconds later, the police Land Rover pulled up outside the church gate.

Carol Manning jumped from the driver's seat and walked purposefully towards him. She had the look on her face that tried to hide bad news. Her lips were held tight across her teeth, eyes focused on the middle distance, trying to give nothing away.

"You have missed him. Rory Brown has taken Seagrave to Northallerton," Peter said.

"We need to talk. Can we go inside?"

"Of course, what is it?" he asked, sensing something was very wrong.

Manning didn't speak until they got inside the church. She looked around the walls covered in paintings that had been whitewashed by Puritans and discovered again during the restoration.

As she calmed herself, Manning took a breath.

Peter locked every muscle in his body. He knew what he was about to be told.

"Mary. A lorry. Head-on collision," Manning said, her voice quivering.

"The children?" he asked, knowing his wife was dead.

"Yes," she whispered the words. "I am so sorry."